D0049116

OATH OF HONOR

ALSO BY MATTHEW BETLEY

Overwatch

OATH OF HONOR

A THRILLER

MATTHEW BETLEY

EMILY BESTLER BOOKS
—
ATRIA
NEW YORK LONDON TORONTO SYDNEY NEW DELHI

ATRIA BOOKS

EMILY BESTLER BOOKS

An Imprint of Simon & Schuster, Inc.
1230 Avenue of the Americas
New York, NY 10020

First Emily Bestler Books/Atria Books hardcover edition March 2017

EMILY BESTLER BOOKS / ATRIA BOOKS and colophon are trademarks of Simon & Schuster, Inc.

For information about special discounts for bulk purchases, please contact Simon & Schuster Special Sales at 1-866-506-1949 or business@simonandschuster.com.

The Simon & Schuster Speakers Bureau can bring authors to your live event. For more information or to book an event contact the Simon & Schuster Speakers Bureau at 1-866-248-3049 or visit our website at www.simonspeakers.com.

Manufactured in the United States of America

10 9 8 7 6 5 4 3 2 1

Library of Congress Cataloging-in-Publication Data has been applied for.

ISBN 978-1-4767-9925-4
ISBN 978-1-4767-9928-5 (ebook)

This novel is for all those in the military, law enforcement, and Intelligence Community who toil against the endless threats our country faces. Your perseverance, dedication, and sacrifice keep us safe and preserve our way of life in these dark times. Never yield to those who wish to do us harm and replace liberty with totalitarianism and fear. Your fight is a good and just one. Semper Fi.

PROLOGUE

Akutan Island, Gulf of Alaska

The 130-foot research boat rocked back and forth in the frigid water as the sky darkened and the last remnants of dusk vanished. Rain fell nearly horizontally, battering everything it touched. An occasional wave from the winter storm crashed over the railing, spraying the deck with frost and foam.

Anchored only a few hundred yards off the north side of Akutan Island, its captain had wisely chosen to seek shelter as the gulf side of the island succumbed to a relentless pounding. Unfortunately for the crew, the storm wasn't the only force of nature stalking the prototype research vessel.

From a perch nestled among the nooks and crannies of several large, craggy rocks on the severe slope of a cliff, a pair of night-vision, military-grade binoculars was trained on the boat. Their owner stared through the lenses and looked at the illuminated dials on his watch.

A few more minutes and visibility will be less than twenty yards. Almost time to go.

The team commander wasn't comfortable on American soil, but his orders had been issued from the top of his chain of command, a chain that didn't exist in any operational publication. His team operated outside the conventional services which his country boasted and was only called upon to execute missions in the most extreme circumstances.

He didn't question his orders. Assuming command of his elite team years ago, his first order of business had been the removal of all questions of morality and objectivity. The success of each individual mission was all that mattered, and he had yet to fail. Tonight would be no different.

There were no signs of life on deck. The crew of six, including the captain and the two researchers, was riding out the storm below deck or in the wheelhouse. It was an advantage for him and his team—the weather would mask their movement.

The commander spoke quietly in English into a slim, waterproof microphone that wrapped around from his ear to his mouth. "We go in two minutes. Conduct one last gear check to ensure no loose items. Radio silence until we make contact. And no matter what, the rules of engagement must be followed. No deviations." He knew there wouldn't be any, and although he'd never had to reiterate his instructions before, his superior had emphasized the point to him. Above all else, he followed his orders to the letter. "Wolverine, out."

The rain gathered in intensity as the final vestiges of light slipped away. Moments later, four dark figures nimbly crept down the steep slope toward the churning water below. Wraiths in the night, they vanished into the gulf waters.

———

Onboard the oceanic research vessel *Arctic Glide*

"Jack, how long is this shit supposed to last again? I thought I was getting used to this boat, but I guess not. I feel fucking awful," said Colin Davies, a research scientist on loan to North American Oil. Rumor on the boat was that he was some sort of mad scientist for the government, but he'd refused to confirm or deny it. He stood in the wheelhouse and tried to maintain his balance as the boat swayed back and forth.

A satisfied smirk spread across the captain's face. He'd spent a lifetime in and around these waters. He never tired of watching a land walker—as he referred to anyone not from the Aleutian Islands—get seasick on his boat. *Although this baby isn't really your boat now, is it, Jack?* he told himself.

"Supposed to pick up steam over the next twelve to eighteen hours. After that, should dramatically drop off in intensity. I'd say we're back out in open water within twenty-four hours." *And if it weren't for your weak constitution, we'd still be out on the water.*

After years of running a crab boat out of Dutch Harbor, Jack Dawson had retired, only to be hired by North American to skipper their latest research vessel built with cutting-edge oil and satellite exploration technology. It carried self-contained, stand-alone servers and closed networks. It was designed especially for these frigid waters, with a reinforced hull and a sloping bow to force ice down and away from the ship.

Its current mission was to test the communications, navigation, and satellite research capabilities onboard in all weather conditions. The captain knew that Colin Davies had developed some of the software—thus, his required presence—and he was also reported to be close friends with one of North American's CEOs, which was why Jack enjoyed giving him so much grief. *A land walker* and *a suit in disguise.*

Colin nodded and started to speak, but a sudden gust of wind rattled the wheelhouse as a wave crashed into the side. He slipped on the shifting floor. As he fell, he grabbed the back of the copilot's chair. The chair turned on its pedestal and—as if mocking him—shook off his hand, spinning him to the deck. He slammed down on his haunches, his legs splayed out in front of him.

Jack laughed out load. "Are you having fun yet?"

"Goddamnit!" Colin shouted. He struggled to his feet. "I'm going down to the galley with Tom and the rest of the crew. Enjoy the storm." As Jack watched in bemusement, Colin turned and carefully exited down the steep stairs from the bridge to the main deck.

"Blessed silence," he muttered to himself. He sat in his chair and stared out the window. Night had finally fallen. He watched the swirling rain envelop his boat. He turned around to look back at the stern, intending to confirm that the minisub had not shifted on the open deck aft of the wheelhouse.

A sudden movement on the main deck just below his observation window caught his attention. He was certain he'd seen a dark figure vanish under the overhang near the hatch to the main structure. *Who the hell went outside on the deck without telling me?*

As Jack Dawson moved to the staircase, he heard the hatch open, followed by a loud whooshing as the wind fought to enter the boat. It was followed by a dull *thump* as the hatch was secured behind the reckless crew member.

"Hey, which one of you guys is that?" he called out. "Next time you get suicidal and decide to take a stroll outside, you better friggin' let me know, okay?"

No answer.

"You hear me down there?"

Still no response.

The sound of quickly moving soft footsteps echoed up the stairwell. *What the hell?*

Jack walked over to the head of the stairs and peered into the darkness below. What he saw froze him in his tracks, and his mind took a snapshot in time.

A black shadow in the shape of a man stood on the stairs, its right arm pointed accusatorily at him. The whites of the eyes blazed at Jack out of the darkness. But it wasn't the eyes that grabbed Jack's attention—it was the black pistol in the man's hand, a menacing shape that ended in a long cylinder with a tiny opening. *Oh no . . .*

He heard a soft *thwap* as the weapon fired point-blank into his body. A heavy punch hit his chest, and he staggered backward, as much from the shock as from the pain. He fell against the stack of radio equipment behind his chair and slumped to the floor. As his attacker stood over him, Captain Jack Dawson's last thought was *Who the hell are you?* And then . . . nothing.

PART I

THE LAST FRONTIER

UNALASKA, ALASKA

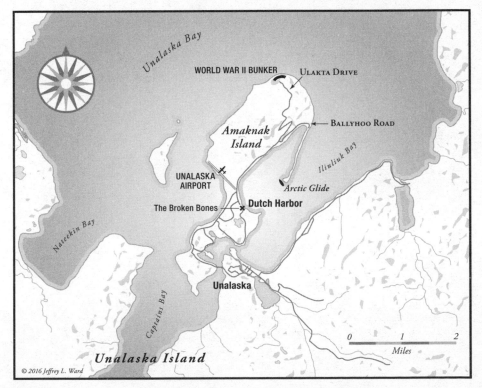

© 2016 Jeffrey L. Ward

CHAPTER 1

Khartoum, Sudan

Namir Badawi absently studied the Nile River through his office window, lost in his thoughts. A midafternoon storm was building to the south.

A statuesque figure with a slim build and bald head, he watched the roiling clouds move toward the Republican Palace. But his thoughts were focused on a different type of storm, one aimed directly at the heart of his suffering country.

After nearly four decades of fighting, the rebellious southern region was holding its crucial referendum next month. The outcome was a foregone conclusion. There was no doubt in Namir's mind that the people would vote for independence. *They always do, even when it's against their best interests,* he thought.

John Garang, the deceased leader of the Sudan People's Liberation Army, would finally achieve his goal, albeit from the grave. *I hope you're burning in Jahannam for all the pain you caused from your self-righteous, sanctimonious belief in independence,* he thought. *After all the fighting, it's a helicopter crash that wipes you from the face of the earth.*

Namir knew better than to think that the South would declare its independence and stop fighting, not with everything at stake along the border. Treasured oil was buried in the territory over which they fought. No peace agreement could prevent further atrocities and bloodshed. It was naïve to believe otherwise. *And I am not naïve.*

Independence would be declared, but unimaginable human suffering had become a staple for the Sudanese people in those contested regions.

In addition to the war with the South, his government had faced an uprising that started in 2003, when members of the Sudan Liberation Movement, supported by the Darfur Liberation Front, attacked the al-Fashir airfield in western Sudan. They'd destroyed four Hind attack gunships and killed most of the soldiers living on the base.

Khartoum's response had been swift and severe in the form of a ruthless genocide. They'd recruited the Janjaweed militias to exact revenge upon anyone unlucky enough to be associated with the rebels in any way.

Namir had personally planned several operations that had resulted in tactical successes—with an intentionally large amount of collateral damage and civilian deaths. His methods had pleased his leadership and, ultimately, the president himself. His reward had been his selection to lead the Al Amn al-Dakhili, the organization responsible for Sudan's internal security.

Unfortunately, the meddlesome international media had leaked images of the horrors to the United Nations and other intrusive organizations, and Namir had been forced to scale back his aggressive assaults. The UN indictments were jokes to the president and his advisors, reminders of the ineffective bureaucracy and hypocrisy institutionalized in luxurious office buildings in New York City.

Neither politics nor moral condemnation from others mattered to Namir. Things had quieted down after the 2005 Comprehensive Peace Agreement with the South and the 2006 agreement with the Sudan Liberation Movement in Darfur.

As the director for internal security, his singular responsibility was clear—protect the Republic of Sudan and preserve the Islamic way of life. And it was those two duties that had him concerned as he waited for his next appointment.

A knock at the door was followed by the sound of creaking hinges as the large, ornate panel to his second-floor office swung inward.

"Sir, your two o'clock appointment is here. Shall I bring him in?" asked a young female voice.

"Yes, please, Alya. Thank you." He smiled at his secretary and nodded.

He turned back toward the enormous double-paned window and noticed that the storm clouds had darkened. *So fast. A storm is rare indeed for late December.* He stepped away from the view, intending to seat himself behind his desk before his visitor entered. He stopped midstride. His visitor was already here.

Standing motionless before him was a young Chinese man who looked no older than twenty-five. He wore dark gray trousers, a white short-sleeve polo—well-defined muscles bulging under the sleeves—and a pair of black dress shoes tightly laced and impeccably polished.

Impressive. I should've heard him, Namir thought to himself. After years of training and field experience, his senses were sharp. The last person that had surprised him like this had ended up in a Kenyan river with a knife through his rib cage. He smiled at the memory.

"Major Lau, I presume," Namir said in English and moved toward the young man, hand extended. Major Lau immediately placed both feet together. He extended his right hand in a fist and covered it with his left hand. He nodded slightly and spoke.

"Director Badawi, it is my distinct honor to make your acquaintance." His delivery and enunciation were as crisp as his appearance.

"Major Lau, while I appreciate your show of respect, please, have a seat. We have much to discuss." *His English is as good as any American's I've met,* Namir thought.

The young man relaxed slightly and sat down in a high-back leather chair that faced the window. His posture was purposeful, intended to display a sense of professional confidence. Namir settled into a second chair across from him.

He studied the trained soldier and killer, a man who'd risen quickly through the ranks of the Ministry of State Security of the People's Republic of China. The MSS was legendary for its ferocious, methodical training. It had recently produced some of the most ruthless and successful undercover intelligence agents in the world. The one in his office was supposed to be one of the best they'd developed. He would tread carefully.

"Major Lau, your terms have been agreed to. The only question I have left is the time line. How soon can it be done? The referendum is only a few weeks away, and I'd like to advise my president as soon as this joint mission is complete. He'll never know the details—just the end result. But it has to be soon, or we won't be able to control it. Do you understand?"

"Sir, I completely—" was all Major Lau uttered before Namir interrupted him.

"Please, call me Namir. This partnership is unofficial. There is no record of this meeting, of my phone conversations with your government, of any of this. If there were and were we to be discovered, we'd both end up indicted by that worthless International Court at The Hague. I've been doing this a long time. I know what you are, and I assume you know what I am. We're both professionals. Agreed?"

Major Lau exhaled and released some of the tension in his frame, a dangerous but genuine smile gracing his features. "As you wish, Namir. Please call me Gang, and I do have a time line. If all goes as planned—although you and I both know it hardly ever does—we will have confirmation and positive control well before the referendum. Once we do, it should provide you with guaranteed security, no matter what the South does."

"How soon can you begin?" Namir inquired quietly.

"My men are here, and I've been informed that the software and equipment should be acquired within the next twenty-four hours. Once they have it, it will be shipped to a safe location, transported over land in our control, and flown here directly via private charter," Gang said.

Namir raised his eyebrows, an unspoken question forming on his lips.

"There is no electronic trail of the shipment," Gang said, reading his subtle expression. "I assure you. I'll have a team I personally selected accompany it the entire time once it reaches Europe. I should have it in my custody in no more than five days."

Gang hadn't told Namir about the second team in the US—a team with a different but related mission—that had gone dark, and he didn't need to. It was that part of the operation that had him concerned. The upcoming American holiday season and the general focus on other threats to their homeland were weaknesses he intended to exploit. Once he gave the order, there would be no turning back.

"If this operation succeeds," Gang said, "and there's no reason to believe it won't—I've secured additional measures just in case—the prosperity of our countries will be guaranteed for decades to come, our financial fates sealed and intertwined."

Gang was confident they'd be successful, but success was not enough. He wanted to humiliate the United States on the global stage. American arrogance would wither under the Chinese technological and industrial heel. A new world order was barreling toward the globe, a freight train of change and equality. He felt the fury rise in his stomach, a feeling he experienced at every glimpse of the American flag, a hypocritical symbol of opulence and superficiality.

Namir nodded thoughtfully. The plan was sound and compartmented. The president and the first vice president had plausible deniability if things went wrong. And with as many moving parts as this operation had, things easily could go awry. *Glory is reserved only for those willing to seize it.*

The stage was set, the actors in place, and it was time for the curtain to open. "In that case, Gang, let's begin." He grinned broadly, his own smile as cunningly lethal as the young killer's.

CHAPTER 2

Unalaska, Alaska

Logan West stepped off the FBI's Gulfstream jet and onto the tarmac of Unalaska Airport. His green eyes struggled to adjust to the bright glare from the recent snowfall.

The storm had exited the area and moved south, but the temperature had dropped twenty degrees as a consequence. With the wind-chill factor, it felt closer to zero than eighteen, but his short brown beard provided a thin barrier to the cold. The beard also covered up the long scar down the left side of his face, a memento from the events of two years ago.

So much for skiing in Colorado. His and Sarah's trip had been abruptly cut short by work, and he'd been forced to leave her in Aspen. He smiled at the thought. Rather than fly back to Maryland, she'd chosen to stay there for the rest of the week.

"If Dutch Harbor turns out to be another wild goose chase, tell the FBI to send you back here, and we'll finish our vacation. I don't need to go back for a few days yet." She'd smiled wryly and added, "*And* I don't always need *you* to have a good time."

He loved her deeply for that independence. The attack on their home two years ago that had nearly triggered another war in the Middle East—this time with Iran—had driven them closer. It'd also solidified his sobriety. He hadn't had a drink since that fateful day. *And today's another one-day-at-a time like any other. Just keep moving forward.*

His reflection was interrupted by a shout from his left. "What the hell is this? The FBI sends me commercial with a lousy turboprop connector from Anchorage, and you get their Gulfstream? This favoritism thing sucks, brother."

Logan grinned at the swiftly moving, athletic figure of John Quick. "Yeah, well, as I keep telling you—next time, *you* can almost get killed by a megalomaniac with a nuclear suitcase."

"Whoa. Whoa. Whoa, killer," John said, putting his hands up in exaggerated protest as he reached Logan. "You seem to forget I was blown up and *out* of my house—literally. I'm worried about your selective memory. You've been hit in the head too many times."

"Tell me about it," Logan said, shaking his friend's hand. He spotted the police vehicle, a Ford SUV that looked as rugged as the windswept, barren terrain. "I see you already introduced yourself to the locals," he said, nodding at the SUV.

"It's the police chief's. He's a good guy. Charlie Phoenix, if you can believe it. It's a freaking fantastic name. Suits him, too. All he knows is that he's been ordered to assist 'two FBI officials' any way he can. I couldn't tell him anything since I don't even know what the hell's going on myself. So what is it this time?" John asked.

After the horrific attack in Washington, DC, that had killed several innocent civilians and Cain Frost, the founder of the largest private security company in the world and the man responsible for the near global catastrophe, Deputy Director Mike Benson, Logan's close friend and one of the few people on the planet he trusted completely, had created a specialized FBI task force, and Logan and John were the lead investigators.

Task Force Abel—named at John's suggestion after the biblical son of Adam killed by his brother Cain—had pursued multiple leads. Every turn in unraveling the convoluted case had led to disparate revelations about the organization behind the conspiracy to attack Iran, until the already-tangled leads suddenly dried up. It'd been six months with no progress, and the Department of Justice was no closer to uncovering the truth than on the day of the attack. Even the Intelligence Community had stumbled into a proverbial brick wall.

All-source reporting indicated several international ties—a possible link to a foreign embassy in Brazil, an arms dealer in the Ukraine, and even a rebel leader in Uganda. But each lead had evaporated, leaving no physical trace or virtual fingerprints. All evidence had been magically wiped away, a conspiracy theory whispered about in the halls of Congress and the White House. There was nothing to show for twenty months of solid investigation, at least until two days ago.

"You remember that assassination in the Ukraine a few years ago?" Logan began. "A Russian dissident who spoke out against the president of Russia? He was killed with some crazy radioactive material. They never caught the assassin, but everyone thought it had to be an agent of the FSB."

John raised his eyes doubtfully. "So what does that have to do with us on this beautiful, isolated landscape?"

"Check this out," Logan said. "Two days ago, an NSA analyst got a hit on a cell phone number, a number he'd received from a CIA report after that assassination. Apparently, when the dissident was killed, our embassy in Ukraine had a walk-in informant who claimed he was a former KGB officer and knew who was responsible for the hit in Ukraine. Our guys vetted him, but he was an alcoholic, and he didn't pass any of their tests."

"You never can trust an alcoholic," John injected, patting Logan on the shoulder in a brotherly way.

"Uh-huh," Logan said. "Anyhow, the chief of station took the report, and it made its way around the IC. The number ended up on tasking somewhere in NSA's databases. By the time it popped up in this analyst's queue and he got around to looking at the call two days ago, he realized it was coming from the coast of Akutan Island, the next island northeast of here. He knew it had to be on a boat, but he couldn't figure out which one. So he called the boys at Langley, and after some legal wrangling since the number was now on US soil, they did their own research. They discovered that the number was associated with multiple HUMINT reports about a secret Russian black ops team. These reports read like spook legends. Mike told me that one of the reports was linked to that South American trip we took last year."

John shook his head, remembering Task Force Abel's deployment to Brazil to uncover an alleged smuggling ring connected to an Eastern European weapons network. "So it's the Russians I have to thank for this vacation?"

"Not sure, my friend, but here's the best part—the last HUMINT report indicated this team was pursuing some sort of new technology that the US government possesses. I wasn't given the details, but apparently this phone number got someone's attention in DC, and the next thing Mike knows is he's getting a phone call from his uncle asking him to send us up here to investigate."

John looked around and then returned his gaze to Logan. "Brother, this is an island. The locals would immediately spot anything out of the ordinary. If there's so much as a new boat in town, any of the fishermen or crab boat captains will know about it."

"And where do you think we might find those types of people in a place like this?" Logan asked.

John immediately knew the answer. Still, he waited a beat before he sarcastically replied, "Great. I fly all the way to Alaska, home of the grizzly bear and bald eagle, and you want to take me to a bar. How long you been sober again?"

"Really? You want to go there?" Logan asked, laughing. "Fuck you," he said.

"No, thanks. You're not my type. Your hair's too long." He slapped Logan on the back. "Now let's go get that drink."

CHAPTER 3

The Broken Bones

One of only three bars in Dutch Harbor, the Broken Bones was aptly named, as it all too often delivered on its sign's promise. Though the town was a famous tourist destination as the result of documentaries and reality TV shows filming the frontier way of life, it was the only establishment avoided by tourists, as well as producers and cameramen from the Discovery Channel. It was renowned for three things—violent fistfights, drinking escapades that would make any practicing alcoholic proud, and a particular distaste for outsiders. An unofficial policy by the police allowed the mayhem to continue, except in the most extreme cases. The last visit by the chief had followed a fight between two deckhands that had escalated wildly to the point that one of the men broke the other's jaw with a fish bat, only to have his right hand smashed by a crab hammer.

The only silver lining was the bar's location on the harbor side of Gilman Road, across the street from the dental clinic, which profited from the steady influx of patients. A percentage of those charges went right back into the Broken Bones's coffer.

Chief Phoenix had delivered Logan and John to the Grand Aleutian Hotel shortly after Logan's arrival. He'd offered to drive them around the island. They'd declined, instead choosing to rent a pickup truck from the hotel, which offered the service for its guests since the island wasn't large enough for a car rental agency. They'd also been provided directions to the island's three bars. The Broken Bones was first on their list.

Logan and John walked through the double set of glass doors and into a different era. As the door shut behind them, all conversation stopped. Logan thought, *Just like a scene out of the Wild West. This is going to be fun.*

Even in the middle of the afternoon, the number of patrons was surprisingly large. They occupied at least half of the establishment.

The main bar to the left of the entrance ran the entire length of the space. The opposite wall was solid glass from floor to ceiling. The central floor had several high tables with bar stools randomly positioned, and a set of stairs at each end connected to a lower level with several hardwood booths scattered along the picture window.

Beyond the glass was a gorgeous view of Dutch Harbor's largest bay. Two main waterways served as entrances to the harbor, and fishing boats of all sizes were moored to pylons and piers along the water.

Logan and John ignored the silence and maneuvered their way through the tables and astonished stares of several patrons. Logan's peripheral vision picked up a man in his sixties with his jaw agape at the sight of the two interlopers. Logan nodded at him and kept moving.

They reached the bar, to be greeted by a small, wiry man with thinning white hair that hung from the back of his head to his shoulders.

"Listen, guys, it's obvious you're not from around here. So let me be blunt," the bartender said. "This place is not for *you*."

"Logan," John said, "do you mind if I handle this situation and educate our new friend?"

"Be my guest," Logan said, and motioned for John to continue. He stood back and crossed his arms over his chest, smiling at the bartender.

The bartender grew uneasy. Something in the man's green eyes set his nerves on edge. *This is not going to go as I thought.*

"Sir, what's your name?"

The man answered, "Will, but everyone calls me Willy, like the killer whale."

"That's great, Willy. My name's John, and this here is my partner, Logan. And believe it or not, we're with the FBI investigating a possible threat to national security, as crazy as that sounds."

Willy's eyes grew wide. "You've got to be kidding me. Nothing goes on up here except that TV show and tourists who want to see where it's filmed. Are you talking about some kind of *terrorist attack*?" he asked incredulously.

"Willy, I can't really tell you much more than that, but what I really need to know is if you or any of your guests here have seen anything unusual since the storm."

Logan watched John cajole the bartender as he observed the patrons behind them in a large mirror behind the bar. At a table near the middle of the floor, two large men quietly stood up.

Great . . .

"What do you mean by 'unusual'?" Willy asked.

The two men slipped through the tables, covering the distance quickly. They were almost directly behind Logan and John.

"By unusual, I mean any—" John continued before Logan cut him off.

"We have company," Logan said quietly, nodding at the mirror.

"Always has to be one or two, doesn't it?" John said, a wicked grin on his face.

"With us? Of course it does," Logan replied, and both men turned around.

John opened his arms wide, welcoming the newcomers, who now stood in front of them. The man in front of John was close to six foot four inches tall and weighed more than 240 pounds, an unhealthy combination of fat and muscle. His black hair was pulled back in a ponytail, and he wore a beard that reached a burly chest covered by a black Harley-Davidson T-shirt.

The second man was Logan's height and more physically fit than his partner. His brown hair was slicked back in homage to the 1950s, and he was clean-shaven. It was also obvious he'd been drinking for several hours. He looked like a cliché, an angry man looking for any excuse to fight for a temporary distraction from his empty and frustrated life. Logan had felt that way once, before sobriety had finally clicked and slowly filled that lonely void in his soul.

"Gentlemen, I'm going to make this as simple as possible for you both," John explained. "We're with the FBI, and we're trying to have a private conversation with this fine, upstanding citizen. So, do you really want to do this right now? I strongly advise against it; however, if that's what you really want, then I guess I can use the sparring practice. It's your call."

John stared up at the bearded man, all emotion drained from his expression. It was a hardened look Logan knew well.

The giant of a man turned his head to his left but kept his eyes on John. "You believe the bullshit coming out of this guy's mouth?" He looked John squarely in the eyes and leaned down into his face. He growled, "You're going to regret walking through those doors. As Willy said, we don't take kindly to outsiders, especially tiny specimens like you." The last words were spat with contempt.

It was all John needed. The time for talking had passed. At 180 pounds and five feet ten inches, he was incredibly fast. He and Logan acted simultaneously.

With blinding speed, John reached out and grabbed the big man's beard with his left hand. He yanked forward viciously and pivoted on his left foot as he lowered his center of gravity. He completed the turn and pulled even harder. The momentum he created sent the man crashing headlong into the front of the bar.

A loud *crunch* stunned the other patrons as the man's nose was crushed by the rounded corner of the marble countertop. Blood splashed onto the bar and down his shirt. He seemed to bounce backward, and as he did so, John stuck out his left leg, almost casually. The man tripped over John's ankle and fell to the floor. The impact knocked the wind out of him, and he lay on the ground, dazed. He stared at the ceiling as blood continued to flow from his shattered nose.

Logan's actions were less graceful but no less effective. He delivered two quick jabs squarely to his opponent's face and split both upper and lower lips. The man reeled in surprise and raised his hands in self-defense.

Logan used the sudden distance between them to deliver a spinning back kick that landed on the man's sternum with tremendous force. The kick launched the man rearward, and he flew into a table, which caught him squarely in the middle of the back. He seemed to scream in pain as his arms flailed, but there was no air left in his lungs to make a sound.

Logan was mildly amused to see the guy stagger forward once more, somehow still on his feet. *Oh well . . .*

Logan stepped forward and delivered a powerful punch to the man's midsection. There was an audible gasp from around the room as the second aggressive local fell to the floor, facedown.

Silence engulfed the Broken Bones, the patrons shell-shocked at the vicious display of precision violence. Two of their own had just been dispatched with what seemed like completely effortless action. They stared at the intruders. John Quick didn't wait for them to recover before he spoke.

"As I tried to tell these two gentlemen, we're with the FBI looking for anything unusual. A new crew none of you have ever seen before, a new boat in town, anything at all. . . . Now I don't want to have to repeat what just happened, and if you want us to get out of here quickly, someone's going to have to tell us something." John looked around the room, making eye contact with each man.

"Why do you think we came here first? We know who you are, what you're about. Hell, when I'm not doing this, I live in Montana in the middle of goddamn nowhere so I can hunt and fish in seclusion. I respect your lifestyle." John could feel a change in the room, a softening of the hostile atmosphere. He continued.

"We know that you'd know if somebody new was on the island, someone not from around here." He paused to let the words sink in to their dazed psyches. "Believe it or not, guys, we're on the same side. So I'm going to ask one more time—no bullshit—does anyone know anything that can help us out?"

The assembled men looked at each other. Logan saw comprehension, fear, and respect all at once. Logan and John had made their point and proven their mettle and determination.

It was why he'd insisted to the police chief that they do this alone. He knew that with men like these, there was often only one way to gain their trust. Dutch Harbor men were hard. They valued toughness and resilience.

A rumble of approval reverberated through the bar, even as the two locals lay on the ground.

After a few moments, a man in his late twenties sitting in a booth along the window quietly said, "The *Arctic Glide*."

Logan walked over to the railing at the edge of the main floor and looked down at the man. "I'm sorry. I could barely hear you back there. What did you say?"

The young man gained confidence at the sound of his own voice and repeated, "The *Arctic Glide*. I think that's what you're looking for."

CHAPTER 4

Timothy Lawrence, also known as Tough Tim around Dutch Harbor, sat across from Logan and John. He was a deckhand and engineer on one of the local crab boats, and his endurance was legendary, even at the young—but veteran in crabbing years—age of twenty-seven.

"I did several trips on Jack Dawson's boat over the past few years. My current job is almost up, and even though I like the captain and the crew, I never made more than I did as the engineer on the *Glide* when they were testing her up here last year." He took a sip of the half-finished dark ale in his mug and studied the former Marines.

"When I saw Dawson's boat come back and dock in the main bay after the storm two days ago, I went to see him. There was some tough-looking guy working on the deck. I asked him where Jack was, and he told me—and I quote—'Something got him in the back of the head during the storm. He's fine, but he's resting down below.' I didn't think anything about it. Shit like that happens all the time out here. The guy didn't give me his name. He just told me he'd been hired on last-minute out of Anchorage and asked if he could take a message. There was something about him—an edge, kind of what you have," he said, nodding at Logan. "So I let it go and didn't think twice, until you two showed up."

Logan pulled out a tourist map of Dutch Harbor. He'd grabbed it from the hotel as they'd left. "Where's the *Glide* docked?"

Tough Tim straightened the map out and pointed at a thin, mile-long piece of land jutting out into the middle of Iliuk Bay. "In the last slip here," he said, gesturing to the west side of the land. "The guy on deck told me they broke a prop and were waiting for the replacement. He said they'd hopefully be back out on the water sometime today, I think."

"You see what I see?" John asked. Logan nodded. "If they're still here," John went on, "they've got a clear line of sight in all directions. They'll see us coming."

"Which is why we approach as casually as possible, as if we belong there. The more obvious, the better, and I have just the idea how," Logan said, smiling at John.

"Logan," John said, shaking his head, "I really, *really* hate it when you get ideas. People seem to die and things usually explode, often right next to me."

"There might be a bit of truth to that, but usually they're bad guys," Logan responded wryly.

"Exactly!" John almost shouted. "*Usually . . .*"

Tough Tim sat quietly at the table and listened to the exchange. *Who the hell are these guys?*

———

Logan and John left the bar. The afternoon was growing colder, seemingly by the minute. The skies had darkened to a dull gray. "Looks like snow," Logan said.

"I agree. But hey! We're cold-weather warriors, hombre. We can put all that cold-weather survival training from MWTC to good use," John said, referring to the Marine Corps's Mountain Warfare Training Center in Bridgeport, California. "We like this shit."

Logan pulled out his cell phone. He dialed the police chief's personal number. When Captain Phoenix answered the call, he said, "Chief, we think our boat is the *Arctic Glide.* It's docked in the main part of the bay in the last slip at the edge of that thin peninsula."

John heard a voice reply, and Logan nodded.

"I understand. No worries. We should be able to handle this ourselves. Just meet us there when you can. Hopefully, we'll know more by the time you get there. Hope everything turns out okay on your end. See you in a bit."

John looked at Logan quizzically. "What's up with our local law enforcement?"

"There was an accident at one of the World War Two bunkers on the main island a few miles south of here. They're evacuating a man who fell from the top of the bunker. Spinal injury. It's going to take some time to get him out due to the rocky terrain. He said he'd get there as soon as he could."

"Great," John exclaimed. "So once again, we're on our own."

"Would you have it any other way?" Logan asked.

"Actually, no," John answered.

"That's what I thought. So let's get moving before these assholes get a chance to leave. We're burning daylight," Logan said, and hopped into the driver's side of the pickup truck.

"Always in a hurry," John said, as he opened the passenger door. "You know you're gonna give yourself a heart attack one of these days. You're getting old. You need to slow down."

Logan looked at John grinning at him through the cab of the truck. "Just get the fuck in the truck."

CHAPTER 5

The *Arctic Glide*

The Wolverine was in a hurry to leave. He stood on the deck near the stern and surveyed the harbor and its surrounding terrain. A man unaccustomed to sentiment, he felt a fleeting emotion, a brief nostalgia for his homeland.

The terrain was rugged and severe, forged by unforgiving elements. He related to the transformative and relentless powers of Mother Nature. *Getting soft in your middle years?* he asked himself. He shrugged off the thought and concentrated on the task at hand—preparing the ship to depart in the next few minutes.

Even though they were the only ship on the peninsula, he'd felt exposed for the last two days, a floating target. Of course he'd chosen this precise location because it afforded him the luxury of a clear field of view in all directions.

What he'd told the inquisitive young fisherman was true—the *Arctic Glide* had sustained a broken propeller, and he'd had to wait for one to be flown in from Anchorage. Once it arrived, his team had used the diving equipment on board and replaced the part earlier in the day.

While waiting in plain sight for two days had not been part of the plan, the delay had provided a plausible cover story for his men to ship their newly acquired equipment from a local carrier to Anchorage. The Pelican cases containing "research equipment" had arrived safely in Anchorage, where they'd been transferred to a commercial carrier to be flown across the United States and beyond. He'd checked the tracking number provided by the carrier, and the current status was "in transit." The freight was currently over the Atlantic Ocean. Unless the plane crashed, its cargo would reach Europe shortly, and then it would be someone else's problem. His mission was almost over. It was time to clean up.

Once they left the harbor, the plan was simple—take the *Arctic Glide* to an isolated location near one of the other islands, send her to the bottom of the Bering Sea with her crew on board, and head to the offshore rendezvous point, where a stealth submarine awaited their return.

He untied the line from the port side of the boat and stepped onto the dock, dragging the heavy rope and coiling it on the ground for the next vessel. Finished, he started walking toward the other dock line when he heard someone shouting from behind.

He turned and spotted a man in a dark blue coat and khaki cargo pants running toward him, waving his arms wildly. Approximately fifty yards behind the running figure was a blue-and-white Chevy pickup truck with Al's Marina Repairs & Services painted on the side. Another figure waited in the driver's seat. "Hey, mister! Hold on a second! I need to talk to you about the propeller! Hold on a sec!"

The engine shop where we purchased the propeller? What now? The Wolverine's senses immediately transitioned into a heightened state of alertness, and he stared hard at the approaching figure, mentally evaluating the man for any threat. *Obviously athletic, moves quickly and with ease . . .*

The man reached him and bent over at the knees, breathing hard and looking up into the Wolverine's face. The Wolverine noticed a scar down the left side of his face, partially concealed by a short beard. Intelligent green eyes met his gaze.

"Thank God! I thought you guys were going to take off, and then I'd have to deal with my asshole boss back there in the pickup truck," he said sheepishly, glancing over his shoulder. "Sorry about the dramatic entry. Just didn't want to miss you." He paused and seemed to catch his breath again. He stuck out his hand, "I'm Tom Mackey from Al's Marina where you guys bought the prop." He motioned over his shoulder with one hand. "And I hate to tell you this, but there's a problem with the credit card your man used."

The Wolverine shook the man's hand. *Firm, confident . . .* "Problem? What kind of problem?" he asked in perfect, unaccented English.

"We thought that the card went through initially when you guys picked it up and paid, but it turns out that due to the storm, all transactions weren't actually getting processed. They got stuck in transit somewhere and never made it to the credit card company. I'm not surprised, really. Those companies know how to fleece a man to death. Anyhow, they called us less than an hour ago and told us they need to rerun the card. I hate to do this to you—and I completely apologize—but is there any way I can get that card again? I even brought the reader with me," Tom said, smiling and holding up an iPhone with an attached credit card reader.

The Wolverine's mind raced through the probabilities. Tom seemed sincere. Other than his physical fitness and alert eyes, his story was plausible. He realized he had two options—kill Tom on the spot and try to stop the man in the pickup from fleeing; or play along, provide the credit card, and leave as soon as Tom and his friend left. He made his choice.

"Tom, I'm Martin. Please come aboard. We'll head up to the wheelhouse, and I'll get you the card. And then when we're done—and I don't mean to be rude—we need to get back out. That storm put us behind schedule by a couple of days."

"Fair enough. I'll get out of your hair as quickly as possible," the man said as he stepped aboard the *Arctic Glide.*

The two men crossed the flat deck, and Tom studied a submersible submarine suspended by a crane over the middle of the deck. It was painted a bright yellow in the tradition of deep-sea exploratory vehicles.

"Nice sub," Tom said. "What are you guys using it for, if you don't mind me asking?"

The Wolverine glanced back, saw genuine interest on Tom's face, and said, "Not at all. And honestly, I couldn't tell you all the details. The oil guys have been using it for underwater research. They've got so much gear on this boat it makes my head hurt thinking about it. I'm just hired help," he added, smiling at Tom.

"I hear you," Tom said, and continued to look around the deck at the other pieces of machinery and equipment. "You sure do have a lot of gear," he agreed, spotting three Quadcon industrial containers near the stern of the boat.

The two men reached the entrance to the wheelhouse. The Wolverine lifted the handle up and opened the heavy door. He walked through the entrance and began to climb the metal stairs. Tom trailed close behind him.

A loud *clang* resounded through the tight, enclosed space. The Wolverine whipped his head around and looked down at the man on the steps below.

Tom still held the iPhone in front of him. It wasn't that device that had made the sound. And then the Wolverine saw it. A bulge on the right hip, concealed by the dark blue Al's Marina jacket. *Gun,* his mind screamed at him. He examined the man's face and saw something even more alarming in the green eyes that now stared back at him. *Predatory alertness, cold and calculating.*

Without hesitation, he acted, and the desolate landscape of Dutch Harbor, Alaska, quickly turned into a battleground, an eventuality for which the islands had prepared during World War II but had never experienced—until today.

CHAPTER 6

After what felt like a lifetime in this business, Logan West had seen the man for what he was—a trained operator that stood over him in the stairwell, ready to react. *Murphy, ever the saboteur,* Logan thought, the image of a wall-mounted poster of Murphy's Law flashing in his head.

The stairwell was tight, and he'd turned too quickly. The butt of his Kimber Tactical II .45-caliber pistol had struck the steel bulkhead.

Logan watched Martin's face for his reaction to the sound. The man's blue eyes skittered to Logan's hip, then back to his face. Recognition dawned as the true threat was revealed.

Logan sprang into action first. His right hand shot under the blue jacket and grasped the handle of the Kimber. He was fast—Wild West gunslinger fast—but the man above him reacted almost as quickly.

As Logan pulled the pistol from its holster, the man he'd just met as "Martin" moved into action and screamed something in Russian. He lashed out with a kick that connected squarely with Logan's chest. The impact sent Logan sprawling down the two steps behind him, and he crashed to the floor. He pulled the trigger of the Kimber, which was now aimed up the stairwell.

Bam! Bam!

The shots were deafening in the confined space. Sparks flew off the ceiling inches above his enemy's head. Martin retreated to the safety of the wheelhouse above as Logan cursed to himself. He'd just lost all tactical advantage. *Great . . .*

Things grew worse as Logan heard the sound of running footsteps from the twenty-foot passageway to his right. Three men appeared at the end and moved toward him with military precision. The man in the lead held a short, black submachine gun in front of him, aimed toward Logan.

Logan rolled to his left toward the open hatch as the point man opened fire. Bullets ricocheted off the floor and metal frame, showering him with sparks and steel fragments.

Christ! Move! Move! Move! He finished his combat roll and dove through the opening. He landed on the rough nonskid surface of the deck and scrambled to his feet. He searched for cover in the few seconds he had before the gunmen reached him.

In addition to the submersible suspended above the deck, a crane operator's station was to his immediate right. Several small wooden crates were to his left. *No good—bullets will go right through those.* He needed something solid. He sprinted across the deck and never looked back.

As he ran, outgunned and outmanned, he prayed, *Please, God, just give me a fighting chance.*

———

John had observed Logan through the windshield of Al's pickup truck. Al had been in the shop, and as a veteran of Operation Desert Storm, he'd been more than happy to help them in any way possible. He was a realist and understood that evil still existed in the world, posing a serious threat. *He even threw in these snazzy jackets,* John thought.

When Logan reached the man untying the *Arctic Glide,* John

had grown uneasy. He recognized the way the man carried himself, self-assured and physically powerful. There was no doubt in John's mind the man was a practitioner in the deadly profession with which he and Logan were intimately acquainted.

Following his instincts, he'd called Captain Phoenix and told him that they'd found the *Glide* but would know more in a few minutes. He knew they'd need backup, and he'd told him to hurry.

So it was no surprise to John that moments after Logan disappeared, he heard the distinctive sounds of gunfire from inside the wheelhouse. Even as Logan tumbled out the opening and scrambled to his feet, John leapt out of the pickup truck and sprinted for the boat. His M1911 .45-caliber pistol was in his right hand as he ran across the gravel road.

John had reached the halfway point to the boat when three men holding PP-2000 submachine guns exited the main structure and fanned out across the deck. They fired and moved as a cohesive unit. *Only years of training could produce that kind of synchronicity,* he thought.

He saw Logan slide behind two all-steel Quadcon containers near the stern.

John knew he only had a few more seconds before the men saw him. He had two choices—try and get closer to get a better shot at the small assault team or take a shot now. As the team closed in on Logan, he realized the clock had run out.

He slid to a stop on the loose gravel and dropped to one knee, his right leg extended behind him. He heard shouts in Russian and glanced at the wheelhouse. The man Logan had approached, the one who had to be the leader, was screaming and pointing at him. *A little too late for at least one of your guys, asshole . . .*

He sighted on the man closest to him just as the other two attackers turned and pointed their weapons at him. John pulled the trigger quickly but smoothly as the two men opened fire. His first shot struck the man in the side of the neck, but John didn't wait to see the results of his handiwork. Instead, he dove for cover behind a stack of thousand-pound crab pots.

Enemy bullets ricocheted off the enormous cages and careened into the Alaskan air or impacted the ground on either side of John's crouched figure.

At least I got one . . . I think. And then more bullets forced him further down.

———

Logan hid behind the eight-foot, dark-green Quadcon container. Even as he assessed the full gravity of his situation, he couldn't help but wonder what an oil exploration vessel was doing with military-grade cargo containers.

As grateful as he was for the temporary protection, the Quadcon containers were the *only* cover near the stern. There was no place left to hide, and the assault team now had him boxed in. If he tried to run for the dock, he'd be torn apart by automatic gunfire. He thought about jumping overboard, but the frigid water temperatures would immobilize him in minutes without a wet suit on under his clothes. He didn't feel like dying cold and wet. That left one option—fight until he ran out of bullets and then reassess his options. *If you're still alive, that is.*

He peered around the corner of the Quadcon just in time to see two of the gunmen point their weapons toward the dock. The third man still had his weapon trained on Logan's location, and Logan saw he was about to pull the trigger. *I looked too soon. Rookie mistake,* he thought, and realized the tactical error might be his last.

The left side of the man's neck suddenly spurted blood as a bullet tore through his throat and carotid artery. The man staggered, but he managed to pull the trigger of the PP-2000. His body seemed suspended for a moment, a dying dancing puppet, surrounded by an explosion of sparks as the rounds struck the deck all around him. But then the magazine emptied, the gun out of ammunition, and he fell forward, dead.

Logan focused on the other two gunmen, who now concentrated their fire toward John's position, which Logan saw was approximately fifty yards away behind a stack of crab pots. *At least now it's a fair fight, unless their leader joins in on the fun.*

Logan heard more screams in Russian and more gunfire directed at John. Then—to Logan's horror—the boat's engines started.

Logan glanced at the wheelhouse as the Russian commander slid open the window and pointed a PP-2000 in Logan's direction. He barked short instructions to his men and opened fire.

Bullet holes appeared above Logan's head in the Quadcon's surface. *He's got armor-piercing rounds. Fantastic.*

Logan flattened himself on the deck and out of sight, hoping to remain unscathed from the intense attack. John would have to fend for himself. He had bigger issues to worry about, especially if the remaining two men flanked him from both sides.

An image flashed through his head—a memory of a soccer stadium in Haditha. He'd subdued Cain Frost, the CEO of the largest private security company in the world turned international terrorist, only to have two insurgents surround him as he used Cain's body as a human shield. Had it not been for John's timely arrival, Logan would have died. The difference now—*thank God*—was that John was already here, and both sides were relatively matched in manpower, if not in weapons.

Logan's face was inches from the deck. The gunfire from the wheelhouse stopped, and Logan briefly peeked around the corner.

The man in the middle was no longer focused on Logan. Instead, he ran across the deck, and Logan watched as he leapt over the widening gap between the boat and the dock. He landed on his feet and kept moving, never losing stride. *He's going for John.*

Instead, the man ran toward a stack of crates parallel to John's position as the remaining shooter on deck provided covering fire.

The hail of bullets kept John pinned down behind the crab pots. The second man disappeared behind the large stacks. *What the hell?*

More bullets tore through the Quadcon, and Logan squirmed his way backward on his belly, eager to minimize his target profile. The boat moved further away from the pier as the team leader expertly turned it toward the opening of the bay.

Logan's options had dwindled to one—stand and fight. *At least now it was only two on one, but I think I can even those odds.* His last glimpse of the deck beyond the Quadcons had given him an idea, one that would require perfect timing.

He knew he couldn't risk a direct assault on his attacker. A submachine gun in the hands of a trained professional was lethal, no matter who the target was. Instead, Logan smiled and rotated his body on his stomach. He quickly slithered across the rough surface toward the other end of the adjacent Quadcon.

———

John was frustrated. The sustained fusillade of bullets had kept him pinned down for the last minute of the gunfight. He was irate, suffused with a cold fury he wore like armor. *Okay, motherfuckers. You better pray one of those bullets hits me, because if not, I'm going to kill all of you, one way or another.*

The onslaught stopped. Silence shocked his senses, and he shook his head as if to clear it. *I'm not sure if that's a good sign or not.*

John looked around the edge of the crab pots and saw the *Arctic Glide* pull away from the pier. From his vantage point, he saw Logan crawl on his stomach toward the left edge of the Quadcon. Something was wrong, and then he realized what it was—there was only one shooter. *Where's the other one?*

A loud engine roared to life behind a huge stack of crates forty yards ahead of him. A moment later, a dark-blue Ford F-350 pickup truck accelerated around the corner of the crates. It gripped the gravel for traction and rocketed toward John. The driver aimed his PP-2000 out the driver's window and opened fire.

John dove toward the ground to avoid the bullets, careful to keep the crab pots between himself and the rapidly approaching pickup. He scrambled to his feet and shuffled around the large stack of steel traps. The Ford passed his location, and the driver fired his remaining rounds toward John.

The pickup gained momentum as it sped away. Its driver was now obviously intent on a secondary objective. *One which apparently doesn't involve killing me. Guess I'm not that important after all.*

John glanced back at the boat. It was already more than 150 yards from the pier, and Logan was no longer behind the Quadcon. Whatever was happening on the boat, he couldn't do anything for his friend from here.

He turned and sprinted toward Al's pickup. He jumped behind the steering wheel and turned the ignition, keeping his foot on the clutch. The engine growled, and John released the clutch, shifting through the gears and accelerating after his new target. *Don't worry. I'm going to catch up to you, and then we can sort this whole thing out.* He cracked a smile. *On second thought, I'm not really in the mood for conversation.*

He floored the gas pedal and caught a quick glimpse in the mirror of the boat behind him. His own burning, intense eyes stared back at him, and he redirected his gaze toward the road and focused on the Ford, which was now a quarter mile ahead of him. He was gaining ground already.

———

Neither of his attackers had seen Logan low-crawl to the other end of the stack of Quadcons. Bullets struck his previous location and tore through the sheet metal where he'd been moments before.

Logan couldn't see his attacker from this angle, but it didn't matter.

If he'd calculated correctly, the man would be where Logan needed him in just a few seconds. He waited. *Five . . . four . . . three . . . two . . .*

Logan moved from behind the Quadcon into a steady crouch on one knee and aimed the Kimber .45. He fired three quick, precise shots.

Bam! Bam! Bam!

Logan was a world-class marksman, an elite shooter among the best anywhere, and all three bullets struck his target. Sparks scattered across the deck and were followed by a high-pitched *zzzzzzzz!*

The yellow submarine suspended thirty feet in the air suddenly plummeted to the deck below. As it fell, Logan stepped around the front corner of the Quadcon, his pistol up and ready to engage the last attacker.

Though he knew it would be a great diversion, he was still pleasantly surprised when the submarine crashed to the deck with a tremendous *boom!* that shook the boat.

The gunman had been closer to the sub than Logan had anticipated. He'd realized what Logan's target was and had tried to dive out of the way, only a moment too late.

The submarine's front left ballast tank crashed down on top of the shooter's legs. The tremendous weight crushed his knees and pinned him facedown on the deck. He screamed in agony and tried to wriggle free from under his own personal paperweight.

Logan quickly combat-walked toward the fallen man with the intent of disarming him and keeping him alive. Unfortunately, like a desperate, caged animal, the man roared in pain and outrage, spotting Logan. The man glared at him with a fury and hatred Logan recognized—he'd seen it in the faces of men about to die, men intent on going out with one last gasp of violence in accordance with the lives they'd led.

The man pushed himself up. He reached out for his fallen PP-2000, which lay inches from his outstretched right hand.

Logan looked the man squarely in the eyes, aimed, and fired. The bullet struck his adversary in the right temple and snapped his head back. Blood sprayed a bright-red mist across the nose of the yellow submarine. The dead man slumped back down to the deck.

Logan looked toward the wheelhouse. He saw the team leader watching him. There was a look of puzzlement on his face, perhaps mixed with professional admiration. Logan thought he saw a small smile, but at this distance, he wasn't sure. He didn't have time to consider it because suddenly the man disappeared from sight and slunk into the shadows.

Now it's your turn, Logan thought as he moved determinedly toward his final target.

———

John concentrated on the road and kept the Ford in sight. The other driver expertly maneuvered the pickup along the peninsula till he reached the island and turned left. John accelerated after him.

Moments later, John skidded around the corner onto the main thoroughfare that ran along the waterfront. Boat repair shops, warehouses, and other businesses that catered to the fishing trade lined the right side of the road. To the left was the open water of the bay.

Fortunately, the road was empty. *I doubt there's ever traffic here. My kind of place,* he thought.

He pushed the pickup truck harder and reached seventy miles per hour. He picked up Logan's phone and pressed the speaker button. He dialed Captain Phoenix's number and was relieved when the police chief picked up on the first ring.

"Mr. West, how goes it?" the police chief asked.

"It's John Quick, Chief. It turned into a gunfight at the dock. Logan's on the boat right now, which just left the pier, and I'm in pursuit of another suspect in a dark-blue Ford pickup. We're on the main road along the waterfront. He's a pro, but I'm slowly gaining on him. Where are you?"

A moment of silence passed as the police chief processed the information. "It's just me and one of my men. The other had to go to the hospital with the injured tourist. And that's Ballyhoo Road you're on. We're still on the other side of the island. Heading in your direction. Be there in five minutes."

John heard sirens in the background. Storefronts flashed by in his periphery. Suddenly, the Ford's brake lights illuminated, and the vehicle slowed. It fishtailed as it turned right off the main road.

"Shit," John said. "Chief, he just turned right up a small road that leads up into the hills."

"That's Ulakta Drive. It goes to the World War Two Historic Area. There's nothing out there but old bunkers that overlook the water. It's steep, rugged terrain, especially at the waterline."

John thought for a moment. *Why would the boat leave? Their commander had to know he couldn't come back to the bay. And this guy was risking capture by fleeing in a pickup. Both vehicles had to be headed somewhere specific, someplace where they could link back up. But why send one man across land?* He didn't know.

"Chief, are there any caves, grottos, any place you could hide a small boat? This guy has to be going somewhere. They're not the type to go on a suicide run. These are pros. He's going to have to link up with the rest of his team somewhere."

Silence. "The Lookout," the police chief said, almost in disbelief. "It's an abandoned bunker built into the side of a cliff a hundred feet above the water. There's a small tunnel about a hundred yards long that leads to it, but it's off-limits to tourists because the tunnel has some structural issues."

"What's below it?" John asked.

"Nothing but jagged rocks, although there is a small area that curves under the cliff where I guess someone could hide a boat. It'd be concealed by the rocks. But there's no way to get from the bunker to the water."

"Chief, these guys are good. I guarantee they found a way." The

Ford had disappeared in front of him as the curve of the winding road masked the vehicle. *Shit.* "Where's the entrance to the tunnel?"

"You can't miss it. When you get close to the water, the road splits. Go left. It dead-ends a short ways after. You'll see a chained gate and the entrance to the tunnel beyond."

"I bet it's not chained anymore. I'm going in after this guy when I get there. He's in a hurry, which concerns the hell out of me." He paused, and added, "When you get there, park and wait outside. I'm sure I won't have a signal in the tunnel. When I come back out, I'll make sure you know it's me. If you see anyone else, light 'em up," John said matter-of-factly.

"Understood. Be careful. It's dark in there."

John smiled. "That's just the way I like it," he responded, and concentrated on the winding road in front of him. The Chevy came around a hairpin curve to the right, and John saw the Y-intersection in front of him.

"Chief, I'm at the intersection now." He slammed on the brakes and took the road to the left, immediately spotting the dead end. The Ford was parked in front of the gate and still running. The driver's door was open. John caught a glimpse of a fleeing figure entering the tunnel entrance. *Motherfucker's moving fast.*

"I'm here. The suspect is already inside the tunnel. I'm heading in after him. Hanging up now. Hopefully, I'll see you shortly." He paused before he hit the end button. "Like I said, don't hesitate. If anyone other than me comes out, shoot him. These guys are trained killers. You don't want to give them a moment to react. You understand?"

"Got it. Good luck," the police chief said.

He slammed the brakes of the Chevy and skidded to a halt. *Showtime.*

———

The Wolverine crouched in the corner of the wheelhouse and assessed his options. He couldn't go downstairs. The hatch was still open, and the man on deck would have a clear shot at him the moment he left cover.

Whoever he was, he was no amateur. The man with the green eyes had eliminated Dimitri, right after his partner had shot and killed Nikolai. They had to be US federal law enforcement, probably with Special Ops training—they were just too good. He also knew they'd have backup, but one incomplete task remained before he could leave. *Which is why I need to kill him as quickly as possible.*

Another door to the wheelhouse led to a walkway and the bow of the boat. If he positioned himself on it, he'd have a view of the entire bridge, including the top of the stairwell. Whoever this man was, he'd have to come up the stairs, eventually. The Wolverine was a patient man, having once spent two days in a field outside Grozny to kill a Chechen commander from more than a thousand yards away. He'd wait as long as it required.

He opened the door to the walkway and pushed the door against the exterior bulkhead. He crept silently backward as the cold air and wind assaulted him. Once outside, he flattened himself on the walkway.

The PP-2000 was aimed directly at the top of the stairs. He knew he couldn't miss at this range, even if he closed his eyes. The Wolverine stilled his body and lowered his heart rate. His breathing slowed. *This engagement will be over shortly.*

Minutes passed. The boat rocked back and forth as it proceeded through the mouth of the bay. He'd put it on autopilot to the preprogrammed destination. The Wolverine heard nothing but the roar of the engines and the wind, amplified by the boat's speed.

He has to come up. It's the only way. He forced himself to remain motionless. To move could reveal his location and likely result in his death. He knew that's what the American wanted—for him to make an amateur mistake.

Thud!

The Wolverine felt the walkway shake from a sudden impact behind him. A shadow engulfed his figure, stretching out in front of him. *Impossible! There was no way to reach the roof of the bridge from the deck.* And yet, his opponent had flanked him from behind. The man's tenacity was impressive.

Now I really only have one choice, he thought grimly.

———

Logan had known that the Russian team leader—as Logan thought of him after hearing his orders issued in that Slavic language—wouldn't be drawn out from the wheelhouse. It would've been foolish to surrender his tactical advantage. Consequently, Logan's dilemma had been a simple one—reach the bridge without being spotted.

The stairwell was his enemy's personal target range, to be avoided at all costs. There had to be a way to access the bridge from outside and still remain unseen. He'd been stumped, at least until he saw the crane. After it had dropped the submarine, its arm had swung back toward the main structure and remained suspended a few feet above the roof of the wheelhouse.

Logan had scaled it quickly and climbed on top of the long arm. Running across the narrow steel beam, he'd spotted the open door in the back of the bridge and instantly identified an ideal ambush position. He'd leapt across the gap to the roof and landed softly. For a moment, he'd thought his enemy had seen him. Logan had frozen, waiting, until he realized he was in the clear, and had crept across the roof as quickly as he could manage in the shifting seas.

When he had reached the edge, he'd looked down and saw the prone Russian, his weapon aimed through the bridge at the stairwell. Since Logan had killed his previous target, his intent was to take the team leader alive. And so he'd dropped onto the walkway, directly behind him.

Hoping to avoid lethal action, Logan spoke in a low voice. "I'm going to give you one chance before—" was all he had time to utter.

The man was lightning quick. He released the submachine gun and used his arms to launch himself up and forward before scrambling on all fours and propelling himself halfway through the open hatch.

Seriously? Logan thought as he raised his Kimber to fire, then hesitated. *If you want him alive, you can't shoot him,* an inner voice warned. Logan West heeded the warning and obeyed his alter ego—it had proven reliable and saved his life too many times to be dismissed.

Logan holstered the Kimber and took two purposeful steps toward the Russian. Without breaking stride, he delivered a powerful kick to his left hip and was rewarded with a grunt of pain.

Unexpectedly, his adversary kept moving through the doorway on his hands and knees. Logan followed him into the wheelhouse. *I need to end this,* he realized as he shot a glance through the bridge's window. The boat was nearing the north end of the island, and Logan didn't want to discover what other surprises the *Arctic Glide* had in store for him.

Logan reached out and grabbed his assailant by the shoulders. He intended to slam the Russian into the boat's controls when his opponent delivered an elbow to Logan's face. Logan turned his head to the right in an attempt to avoid it, but the elbow glanced off his head nonetheless. He felt an all-too-familiar ringing in his ear.

Logan rotated his body toward his prey and pulled his left foot backward, hooking his right arm under and around his opponent's left arm and securing it at the elbow. He whipped his body completely around and pulled as he pushed his body upward in a judo hip throw.

The man who called himself Martin was lifted off his feet, propelled partially by his own momentum, as Logan flung him over his right shoulder. He crashed to the floor of the bridge and rolled to a stop at the base of a computer rack along the back wall.

The Russian shook his head to regain his focus.

Seizing the moment, Logan stepped forward and delivered a short roundhouse kick to his face. The kick was expertly executed, but somehow the man blocked it with both arms and used the computer rack as leverage to launch himself at Logan's midsection.

The Russian struck Logan in the stomach and pushed him backward. Logan's back collided with the instrument panel in front of the captain's chair, and he felt a lever shift beneath his weight. The boat accelerated.

Logan clasped his hands together and brought them down viciously between his attacker's shoulder blades. He felt the blow stagger the Russian, and Logan risked a quick look backward out the window of the wheelhouse.

Oh no. The currents around the northern corner of the island, combined with the speed of the boat and the pounding waves, had redirected the *Arctic Glide.* To Logan's horror, the boat was now on a collision course with the island, aimed directly at an outcropping of jagged rocks at the base of a cliff two hundred yards away.

We've got thirty seconds at the most, he thought as he delivered a knee to the Russian's stomach, hoping it would put him down for good.

But he had no such luck.

————

John moved silently through the tunnel, alert for any sign of his prey. He'd forced himself to wait one minute, tightly squeezing his eyes shut to adjust to the dark, dank environment. It was a trick he'd used during his time in the Marine Corps. He just hoped it'd help now.

The man he chased had a head start, but an extra minute wouldn't matter since his quarry would've used a light to guide his way through the tunnel. As the pursuer, John didn't have that luxury unless he wanted to broadcast his presence. He knew that meant that his target was already at the end of the tunnel and likely waiting to ambush him. *All I have to do is just walk right into it. Awesome.*

The walls' gray outlines were visible, but only when he peered straight into the darkness.

A slight, cold breeze wafted through the tunnel, and the faint roar of waves crashing into the rocky cliffs reached him. Fortunately, the sounds of the environment masked the soft *thwap thwap thwap* of his Oakley hiking boots, a pair similar to those he'd worn in Force Reconnaissance.

The tunnel gradually lightened. *Almost there . . .*

He rounded a curve and heard two voices speaking Russian in quick, short phrases. It was a distinctive language, and a trip to train the military in the former Soviet republic of Georgia had ingrained it in his mind.

Directly in front of him, the tunnel curved again to the right. The sounds of the ocean had grown louder, and John knew the bunker's entrance lay beyond the last turn.

He pressed himself against the gnarled and jagged wall and moved cautiously toward the bend in the tunnel, preparing himself for what came next—he'd stick his head around the corner to assess the situation and hope he didn't get it blown off.

John never got the chance. A loud *thwack* shattered the relative silence of the bunker facility. The sound was distinct, as if a heavy book had landed on a wooden table. It was immediately followed by a brief shout of surprised pain and then a softer, duller *thud.*

Oh no, John thought as his brain processed the sounds.

Unlike in the movies, a silenced weapon didn't make a soft *hss* or *pfoot.* As he knew from experience, it was much louder due to the explosion of the round in the chamber and the ejection of the shell casing. But it was the second sound that had chilled him. It was the sound of a body hitting the floor.

Someone had just been executed.

And then a second *thwack* followed by another *thud* echoed through the dark.

All thoughts for his personal safety vanished. Whatever ideas he'd had about this team of mercenaries were gone. They weren't soldiers. They were cold-blooded killers, executioners masquerading as professionals.

He didn't know who was dying, but he thought it was likely the *Arctic Glide* crew members the killers had captured. Unlike the times in Iraq when their Force Reconnaissance platoon had been too late, he was here now when the killing was starting. And he'd do everything he could to stop it.

The ice in his blood turned to fire as a familiar emotion took control. The battle rage he'd experienced several times in his life fell over him like a protective cloak and sharpened his senses to a scalpel's edge.

Without wasting another moment, he dashed around the last corner with his Colt .45 in front of him, seeking blood and vengeance.

Logan's blow dropped the Russian to his knees, but instead of falling fully to the floor, the man delivered a punch to the inside of Logan's right knee. Logan's leg buckled from the pain, and he started to slump to the deck.

As Logan fell, he had the presence of mind to reach under his enemy's head and secure it in a tight guillotine choke hold. His right hand applied strangling pressure, and he pulled upward with all his strength.

The Russian struggled violently, striking Logan on both sides of his rib cage as he flailed for air. Logan glanced over his shoulder and tightened his grip. He squeezed harder.

The jagged rocks now filled the entire view. There were only seconds left for Logan to avoid a disastrous collision.

The man's struggles quickly subsided, and he pawed at Logan's waist. *Finally,* Logan thought. He redoubled his efforts, and the Russian's arms went limp. Logan released the man's neck and turned around.

The boat was twenty yards from the rocks. He slammed the throttle into reverse and yanked the steering wheel to the left. The impact was imminent, and he dropped to the deck of the bridge. He braced himself against the console for support. *We're not going to make it.*

The 130-foot vessel's speed and momentum propelled it forward with lethal intent. And then the big boat began a gradual turn to the left . . . but not enough to avoid the rocks.

The boat's starboard side struck the rocks with a tremendous, metallic crunch. A long, painful *screeeeeech* followed as the hull was torn open under the waterline, even as alarms began to blare throughout the ship.

The impact knocked the breath out of Logan's lungs.

Logan struggled to stand, knowing he needed to assess the damage, but he was flung off his feet as the boat surged forward, suddenly free of the jagged boulders that had torn a gaping wound in the hull.

He scrambled for balance, and the boat finally slowed, the speed quickly dropping as water poured into the underwater compartments.

The boat was now less than thirty yards from the cliff and sinking quickly, even as it slowly drifted toward the rock-face wall. There was a rock shelf visible just above the waterline. Logan calculated he had less than two minutes to escape the sinking boat.

He inspected the prone figure of the team commander—his only remaining suspect—and turned the man over. Vacant eyes stared up at him. The man's unconscious body had been thrown into the base of the bridge's instrument panel. His head had struck the console, breaking his neck and killing him.

"Not good," Logan muttered to himself, not out of sympathy for the dead man but for the fact that he'd lost his last source of action-able intelligence.

The boat tilted dramatically to the starboard side as the weight of the assaulting water forced it under. *Less than ninety seconds. Time to get the hell off this floating tomb.*

He ran toward the stairwell with one last item to attend to before he abandoned the sinking ship.

———

The only thing that saved John Quick's life was the sound of a tre-mendous crash and the subsequent roar of metal bending against its will. He didn't know what had happened in the waters below, and he didn't care. It was the scene in front of him that held his attention.

Old and worn concrete blocks fortified a large rectangular en-trance, which shook and crumbled in unison with the explosions below. Beyond the opening was an enormous space at least thirty yards across and twenty yards deep. The entire back wall was curved and contained a concrete opening at least three feet tall at shoulder height that ran the entire length of the wall.

Two bodies lay on the ground in the center of the room. Fresh blood mixed with the dirt and dust of the bunker. A man in black apparel stood next to the bodies and held a pistol aimed directly at John's head.

I'm done, he thought. *I knew it was suicide, but at least I tried.* But to his surprise, the man's head was turned toward the sea. He'd been distracted by the cacophony below.

Behind the combatant with the pistol, John spotted another man in the far right corner at the base of the opening, also clad in black tactical gear. He stood over a pile of smashed computer equipment and held a round object in his right hand, appearing to pull on it with his left.

With precious seconds at stake, John dropped to his right knee and dealt with the most immediate threat first. The man with the pistol started to turn back toward the bunker's opening, but the Colt .45 thundered in the confined space.

Bam!

The first round struck the man in the left side of his jaw, which exploded into chunks of bone and flesh. Grimly satisfied with the gruesome wound he'd inflicted, John fired again and mercifully ended his opponent's agony. The killer's body collapsed, his legs bending to the left as his upper body fell to the right.

The second man reacted too slowly. Even as he tried to release the round object—John now realized it was some kind of incendiary device—John aimed and fired three shots in quick succession.

Bam-bam-bam!

All three bullets struck the man's chest as he dropped the grenade, and he crumpled to the ground in a sitting position. The grenade plummeted in synchronicity with his fall and landed squarely between his legs. It wobbled for a moment as the dying suspect stared at it in amazement, as if mesmerized by the languid motion.

Suddenly, a brilliant light engulfed the dying man, and John felt a rush of heat assault him as he looked away from the temporary sun he'd created inside the bunker. The man had pulled the pin too soon. *Too bad for you.*

The man screamed in agony as the thermite grenade produced a stream of molten iron and aluminum oxide that burned through his clothes and consumed his body. Seconds later, the screams stopped as the four-thousand-degree Fahrenheit fire melted flesh and bone. All that remained was a melded pile of human debris.

Acrid smoke poured out through the opening as the blinding white light devoured the natural darkness of the bunker. John's eyes burned from the intensity, and then the light vanished just as quickly as it had appeared.

John opened his eyes and surveyed the carnage he'd created. He looked around the bunker as the smoke slowly dissipated, and walked over to his first victim, kicking the pistol away for good measure.

Several small Pelican cases were stacked along the back wall under the opening. The right corner now contained a burning hulk, a grotesque statue shaped from the second dead killer and a pile of melted computer parts that had been too close to the thermite grenade. *What a mess.*

A groan emanated from one of the two captives who'd been shot point-blank.

John hurried over to the man and knelt down. He'd been shot in the chest, and blood slowly leaked from a hole in his dark blue parka. His face was ashen, and sweat poured down his forehead. His eyes danced wildly with a fierce determination and awareness.

I can't believe he's still alive. John crushed the thought and said, "My name is John Quick, and I'm with the FBI. I've got you now. You're going to be okay, but I need to check this wound."

He started to open the man's coat, but the man suddenly grabbed John's hands and squeezed tightly, forcing John to look into his face. He stared intensely into John's eyes and pulled him closer.

An unsettling feeling of déjà vu washed over John—he'd watched this scene play out before. The man knew he was dying but clung to life through sheer will. Whatever this man had to tell him—a confession, an explanation, a prayer—he'd listen. John hadn't been able to save him—he'd been seconds too late—but he'd listen to his final words and provide whatever comfort he could in these last moments.

John let himself be pulled to within inches of the man's face. He could feel the man's life force blazing away beneath him. "I'm here with you until the end." He squeezed his hands tightly to emphasize the point. "I won't let go."

The man nodded, and an unspoken bond formed between them. He inhaled a deep breath, and John heard it catch in his chest. *It's close now.*

"Do you want me to say a prayer?" John asked. Some men sought religious comfort in their final seconds. John often wondered why.

He thought it might be some last-ditch effort to seek forgiveness for lives filled with sin, final hopes for salvation and entrance into whatever version of heaven they yearned to reach.

The man smiled and shook his head slightly. John smiled back at him, completely focused on the dying stranger.

"Fair enough." He paused. "I promise you this, my friend. We'll find whoever's responsible for all of this, and we'll stop them. I assure you. You won't be forgotten. I will avenge you."

The man's eyes widened. *Here it comes.* And then he spoke his final words, whispering them into John Quick's face.

"You . . . need to . . . talk . . . to DARPA," he said, and died holding John's hands.

John laid the man's head on the ground and closed his eyes. He folded the stranger's hands over his chest and stood up.

The Defense Advanced Research Projects Agency? What the hell do they have to do with this?

A scraping noise from the far left corner of the bunker snatched his attention, and his training took control once again. He whirled on his heels as the Colt .45 searched for another target.

In a nook carved into the wall stood a shadow-shrouded Logan West. He was soaked from head to toe and held his Kimber pistol in one hand and a black backpack in the other.

John lowered the weapon. "I see you're still alive. What did you do? Blow up the boat? I assumed that was your mess that shook the mountain. You never knew how to make a silent entrance." He paused, and added as he looked back down at the dead man, "Thanks, by the way. It distracted them just long enough to save my ass and end theirs."

Logan processed the aftermath, and his eyes were drawn to the two dead men at John's feet. "They killed the hostages." It was a statement, not a question. "Motherfuckers . . . I hope you made them pay before you sent them on their way." And then he saw the burning pile of smoldering bone and plastic on the other side of the bunker.

"I guess you did." He saw the somber look on John's face. "Hey, you okay?"

John nodded. "This man just died in my arms. Not the first time, probably not the last . . . I held him through his final moments. Hell, he should've been dead already." He shook his head slowly. "He said something at the end, and it's throwing me for a loop."

"What's that?"

"He said we need to talk to DARPA, and then he died. Didn't want to pray. No 'Tell my wife I love her'—nothing like that. Instead, he told us to talk to DARPA." John looked at him. "What the fuck, Logan?"

Logan stared back at him even as his mind raced through countless possibilities, none of them good. "Do you have my phone?"

"As a matter of fact, I do. But it's back in the truck, probably with Chief Phoenix and his men, if they've shown up." He paused. "Why?"

Logan never hesitated. "Because we need to call Mike right now. Let's go." He ran toward the tunnel entrance, a wet apparition disappearing into darkness.

John followed. *A Russian special ops team, oil researchers, and now the DOD's DARPA? Wherever this one goes, it's not going to be good.*

CHAPTER 7

Hangar 7, Unalaska Airport

The images were grainy and shaky, taken from the main road, but the video clearly captured the significant events of the gunfight on the pier. The cameraman had remained surprisingly silent as he filmed the unfolding battle.

After John had pursued the fleeing pickup truck, the cameraman had chosen to follow the fleeing *Arctic Glide*. From his angle ashore, he'd had a direct line of sight into the rear of the boat, albeit at a distance.

"Here comes my favorite part," John said to Logan as they watched the video on a large-screen TV in the middle of the constant activity of the airport's makeshift command center. The camera zoomed in just in time to film the yellow submersible crash to the deck and crush the remaining gunman. "Ouch. That had to hurt," he added.

Logan just shook his head at his friend's morbid joke as the boat disappeared around the peninsula toward the north point of the island, moments before Logan had put a bullet in the wounded shooter's head. *Thank God he didn't get our faces. After the events of two years ago, that's the last thing any of us needs.*

The cameraman was a producer for a popular TV show filmed during crab season. His boat had returned for a repair that morning, and he'd happened to be leaving one of the local stores when the gun battle occurred.

To his credit, as soon as the State Police and FBI had descended on the isolated island within hours of the incident and set up operations at the airport, he'd brought them the video.

After confirming the legal fact that Logan and John had engaged in a justifiable use of force, the FBI technicians had copied it and continued to examine it for any evidence. The FBI requested that the cameraman wait twenty-four hours to release it publicly—which he had—but now here they were, watching it for what to Logan felt like the hundredth time in less than forty-eight hours.

"Fuck him," John said. "He would've gladly killed you and fed you to the killer whales up here."

"Agreed," Logan said. "They all got what they deserved, although it would've been nice to question one of them." He paused. "Regardless, the world's definitely better off without this team in it."

One of the classified phones on a communications table suddenly rang, and a digital *chirp* was heard throughout the command center. All heads turned, including Logan's and John's.

DC—must be Mike. Hopefully he's got some good news, Logan thought. He stood up as a young FBI agent answered the phone.

"Roger, sir. I'll put him on," Logan heard the agent say. The young man turned toward Logan and said, "It's Deputy Director Benson for you, sir."

In the last twenty-four hours, FBI and US Coast Guard divers had recovered all the bodies of the assault team and the *Arctic Glide*'s real crew. The Russian team had killed the men and stored their bodies below deck in one of the staterooms.

Logan accepted the handset and raised it to his ear. "Mike, please tell me you've got something back there. What about Colin Davies's last words about DARPA? There has to be something. We're running out of evidence up here."

The nationality of the assault team had indeed been confirmed as

Russian. The CIA had even identified one of the team members, a former FSB operator who had supposedly retired several years ago, but those facts were being kept under wraps at this point in the investigation. Their weapons linked directly to a black-market arms dealer in South America who was now dead, and their communications gear was state-of-the-art but available off the shelf.

"As a matter of fact, we do, but it's too sensitive to discuss over the phone, even a secure one. I need you and John back here as soon as possible," Mike stated.

"As in do-not-pass-go-do-not-collect-two-hundred-dollars soon?" Logan joked. "Sarah's going to be pissed," he added, thinking about his wife and his futile hope to join her back in Aspen.

"I'll call her myself if you want, but I need you here at my office in DC by zero seven tomorrow morning. We have a meeting at seven thirty. I'll fill you in when I see you both. Use the agency's Gulfstream. I know you're four hours behind, and it's two o'clock there, which means you're going to be flying all night and coming straight here when you land. I'll have a car waiting."

Logan looked at John and lowered his head in mock defeat. "John might be more upset than Sarah. He was starting to fall in love with this place. He was even thinking of converting one of these bunkers into a summer home, living off the land, and writing his own manifesto."

John flipped Logan the middle finger in response and silently mouthed, *Asshole.*

"Tell John I'm surprised he knows how to write," Mike replied. "More importantly, tell him—and this goes for you as well—to get some rest on the plane. You're both going to need it."

"Will do. Anything else before I go?" Logan asked.

"Now that you asked . . . you wouldn't happen to have your passport on you, do you? Both of you are going to need them."

"No. Mine is back in Maryland." He mouthed, *Passport?* to John, who immediately understood but shook his head and mouthed *DC.*

"John's is in DC," he added. "So we're taking the Logan and John show global? I always wanted to be a spy, a sort of roguish double-O seven."

"Stop talking about your IQ," Mike retorted sharply. "See you tomorrow." And he hung up.

Logan had detected an edge to Mike's voice. *Something's got him concerned.* He looked at John. "Whatever's going on, Mike's worried."

"I guess we'll know in the morning." John added, "And Logan, you'll never be James Bond. More like Maxwell Smart."

"Always have to bring me down, don't you? Crush my hopes and dreams . . ."

"I just don't want you to have any unattainable aspirations," John said, and smiled. "I'm looking out for *you*," he emphasized.

"Thanks. I can tell," Logan said wryly. "My heart's all aflutter. Now let's get to the plane. We just got voted off the island."

CHAPTER 8

Republican Palace, Khartoum

Namir had watched the video of the gun battle countless times through Sky News via his satellite provider. It had only started running within the last few hours, but Gang had informed him that the battle had occurred more than two days ago. He hadn't asked Gang about the team that had been killed. He didn't need to. He knew that Gang would only have involved professionals, a fact which meant that whoever the Americans were, they were good.

It didn't matter. Even if the Americans were on their trail, the plan was already in motion. The team had succeeded. The equipment was in Europe and awaiting ground transportation to a private airfield that Major Lau had selected. Namir didn't know or want the details. The less he knew about the movements of the equipment, the better.

What was most critical was that by tomorrow, it would reach his beloved continent and embark on the last leg of the journey to Sudan.

And once it's here, there's nothing anyone can do to stop us or the Chinese. Not the US, not the international community—no one. They don't have the stomach for it.

His cell phone rang. It was Gang.

Namir answered. "I assume you've been watching the news?"

"Of course," Gang answered tersely. "No matter—the team served its purpose. My operatives in Europe have collected no intelligence that indicates the Americans know we have it. The package leaves tonight for the airfield and should arrive tomorrow morning."

"That's good to hear," Namir replied.

"The equipment should fly out tomorrow or the next day. There's a weather system that may delay them," Gang said.

"These things happen. A small delay, nothing more. I have full confidence in your ability to deliver," Namir said.

"As you should," Gang said, "since I've never failed to meet an operational deadline." He hesitated, and added, "I assure you. We will succeed. No matter what obstacles land in our path, we will overcome them. America's status as a superpower will be no more by the time our countries are done with it. The oil will be ours, and the largest influx of money your country has ever seen will be yours."

He is driven by something other than Chinese nationalism, Namir thought. He recognized the intensity and hatred in the young man's voice. *It's personal for him.*

"I believe you. Keep me posted if anything changes."

"I will. If you hear nothing from me in the next twenty-four hours, we're on schedule. I'll update you next when the plane takes off for Sudan." Gang hung up.

Namir stared out the window at the sluggish waters of the Nile River, which patiently wound its way north through his country and ultimately fed into Lake Nasser. He prayed for that type of steadfast patience to carry him through the next two days. Now the most difficult part of any operation—the waiting—had begun.

———

Gang dialed another number the moment he disconnected the call to Namir. The call was answered on the third ring.

"Hello?" the American said cautiously and somewhat sleepily. It was the middle of the night on the East Coast.

"The equipment is in Europe. It leaves tomorrow for here. We're in the last leg of the operation. Does your government know anything yet?" Gang asked.

"Only that the team was Russian, but that was always part of the plan," the American said. "If they take the bait, it will guarantee your success."

"Is there anything that can lead back to you?" Gang asked. The American was one of the most highly placed double agents Gang had encountered in his career in the clandestine world. The compromise of his identity would be nearly as catastrophic as the failure of their main mission.

"Negative," the American said. "The team is dead, and my source in Moscow has gone dark now that the team has been identified. He's as good as gone, even though he set the whole thing in motion. As for the researcher, I convinced him we needed an actual trial before we could go operational with the equipment. I managed to persuade him to keep it from his superiors, reassuring him that he'd be more than rewarded by his government with limitless funding when the appropriate time came. The ironic part is that it was his idea to use the *Arctic Glide* through the contacts *he had* from his oil exploration consulting. And now that he's dead, it couldn't have worked out any better."

"That's very smart," Gang said.

"I've covered my tracks. Don't worry. I've been doing this long enough. But I should know more in a few hours. I've got a meeting with several of the key players."

"Please keep me informed when you know what your government's plan is," Gang said.

"I will. Now I'm going to go back to sleep. The next few days are going to be long," the American said. "I'll let you know when I have something."

"Very well. But be safe," Gang emphasized. "My leadership cares greatly about your position."

"I understand, and I will be," the American replied, and hung up.

The false flag is set, Gang thought. Now it was time to see if the American government tried to capture it. If they did, it nearly guaranteed his success, even in a brutal business that often had no guarantees other than death and betrayal.

PART II

SHELL GAME

WONJO BUHWAL

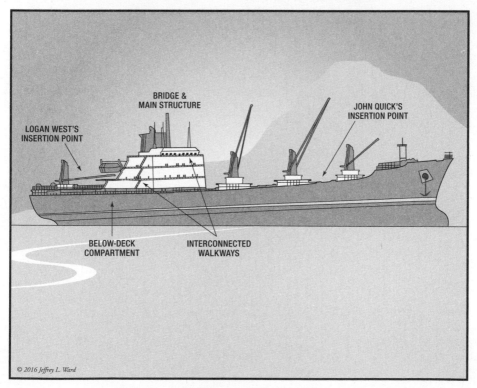

LOGAN WEST'S
INSERTION POINT

BRIDGE &
MAIN STRUCTURE

JOHN QUICK'S
INSERTION POINT

BELOW-DECK
COMPARTMENT

INTERCONNECTED
WALKWAYS

© 2016 Jeffrey L. Ward

CHAPTER 9

Arlington, Virginia

When Mike Benson's chauffeured and armored SUV picked them up at Dulles International Airport, they'd immediately known it was a major crisis. Mike looked like he'd barely slept, and he hardly spoke on the drive to DARPA's headquarters, a massive building of black glass and brown stone.

He'd only informed them of their audience and the organizations it represented as they pulled into the underground garage.

Logan and John now sat at the conference table on the twelfth floor and listened as the director of DARPA, Dr. Anita Mackenzie, continued the brief.

In addition to FBI Deputy Director Mike Benson, the other attendees for the morning meeting included the deputy director of the Central Intelligence Agency, the national security advisor, and the director of DARPA's Tactical Technology Office.

A fit man in his midthirties sat in a chair along the wall and observed the discussion. He hadn't introduced himself, but Logan identified him as military or covert operations. Even with long, black, combed-back hair, it was hard to conceal the mannerisms of a professional warrior.

Logan suddenly recalled a brief period several years ago when he'd let his hair grow out and hadn't shaved for three months. He'd been at a bar in Baltimore when an extremely attractive woman beside him had initiated a conversation. "So which branch of the service are you in?" He'd been surprised and asked her why she thought he'd been in the service. She'd leaned in to him and said, "I can always tell. No matter what you do to hide it, it's always written all over you guys like a flashing neon sign."

Refocusing his attention, Logan struggled to comprehend the highly technical aspects of the brief, but he'd already grasped the major points, as well as the global implications and imminent threat to national security. *I knew this was going to be a bad one,* he thought. *I hate it when I'm right.*

Now clean-shaven, Logan spoke to Dr. Mackenzie. "Ma'am, are you telling me that you had *no idea* Colin Davies was testing the equipment on the boat in Alaska? How'd he get it out of the facility?"

Dr. Mackenzie sighed and placed her well-manicured hands on the table. "Mr. West, the facility was only one of our computer laboratories in the DC area. We have several. Mr. Davies—who pointed you to us before he died—was the program lead for ONERING, and he had complete access to all areas of that facility. Due to the sensitive nature of our work, it's not uncommon for employees to transfer equipment between facilities or even take computers home."

Logan raised his eyebrows. "Dr. Mackenzie, you may want to reconsider that policy." The deputy director of the CIA, Roger Brock, shifted uncomfortably in his seat.

Dr. Mackenzie responded, without any notice or offense, "Mr. West, not all of our work is classified. Unfortunately, in this case, ONERING is one of the most sensitive and secret projects we have under development. We didn't even think it was fully functional, let alone ready for field testing."

"Why ONERING, Dr. Mackenzie?" John suddenly asked. The program name had raised a curiosity in his mind, and he couldn't shake it loose until he asked the question.

"From *The Lord of the Rings,* Mr. Quick. 'The one ring to rule them all,' or something to that effect."

John stared at her in disbelief. "You named one of the most sensitive classified projects you have after Tolkien?"

"Mr. Quick," Dr. Mackenzie responded, "you'd be surprised at some of the project and program names in the Intelligence Community. I've seen everything from Harry Potter to Hello Kitty. Some of our brightest folks have a rather wry sense of humor."

John looked at Logan and said, "And I thought our recon operations named after brands of beer were clever. Not so much now."

Colin Davies had died in John's arms; however, after learning of the man's activities and the potential threat he'd created with his irresponsible actions, he felt slightly less sympathetic about his fate. He continued to Dr. Mackenzie, "Do you have any indications that Davies actually tested it? Hell, would you even have any way to know if he did?"

"I spoke to the deputy director of the NRO, who built most of our intelligence satellites," Dr. Mackenzie said. "Based on what I told him about ONERING, he reached out to his folks. There was a GPS fail-safe built into it to let us know when it's been activated, but if whoever has it now has found and disabled it, we're screwed. Also, once it's used, there's no way for the target satellite to detect from where or how it's being controlled. As the deputy director said—and I quote—'And you thought this was a good fucking idea how?'"

Dr. Mackenzie only shook her head and lowered her eyes to the table. No one spoke.

Finally, Mike Benson leaned forward, his enormous frame pressing against the table. "John, it doesn't matter. What does matter is the limited information we have at this time and where it puts us. What's even scarier is that if the boat's propeller hadn't broken, the Russian team probably would've taken the equipment off the island via other means. The fact that they used a public freight shipping company rather than wait for that repair tells me they're on a time line."

"I still can't believe they used the same credit card to ship the equipment," Logan said. "Seems like such an amateur mistake."

"They probably never planned for a mechanical malfunction," Mike replied. "They also probably never thought we'd catch on to them so quickly. Fortunately, we did, but unfortunately for us, now we're playing catch-up." He paused. "The equipment reached Madrid, Spain, late last night."

Jonathan Sommers, the President's national security advisor, interrupted and added, "I spoke to Ambassador Santos several hours ago. He personally spoke to the captain of Madrid's National Police Force, who dispatched a special investigative unit to the cargo receiving area of the Madrid-Barajas Airport. Their computers indicated the equipment was picked up within an hour of arrival." He looked down at his watch. "Which means it's now been en route to God knows where for the last five hours."

John tilted his head back and laughed out loud. He looked up at the ceiling of the conference room and placed his hands behind his head. All eyes turned toward him, and conversation stopped.

"Ladies and gentlemen, you are some of the brightest people our government has—the president's national security advisor, leaders in several powerful agencies—and yet here we all are, stuck in the same boat. Since I'm probably dragging the intelligence quotient down a bit, let me see if I can get this straight," he said.

Logan knew John was much smarter than he often acted and probably as quick in his analytical processing as more than a few of the members of their esteemed audience.

"Colin Davies led a program to develop a ground-based anti-satellite weapon that is theoretically capable of hijacking *any* satellite it targets and then controlling that satellite, all the while remaining undetected. He then walked right out of one of your DC laboratories with the test unit, five extremely powerful classified laptops, and a next-generation portable satellite broadcast system. He somehow ended up on the *Arctic Glide* a week later as a result of a connection he has in North American Oil. You have no idea if he tested his equipment, which doesn't matter anymore, since an elite Russian special-ops team killed him and the crew and managed to steal all of the equipment, which is now somewhere within five hours of Madrid, Spain. We have no idea who is behind this or what they intend to do with the system, although the possibilities are limitless and equally sinister. Does that about sum it up?"

It was John's last point that chilled the listeners. All knew the enormous risk to national security if an enemy of the United States could control any satellite it desired and use it for its own purposes. The result would be catastrophic for the US and the international intelligence community. Systems would be compromised; information stolen; and most importantly, people would die. It was an unfathomable scenario. *No. It's a fucking doomsday nightmare,* Logan thought.

"Good Christ, and I thought stopping a war in the Middle East was hard," John said, and looked around the room at the group. "So what now?"

"I think I can answer that. We're going to Spain," Logan said. "And I believe that debonair gentleman in the back"—he paused, and nodded toward the quiet, fit man with long black hair—"will be our CIA chaperone. How's that for some good prognostication?"

"I really hate it when you use big words," John said in a deeply sarcastic tone as Dr. Mackenzie stared wide-eyed at the exchange. John saw her expression and added, "Don't worry, Dr. Mackenzie," in a suddenly serious tone. He looked her squarely in the eyes. "There are few better when it really matters."

The man with the black hair smiled genuinely, and said, "Well done, Mr. West. I was wondering how long I was going to have to sit here."

"I thought about commenting earlier but figured I'd wait for the appropriate moment."

CIA Deputy Director Roger Brock spoke up. "Lady and gentlemen, please say hello to Mr. Cole Matthews, the chief of the CIA's

Special Operations Group." Commonly referred to as SOG, it was the arm of the CIA involved in all high-risk, military, or clandestine intelligence activities overseas. It was a team from this group that had reportedly captured Khalid Sheikh Mohammed, the mastermind behind the 9/11 attacks.

Before Logan could catch himself, he said, "Hi, Cole. Thanks for sharing. Keep coming back." Dr. Mackenzie looked at Logan quizzically. "Just a little AA humor, nothing to worry about . . . too much." He grinned for emphasis.

Cole Matthews smiled back at him and exposed a neat row of teeth set amid an angular jaw and square facial features. *The teeth of a shark, or some kind of predator,* Logan thought.

Mike Benson realized the formal portion of the meeting was at an end. "Play nice, Logan. Cole's your new battle buddy."

Logan and John both looked at Mike and simultaneously said, "Thanks, Dad." Cole was the only member of the audience who laughed. *At least he has a sense of humor,* Logan thought.

CHAPTER 10

Over the Atlantic Ocean

Logan watched the wispy clouds race below the speeding Gulfstream jet. Even at this altitude, he spotted a whitecap wave and the occasional ship. He turned his attention back to the two men accompanying him to Madrid. *Two more hours. I hope the trail's not cold.*

"So the Russians in Spain who picked up the equipment have mob ties," Logan said, returning to their conversation. "I remember reading about two major operations against the Russian mob that captured several high-ranking members."

Cole Matthews nodded. "That's true. The government of Spain pulled off a coup. They captured four of the Russian mob's senior leaders and dozens of mid- and low-level enforcers. Unfortunately, they also discovered that the Russians were embedded in almost every branch of the government, and they're still rooting them out."

"If nothing else, you have to admire the Spanish resolve," John added. "But what I don't get is why the mob would help a Russian covert team that's being directed by the government in Moscow."

Cole smiled, and said, "Until recently, that puzzled us as well; however, thanks to that jackass kid who gave all those documents to WikiLeaks, we have an answer. As much as I'd like to put a bullet in his head for compromising the identities of numerous operatives in various agencies, one of his documents revealed that the Russian government is *closely* connected to the Russian mob. We now know the Russians are using the mob as proxies wherever and whenever it suits their interests, both home and abroad."

John replied, "And I thought the Russian government was a lover of democracy and free-thinking individuals. You know, for a CIA guy, you're not half bad." He looked at Logan and then back at Cole.

"We don't exactly have a great track record with the CIA," John continued. "One of your ilk led us into an ambush in Fallujah in '04—an ambush that led to the violent deaths of most of our Force Recon platoon."

John knew Logan still harbored the same resentment and anger that he felt toward that agency.

"That same man then supported a megalomaniac who wanted to start another war in the Middle East, all to settle a personal score with the Iranian government," John said.

Cole nodded. "Trust me, Mr. Quick. I'm well aware of what Mr. Carlson did to you, your unit, and this country. I'm disgusted as anyone by his despicable actions. If Mr. West hadn't ended his life in Haditha a few years back, I'd have been tempted to sanction an off-the-books action on him." He looked to Logan. "Fortunately, you took care of that for me."

Cole turned to John. "You don't know me. I know you don't trust me. And I don't blame you. I wouldn't either. What I can tell you is that I spent over a decade with that unit at Fort Bragg everyone loves to glorify, and my current job was a personal calling for me after something went south on a mission."

Logan wondered what could've forced a Delta operator out of the community on his own volition but knew better than to ask.

"Most importantly," Cole continued, "you need to know I'll do whatever it takes to protect our country from all threats, whatever the origin."

John studied the man for a moment and then shrugged. "Works

for me. I figured you can't all be bad. And I just hope for your sake you're as good a shot as you were in Delta." He paused, and added, "I hear you can get soft as a civilian."

"From what I hear about you two, you're not that soft, even at your advanced age *and* as civilians." Cole smirked.

"Well played, Mr. Matthews," John said.

"Are you two done? Or would you like me to join the pilots so you can hold hands and cuddle?" Logan asked. Something still nagged at him about the Russians. "So what should we expect in Valdemoro?"

Cole looked at John. "Is he always like this?"

John laughed. "This is on a good day. Sometimes he gets *really* serious, and then the fun begins, usually with explosions, screams, and bodies."

"Great. Okay then." Cole shifted in his chair, and said, "Down to business. We know the Russian mob still has several networks that continue to operate throughout Spain. Like cockroaches, it's hard to kill them all."

"Sure, but we can always try," John said.

"Spanish police traced the license plate of the white box truck that picked up the equipment to a Madrid Chinese restaurant."

Logan interrupted. "Chinese?"

"Turns out, like in all major cities, there's quite a Chinese population in Madrid. Anyhow, they thought the restaurant was a dead end until they checked with their organized crime task force, who realized it was a money-laundering front for the Chinese mafia. The head of that Chinese family also has an arrangement with a team of Russian businessmen who just happen to operate an illegal casino in the same district. The Spanish police raided the casino with a small unit from their Special Group of Operations, the Grupo Especial de Operaciónes, referred to as GEOs. They're equivalent to the FBI's HRT." Cole paused, and added, "I understand you're both quite familiar with them."

This guy seems to know a lot about us, Logan thought cautiously.

"From what the embassy told me, after less than ten minutes of 'persuasive' conversation, the Russian mobster they cornered at the casino gave up the location of a safe house in Valdemoro. He said he'd received a phone call earlier in the day from his leadership in Moscow to arrange for pickup and delivery of a shipment from Barajas Airport. His men had specific instructions to pick up the shipment, head to Valdemoro, and wait for follow-on orders. He provided Moscow with their cell numbers, and for all he knows, they've already received their instructions and are gone."

"Great. You know, I really, really hate playing catch-up," Logan said. Changing subjects, he asked, "Do the GEOs—or anyone for that matter—have the safe house under surveillance?"

"As a matter of fact, they do. There's a car waiting for us at the airport. It's going to take us directly to Valdemoro, where the team leader has orders to assist us in any way possible."

"I'm sure he'll love that," John said.

"Depends on how professional he is. In my experience, these guys are like us. They're just a different flavor of the same candy," Cole said.

"Agreed," Logan said, and then stuck out his hand. "And the name's Logan, and this is John. I don't want my battle buddy using 'Mr. West' and 'Mr. Quick.' Sounds so fucking formal."

Cole shook his hand firmly and said, "Please, call me Cole. It actually is my real name, by the way."

"Good to know you are who you say you are," Logan said. "And now that introductions are over, I'm going to sleep for an hour before we gear up and hit the ground."

CHAPTER 11

Policía Municipal Headquarters, Valdemoro, Spain

Logan studied the commercial satellite image on the inspector's iPad. In the center was a farm on the eastern outskirts of the city's main municipal district. The farmhouse was set back more than a hundred yards from the nearest road, with a barn and garage in close proximity. It was surrounded by slightly rolling hills and wheat fields, the main crop of the sleepy commuter town.

No observable cover in any direction. No avenues of approach, Logan thought.

Inspector Adan Antonio Romero, a man in his early forties with dark-brown hair worn in a crew cut, seemed to read Logan's expression as he examined the topography. "Señor West, the climate is too dry, which makes it difficult for any trees to survive."

The inspector was the commander of the GEO team that had executed the raid on the Chinese casino. His instructions from several rungs above him had been clear—assist the Americans in any way possible; recover the truck at all costs; and arrest all Russian mafia members.

He didn't know what was in the truck, but whatever it was, it had members of his government concerned. And that was really all he needed to know. A loyal Spaniard to the core, he served the monarch of Spain and was sworn to uphold the Spanish constitution. Romero was duty bound to fulfill his obligation to his newfound international friends.

"I'd hoped at least for some cover," Logan said. "The nearest building is over half a mile away." He pointed to a small industrial shed surrounded by a small fence. "If we want to find out where the truck is, we need to take someone alive. If they see us coming, that possibility goes out the window. That leaves only one other option."

"And what exactly is that?" Cole asked.

"I know," John said, sighing loudly. He looked at Logan. "You want to go in like Dutch Harbor again, don't you?"

Inspector Romero asked, "What's Dutch Harbor?"

"You mean you haven't seen the news coverage?" Cole said in mock disbelief. "Sorry, inspector. Bad joke. It's not a *what*. It's a *where*. Logan here, two days ago, initiated a gun battle and boat chase by posing as a marina worker. I'm guessing he already has something in mind."

"I do," Logan said, taking a deep breath before continuing. "I pose as a tourist with a broken-down car."

The men standing around the table stared at him in silence. Finally, John said, "You're fucking kidding me. A tourist? Why not just wear a sign that says 'American cowboy and law enforcement officer. Shoot me in the head now, please.' It's too obvious."

"That's exactly my point, John. It *is* obvious, but only to us. If the Russians are still there, they're on edge waiting for their instructions. They're going to assume anyone coming on their property is Spanish law enforcement. They're not going to suspect US involvement. A lost American, especially one whose car blows up in front of their farmhouse, might not raise any suspicions. And if the truck is gone, the guys left behind are going to be even less suspicious. They won't see it coming. No way. And after all, all I need is to get to the front door without getting gunned down in the dirt."

Logan looked at Inspector Romero and said, "This is your country. You know these people. What do you think?"

"I think, Señor West, you are a very brave and foolish man," Inspector Romero said.

"Inspector, I could've told you that," John interjected.

"However," the inspector continued, "it might work. Tourism is common all throughout the country. The proximity of Valdemoro to Madrid makes it a stop on the commuter rail, as well as a sort of—how do you say it?—gateway to the rest of the country. You wouldn't be the first lost American they've seen."

Logan smiled triumphantly at John. "See?"

"Don't declare victory just yet, Señor West. In order for this to work, you still have to be convincing. But once you get to the door, what's your plan?"

"Yeah, smart guy, what's your plan? Politely ask them to throw down their weapons and come out with their hands up?" John asked.

Logan studied the iPad's map, shifting the image around and studying the terrain. "That's *exactly* what I intend to do," he said emphatically.

Cole glanced at the positions Logan had just examined on the iPad, and comprehension dawned. *Very nice, Logan. Very nice indeed . . .*

———

Even by local weather standards, the day was especially moderate, with the temperature in the low fifties. The sun added an additional layer of warmth as Logan casually walked up the dirt driveway to the secluded farmhouse.

He held a cell phone to his ear and pretended to be engaged in an animated conversation. In reality, he spoke to Inspector Romero and provided real-time intelligence as he moved. They'd made the decision to avoid radios in the event the Russians were monitoring police communications.

Logan wore blue jeans, a khaki, lightweight coat that ended below his belt and covered a dark tee shirt, and tan Oakley hiking boots. His Kimber .45 was hidden on a belt holster, which was further back on his waist and tightly secured after the incident on the *Arctic Glide*. A concealed combat harness under his jacket held his Mark II knife in a sheath, two extra magazines, and a flashbang grenade. He hoped to use none of it.

He kept his eyes focused on the white stucco house covered by a gray slate-tile roof, a trademark of Spanish homes that helped to effectively reduce the oppressive summertime heat.

Behind him, parked alongside the main road near the driveway's entrance, smoke poured from under the hood of a dark-green Spanish SEAT León sports hatchback. The incendiary device's timer was set to diminish in intensity over a two-minute period before the smoke disappeared completely.

As he waved his arms in mock frustration and glanced back at the car, he said, "Fifty yards from the front door. No signs of movement in the main house, the garage, or barn. Stand by. Here comes the award-winning performance."

"Roger," replied Inspector Romero.

"He's a horrible actor," Logan heard John say in the background. "Although he did once convince a man he was going to drown him. But then again, he did have him underwater at the time." Logan smiled. *Hopefully, I won't have to do anything like that this time around.*

As Logan closed the distance to the front door of the house, he shouted into the phone, "How soon can you send another car? I'm supposed to be in Madrid in two hours to meet my fiancée. This is ridiculous!"

He stopped on the driveway at a small gravel walkway that led to the front door. He spoke loudly once again as he heard movement inside the extra-wide multicar garage. *Bastards had someone in there the whole time, must have gone around back when I started up the driveway. Could make things a little more interesting.*

"Okay. No problem. I walked to the nearest house on Ronda

Prado Road. Looks like the house number is fourteen-oh-three, and I'm about to knock on the door. Hopefully, I can wait here. You think an hour or so?"

He paused a moment longer.

"Sounds good. Thanks, Armando. I'll see your driver soon." Logan pretended to hang up the phone but still held it in his left hand as the black front door of the house opened. *Showtime . . .*

Logan turned to the house and almost stopped in his tracks. *Holy Christ. This may not be as easy as I thought.*

A young behemoth in his early twenties completely filled the doorway. He stood at least six foot eight inches tall and wore a black tee shirt that barely covered his engorged muscles. His size dwarfed Logan in comparison. *He's got to be at least two sixty and all muscle— probably steroids. Great, an unstable giant, just what I need.*

He glared at Logan with dead, black eyes, his short black hair cut in a flattop that would have made any Marine Corps barber proud.

Logan heard the sounds of a soccer match coming from a TV somewhere deep inside the house. He couldn't see past the slab of meat in front of him, but he thought he heard movement. *There are at least three of them here. No point in delaying the inevitable.*

Logan spoke in a friendly manner. "Hi, my name's Mark. Do you speak English?" He paused and then added for effect. "I really hope you do. I could use a break the way my day's going."

No response. The man stared at Logan and then scanned the property behind him. His eyes stopped on the smoking car. He smirked and returned his gaze to Logan.

"You're an American," the man stated in a flat, thick Russian accent. "What do you want?" The expressionless tone raised the hair on Logan's neck, not out of fear but in recognition of the sociopathic quality to his voice.

"I'm really sorry to bother you, but that's my rental car out there in front of your property. I was supposed to be in Madrid meeting my fiancée for dinner in a few hours, but the engine blew. I just got off

79

the phone with the rental car company, and they're sending another one, but the guy told me it's going to be an hour."

Before Logan could continue, the mountain spoke again. "How is that my problem?"

"Well—and again, I'm sorry to interrupt your day—I was wondering if I could wait here until they showed up?"

"No," the Russian answered singularly, and stepped back to close the door.

"Come on, buddy. Cut me my some slack here. There's nowhere else for me to go. I hate to ask, but I really need to use a bathroom too. You don't want me going in your yard, do you?"

Silence. And then the man emerged from the door and lumbered down the front porch like a mythological god stepping down from Mount Olympus. He towered over Logan, now within arm's reach on the walkway.

"Listen, American, you cannot stay here. Go back to your car and wait there." The Russian accent was extremely thick now, almost to the point of being comedic. "Don't make me tell you again."

Logan glanced around the giant. Another man lurked in the shadows of the hallway, his hand behind his back.

Logan's demeanor and posture changed. His back stiffened, and he assumed a combative stance the Russian recognized immediately for what it was—hostile. Most dramatically, the carelessly casual visage he'd worn up the driveway was replaced by the hardened, calculated expression that was his natural countenance. Green eyes blazed at the younger man, who visibly reacted at the sudden transformation.

Logan's voice was suddenly as expressionless as the titan's. "Here's the deal, Yuri, or whatever the hell your name is. I am an American, but I'm here with the Spanish National Police, specifically, the GEOs. This place is surrounded. There's nowhere for you to go." He paused for a second to allow the information to sink in. "You have two choices—one, tell us where the van is, or two, die on this farm. I'm not going to ask again."

His body coiled, preparing to act.

The man looked around the property again. Seeing nothing suspicious or alarming, he made his fateful choice.

"Fuck you," the man growled, and reached down to grab Logan by the shoulders.

The man was surprisingly fast for his size, but Logan was faster. He dropped to the ground on his left knee as he let the cell phone fall from his hand. Logan used the height difference between the walkway and the porch to his advantage and delivered a vicious hammer fist to the outside of the man's knee.

The Russian buckled but didn't fall.

Logan heard rapid movement from inside the hallway and looked into the home as he delivered a second blow. The second man lurking inside the shadows ran toward the doorway, a black pistol aimed in Logan's direction.

Logan reached around the giant's right leg and yanked hard on his ankle.

The young giant slammed to the stone porch on his haunches as his comrade opened fire behind him. *Bam! Bam! Bam!*

Logan ducked in front of the Russian as the bullets struck the man in the upper back with wet thuds. His eyes looked into Logan's and widened with horror as his body registered the pain and realization that he'd been shot. *The bigger they are . . .*

Logan drew his Kimber .45 and leaned to his right, exposing himself to the second assailant. His pistol roared on the front steps as he fired three quick shots at the running figure.

The slugs struck the man squarely in the chest as his forward momentum carried him through the doorway. His right foot stuck on the door frame and tripped him.

To Logan, it looked as if an invisible force had yanked the shooter's feet from under him. His upper body kept moving as if he were being pulled to the ground, while his lower body remained secured to the door frame. He crashed to the front porch face-first behind the behemoth. The gun skittered across the porch and down the steps. The man didn't move.

Logan looked back at the behemoth just in time to see his eyes roll up in his head. He toppled backward and landed on top of the second man's head and neck. Logan cringed as he heard a *crack*.

If his friend wasn't dead from my bullets, he is now.

He kept the Kimber trained on the doorway and picked up his cell phone. Before he could speak, he heard the high-pitched revving of a small engine from the separated garage. He looked over and saw the garage door had been raised.

From within, a Honda all-terrain vehicle exited and flashed by Logan before he could react. *There's nowhere to run, moron. I told your friend that and look what happened to him. I guess now it's your turn.*

———

Inspector Romero lay on a hilltop four hundred yards away and watched the speeding ATV accelerate down the driveway toward the street. He adjusted a dial on top of his spotter's binoculars and kept the illuminated reticle on the fleeing figure.

"Three seventy-six, three-seventy, three sixty-five . . . ," he told the prone figure in camouflage holding a military-grade Heckler & Koch PSG-1 sniper rifle.

The shooter exhaled, released all tension in his upper body, and gently pulled the trigger. A singular *crack!* echoed down the hillside.

Inspector Romero caught a momentary glimpse of the 7.62mm bullet's vapor trail as the round flew toward its target. The bullet struck the front right tire of the ATV, and both men watched the resulting carnage unfold.

The tire exploded from the impact, and the nose of the ATV changed direction, lurching down and to the right as if the vehicle were trying to tunnel into the ground. The front right tire served as an anchor as the rear of the vehicle hopped up and swung around toward the front. The left tires touched back down, and the vehicle's momentum caused it to flip over sideways, executing four full barrel rolls before it smashed upside down on the edge of the driveway.

Fortunately for the driver, he'd been flung into the air with the first flip. He landed on his side with one leg bent awkwardly beneath him and lay still.

Madre de Dios, Inspector Romero thought and picked up his cell phone. "All units converge on the farmhouse."

Both men stood up and watched as the figure of Logan West ran to the front door of the house and looked inside. Apparently satisfied that no other hostiles were present, he leapt down the steps and moved into the garage.

Inspector Romero turned to the shooter and said in English, "Excellent shot, Mr. Quick. Excellent shot indeed. Now let's go see if that Russian has anything interesting to say. If he's still alive, that is."

"Show-off," Cole added from a prone position behind them, a radio in his hand.

John Quick smiled at the GEO special forces inspector, ignoring his new CIA friend, and said, "Thanks. I try. That sure looked like a nasty spill, but if he needs it, I'm sure Logan can give him mouth-to-mouth."

———

That had to hurt, Logan thought as he ran down the driveway, figuring that anyone left inside would've made a break for it by now or come out with guns blazing.

You better be alive, asshole, he thought as he reached the ATV driver. Through the open garage door, he'd seen a parked black sedan, and he'd gone inside to investigate. He'd opened the trunk only to discover a spare tire and an old tarp. *God knows what that has been used for.* More importantly, he'd confirmed that the van and its vital contents were gone.

The Russian was unconscious but breathing steadily. A small rivulet of blood streaked down his upturned face. *You're lucky you're out because that's going to hurt like hell when you wake up,* Logan thought as he looked at the broken left leg.

The man's pant leg jutted out at the shin. The misshapen fabric indicated he'd suffered an open compound fracture—the bone had broken through his skin. His left arm was positioned at an awkward angle, and there was a huge laceration on his forearm.

Logan heard the black tactical police vans roar down the street, sirens wailing. A Spanish National Police SUV pulled into the driveway and stopped. Two black tactical vans pulled in directly behind it. Three doors of the SUV opened as John Quick, Cole Matthews, and Inspector Romero exited the vehicle.

"Nice acting, Brando. You really fooled them," John said.

"Hey, cut me some slack. I made it to the front door before the shooting started, which is all we wanted. Unfortunately," Logan said, and sighed, "they didn't want to come out nicely."

"At least this one's alive," Inspector Romero said as a GEO medic hopped out of a van and ran over to attend to the wounded man. The inspector smiled at the Americans and said, "We can hold him up to thirteen days, but I'll only need thirty minutes to interrogate him effectively. We should know what he knows within the hour."

John studied the hardened Spanish GEO, smiled broadly, and said, "You know, I really think I'm beginning to like this country."

CHAPTER 12

Policía Municipal Headquarters, Valdemoro, Spain

Inspector Romero exited the concrete interrogation room and smiled at his guests in the police station hallway. "Did you know that a form of waterboarding was widely used during the Spanish Inquisition? I guess after all these centuries, it's still an effective technique."

John stared at the GEO team leader with raised eyebrows. "I thought we came up with that idea all on our own. So much for American ingenuity," John said with mock disappointment. "More importantly, are you telling us that you just waterboarded that Russian bastard inside that concrete box? Wow. That's awesome, but don't let our ACLU hear that. They'll come after you as if you were Hitler."

"What is this 'ACLU'?" Inspector Romero asked.

"It's this group of lawyers in our country," Cole answered. "Bottom line—they're not all bad, but they often protect the wrong people at the expense of others."

The inspector nodded his head in contemplation and said, "We have that here as well. We call it 'Congress.'"

Logan laughed and said, "In America, the lawyers would be offended by the comparison. Right now, our politicians have about the popularity of the plague, and even that might be considered insulting to the Black Death."

Inspector Romero seemed to appreciate the metaphor. "Setting aside our countries' political problems, I'm sorry to disappoint you, Mr. Quick, but I did not actually torture Mr. Yuri Gagolin."

"Wait a second," Logan interjected. "His name is actually Yuri? That's funny because that's what I called the big guy back at the farmhouse before his buddy killed him."

"Not so funny for him," John said.

"Fuck him if he can't take a joke—or couldn't," Logan said, and smiled.

"You two are somewhat crazy," Inspector Romero stated drily. "Regardless, I only convinced him that if he didn't cooperate immediately, he'd soon have a new appreciation for the historical significance of water torture. It helped that he's disoriented from the pain medications our medic gave him."

"You guys don't mess around," Logan said. "I like that. Out of curiosity, would you have done it if he didn't crack right away?"

"In a situation like this, I would do whatever's necessary to obtain the information I need," Inspector Romero replied, with a look that confirmed Logan's suspicions. *This is a serious man.*

Logan nodded but didn't get a chance to speak, since Cole asked, "What did he tell you, Inspector? We're running out of options, and I hope he's got something useful."

Inspector Romero nodded and said, "He says that two of his comrades left the farmhouse this morning with the van for a port in Cartagena. Our friend in there wasn't supposed to know the details, but he overheard his two friends talking. The one thing he seems to remember was a ship called the *Wonjo Buhwal.* He thinks the van was delivering its contents to that ship."

"You've got to be fucking kidding me. No way," John said, his head whipping to look at Logan in disbelief.

Logan's eyes widened for a brief moment and then narrowed intently at Inspector Romero. "Are you sure—absolutely sure—that's what he said, Inspector?"

Inspector Romero nodded and held out a yellow legal notepad. In small capital letters was printed WONJO BUHWAL. "Do you know this vessel?"

"Both John and I do, unfortunately. It means 'aid bringer,' ironically. In 2003, our Force Reconnaissance platoon was sent inside Iraq near the western border three months ahead of the invasion. Our mission was to probe Iraqi defenses near Al Qaim, this town on the border with Syria. When we were done, we were ordered to take a slight detour. There was a North Korean vessel en route to Lebanon with a shipment of SCUD missiles. Our Intelligence Community supposedly had solid proof the missiles were on board, including satellite imagery of the SCUDs being loaded in North Korea. Our JSOC boys and Navy SEALs were busy preparing for Iraq, and we just happened to be the closest unit in the region trained to take down a cargo ship of that size."

"What happened?" the inspector asked earnestly.

"The boarding was routine. We met no resistance, and once we secured the ship, we found no trace of the missiles. But the North Korean captain was belligerent and defiant. I still remember the disgust on his face at the sight of American Marines on his ship. He despised us," Logan recalled.

"I remember that asshole," John said. "We knew the weapons had to be on the ship, but after only an hour of searching, we were ordered off before we could take it into a friendly port. Unbeknownst to us, the Chinese filed an immediate complaint with the UN Security Council, and the UN called our State Department, which caved in to the pressure in typical and glorious fashion."

Logan added, "The captain smiled at us as we left the bridge. He knew he'd won and that we couldn't do anything. We had no choice but to follow orders, which we did, tragically."

"Why? What do you mean?"

"We'd inserted using four Black Hawk helicopters—the Navy calls them Seahawks—and on the way out, there was an accident."

Logan paused in recollection as John shook his head in anger. "There were these four enormous cranes on the deck of the boat—three in the front part of the ship and one aft of the main structure. They occupied the entire area where the cargo containers were stacked. They were secured with these huge cables to keep them from shifting around in rough weather. We'd been careful to avoid them on the way in, but on the way out, one of them snapped—"

"Or was cut loose," John said icily.

"—and it whipped around the deck like a live wire, slicing the tail off one of the Seahawks that had been too close to the deck," Logan finished.

"*Madre de Dios*," Inspector Romero muttered.

"The helicopter struck the side of the boat and burst into flames as it plunged into the Mediterranean," Logan said soberly. "In total, we lost eight Marines, two Navy pilots, and two crew members."

"And to make matters worse, that motherfucker got away. As the burning wreckage lay on top of the water, the North Korean captain turned his ship and sailed away in a big 'Fuck you' gesture, refusing to help with the rescue," John said flatly. "Anyone who might've survived the crash didn't last long because the water was too choppy. By the time the nearest naval vessel showed up, all the wreckage had sunk. We recovered only four bodies. The rest were just gone."

A sudden realization struck the inspector. "How come I don't recall this incident? Something like that would've drawn international attention. I don't remember it in the news at all."

"Because," Cole answered, "the US government considered it an embarrassment and agreed to keep it out of the press." He looked at Logan and John. "I didn't know that was you guys. I remember when it happened. I was in Turkey at the time, and our station chief had been ordered to monitor any communications coming out of Lebanon. After the crash, we couldn't believe the spineless response of our own government."

"Looks like it's time for a little overdue justice," John said.

No one replied. The mood was somber. The day was nearly over, but night waited for no man's reflections.

Inspector Romero looked at his watch and broke the silence. "The clock is ticking. Let's go find a phone. We need to track a ship."

CHAPTER 13

Khartoum

Lau Gang's phone vibrated silently as he received a text message. He watched as his men prepared several vehicles at the small military airfield Namir had provided for their use.

He looked down and smiled. It was the American. *The bait has been taken. They're going after the ship. You're almost free and clear.*

It was his international ties to multiple allies, all of whom shared the same interest, that made the American a critical piece in this violent, global chess match. *Too bad the US doesn't see the board yet,* Gang thought as he deleted the text and put his phone away.

———

The Alboran Sea

Two Spanish NH90 tactical transport helicopters flew low in the dark night across the Alboran Sea. The lights of the *Wonjo Buhwal* served as an illuminated homing beacon less than two miles directly ahead.

Several phone calls from the Spanish National Police to Cartagena's main port had revealed that the North Korean vessel had departed Spain less than an hour after the raid on the farmhouse in

Valdemoro. The Spanish Navy had immediately initiated tracking and confirmed that the ship was headed in the direction of the destination listed on its manifest—Algiers, Algeria.

Cole had raised the well-publicized fact that radical Islam was on the rise in Algeria, but why the Russians and North Koreans would be dealing directly with religious extremists was anyone's guess. In reality, it didn't matter why. There was only one course of action—board the ship and find the ONERING.

Inspector Romero and Logan were onboard the lead helicopter, accompanied by an eight-man team of the Spanish Navy's elite Unidad de Operacionales Especiales, or UOE. The UOE was Spain's equivalent to the US Navy SEALs, trained with the same legendary physicality and unwavering mental discipline. Cole Matthews and John Quick led a second UOE team on the following NH90.

Four smaller four-man UOE teams riding combat rubber raiding craft equipped with baffled engines supported the two helicopters. The four teams had launched from the Spanish-flagged landing platform dock *Castilla* ahead of the helicopters in order to synchronize their arrival at the North Korean ship.

Logan leaned forward and looked out the cockpit window of the NH90 but only saw blackness below the windows. Inspector Romero's voice crackled in his headset. "The teams are less than a half mile from the ship. Two minutes to target." The update was broadcast to the other helicopter through the internal communications system. Once they landed on the ship, the teams would switch to their tactical radio network.

Logan turned toward the rear of the helicopter. Inspector Romero signaled the team as the helicopter accelerated toward the target. Logan quickly switched the radio channel and spoke into the microphone. "John, less than two minutes. We'll take the bridge. You search the cargo. See you on deck. Be safe."

"You too. Out," John replied over the reverberation of the aircraft. The time for joking had passed.

———

Captain Kim Sung Baek was aggravated with Pyongyang. He'd been the captain of the *Wonjo Buhwal* for twenty years, but today's events had been a first. He'd received new orders earlier in the afternoon—"Sail immediately for the port of Algiers. Do not stop under any circumstances if anyone tries to board you. Eliminate all hostile forces. It is of the utmost importance that the ship not fall into enemy hands. Fail-safe option should be exercised if necessary. Office 39 is depending on you. Long reign the Korean Workers' Party!"

The last part of the message had frozen him in his tracks. Office 39 was the main office of the Central Committee, which took its direction from the highest levels of leadership in the North Korean government, including the Dear Leader.

He knew that his strong family ties to the military generals in Pyongyang wouldn't save him if he didn't follow orders. His family would be executed—if lucky—or worse. Captain Baek had done the only thing available to him—set his navigation system for Algiers and left the port of Cartagena immediately. He'd left so quickly, he'd stranded ten of his thirty-five-man crew ashore. Orders were orders, and he knew these were anything but normal ones. Whatever Pyongyang was orchestrating somehow involved him and his ship, and he didn't intend to fail his country or—more importantly—his family.

It was now past 2200 local time as he scanned the sea around him. The nearest ship was three miles to his stern, and nothing lay in front of him. He walked to the port side of the bridge and looked back across the enormous, open cargo area.

So far, so good, he thought as he peered into the darkness behind the ship through high-power binoculars. He stopped his lateral motion as his eyes spotted four dark, blurry shapes contrasted against the moving sea. *It's not possible.* They disappeared. He squinted into the lenses. There they were again, but this time, the shapes were closer. Four small boats were aimed directly toward his ship.

"Get me the chief security officer. Now!" he barked at his executive officer. He looked back out the window, and that was when he saw it—*them*. Two low-flying shapes behind the boats were moving quickly toward him. He recognized them immediately as helicopters. Even though their running lights were off, his hawkish eyesight picked up the soft glow of their instrumentation.

He dropped the binoculars, grabbed the handset to the ship's intercom system, and spoke calmly but quickly. His men were trained for such matters.

If there's one thing we're good at, it's keeping secrets. Unbeknownst to the United States Intelligence Community, Captain Baek and his crew had been operating as a clandestine counterespionage unit managed by North Korea's Ministry of State Security for over twenty years.

After all this time in the shadows, they were about to engage the enemy directly, and Captain Baek relished the possibility, hoping it was the Americans or the British. They were the real enemy he longed to humiliate. He'd done it before, and it seemed he'd been gifted the chance to do it again.

CHAPTER 14

"Twenty seconds to target. They're still not responding to our calls. Be prepared for anything," Inspector Romero screamed into his headset.

Logan pulled the charging handle on his Heckler & Koch MP5K-PDW and chambered the first 9mm hollow-point round. He checked the safety and ensured it was still on. He didn't need a negligent discharge on a Spanish Navy helicopter.

A sudden rush of wind filled the cabin as the two crew chiefs slid open the side doors on both sides of the NH90. The helicopter suddenly banked to the right, and Logan caught a glimpse of the ship, an illuminated behemoth lurking below the helicopter. *It's still a piece-of-shit-looking rust bucket.* And then something else struck him. *That's odd. No movement on deck.*

A heavy rappelling line dropped from each side of the helicopter, and UOE members descended in a synchronized maneuver.

Logan refocused on the immediate task, removed the helicopter's internal communications headset, and shuffled to the door. He waited as Inspector Romero exited the helicopter and moved into position.

The sound of the rotors filled his ears as he grabbed the rope between black-gloved hands and stepped across empty space off the

NH90. He cinched the rope between his feet in a J-hook, pinned it against his left boot, and pressed down with his right foot.

As he rapidly descended, he spotted the second helicopter hovering three hundred feet away on the forward side of the ship's bridge.

Twenty feet to go, he thought as the rope slid through his hands with growing heat. Suddenly, darkness engulfed the ship.

A bright flash originated from one of the main structure's decks, immediately followed by a smoke trail as a rocket-propelled grenade streaked toward the stationary helicopter.

Not good, Logan thought, reacting swiftly. He let go of the rope and dropped like a stone as the RPG reached its target.

———

John and Cole had exited the helicopter first and were already on the deck when the lights went out. Four more UOE team members surrounded them and scanned the cluttered stacks of the cargo area for immediate threats.

"What the fu—" were the only sounds John was able to utter as automatic gunfire shattered the night. Bullets cracked overhead as unseen attackers targeted the helicopter.

John heard several impacts as the NH90 was struck. He looked up and watched as the pilot tried to veer away from the ship. Unfortunately, the fifth UOE member hadn't reached the deck, and the violent motion shook him loose. John watched in horror as the man plummeted thirty feet, crashed to the deck, and lay motionless.

Cole ran to the fallen operator and checked his pulse. "He's still alive!" he shouted over the roar of the gunfire and rotor blades.

A loud, wrenching metallic sound filled the space above them. *Crrraaannngggg!*

Something in the helicopter's engine exploded, and the rotors ground to a halt in a horrendous cacophony of sound. The NH90 pitched away from the ship, hovered momentarily at an awkward angle, and then dropped from the night sky. They watched as their ride disappeared below the railing. Moments later, a loud splash echoed up as water sprayed the side of the ship.

Motherfuckers! We should've sunk this boat years ago, John thought. He looked toward the bridge and saw four men lying prone on an elevated platform at the base of the main structure. The dim ambient light from the night sky illuminated their position. Three cranes and a distance of two hundred feet were between their team and the North Koreans.

With the helicopter in the water, the sounds of a battle from the aft side of the bridge reached their ears. John couldn't worry about Logan and Inspector Romero. He had to attend to more pressing matters.

"Cole," John spoke calmly, "we need to take that position out. This entire area is their kill zone. We can't do anything until they're gone."

Bullets suddenly ricocheted off the deck behind them. John whipped his head around in time to witness two UOE members drop to their knees and fire in simultaneous, short bursts.

Brrrp! Brrrp! Brrrp!

John looked past them to see four men who had been hiding near the bow fifty feet away collapse to the deck. Cole and John exchanged a glance. "Nice shooting, boys," Cole said softly under his breath.

Gunfire erupted from near the bridge of the ship once again. John, Cole, and the four UOE members crouched down in a futile attempt to hide from the automatic fire. *They finally see us,* John thought.

But no bullets struck anywhere near their location. *What the hell?* John thought, but then he saw the enemy shooting into the water on both sides of the ship. *They've spotted the UOE teams in the rafts.*

John assessed the situation. "Now's our only chance, while they're distracted. Use the darkness and shadows of the cranes to close the distance. I'll take the lead. Move when I move. One of you needs to stay here with your injured man. Let's go," he spoke quietly. The safety off on his MP5, he stalked his way forward with Cole and the UOE team close behind.

Logan crashed down on top of a heavy tarp covering one of the ship's lifeboats. The impact knocked the wind out of his lungs, and he lay on his back, momentarily dazed.

Above him, he watched as the pilot yanked the NH90 up and to the right in a last-ditch effort to avoid disaster. The RPG streaked underneath the helicopter, missing it by inches, the light from the rocket's trail illuminating the rivets in the helicopter's underbelly.

Gunfire suddenly erupted from three levels of the main structure. It was directed toward the remaining NH90. It spurred Logan into action, and he rolled off the lifeboat and landed on the deck next to Inspector Romero and four UOE members.

The main structure of the *Wonjo Buhwal* lay directly in front of them, a hulking tower at least eighty feet tall and built with four levels, each with its own walkway connected by ladders to the levels above and below. At the top was the ship's bridge, where Logan was certain the North Korean captain coordinating the ambush lurked. He spotted at least twelve shooters spread out in teams of two among the walkways.

The fourth massive crane rested on top of a supporting platform directly to their left. He and the team were currently hidden in its shadows, but once they moved forward, they'd be exposed to the gunmen arrayed on the main structure.

"This just turned into a clearing operation," Logan said. "Until we eliminate all hostiles, we can't secure the ship or look for the cargo."

"What do you suggest?" Inspector Romero asked.

Logan turned to Lieutenant Commander Fernando Alexia, the senior UOE commander, and said, "You still have comms with the teams on the rafts?"

"Yes," the veteran leader said. "They're about to board the ship on either side back here with us."

Logan shook his head and spoke intensely. "Negative. Wave them off. If they board here, they'll give us away and then be sitting ducks just like us. Tell them to move forward on each side directly next to the main structure. As soon as they're in position, we'll provide covering fire so they can board."

"But what then?"

Logan pointed at the walkways. "The walkways wrap around the side of the structure. We should be able to provide them enough time to climb up and flank these fuckers from both sides. And then, between us and your two teams, we should be able to take them all down."

Inspector Romero and Commander Alexia nodded, and the UOE commander issued quick instructions in Spanish into his throat microphone. He looked at Logan and said, "Twenty seconds."

"Good. Let's get into position." Logan looked around for cover. The enormous metal cargo doors that covered the massive storage area below deck were retracted. *That's odd, but we can use it to our advantage.* The accordion-folded roof created a thick metal barricade at least four feet tall that would provide solid cover for them in the coming firefight.

With Logan pointing the way, they fanned out in a short line behind the steel barricade, concealed in the shadows and waiting for the commander's signal.

Logan rested his left arm on top of the metal door and laid the red dot of his reflex scope on a prone figure on the second-level walkway. *Steady . . . steady . . . breathe . . .*

"Fire." At Commander Alexia's word, their automatic weapons chattered loudly in a symphony of death for the unsuspecting gunmen who'd seen them rappel from the helicopter but had lost sight of them once the lights went out.

Darkness works both ways, assholes, Logan thought as he pulled the trigger. His first burst struck his target in the head and shoulders. He couldn't see the resulting damage at this distance, but it wasn't necessary. The man went limp and dropped facedown on the walkway.

Logan shifted the weapon slightly and aimed at the dead man's partner. He opened fire, but his rounds went high and struck the railing. Sparks erupted in a bright shower and fell to the main deck. He adjusted his sights, and his second burst struck home, dropping the target.

Those who weren't killed by the sudden onslaught of bullets returned fire. Bullets struck the metal barricade, and Logan ducked behind it. He glanced left to see Inspector Romero crouched and reloading his submachine gun. Two UOE members on the other side of him emptied their magazines and began to reload as their teammates next to them continued to fire.

With each burst from their weapons, the returning fire diminished in intensity. Logan heard the sounds of the NH90's rotors as it hovered near the side of the ship. *So it didn't crash. Thank God.*

Logan popped his head up in time to see two men on the third-level walkway lift a Chinese Type 67 7.62mm machine gun. One man stepped behind the crew-served weapon, grabbed the handle, and opened fire.

Even though Logan couldn't see the helicopter from his position, he heard several impacts and the tearing of sheet metal. He stood to provide cover when a second two-man team lit up the entire barricade with another Type 67.

Bullets slammed into the metal and penetrated several folds of the steel, although none passed all the way through. Logan and the rest of the men dropped to the ground behind the folded door. The first machine gun strafed back and forth in a relentless barrage. A moment later, the second Type 67 team, having successfully driven the NH90 away from the ship, joined the assault on Logan's position.

Logan was almost certain the only remaining shooters were the two-man machine gun teams. Unfortunately, both were on the third level just below the bridge and had unobstructed fields of fire. There was no chance Logan or the Spanish team could approach without being torn to pieces.

Inspector Romero shouted, "The helo's hit but still flyable! He's pulling back because he can't take much more!"

What now, Logan? Think! Think! Think! His mind searched for options. He low-crawled to the right edge of the barricade, paused, and glanced around the corner. The sight before him told him the tide was about to turn, even as bullets struck only a few feet away from his head.

The aft UOE teams had successfully boarded the ship undetected. With predatory appreciation, Logan watched four men dressed in black combat fatigues slowly work their way up each side of the main structure. They reached the third-level walkway and moved forward toward the corners where it joined the open area behind the structure.

"Commander, tell them it's only the two machine gun positions. I don't see anyone else moving on the walkways." Even as Logan spoke, the intensity of the fire diminished. "Tell them to go now while they're reloading!"

Commander Alexia issued the orders, and Logan stuck his head back out to watch the attack. It wasn't an assault so much as an execution, but Logan was relieved just the same. *Better them than us.*

The two lead UOE shooters simultaneously stepped around the corners of the walkway from each end. The UOE member from the right side of the ship fired first, killing the North Korean manning the Type 67 machine gun. Even as the North Korean's body slumped backward against the exterior bulkhead, the UOE member aimed and fired three rounds into the gunner, who was in the process of reloading the weapon. *One team down,* Logan thought.

The UOE team from the left was just as efficient and had an easier time, since their targets were still prone on the walkway. The lead shooter dispatched the man pulling the trigger with three shots to the back, and the machine gun fell silent. His partner managed to roll onto his side, hoping to return fire, only to die on his back from the three bullets that struck him in the chest and head.

Logan exhaled in relief as silence fell across the aft side of the ship. He heard the sounds of battle from the forward side of the structure and hoped John and Cole had the situation under some semblance of control.

Logan and the rest of the team rose from behind the barricade. "Commander, tell your two shooters nice job and ask them to hold fast on the third level. We'll make our way to them, and then we'll assault the bridge."

Inspector Romero stared at Logan. "I guess you do really live up to your reputation, or at least the parts they told me about." He smiled, both in victory and from the unique relief all warriors who just survived battle experience.

Logan grinned back at him. "Don't believe everything you hear, Adan," he said, and winked. "This isn't even the first ship I've taken down this week. Regardless, I'd say the UOE deserves the majority of the credit. Some great shooting. Now let's cut the chitchat and join the rest of the team, shall we?"

"Whatever you say, Señor West."

Logan smiled in response, stepped around the folded door, and quickly jogged toward the main structure. As Inspector Romero and the rest of the UOE team followed, a steady *thrum . . . thrum . . . thrum* built in intensity. The entire deck of the ship vibrated violently beneath their feet.

The sound engulfed them from all sides, but Logan thought it originated from below them. *Oh no,* he thought. *That's why the door was open.* In a moment of horror, he realized what it was. As he turned to run from the new threat, he screamed, "Run toward the structure *now!* As fast as you can! *GO! GO! GO!*"

Inspector Romero and the UOE team were trained to know exactly when and how to follow certain orders. They sprinted behind Logan toward the middle of the ship.

But they weren't fast enough. From the enormous open cargo chamber beneath them emerged a hovering monster, a black Boeing light attack AH-6 helicopter armed with two .50-caliber GAU-19 machine guns and two 70mm rocket pods.

The pilot opened fire, shattering the temporary sense of safety they'd felt only moments before.

John led the UOE men along the railing, concealed by the monstrous metal cranes and their accompanying shadows. With Cole and the three remaining UOE members behind him, he covered the distance in fifteen seconds.

During that short time, the four North Koreans on the superstructure had split into two teams and now defended each side of the ship. They fired into the water below with alternating automatic weapons fire.

For the UOE teams' sakes, John hoped that the darkness of the night and the movement of the ship were throwing the North Koreans' aim off target. *Just hold on for a few more seconds,* he willed the Spanish Special Forces.

He reached the base of the last crane undetected and halted. Cole and the Spanish team stopped next to him. The last crane was now directly between them and their attackers.

"Cole and I will break right and take the team on the right; the three of you move left and take out the other team." John spoke rapidly, and all heads nodded at once. "On my mark," he said, and turned as he raised his MP5 to his shoulder. "Three . . . two . . . one . . . now!"

The North Koreans were completely focused on the boarding teams and never saw their deaths approaching from the darkness.

John took two quick steps, stopped, aimed at the North Korean closest to the corner of the railing, and opened fire. His target was dead before he knew what hit him.

John glanced to the left side of the walkway. The other three North Koreans were facedown and motionless, dispatched by Cole and the UOE shooters. The battle for the forward part of the ship was over. *At least for now,* he thought.

He turned to Cole and said, "Let's let the UOE teams know it's clear." He looked at the UOE team member with the internal radio on his harness. "Radio the remaining two boat teams that it's clear." Even as he finished the order, a young UOE member in his late twenties quickly spoke Spanish into his microphone.

He looked up at John and said in English, "It's done. They're coming up now."

John nodded. Before he could utter another word, the high-pitched whine of a large-caliber, electrically driven machine gun reverberated from the aft side of the ship.

"What in God's name?" Cole uttered. And then he heard the steady *thwap! thwap! thwap!* of a helicopter. It sounded different from the NH90s they'd ridden to the ship. Even as Cole processed the sound, John had already reacted and was two steps into a full-out sprint toward the main structure.

Trouble certainly seems to find you guys, Cole thought as he ran to catch up. The UOE members followed them once again.

———

As Logan ran for his life, there was a sudden scream of pain from behind, but he didn't dare turn around. He knew from experience that he couldn't help whoever had been hit until he had eliminated the immediate threat.

Insurgent snipers used wounded US servicemen as bait, often killing two or three more who tried to help before finishing off the initial target. That brutal and gut-wrenching lesson had been ingrained in every military member who stepped foot on Iraqi soil, and this situation was no different. Logan knew if he stopped, he and the others would likely die.

The high-pitched roar of the twin Gatling guns was deafening. Bullets tore into the deck around them. Large chunks of nonskid surface flew into the air and peppered their backs and legs. Logan briefly recalled sprinting the length of the inner cavern of the Haditha Dam two years earlier and redoubled his efforts.

An open hatch to a small observation room on the first deck was directly in front of him. He ran faster. *Just a few more seconds. Please God.*

Logan dove through the dark opening as the large glass window disintegrated under the withering fire. He landed on his side, slid on the smooth floor, and scrambled furiously to hide behind the observation room's wall.

Two figures burst into the room behind him and found cover even as bullets devoured the entryway. Inspector Romero and one UOE member crouched next to Logan.

"Where's Alexia?" Logan shouted over the din of the barrage.

Inspector Romero shook his head. "No idea," he exclaimed, breathing hard. "But it doesn't matter, because if we don't figure out a way to take out that bird, we're all dead."

Logan nodded, cringing as .50-caliber slugs struck a flat-panel monitor on the wall across from him. It exploded in a shower of sparks, flame, and smoke. *Smoke.*

"Hold on a sec," Logan said, and grabbed an M18 smoke grenade off his vest. "This might at least buy us a little time," he said as he pulled the pin and lobbed it out the shattered window.

Logan heard a small *pop* followed by the *hssssss* of white smoke escaping the canister. He looked around the room for options. Another hatch opposite the doorway led deeper into the ship. *No good.* And then he saw it—a metal ladder in the far corner of the room led up a small well secured by a hatch. It led to the roof of the observation area. *Bingo.*

"You know how to use that effectively?" Logan asked the surviving UOE member as he pointed at the XM25 automatic grenade launcher slung across the commando's back.

"Absolutely," the Spaniard replied.

"Good. Follow me." Logan glanced through the doorway and saw a haze of white smoke thickening by the second. He knew it wouldn't last long, especially if the AH-6 moved closer.

As he crawled toward the ladder, he turned to Inspector Romero and said, "As soon as we open fire, do the same. If we're lucky, we'll knock him out of the sky; if we're not, we'll likely be dead."

Logan reached the ladder and climbed. He grabbed the hatch, twisted the lever, and pushed upward. Another burst from the Gatling guns lanced through the smoke and struck the room below.

Fate was on their side, at least for the moment. A large exhaust vent directly adjacent to the hatch concealed them from the view of the AH-6 pilot.

Logan emerged from the opening onto the roof and transitioned into a prone position next to the vent. The UOE commando slid next to him and removed the XM25 grenade launcher from his back. He made an adjustment on the weapon and waited.

The smoke had thickened into an amorphous white barrier that seemed to shift with the movement of the ship. The helicopter was hidden in its midst, a flying predator waiting to strike. *Won't last much longer.*

"Wait for it. As soon as you have its outline, take him out," Logan said to his UOE brother-in-arms as he aimed his MP5 toward the AH-6's anticipated position on the other side of the smoke. They didn't have to wait long.

Instead of slowly dissipating, the smoke screen was blasted apart by a sudden gust of wind. It disintegrated into tiny wisps of translucent haze that danced on the deck before vanishing completely, mesmerizing and terrifying them at the same time.

Oh shit, Logan thought. They were now completely exposed. His fear was confirmed as the nose of the AH-6 suddenly tilted upward and aimed the twin Gatling guns at them.

"*Now!*" Logan screamed as he stared directly into the menacing face of the AH-6. *It's too late.* And then he saw what loomed behind the war machine, and his jaw dropped in disbelief.

From behind the AH-6, the enormous steel arm of a crane slammed into the tail of the helicopter like an angry metal giant swatting an annoying insect.

Logan heard several bursts of automatic gunfire from the observation room, but he also thought he heard guns blasting away from other positions on the deck.

The impact from the crane violently turned the helicopter sideways and exposed its left side to Logan and the UOE commando, who pulled the trigger on the XM25.

Thwoosh!

The 25mm grenade sailed toward the hovering killing machine with expert aim and into the open-air compartment behind the cockpit. The UOE commando had set the detonating distance to match that of the AH-6, and the high-explosive airburst round exploded in a magnificent display of destruction.

BOOM!

The supersonic shockwave shredded the interior of the helicopter. A secondary explosion as the fuel tank ignited split the wounded bird in half, engulfing the rear section in flames. The back half was propelled away from the cockpit and fell to the deck. An earsplitting metallic screech reached them as the gearbox disintegrated and the rotor blades were torn apart.

Logan watched in amazement as a large chunk of one blade sliced into the cockpit on the pilot's side and lodged itself halfway through the glass. Grimly, he thought, *I hope he was already dead.*

The front half of the AH-6 plummeted to the deck and bounced forward. It came to rest against the ship's railing, a dead metal husk.

The sounds of battle were silenced. The helicopter's wreckage sizzled and popped on the deck. The stench of cordite, smoke, and fuel filled the air. *At least the bullets have stopped. Time to take the bridge,* Logan thought.

"Let's go," Logan said to the UOE commando, then paused and

added, "'Absolutely' is right. Nice shot—but how'd you get it to detonate inside? I thought they were airburst grenades."

The professional killer smiled. "They are, but I got his distance from the laser range finder the second I got up here and set it. The damn gun's so smart, it transmits the data to the grenade itself." He gestured dramatically with one arm. "And voilà!" he said, and looked at the remains of his kill with the pride of a veteran hunter.

"Good to go," Logan said, and climbed back through the hatch down to the observation room.

Inspector Romero stood outside and looked up at the bridge four levels above them. The fiery wreckage emitted an eerie glow that illuminated the deck and distorted the shadows. "We need to get up there," he said as Logan and the commando joined him.

Logan looked up to see the other UOE commandos slowly working their way up the outside of the structure. Before he could reply, a voice spoke from nearby. "Logan, you really know how to make an entrance," John Quick said as he approached with Cole Matthews and the UOE team in tow. "I came around the corner just in time to see your new friend fire the grenade launcher as the crane batted the bird out of the sky. It almost wasn't a fair fight," he finished, grinning crazily.

"As always, a day late and a dollar short," Logan responded sarcastically. "Sounds like you had some excitement on your side of the ship." He paused, and added seriously, "We lost at least one man and our helo got knocked out of the sky into the sea. Status unknown, but it didn't sound good."

"We took one casualty, but he should make it. There's a man with him now."

The sound of running footsteps interrupted the impromptu reunion. Through the smoke and flames of the wreckage, the running figure of Commander Alexia appeared.

"What happened to you?" Logan asked with relief in his voice. "I thought their bird got you." And then it hit him—*the crane operator.* "That was you on the crane, wasn't it?"

Commander Alexia nodded grimly. "Sergeant Artiga didn't make it. The gunfire got him as we dove for cover since we knew we couldn't make it to the structure. We were too far back to make a run. So I circled back to the crane along the starboard side."

Logan was impressed.

"Like your Navy SEALS, taking a ship is a primary mission for us. You never know when you'll need to know how to use a crane."

"Indeed, Commander Alexia. Nicely done, and I'm truly sorry about your man," Logan said sincerely. "But we need to secure the bridge as soon as possible. Can you radio the raft teams and tell them to secure the deck and begin evacuating casualties? See if you can get the surviving helo to radio the *Castilla* to send a rescue team to search for survivors where our bird went down. Ask our pilot to stand by near us, though. Also, ask the raft teams not to search the ship until we know it's clear. There could be more of these guys hiding or setting up booby traps. Please order the team on the structure to remain outside the bridge until I get up there. I want to be the first one in to talk to the captain. I'll find out if he has any other surprises in store for us."

Commander Alexia nodded and turned to speak quickly into his throat microphone.

Logan looked at John, Cole, and Inspector Romero. "You guys ready to finish this thing?" he asked. Reflected flames flickered across his green eyes and magnified the intensity of his gaze.

"The sooner the better," Cole answered.

"Good," Logan said, and turned to climb the nearest ladder to the ship's second level.

CHAPTER 15

Logan crouched on the right side of the bridge door below the ledge of the windows. He held his Kimber .45 at an angle in front of him. John, Cole, and Inspector Romero stacked up behind him in formation.

There was silence from inside.

Logan signaled the UOE commando on the opposite side of the doorway and held up his left fist before making a knifing gesture toward the door and grabbing the levered handle.

The commando pulled the pin on an M84 flash grenade and waited.

Logan pulled the lever quickly and pushed the door inward.

Shots from inside shattered the window of the door as the hardened UOE commando threw the flash grenade into the enclosed space. Moments later, the relative calm that had settled over the embattled ship was blown away.

BOOM!

The sudden blinding light was followed by the concussive force of a 180-decibel explosion. The remaining windows shattered, and glass fell on the UOE commandos surrounding the bridge.

Logan's ears still rang as he entered the bridge with his pistol up and surveyed the scene.

Only one occupant remained. A man Logan recognized as the captain from all those years ago knelt on his hands and knees near a control panel fifteen feet to the right of the doorway. The grenade had detonated less than two feet from him. He shook his head from side to side in an obvious attempt to clear the ringing in his ears. Logan saw blood trickling from his right ear. *Shattered eardrum—our bad,* he smirked unsympathetically.

The captain sensed movement from his right and staggered to his feet. He whirled to face his attackers. As he turned, Logan glimpsed a small device in the captain's right hand. *A trigger detonator,* Logan thought in horror, and his reflexes took control.

Logan raised his pistol so quickly that to John it looked like he was still extending it as the Kimber roared to life with a single loud shot. The bullet struck the captain directly between the eyes and created a small hole that immediately oozed dark blood. The captain's head rolled back as death gripped him and his hands tensed in response. It was just enough to compress the trigger in one last destructive act of defiance.

"I wish we'd done that the first time we met that asshole," John muttered.

Logan didn't have time for a response. From deep within the bowels of the ship, a series of muffled explosions rocked the North Korean vessel. The thunderous crescendo built in intensity as the large cargo ship suddenly lurched to the port side.

"Everyone off now! She's sinking and going fast! Get the helo up here. I don't want to swim back to Spain." Logan looked around the bridge. *Come on—come on—come on. There has to be something that we can use.* Then he saw it—*gotcha!*

He scrambled to the control panel, grabbed the folded laptop computer, and threw it into the small black backpack he wore. *Better than nothing at all,* he thought, and exited the bridge for the last time.

The UOE commandos had recognized the imminent danger after the first explosion. By the time Logan joined the rest of the men on the walkway, the Spanish operators were halfway down the structure. Inspector Romero and Cole were with them. John was the only one waiting.

"We're not having good luck with ships this week. I hope you're still swim qual'd, because if we don't move quickly, we're going to get wet," John said, sarcastically referring to the swim qualification requirement that all Marines maintained.

As if on cue, the bow of the ship slowly began to lower into the black sea, lifting the stern slightly out of the water.

The two men rushed down the ladders to join the rest of the assault force, which had already evacuated onto either the boats or the remaining NH90.

Another muffled explosion reached their ears as they hit the deck. The rate at which the ship was sinking suddenly increased, and Logan and John found themselves facing a thirty-degree slope.

The NH90 helicopter hovered forty feet away. It was blocked from moving any closer by the crane's enormous arm, which had come to rest on the deck after knocking the AH-6 out of the sky.

Logan and John scrambled up the deck's nonskid surface. A loud, wrenching metallic shriek mixed with the roar of rushing water.

This is going to be close, Logan thought, and pushed himself harder.

The ship suddenly lifted higher and tilted portside. Logan and John were knocked off their feet and began to slide down the deck's surface toward the ship's main structure.

As they fell, they grabbed the railing that ran along the base of the crane, hanging suspended at a precarious angle.

Logan looked up and behind him to see the enormous stern of the ship sticking out of the water like some monstrous creature yearning to touch the sky. The stars and moon in front of him were disorienting, and he looked around for options. He didn't see the helicopter. *At least the pilot got the rest of the team out. Only a few more seconds, and we're going under,* he thought.

"It's just like fucking *Titanic!*" John screamed.

Logan smiled at his friend. "Maybe, but I'm not holding your hand! If we're lucky, we can break the pull and kick our way to the surface." Both men knew the biggest threat would be the moment the ship went under the surface. The suction created by the sinking vessel would pull them and everything else near it to the bottom, even if they let go of their death grips on the railing.

A loud screeching grabbed their attention, and they looked up just in time to see the crane's gigantic metal arm arcing toward them as gravity pulled it downward.

It swung over their heads and stopped, the metallic arm pointing directly into the water, which had engulfed the base of the super-structure. They watched in disbelief as the sea appeared to devour it, slowly rising up its outer surface. The churning water was an angry, amorphous leviathan eager to claim its prize.

The sudden sound of rotors and the downdraft of the NH90 broke their fascination. As soon as the crane had shifted, the pilot—who'd pulled the helicopter away from the ship as it rose up from the sea—seized his opportunity and moved in closer to them.

The helicopter hovered fifteen feet away and directly in front of them. Logan saw movement in the open passenger compartment. *What the hell?*

Something long and heavy unfurled in the air like twin snakes striking and crashed into the deck six feet below them. *A rope ladder!*

The lights on the ship went out, and their world became a dark roar of rotor blades, rushing water, and screeching metal. Logan felt the wind increase as the waterline closed in on them. *"Now!"* he screamed, and released his grip. He fell into the shifting shadows.

I don't need to be told twice, John thought, and let go. He plum-meted a short distance and felt the nonskid surface grab at his clothes. He held his arms out in front of him. *Please, God, be there.*

Thwack! A rung from the ladder smashed into John's forehead, but he felt his left arm slide between two other rungs below it. He secured his left arm to his chest with his right and held on for dear life. Freezing water suddenly drenched his boots and engulfed his legs. An unfamiliar panic gripped him. The violent din of the water consumed his world, and he squeezed the rope ladder even tighter.

The ladder went taut, and John was violently pulled upward and out of the roiling sea below. He swung freely on the ladder and wrapped his right leg through it—and struck something with a wet boot. He looked down to see Logan dangling from the rope ladder several rungs below him, soaking wet. He'd accidentally kicked him in the face.

"Nice of you to join me!" John shouted into Logan's upturned face. But his sense of humor failed him as he glimpsed the deathtrap they'd barely escaped.

Logan turned back toward the ship below just in time to see the top of the bridge disappear under the surface. All that remained visible of the cargo ship was the stern. Flashes of light danced across the submerged ship as major electrical systems failed. As the stern slipped into the dark abyss moments later, a burst of light erupted under the water, illuminating the ruined ship in one last garish, ghostly image. And then it was gone, descending to the bottom of the Alboran Sea and Davy Jones' Locker. The *Wonjo Buhwal* was no more.

CHAPTER 16

Combat Operations Center, LPD *Castilla*

The men stared at the wall of high-definition monitors feeding the ship's operational nerve center. Six screens formed one infrared image that was fed from a Spanish UAV flying at five thousand feet. Two helicopters and four small boats circled lazily back and forth in a search pattern, looking for the lost NH90.

"The area isn't as deep as the rest of the Alboran, but it's still at least eight hundred feet," Captain Lorenzo Salazar, the ship's commanding officer, said. "We'll get our submersibles down there in the daylight. They'll have several types of high-accuracy sonar to support them. In all likelihood, they'll have the helo's exact location before they enter the water. Hopefully, the minisub can remove the bodies of the pilot and copilot, trigger their life vests, and send them to the surface." He paused. "If not, we'll send a diver down."

"A diver can go that deep?" Cole asked.

"Our divers use atmospheric diving suits that can go down to twenty-three hundred feet, just like your navy. If that's what has to be done, so be it."

"Sir, you have our condolences for the loss of your men," Logan said somberly. He shifted his stance as the boat gently swayed. His boots still squished from the water they'd absorbed. "John and I lost more outstanding young men under our command than I care to re-member. Each loss still hurts, even to this day. My Marines swore an oath and knew the risks, but knowing and dying are two completely different things." He looked the Spanish captain squarely in the eyes, and said, "I can promise you one thing—their sacrifice will *not* be for nothing."

The captain nodded briskly and glanced at the search efforts under way. "I appreciate that, Mr. West. This is a dangerous business, and the state of play in the world seems to get worse every day." His face hardened. "Quite honestly, it sickens me. My headquarters ordered me to help you in any way possible. I don't know what this is all about, and I'm sure you can't tell me, but whatever you need, you have. What's next?"

"My guess is that what we're after wasn't on that ship," Logan said with disgust. "I have a horrible suspicion that this was a wild-goose chase meant as a diversion. After what the Russians went through to steal what they stole, there's absolutely no way they'd let us get this close and risk everything they have to just send it to the bottom of the sea. They have to know we can retrieve it from down there."

The bitterness of having been duped was sickening, and the cap-tain grimaced at the thought of his men being sacrificed as pawns in a larger geopolitical game.

"More importantly," John said, "it also means our Russian friend, Yuri from Valdemoro, lied to us. He played us this whole time." He looked at Logan. "This is like Fallujah 2004 all over again. My gloves are about to come off." He turned to Inspector Romero. "What do your laws say about Americans questioning suspects on Spanish soil? I'd *really* like a chance to have a heart-to-heart with our good Russian friend."

Inspector Romero considered for a moment and then said, "He's been transferred to our headquarters in Madrid. If we get back there tonight, I'm sure the lawyers can answer that question . . . tomorrow," he said with a straight face. The implication was clear.

"Good," Logan said, "because we also need to get this back to the FBI's digital forensics lab in DC." He held up the North Korean captain's laptop.

"Actually, we don't need to send it back to DC," Cole said, and turned to Captain Salazar. "Sir, can you please get us back to Madrid as soon as possible? I know how we can handle it from there."

Captain Salazar turned to a junior officer standing next to a bank of communications equipment. "Lieutenant Rodriguez, please order the NH90 back to the ship and have him stand by on deck for passengers. Tell him to make sure he's got enough fuel to get to Madrid. Once he drops our friends off, he can refuel at Torrejon Air Base and then get back here."

"Roger, sir," the lieutenant answered, and issued instructions into the ultra-high-frequency encrypted radio.

Captain Salazar turned back to the four men. "Let's get up on deck. You've got a ride to catch."

CHAPTER 17

Khartoum, Sudan

Namir's chambers were completely dark. It was a luxury he relished. As a child, his central hut in his small village had let in ambient light and noise from all directions, mainly from the village's prized possessions—three portable generators that had run at seemingly random times he didn't understand. He'd grown to detest the sleepless nights. Now, no matter how chaotic the day's events or the pressure of an impending operation, he always slept deeply.

His personal cell phone suddenly lit up and issued the melodious chirp of a digital bird, a more pleasant remembrance from his childhood.

Years of training dictated his automatic response to the intrusive yet harmonious tone. He sat up and reached for the phone, even before he opened his eyes to the darkness.

"Yes," he said quietly, after he had deftly pushed the talk button with one thumb.

"The Americans took the bait," Gang reported calmly. "I have confirmation from my source that the North Korean ship was about to be boarded thirty minutes ago. They soon lost contact but assured me that the captain would follow his orders, *my* orders. The ship is likely at the bottom of the sea right now, or soon will be."

Namir pondered the news for a moment. "Your captain would sink his own ship and sacrifice himself and his men?" He heard the distant engine of a truck in the background as he waited for a response.

Silence, as if Gang were deciding how to answer the question. "The North Korean leadership can be very persuasive, especially when they have one's entire family at their disposal. I can guarantee you that if they ordered him to sink the ship, he did. We'll know tomorrow morning, hopefully from the international media." Another pause. "Unless they try to hide it to serve their purposes."

"What purposes would those be?" Namir asked.

"The Americans probably think they're close to reacquiring the equipment. And if they suspect otherwise, it will take them a few more days to search the cargo vessel and confirm the equipment's not on board, which means—"

"Which means they won't want to show their hand too quickly," Namir completed the thought.

"Exactly," Gang said. "But unfortunately for the Americans and whoever's helping them, it's too late. The device made it out of Spain as expected and arrived at the French airfield a few hours ago. I just received another text. They're wheels up and should be here in a little more than six hours. Go back to sleep. By the time you wake up, your future will be one step closer to being realized. I'll contact you in the morning."

"Thank you for the update," Namir said. "And it's *our* futures that will be realized, not just mine. The time to act is almost upon us. Good night."

Financial and military security for Sudan for decades. A glorious dream about to become reality . . .

Namir lay down and closed his eyes to allow the darkness to take him under once again.

———

"Is the team ready?" Gang asked the American moments later.

"In five days' time, the American people will know fear once again, even if they don't know who triggered it or why. The government will scramble to figure out who did it, and all evidence will point exactly where we want. And then the real war begins." There was no mistaking the satisfaction Gang heard in the American's voice.

"Very well. Let it be so," he said, and ended the call.

PART III

WELCOME TO
THE SAFARI

KHARTOUM WAR CEMETERY

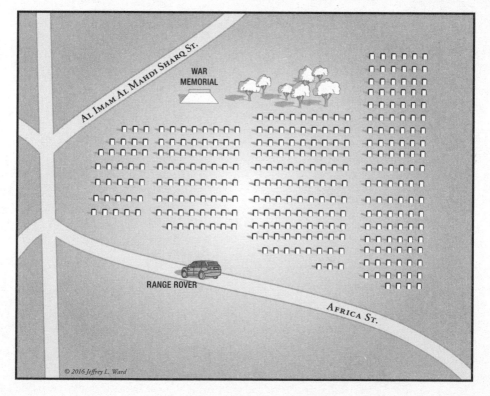

CHAPTER 18

Outside Khartoum
Five Days to Zero Hour

Amira Cerone watched the airfield through a pair of high-power binoculars. Several miles beyond the western outskirts of Khartoum, the small military airstrip was bustling with an unusual amount of activity for seven a.m. on a weekday. *The sonofabitch was right again.*

The airfield was the size of a small US municipal airport, with an additional fifteen-foot barbed-wire fence protecting its perimeter. Two Soviet-era MiG-29 fighter jets were inside the shadows of the hangar, and a hose snaked its way to one of the jets from a large tanker truck outside. The hundred-foot control tower was located at the other end of the runway. The series of connected buildings at its base seemed to have no organizational structure—just oddly sized concrete buildings seemingly positioned at random. But it was the white Gulfstream jet parked at one end of the three-quarter-mile-long runway that held Amira's attention.

Several men in nondescript khaki clothing unloaded dark cases from the underbelly of the jet. The cases were then placed on two five-ton military trucks with canvas coverings over their rear cargo areas.

She repositioned herself in the front seat of the US Embassy's

Land Rover. The dark-green hijab she wore shifted as she focused the binoculars on two men who seemed to be coordinating the transfer. The right side of the veil obstructed her view, and she flung it aside. *I can't stand this custom,* she thought with contempt for the male-dominated culture in which she now operated.

Allowing her to blend in with the local culture, the hijab and the various lightweight, robe-like garments that covered her entire body also disguised her striking features.

The offspring of an Italian-American Washington, DC, homicide detective and a beautiful Ethiopian immigrant, her light skin was perfectly toned to blend in with the Arabic cultures of Northern Africa. Short black hair was hidden under the garments, but other than sunglasses, nothing could hide the pale-blue eyes she'd inherited from her mother. It was the eyes that caused men's breath to catch, and she always looked away to avoid drawing too much attention to herself. The fact was that she was jaw-droppingly beautiful—and just as deadly.

Tired and aggravated, she'd been awakened in the middle of the night by an incessant beeping on her laptop. It wasn't the normal back channel but rather an unbreakable encrypted chat link that originated from one of the most highly classified servers inside Washington.

Before she'd left Langley three months ago, she'd been summoned to the director's office. It was unusual, but not the first time she'd had an audience with him. He'd told her that if the link were ever activated, she was to follow the instructions immediately and without hesitation. He'd also told her there were only a handful of the most senior leaders in the US government who knew about the existence of the link, let alone the compartmented program that covered her mission and existence. It was reserved for extreme circumstances that required an immediate response, often in the form of lethal action. She didn't even know which senior leader sent her instructions, and it didn't matter. She'd begun to refer to the person as Zeus inside her head, since the proclamations seemed to come down from on high.

The last time the chat window had popped up unexpectedly, rebels in southern Sudan had captured the largest pumping station along the Greater Nile Oil Pipeline and shut it off, abruptly stopping the flow of the government of Sudan's most valuable export. She'd been delivering USAID food supplies to a nearby village but had been redirected via a secure satellite to "intervene." She'd gone in alone under cover of darkness.

When she'd walked out of the pumping station the next morning, fifteen rebels were dead from various puncture and cut wounds, and the oil was once again flowing its liquid trek to Port Sudan. She'd spared the rebel commander and ordered him to return to the rest of his fighters—minus two fingers on his left hand—with one message: the pipeline was off-limits. She'd wanted to kill him because of the atrocities he'd committed, but her instructions had been specific, and ultimately correct. The attacks stopped soon after.

Amira refocused the lenses and caught her breath. Both men now stood still and faced her direction. The man on the right—at this distance, she could at least discern short, dark hair—raised something to his right ear and pointed in her direction.

"Damnit," she mumbled under her breath. *Time to go.*

She'd deliberately parked less than a hundred yards from a concentration of fifteen mud and stone homes, hoping the shapes of the structures would camouflage her vehicle. *Guess not.* It didn't matter. She'd confirmed what Zeus had told her. Whatever it was the CIA was looking for was here. Now she just needed to return to the embassy, send a message back to DC, and await further instructions.

She dropped the binoculars on the passenger seat, turned the ignition on, and pushed the gearshift into drive. The tan SUV kicked up dust as she turned around toward the isolated homes.

Her mind wandered to the contents of the cases. Whatever it was, it was important enough to wake her up in the middle of the night and send her on a solo reconnaissance mission.

She drove down the middle of the street and turned right at the main road leading back to Khartoum, only to slam the brakes as a white pickup truck sped toward her. Her reflexes kicked in, and she shifted the gearshift into reverse. She glanced over her shoulder and saw another pickup truck barreling toward her. It was even closer than the first.

She calculated the distance between the vehicles and realized she didn't have enough space to maneuver back the way she came. The pickup truck behind her skidded to a halt sideways, blocking the street between the last two houses. She looked forward and saw the first truck almost upon her. There was nowhere to go. She was trapped. *Which leaves only one option.*

A Sudanese man in military fatigues screamed at her in Arabic as he exited the pickup truck, his right hand holding a pistol pointed toward the dirt. She exited the vehicle and held her hands up, shouting in Arabic in a voice she hoped sounded tinged with fear. "I'm lost! I'm lost! Please don't shoot!" She repeated the phrases over and over as she moved away from her vehicle, her hands never leaving their raised positions.

Slam!

She glanced left to see a second threat and was momentarily surprised by the man's appearance. He wasn't Sudanese. She didn't want to risk a closer look, but he appeared to be Asian at first glance. *Has to be Chinese. They're in bed with the Sudanese for oil, but what the hell is he doing out here with the Sudanese military?*

She didn't have time to contemplate it further as the Sudanese man reached her, his weapon still lowered. He leaned in, his face inches away, and shouted, "What are you doing here? Who sent you? What are you looking for?"

She kept repeating, "I'm lost! I'm lost! Please don't hurt me! I stopped and was looking at a map! I didn't know how to get back. I swear! Please don't hurt me."

Even as she pleaded, she watched the Chinese man walk over to the Land Rover and lean inside the rolled-down window. He pulled out a folded map and glanced at her. *So far so good.*

"I'm with USAID. I swear. I was told there was a village out here in need of food. I must've made a wrong turn." She lowered her arms and put her hands in front of her, bowing slightly in supplication, another concept she loathed.

The Sudanese male turned toward the Chinese man as if awaiting instructions. *So he's the one in charge. Okay then.*

The man stared at her for a long moment, refusing to break the silence, allowing her whimpering sounds to underscore the palpable tension.

"If that's the case, then what are you doing with these?" he said slowly, and held up the pair of military-grade high-power binoculars she'd shoved under her seat. He stared at her, expecting a response.

Amira's mind quieted, abandoning all thought. A sensation like cooling water washed over her entire body, calming her. She glanced at the Sudanese man in front of her and then toward the second man less than ten feet away, still standing next to her car. Her eyes narrowed imperceptibly. Only then did she act.

The man in front of her never knew what killed him. From beneath her dark-green garments, Amira withdrew a six-inch black stiletto and plunged it in a flurry of fabric and speed into the side of his neck just beneath the jawline. She withdrew it just as quickly and felt the warm gush of blood cover her hand.

The Chinese man reacted even as the dead man's blood struck the dirt. She knew he was a skilled professional—it was evident to her trained eye. He reached inside his lightweight khaki jacket, but he'd miscalculated, thinking he'd have to time to draw his weapon and fire. He was wrong.

She took three bounding strides, appearing to float through the air, the flowing robe trailing behind her like streamers. A second stiletto appeared in her left hand as the Chinese man succeeded in pulling a short, black pistol loose from its holster underneath his jacket.

As Amira reached his side, she slashed his wrist, the razor-sharp knife slicing deeply and severing the tendons. He screamed in pain as his now-useless hand dropped the pistol harmlessly to the ground.

With her other hand, she plunged the stiletto into the man's side and felt the blade slide in between his ribs. He shrieked in pain once more, and his body stiffened next to hers as he went into shock. His horrified eyes looked into her face, only to see a fiery blue and unforgiving gaze. She pushed the blade upward, realizing she'd punctured his heart when his body shuddered uncontrollably and his eyes rolled upward into his head. Amira withdrew the blade and allowed his body to crumple to the road.

There was no hesitation as she sheathed both stilettos under her garments and bent over the Chinese man's corpse. She didn't care about the other one. He was Sudanese military and probably just following orders. But this one was different.

She found a black wallet inside his coat pocket, already covered in blood. She carefully opened it and saw a photo ID with Chinese characters printed on it. She'd seen this type of ID before—it belonged to employees of the Chinese embassy in Sudan.

She grabbed the wallet and looked around the street. No one had come out to investigate the sounds of screaming. *It's Sudan, after all. They know better.*

She nodded in silent approval and purposefully strode to her SUV, covering her face once more with the hijab. *Time to go, this time for good.*

As she drove back to the US Embassy, she cursed Zeus for activating the chat alert on such short notice. Unfortunately, what was done was done, and she'd have to notify him immediately. She couldn't have foreseen all of the unknowns—including the eyes that watched through a different pair of high-power military binoculars as she fled the scene of the encounter.

CHAPTER 19

US Embassy, Madrid
Four Days to Zero Hour

"Did I ever tell you how much I detest losing?" John asked no one in particular, his grizzled face set in a look of odd reflection. "You can blame America's pastime for who I am today," he added, smiling with mischievous nostalgia.

Logan looked quizzically at his friend but didn't respond. The only other occupant of the classically decorated conference room on the top floor of the building was the CIA's chief of station, David Everett. The three men waited for Cole to return with an update from Langley.

The embassy's secure communications facility lay elsewhere in the building, but thanks to the sensitivity involved in the current operation, Cole had asked Logan and John to wait with the senior CIA officer.

The three men gazed out the large window at the Madrid skyline, an odd combination of centuries-old architecture, historical land-marks, and modern skyscrapers, including the four tall buildings that stood like sentinels over the city in the Cuatro Torres Business Area.

"You know I wrestled in high school, state champion and all that, but I don't think I ever told you about my foray into the wonderful world of baseball." John laughed as he recalled a younger version of himself, the one the world hadn't jaded with its evil and cruelty.

"I was a Little League pitcher. Back then, that's all I wanted to be when I grew up. Like Nolan Ryan, you know? And I was good, really good. I could throw in the eighties by the time I was thirteen, but unfortunately, I didn't have a good curveball." He grinned, looked over at Logan and the CIA officer, and said, "And what's a good pitcher without a curveball? A one-trick pony," he said, answering his own question.

"So I decided I was going to master the curveball, no matter how long it took. Even though I'd strike out eight to ten batters a game with the heater, I wanted that curveball. You see, I wanted to dominate the other team, not just win. I didn't want anyone to be able to hit my stuff. It was just the way I was wired, although I wasn't aware of that perfectionist trait at the time. So I practiced and practiced with the help of a teammate—Tommy Smithers, I think—who wasn't that good but could throw a curveball as if it were a personal calling. And then one day, I suddenly had it—my own physical epiphany."

Logan and the station chief were now listening intently.

"Now, I'd been throwing more than I was supposed to, especially without the coach's knowledge, and I was supposed to be off the next game. But what did I do? I begged and pleaded for him to put me in. I convinced him I was rested and ready to go. More importantly, I wanted the world to see my new pitch as I took out the opposing team one batter at a time."

Logan pictured teenaged John Quick, full of enthusiasm and youthful confidence. He'd been an enthusiastic young kid himself, as well as a high school track star and football player. He'd also developed the drive to win at an early age. He was fairly certain most Marines did, not because all Marines were born winners, but rather because the Marine Corps attracted a certain type of personality, like moths to a flame, for better or worse.

"The first three innings were flawless. In fact, they were probably the best three innings I ever pitched. Between my fastball and the newfound curve, I was unstoppable. The coach was amazed at the strides I'd made. My dad was as proud as any parent could be. And I felt like the king of the world, a Little League giant that no one could oppose. And I liked it. No. That's not true. I *loved* that feeling." He sighed but continued, a slight edge of regret tingeing his voice.

Logan knew John better than any man on Earth. Despite his vicious sarcasm and ruthless killer's instinct, he was a passionate man, a man who felt things deeply but rarely talked about them. The psychological toll of the things they did was an omnipresent force, the reality in which they chose to exist. For John to speak so openly about anything absent a sarcastic comment or profane remark was nearly an act of reverence.

"In the fourth inning, I'd already struck out the first two batters, and I was facing the league's biggest slugger, this oversized kid who looked like he should've been in high school, not seventh grade. I decided I was going to take him down. He'd grounded out his first time up, but I wanted—no, I *needed*—to strike him out, to make a point. I threw two fastballs down and away, and he missed them both. So, of course, it was time for the curve, and I decided that I was going to add a little something to it. And I did."

His face seemed to lighten a little, the echoes of a fresh-faced boy dimly shining through the hardened features of the man he was. "It was a thing of beauty. I threw the best curveball of my life. I made the kid look foolish. He never had a chance. I knew in that moment that one day I'd be a big-league pitcher like Nolan Ryan." He lowered his eyes briefly but continued. "And just as quickly, it was over. As I completed my follow-through, there was a sudden, searing pain in my arm. I felt something pop, and I dropped to the ground writhing in agony. The rest of that day was a blur. My dad took me to the ER, where X-rays showed I'd severely separated my growth plate, so severely in fact that I needed pins to reattach it. And just like that, my pitching career was over, and along with it, any dreams of being the next Nolan Ryan."

"I'm sorry," Logan said. The words concisely reflected the numerous emotions his friend's story had elicited.

"I'm not. I learned several valuable lessons that day—and I do have a point in telling you this." The boy was gone; the man had fully returned. "You see, I'd overtrained. I'd pushed myself so hard because I didn't know better. In my youthful arrogance to be the absolute best, I'd unknowingly sabotaged myself, which was the true irony. It was as if the universe was saying, 'Nice try. Better luck next time.' I learned a valuable lesson in humility as well. But here's the point." John paused to emphasize it. "Just when I thought I'd won, I actually lost. I lost my arm, my future as a pitcher, and that feeling of domination I'd briefly experienced. And I *hated* it. Even though I'd done it to myself, I refused to accept it." He spat the last words with contempt.

"I mean, I really detested that feeling and I vowed that no matter what, I'd never lose *anything* after that again. I know that sounds crazy, even pathological, but I stuck to it as much as I could. Whatever it was I did, I trained not just harder than anyone else, but also smarter."

Logan glanced at the CIA officer, who sat silent, a wise man with years of interrogation experience who knew when to remain quiet. Logan said quietly, "That failure is what made you—what led you to the Marine Corps, and ultimately, to Force Recon."

"I know, which is why I never forget it. It's a central part of who I am. And here's why I bring it up. Right now, I'm starting to get that feeling again, and I fucking hate it now as much as I did back then. We thought we had our target on that ship, and it turned out to be a wild-goose chase. We're chasing ghosts who are acting on behalf of our nation's biggest enemies, and like a dog chasing its tail, we just can't catch 'em."

The door suddenly opened, and Cole Matthews walked through, an expression of optimism on his face. John ignored him momentarily and continued. "Like I said, I hate it. And unlike my brief fame as a pitcher, failure is not an option here. God only knows the ruin and human misery this technology will reap in the wrong hands. Our best lead is now at the bottom of the sea, and we have no idea where to go next."

"First, I have no idea what conversation I just stumbled into, but you can tell me about your pitching career later. Second, you're wrong on that last point," Cole said.

All three men stared at him. Cole grinned and said, "We *do* know where to go next."

Logan was the first to ask the obvious. "Where?"

"Well, that's a little complicated," Cole said. "But we're working on it."

"Isn't it always," John replied sharply. "So I ask again, O' Wise Man, where?"

"Africa." He looked at John directly and said, "Specifically, Sudan."

"Sudan?" Logan and John asked simultaneously.

"Uh-huh," Cole responded emphatically. "Once we left the US, in addition to the intergovernmental intelligence efforts and the standard SIGINT and IMINT packages supporting our mission, we've also had the support of some clandestine and very sensitive compartmented programs."

"Really?" Logan said. "You CIA boys just can't help yourselves. Always running around playing 'I have a secret.' I don't think it's in the CIA's institutional DNA to want to share." It wasn't stated accusatorily, just as a matter of fact.

Cole shrugged, and said, "Hey, I'm telling you about it, aren't I? And you're right. We don't always tell everyone what we're doing. I've found that a little secrecy sometimes saves lives, and more often than not."

"Point taken. So what happened?" Logan asked.

Cole averted his eyes from Logan and looked to the still-silent David Everett. "Mr. Everett, what I'm about to tell you is compartmented. In fact, it's actually a SAP," he said, referring to the acronym for a special access program. "It was initiated by the director of National Intelligence, whom our boss, the director of the CIA, works for. I just got you and my friends here cleared for it."

John smiled at Cole, a contradiction to the serious and quizzical look on the chief of station's face. John said, "Well, now I'm really intrigued about what you have up your sleeve. Pet rocks? Robot soldiers? Wait a minute—is it a spy shoe like Maxwell Smart had?"

Logan just shook his head. "Ignore him."

"It's slightly better than that. We have trained operatives inserted at several embassies across the world who specialize in wet work and only answer to our director or higher. Sometimes they pose as State Department employees, sometimes contractors. It's always different so that no one—and I mean no one—ever knows the operative's identity except a very few, highly cleared folks back in Langley. The program is called LEGION."

It was Cole's turn to smile as the grin fell from John's face. "What's that, John? No *Quick* comeback?"

"Mr. Everett, don't be upset," Cole continued, now looking at the chief of station, who seemed to have turned a shade of white, either from shock or disbelief. "Most station chiefs never learn of this program's existence, even after an entire career. It's actually one of our most closely guarded secrets. And now it's going to be one of yours that you'll have to take to your grave. Do you understand?"

David Everett nodded his head. "I do."

"Good. Oh, and just so you know, you don't have one currently here. So don't play supersleuth in your head and try to figure out who the secret assassin is. It's a waste of emotional energy and won't serve any purpose, except to frustrate your intellect." He paused for a moment, choosing his next words carefully.

"So here's what I just learned—Langley told me that once we hit the ship last night, they activated the entire network to be on the lookout for unusual air activity. It was a total long shot. Langley didn't expect to gather any intelligence from it. They were shocked when an operative in Sudan reported a delivery from an unmarked private plane at an isolated military airfield several miles outside Khartoum. The operative couldn't see what was delivered but was able to provide one more piece of key information." He shook his head, still processing the unexpected news. "The presence of Chinese intelligence officers."

"Chinese intelligence officers in Sudan?" Logan asked. "Is your person positive? I know China's heavily invested in Sudanese oil, but Chinese intelligence adds an entirely new dimension."

"Positive," Cole responded. "Our operative killed one of them."

"Jesus," John said. "You know what that means, don't you?" he asked, his brown eyes displaying his emotions, anger mixed with concern.

"I do," Logan said quietly. He looked around the room at each of the men before he spoke. "It means this thing's gone global, and we're running out of time. If we're dealing with an international conspiracy comprised of several of our country's enemies, there's an endgame. Someone's got the gear, and they're going to use it, and likely soon."

"When do we leave for Sudan?" John asked.

"I'm glad you asked." Cole turned to the CIA officer. "It actually depends on Mr. Everett."

The mention of his name caused the man to turn his head. "Me?" he asked.

Cole nodded. "Langley already confirmed that the State Department is submitting an emergency request for three diplomatic visas for American IT contractors to repair several crashed servers at the American embassy in Khartoum. They've already emailed you the cover identities to your classified email account. We have our diplomatic passports, but we can't use them. We don't want to tip the Sudanese that we suspect they're involved. There's too much at stake. Langley said you have a talented gentleman who should be able to gin up the appropriate documents within a few hours."

"That's right. I'll get Oscar on it right now." David Everett stood and dialed the closed-network telephone in the middle of the conference table.

"As soon as we have our new identities," Cole continued, "first-class seats on the next available commercial flight, courtesy of the Spanish government, will have us in Khartoum by tomorrow morning, where we'll link up at the embassy with our operative and plan the next move."

"I just hope we're in time," Logan said as he stood from the table, his face darkening. "Otherwise, something very bad is going to happen. It's like you said, John. We're dogs chasing our tails."

CHAPTER 20

Republican Palace, Khartoum

The phone rang in Namir Badawi's office, interrupting his contemplations. *Be patient. Only a few more days . . .*

All was proceeding as planned, and regardless of the incident at the airfield, they were still on schedule. He'd been initially concerned when Gang had informed him that the Americans had seen through the North Korean cargo ship decoy. Namir knew that the Americans had put two and two together. Whoever had been at the airfield had seen something. It was the only explanation for the bombshell that Gang had just dropped on him—the Americans were sending covert operatives to Sudan.

Gang didn't tell Namir how he knew this sensitive information, and Namir had momentarily faltered at the ominous news. But after listening to Lau Gang's explanation and—more importantly—his plan to deal with it, the director was satisfied.

Even though two men were dead, much larger stakes were on the table. And he had a role yet to play—identify the Americans before they arrived. Even covert operatives had to have a cover story, and Namir had ordered his Ministry of Foreign Affairs to be on the lookout for last-minute visa requests, especially from the United States.

This better be good news, he thought, and picked up the phone. "This is Director Badawi."

"Sir, you asked us to notify you in case any strange requests come in," said a voice he recognized. "And while I'm not sure it's strange, it's at least something I thought you should know about."

Namir closed his eyes, already sensing trouble before the deputy minister of the Ministry of Foreign Affairs spoke. *Take a deep breath, exhale, now speak.*

"Mr. Suliman, thank you for calling," Namir said, his voice resonating with graciousness. "Hopefully, it's nothing, but I appreciate the phone call. What is it exactly?"

Namir heard the man inhale, as if praise from the director of Internal Intelligence were confirmation of his significance in the Sudanese government. *Small man in a small position.*

"Sir, we received a request from the US State Department for three contractors. The Americans are apparently having computer issues at their embassy, and the technicians they have here can't seem to fix it," Mr. Suliman said.

"Is that so?" Namir responded, his mind already racing.

"It is, sir. These three contractors were working in Spain and—" Namir suddenly bolted out of his chair behind his desk but maintained the calm in his voice as he interrupted the deputy minister.

"Did you say Spain, Mr. Suliman?" Namir asked, his muscles tensing. He didn't believe in coincidences.

"Yes, sir. They were apparently working on a similar problem in Madrid," the deputy minister responded.

I'll bet they were. The same kind of problem that involves a lost North Korean cargo ship the press hasn't yet reported, Namir thought.

"Should I deny their requests?" the man said, excitement in his voice as he sensed Namir's interest. "It seems routine to me, but if you ask, sir, I can deny it."

Namir knew the man wanted to be of service to him, to please him in any way he could. Deputy minister or not, Suliman knew who wielded the real power in the republic.

"No, Mr. Suliman. I'm sure you're right. It's probably nothing, but I most sincerely appreciate *you* notifying me," Namir said, emphasizing the point.

"It's my pleasure, sir. If there's anything else I can do—"

Namir interrupted the man again. "As a matter of fact, there is," he said, and proceeded to outline the "anything else" for the deputy minister.

When he was finished, he thanked the man once again and hung up the phone. Still standing, he picked up his cell to call Gang with the good news—the Americans had been identified.

More pieces on the board were advancing, but Gang and Namir were still several moves ahead, even as the Americans raced to catch up. Try as they might, Namir knew they wouldn't succeed with what Gang had in store for Sudan's newest visitors.

CHAPTER 21

Khartoum International Airport
1030 Local Time, Three Days to Zero Hour

A man in his midforties with a shaggy head of black hair scanned the arrival terminal with perceptive eyes that looked deceptively vacant. He'd been briefed by the chief of station as to what the three "IT contractors" looked like—as well as their cover identities—and he'd spotted them immediately as they searched for their bags in a luggage pile the porters had hastily created in the corner of the terminal.

The scene inside the arrival area was one of loosely organized chaos. Sudanese nationals jostled one another as bags were thrown aside in impatient searching. Blue smoke wafted through the air as young Sudanese taxi drivers puffed away in defiance of the No Smoking signs near the exit, waiting to be hired by arriving passengers in need of a ride in one of their endless supply of mostly white, late-model Toyota Corollas, a staple of the Khartoum taxi trade. A Spanish national was pulled out of line, protesting loudly, as security opened a suitcase full of clothes and two laptops, the local security suspicious of all electronic equipment.

It never changes, the man thought, amused as he walked toward his human cargo.

As he approached, one of the men, a man in his thirties with slicked-back dark hair, spotted him and said something to his two traveling companions. The other two men, black duffel bags now in hand, turned toward him as he reached their position.

The man smiled, displaying a row of neat, white teeth. "Misters Davis, Johnson, and Greene, I presume," he said, using their cover identities, "welcome to Khartoum. I'm David Cross, with the embassy's information systems security office. We've been expecting you."

Mr. Davis—in reality, Cole Matthews—nodded, recognizing the undercover CIA officer from a photograph he'd been provided the previous night. He reached out and shook the man's hand. "Mr. Cross, it's nice to meet you. We appreciate you picking us up. Saves us navigating the city ourselves. Having been here before, I know how *hectic* local travel can be."

The other two men nodded, and the man with a faint scar down the left side of his face quickly looked around the terminal. *Probably attempting to spot any countersurveillance, but we've already got that covered. We're good,* David thought.

"Gentlemen, I know you're eager to get started. The system is still down," he added for any government eavesdroppers. "So if you'd please follow me, my SUV is parked out front in what passes for a parking lot around here."

"Sounds like a plan, Mr. Cross. Please, lead the way," Cole said as the four men weaved in and out of the bustling travelers that served as a human obstacle course.

As they exited the terminal and emerged into the December morning heat of Khartoum, John said, "Jesus, is it always like this?"

"Wait till you see what traffic's like," David said, and grinned at John. "It'll make this look like an Evening Parade at Eighth and I," he said, referring to the Marine Corps's legendary and perfectly synchronized parades at the Commandant's Barracks in Southeast DC each Friday evening during the summer.

Logan spoke up, his interest piqued. "How would you know

about those? A former life, perhaps?" he asked in a playfully incrim-
inating manner.

"Something like that, Mr. Greene. We all have our pasts," David
said, grinning. He turned and pointed to a white Range Rover parked
two rows from the door. "Come on. That's our ride."

None of them spotted the dark pair of eyes that followed them
across the parking lot.

———

"Wow," John exclaimed, staring out the back passenger seat. "You
weren't kidding. This place makes rush hour in DC look like a speed-
way. We could've crawled on our hands and knees to the embassy by
now."

"We've got a little more than a mile to go. You get used to it, unfortunately, as you do with a lot of things in a place like this," David
responded.

Not sure I agree with that, Logan thought, momentarily reflecting
on a previous tour he and John had done in Somalia—the poverty,
the violence, the children desperately begging for any handout possible. Corrupt governments, rampant diseases, and violence of epic
proportions were commonplace in too many countries on this continent. Africa was not a good place to be these days.

The Range Rover battled its way forward as David tried to merge
with three lanes of traffic from their left. Logan turned around from
the right rear passenger seat and saw a sea of cars. Several Sudanese
men and women weaved in and out of traffic on foot as other drivers
honked furiously at them. *Not a bad choice,* he thought, easing back
into the seat.

He stared out the window and watched the scenery change as the
Range Rover approached a large cemetery full of white headstones
on the right side of the road. Logan opened his mouth to ask about
it when a sudden shrill chirping erupted from a compartment in the

middle console. David slid the panel up and pulled out an Iridium satellite phone.

"Hello?" he asked as all three passengers heard a muffled voice coming from the handset.

"Yes, sir. I've got them now. We'll be at the embassy shortly," David said. A pause. "Okay. Here he is."

David turned in the driver's seat and shoved the satellite phone toward Logan. "It's for you. It's Deputy Director Benson. It's encrypted, and this vehicle has technical countersurveillance measures—as well as armor—installed. So you don't have to worry about what you're saying."

Logan and John exchanged glances as Logan accepted the handset. John mouthed, *Fancy setup.* Logan only nodded and lifted the handset to his ear.

"Hey, Mike. What's up? Isn't it like four in the morning there?"

"It is, but I'm going to be up for quite some time. I've got HRT meeting me at Dulles as soon as I hang up. We're heading to Las Vegas for—"

"Vegas?" Logan interrupted. "Taking a trip in the middle of a crisis? That's not very responsible for a deputy director of the FBI, is it?"

"Fuck you," Mike said.

"Is it the gambling? I wouldn't know. That wasn't my problem. I'm a recovering alcoholic. But remember, always bet on black," Logan quipped as John gave him a perplexed look across the backseat.

"You're an idiot, and I'm going to ignore the lousy Wesley Snipes reference. What I was trying to say is that the Vegas PD received a phone call last week from a local resident, one Mrs. Chambers, an elderly Caucasian woman in a working-class neighborhood who was concerned about her neighbors. She had a history of making complaints against all of them. Apparently, her neighborhood had become a cultural melting pot of immigrant workers, and she didn't like it. Turns out her complaints were usually against African-American or Hispanic families, and they never amounted to anything."

"Sounds like a lovely person," Logan injected.

"Exactly," Mike responded. "Unfortunately for us, she was the Old Lady Who Cried Wolf. Her last complaint was about four Chinese brothers with the last name of Chang who moved into the house across the street from her six months ago. They told neighbors they were here on work visas and all worked at their uncle's restaurant. Nobody pressed them for details because they stuck to themselves."

Logan stiffened in his seat. "Chinese? I'm not liking where this is going."

"You and me both, brother," Mike said. "It gets worse. She told the PD they were up at all hours of the night, working on something in their garage. She also told police she thought she saw one of them with a pistol, but she wasn't sure. The on-duty officer took the report, but because of her history and the fact that the Changs had clean records, at least according to ICE, it got moved to the bottom of the list as a noise complaint. When Vegas PD finally responded to investigate it—this was yesterday—they went to knock on the door. There was no answer, but when the officer looked inside, he noticed that the place looked abandoned, as if they'd left in a hurry. He didn't see anything else suspicious. So he decided to stop by Mrs. Chambers's home and tell her. She didn't answer, but he heard a howling coming from upstairs. Something about the noise set off alarm bells with this cop, and he broke the door down."

"Sounds like a smart officer following his instincts," Logan said.

"Luckily for us," Mike responded. "He found Mrs. Chambers shot to death in her bedroom, locked inside with her cat, which had been making the racket. It looked like she'd been dead for at least two days."

"Good Christ . . . They must've caught her spying on them, which means whatever they're up to is important enough to kill for."

"Exactly. When the Vegas PD broke into the Changs' home, they found several chemicals in the basement used to make homemade explosives. They also canvassed the neighborhood, and the guy who lives behind them overheard them talking about Africa while he was taking his dog out. They didn't know he was there because of the fence, and he thought it was weird since they're Chinese but talking about Africa. It was a few days ago, and he didn't catch any specifics. He didn't think about it again until the PD knocked on his door."

"Go figure," Logan said.

"So I figured since these guys are Chinese and you're now investigating Chinese intelligence agents in Sudan, we have to operate under the assumption that this is not a coincidence. I've got a forensics team tearing their house apart, but these guys were pros. They didn't leave a lot to work with. We've put out an APB on these guys and are going to release their photos to the press."

"You've got to be right. Something's definitely going down, and we still don't have the full picture. Everything we do have seems to point directly at the Chinese government. It wouldn't be the first time the Chinese have had help from the Russians or North Koreans. We just need to figure out what their endgame is, although with the ONERING in play, it could be anything. If we get something on our end, you'll be the first to know." He looked out the window. The Range Rover had progressed only another thirty yards since he'd been on the phone. "We'll be at the embassy shortly."

"Sounds good. If I don't hear from you, I'll assume you're working. Once I'm in Vegas, I'll let you know when I have more information."

"Thanks, brother. Stay safe," Logan said.

"Hey, you're not here, which means no one will be trying to blow me up or shoot me."

"That's very true." Logan laughed. "I do have a way of bringing out the best in people."

"That you do. Okay. Enough chitchat. Happy hunting. Talk to you soon, brother. Take care and out here."

"Roger. Good luck in Vegas," Logan said, and hung up the phone. He handed it back to Cole in the front seat.

"So what's up?" John asked.

"Four Chinese suspects claiming to be brothers—although I'd bet they're not really related—are on the loose in Vegas with weapons and explosives. They murdered their neighbor, and Mike doesn't think it's a coincidence. I agree. It has to be connected. There are too many moves being made by the Chinese at one time *not* to be connected. He's on his way—"

A sudden loud *crunch!* interrupted his explanation.

A white Toyota Land Cruiser had slammed into the front left quarter panel of the Range Rover, which was shoved into the side of a white bus edging its way along the dirt shoulder.

Logan's initial thought as he was jerked toward the middle of the backseat was that some careless, crazy Sudanese driver had miscalculated in the vehicular bedlam.

Both vehicles came to a sudden stop, and Logan opened his mouth to speak when David yelled, "Guns!"

Logan's mind automatically switched into overdrive as he recovered from the initial impact and searched for the threat.

The white Land Cruiser had the Range Rover pinned against the bus. More alarming, two Chinese men armed with Type 05 silenced submachine guns stood next to the vehicle, weapons aimed at the driver's window. A third man aimed a weapon across the hood from the driver's side of the SUV, taking direction from the Toyota's driver, who remained behind the wheel.

They shouted in Chinese, motioning with their weapons for everyone to get out of the vehicle. *This isn't good at all,* Logan thought.

"I don't think they're here to escort us to the embassy," John stated drily, staring into the muzzle of one of the submachine guns. He smiled and waved at the gunman through the window, turned to David, and said, "Get us the fuck out of here, please."

"I don't think he liked your attempt at diplomacy," Logan muttered as the attacker screamed louder at John and tried to open the back door.

"Hold on!" David screamed, and slammed the Range Rover into reverse. The vehicle shot backward, but only made it a few feet before striking the vehicle behind them.

We're boxed in. This was well planned, Logan thought. He turned around and looked through the back of the SUV into the grille of a truck that had nowhere to go.

"There's no way out back here!" Logan screamed. "Find another way!"

"Hit 'em!" Cole shouted from the front seat, but David was already ahead of him.

The Range Rover rocketed forward, the supercharged 510-horsepower engine roaring to life. Even in the confined space, it gained enough momentum that it struck the passenger side of the Toyota and lifted it into the air.

For a moment, Logan thought it'd be enough. But then the Toyota came crashing back down, the passenger side grinding on top of the front end of the Range Rover as if trying to meld the two vehicles together.

"Brace yourselves!" John said suddenly as he watched one of the attackers throw a dark rectangular object under the front of the Range Rover. Even as he shouted "IED!" the small explosive detonated.

BOOM!

The front of the Range Rover was lifted into the air, separating from the Toyota with a metal-rendering *scrreeeech!* The vehicle slammed back to the ground, the engine destroyed by the blast. The instrument panel went dark, and smoke from under the dashboard quickly filled the vehicle.

Logan's head rang from the explosion. He shook it from side to side to clear the buzzing sensation. He looked over to see John doing the same. *We have to get out of here.*

David and Cole had taken the brunt of the blast in the front seats. David was slumped against the driver's side door, and Cole leaned against the headrest, his head tilted backward.

Thwack! Thwack! Thwack! Thwack! Thwack! Spiderwebs appeared on the windshield as the Chinese attackers opened fire.

The gunfire shook loose the remaining cobwebs from Logan's head, and he saw Cole staring at their attackers, awake, but still dazed.

Now we're really out of time. He looked around and realized there was only one option left. *Better than dying in place,* he thought as he unlocked his door and pushed it open halfway before striking the side of the minibus.

The thick smoke inside impaired his vision, and he couldn't see to the front of the vehicle. *Hopefully, they can't see us either.*

"This way!" Logan shouted, his hearing still affected by the explosion. He scrambled out and crouched down behind the rear quarter panel as bullets continued to pepper the SUV amid the shouts in Chinese. John stumbled out behind him, turned around, and reached back inside.

Logan heard shouting from inside the vehicle as he watched the rear of the Range Rover for more Chinese attackers. *Lucky so far . . . We have to go, go, go.*

"What's taking so long?" Logan shouted.

Moments later, John yelled, "He's still out!" and Logan turned to see John pulling David's unconscious form from the vehicle. *Oh, no . . .*

"John, we have about ten seconds. We have to move *now!*"

Cole finally emerged from the smoking vehicle, coughing but giving a thumbs-up gesture as he stood next to them.

John bent over, pulled David into a sitting position, and picked him up in a fireman's carry, hoisting him across his shoulders.

Logan looked at John and nodded. "Cole, up here with me. We'll run point. Let's try to get as much distance as we can between them and us. Let's go."

He turned back around, even as he realized the gunfire had finally stopped. *Damn. They know we're out of the SUV, and they don't want to risk hitting us. If they were willing to shoot, it means they knew we had bulletproof glass.* He realized a moment later what their attackers were doing—*they're herding us.*

Still crouched, Logan moved forward until he reached the rear of the minibus. He peeked around the corner—only to be greeted by another attacker thrusting a Taser toward him.

He reacted instinctively, dodged, and grabbed the man's arm. Logan leaned back and pulled the attacker's arm toward him, using the corner of the minibus as a fulcrum.

Crack! The man's arm snapped. As he screamed in pain, he reflexively dropped the Taser. Logan deftly snatched it out of midair and redirected it into its owner's torso, delivering an initial shock of fifty thousand volts. The man immediately stiffened and fell to the pavement face-first with a loud *smack.*

Logan glanced around the corner of the bus again as he heard footsteps from the front of the Range Rover. The immediate area was clear of additional attackers. He dropped the Taser, knowing it was a one-shot weapon. He didn't have time to search his attacker for extra cartridges.

"Let's go. Be prepared for anything." He moved as quickly and quietly as he could, eyes searching the environment in front of him.

He reached the back of the bus near the dirt shoulder of the road. Moving forward wasn't an option since their attackers were in that direction. In front of him was the war cemetery he'd spotted what now seemed like eons ago. *Lots of tombstones, some trees, a square building in the center—not a lot of cover.* To the right was an endless sea of traffic. Neither were good options. Or they could try to work their way backward toward the airport. *This fucking sucks.*

The decision was made for him when four more Chinese pursuers emerged from the flow of cars fifty yards behind them. Two of the men carried electric-shock batons; two, Type 05 submachine guns. They spotted him and broke into a run.

"Into the cemetery! We have more company coming from the

right!" Logan said, and then dashed across the dirt shoulder and into what a sign informed him in Arabic and English was Khartoum's War Cemetery. *A perfect place for a modern-day showdown.*

Even as he sprinted across the open ground, the thought again popped into his head, prompted by the presence of the electric-shock batons—*they don't want to kill us.* As he ran, he pondered which was worse—death or capture.

CHAPTER 22

US Embassy, Khartoum

Wendell Sharp was still trying to piece together the information and orders he'd received from Langley only hours ago. As the chief of station and senior CIA intelligence officer, he was accustomed to having ultimate oversight of all intelligence operations in his region.

He ran his hand through his graying hair as he paged through the late-morning traffic and updates from his case officers on his classified computer, but his mind kept turning toward the conversation he'd had with the deputy director two hours ago.

A twenty-year veteran of multiple duty stations across the African continent, Wendell Sharp had requested his current assignment for his twilight tour, prior to returning to Langley for one last short assignment and then retirement.

His interest in imperialism and his love for British history had led him to study England's role in Sudan in the late nineteenth century. He knew that the British had conquered Sudan in order to prevent the French from controlling the waters of the Nile. But it wasn't Britain's conquering of the rich land that had fascinated him—it was the revolution that the British occupation had started, a slow and steady quest for freedom that had escalated over fifty-eight years, resulting in Sudanese independence in 1956.

The son of a civil rights activist from Alabama, he identified with the Sudanese people who currently suffered under the oppressive regime in Khartoum. After the horrific, genocidal war crimes in Darfur, he'd hoped to at least make a slight difference, not only in the national security interests of the United States, but also for the people of Sudan.

In the past three years, he and his case officers had made serious inroads into the various ministries. The DC politicians had been especially pleased with intelligence that resulted in the indictment of the current president for war crimes and crimes against humanity.

Through it all, Wendell had operated with the utmost autonomy, which is why the current order from the director's office to provide any and all assistance to the three men under cover who'd just flown in to Khartoum had him perplexed.

What the hell is going on? Whatever it was had to be big, because they'd been able to arrange visas and travel arrangements on short notice. *A coup?* He'd once heard a rumor that the vice president had wanted to overthrow the president, but he'd never been able to confirm it.

More than likely, it was probably the presence of a high-value target. Several Islamic extremist operatives were rumored to be hiding in Sudan, as Osama bin Laden himself had once done. *I'll find out soon enough.*

He was refocusing his attention on a report on a low-level minister who might make a good target for blackmail—he had two mistresses and serious financial troubles—when the secure phone on his desk rang.

"This is Sharp," he said, picking up the handset.

"Sir, this is Holmes down in the communications office. I think we have a problem."

The words sent Wendell's heart into tachycardia. The communications officer went on, "Mr. Cross just triggered his personal locator beacon in his SUV. The vehicle isn't moving, and it's located near the

War Cemetery. Also, he's not answering his satellite phone. I wanted to touch base with you before I activate the quick-reaction force—"

Wendell cut him off. "Do it now. Get them moving ASAP. Also, launch the Draganflyer for overwatch and make sure the operator has a direct link to the QRF commander," Wendell said urgently, referring to the compact rotary UAV the embassy used for force protection. "I'm calling Langley, and then I'll be down in the command center."

He hung up and dialed the senior watch officer at CIA's Operations Center in Virginia.

———

Lau Gang dashed around the stopped traffic, intent on reaching his operatives who were now in pursuit of their targets. He'd watched the ambush from a parked SUV fifty yards away on the other side of the intersection, an elevated location that had provided him with a vantage point over the entire area. The ambush had unfolded exactly as planned, at least until the embassy driver had slammed the vehicle into reverse and tried to escape.

As he'd exited his vehicle, he'd spotted two men moving toward the grounds of the cemetery, but once he'd run into the sea of traffic, he'd lost sight of them. *This should not have been this difficult.*

As he ran through the honking, metallic chaos, he reminded himself once again that operations like this never went smoothly. *True, but they always ended successfully,* he thought, and redoubled his efforts to navigate the mass of angry and panicked drivers.

He *had* to remove the Americans from the playing field and eliminate the threat that they posed. The physical compulsion to control the situation had taken over his actions. The fact that they'd made it this far, even in the face of his carefully crafted plans, was disturbing but not enough to send him into a panic. He was too disciplined for that type of irrational reaction.

The next forty-eight hours would ultimately determine the success of his operation and add another notch in his belt as a Chinese operative, and he wasn't about to leave anything to chance, especially the presence of US agents. Once he had them in his custody, he'd obtain what they'd learned about him, Namir, or the plan. After that, their only other purpose would be to serve as another diversion, ultimately ending up as permanent residents in the fertile soil of the Nile River—*or worse.*

He smiled at the thought, the expression breaking up his normally impassive features, and ran harder.

———

How the hell did we get into this situation? Logan thought as he weaved in and out between the white tombstones. Cole ran next to him, breathing hard.

"I think David triggered an emergency beacon," Cole said in between rapid breaths. "As soon as the ambush started, he flipped a switch inside the same panel where he had the SAT phone. I'm guessing that the embassy knows we're in trouble, and they'll be sending a QRF, if they haven't already. If we can find a way out and a place to hide, we might make it out of this."

Logan opened his mouth to speak when another four-man team suddenly appeared at the cemetery's perimeter fence one hundred yards to their left. A young, Chinese male with short black hair was barking orders.

Logan suddenly stopped, and Cole pulled up beside him. Logan turned to see John thirty yards away, just entering the field of stone. The four men who'd chased them had closed the gap on John, and two men wielding shock batons were only twenty feet behind him. *He's not going to make it.*

"We're almost out of options," Cole said. "They've got us on three sides."

Ignoring Cole for the moment, Logan shouted, "Faster, John! They're on your tail!"

John raised his head to respond, but calamity struck first.

Logan watched in horror as his closest friend's right foot caught the edge of a tombstone and sent him flying across the cemetery lawn. Even in midair, it was obvious that John's concern was for his unconscious cargo. John twisted his body, gripping David's arm tightly, and curled his upper torso to protect David's head and neck from the ground. They crashed onto the earth, their backs absorbing the brunt of the impact. As he slid still, John released David's arm, and the unconscious man rolled off him and onto his back, eyes still closed, unaware of the chase in which he was an unwilling participant.

John sat up as the four pursuers slowly surrounded them. He locked eyes briefly with Logan, momentarily ignoring his attackers. Years of combat experience and the deep friendship they'd developed lay exposed in the hot Khartoum sun. John knew what his friend would do for him, but now was not the time or the place. If they wanted any chance of finding the ONERING, some of them had to escape. And right now, Logan and Cole had the best odds. Today wasn't the day they'd die together.

"Don't even think about it! Get out of here, regroup, and come find me," John shouted. He grinned, looked at the nearest man wielding a baton, and said, "That is unless I kill these motherfuckers myself, in which case I'll be along shortly." He quickly looked back at Logan and screamed as loudly as he could, his voice carrying across the burial ground, threatening to wake the dead, "*NOW GO!*"

The four men to Logan's right had jumped the fence and were now slowly approaching them, carefully covering the entire width of the cemetery. The young man issuing orders spoke calmly into a handheld radio. *He's calling for more reinforcements. They must really want us.*

Voices suddenly emanated from the south side of their position, and Logan whirled around to see three more armed operatives navigating the tombstones. *We're surrounded.*

Logan glanced back at John, who now stood in the center of his attackers. *Goddamn you, John. You always have to be the hero.*

"Let's move," Logan said. He didn't look back as he fled toward the back of the cemetery where a smooth, white marble rectangular memorial stood near the back fence. The two other teams were in pursuit, executing a foot-mobile pincer movement designed to cut off their last chance of escape.

CHAPTER 23

QRF Convoy

Retired Army Major Tim Greco watched the dash-mounted laptop screen in silence from the passenger seat of the beige MRAP, a mine-resistant, ambush-protected vehicle that laboriously worked its way through the Khartoum traffic.

As the embassy's regional security officer—commonly called an RSO—he was the senior officer assigned by the Diplomatic Security Service, the DSS, in charge of all embassy security and force protection, including the safety of all US personnel assigned to Khartoum.

Less than five minutes ago, he'd been sorting through the daily intelligence, assessing the validity and severity of the multiple local threats the embassy received on a regular basis. Almost all turned out to be nothing, either the result of bad information or intentional disinformation from local bad actors hoping to probe the embassy's security posture. The last real threat from a local Islamist extremist group had been neutralized by the Sudanese government after he'd fed the Sudanese National Intelligence and Security Service information leading to their safe house.

A former enlisted Army Ranger with the 3rd Ranger Battalion, Tim knew the risks of complacency in enemy territory. He'd been a young Fire Team leader in Somalia in 1993 during the Black Hawk

Down battle. His convoy had been sent into the city from the airport after the second Black Hawk had crashed. His Humvee had come under intense fire, and his radio operator had been killed in the seat behind him.

To this day, he still blamed the presidential administration for denying the requests for Abrams tanks and Bradley armored fighting vehicles. There was no guarantee Specialist Mike Airesdale would've survived, but at least he'd have had a fighting chance. The Humvees of the early nineties hadn't been built to sustain the kind of damage inflicted by Aidid's militia.

Months after the battle, he'd decided to become a commissioned officer and dedicate his career to providing the appropriate level of force protection for US personnel stationed around the world. It became his personal mission and ultimately landed him in the DSS, utilizing his knowledge and skills to become one of the best RSOs in the agency.

When his phone rang and the chief of station told him an emergency beacon had been triggered by one of his case officers, Tim had been able to launch a two-MRAP QRF convoy comprised of both Marine Security Guard forces and civilian DSS personnel in less than five minutes.

Training and preparation always pay off, he thought as he watched the live feed from the Draganflyer UAV hovering five hundred feet above the cemetery. Two small dark figures ran toward a rectangular marble building Tim recognized—he'd visited the cemetery multiple times; all warriors have a respect for the war dead—pursued by running figures from both sides. Two others remained near the main entrance, surrounded by four other attackers.

Who were these guys? But the chief of station hadn't told him, and it wasn't relevant to his mission. All that mattered was their safe recovery.

But then something else caught his attention from outside the fence in the back of the cemetery. *What the . . . ? Oh no.*

"Brian, you better drive as fast as you can. Run them off the road if they won't move. This is going to be over in the next few minutes, and we're still a half mile away," Tim said urgently.

His second in command responded by pressing the accelerator to the floor. The 9.3-liter engine roared, a living beast eager to devour anything in its path. The MRAP struck a small white Toyota blocking the shoulder and flung it aside, its driver staring in amazement as the gigantic tactical vehicle passed it on the inside.

Tough luck, buddy. Should've stayed on the road.

Tim spoke into the microphone mounted on his Kevlar helmet and issued instructions to the second team in the MRAP behind him.

———

John was itching for a fight. Getting ambushed in the middle of Khartoum had triggered a reaction he reserved for special occasions, ones usually involving the use of especially lethal force. To put it bluntly—he was pissed off.

It wasn't the assault on their Range Rover. It wasn't even the fact that he was now surrounded by four men with modified electric-shock batons and submachine guns. He couldn't blame them. They were following their orders, although how their enemy had so quickly identified Logan, John, and Cole when they themselves had only realized they were coming to Khartoum mere hours ago was extremely disturbing. He'd save that mystery for a later date.

No, he was enraged—pure and simple—because he'd tripped. He was furious with himself for being so careless, especially when he'd charged himself with the safety of David Cross. *I'm getting old,* he thought, although he knew his "old" was good enough to take out most men decades younger. *It doesn't matter. I stumbled, and I shouldn't have. Goddamnit!*

"Okay then, boys," John said, assessing the situation. David was semiconscious where he'd fallen near a headstone, and he began to stir, a low groan rising from his form.

One attacker with a baton was just out of John's reach to his right, the other baton-wielding man to his left. The two men with submachine guns stood in front of him a little more than ten feet away. The muzzles were angled down, as if to remind him there was no point in fighting, that there was nowhere to go.

Oh yeah? Fuck you. We'll see about that. He picked his target.

"Don't just stand there with your dick in your hands, junior. Let's get on with it," John said icily.

The man was the youngest of the four. John figured he couldn't be more than twenty, maybe twenty-five. A brief flash of anger raced across the young man's smooth forehead, and then he gripped his weapon tighter. He raised the submachine gun at John's head and nodded slightly to John's side.

"Take him," the young man said in crisp English.

Gotcha, asshole, John thought, and smiled, waiting for the attack.

The young man saw the smile and faltered, recognizing too late that it was what his target had been hoping for.

The man with the black baton took a quick step forward. In a flash, John moved to the right and closed the distance between them.

The electric baton came rushing toward John's chest—as he'd expected—but he was too quick for his attacker. Like a professional boxer, he sidestepped as the baton sizzled past him in the air, and he looped his left arm over his attacker's, securing the baton against his side and protecting himself at the same time.

John heard the other two men move behind him. He had to eliminate this threat before he could deal with them, unless they got to him first.

Acutely aware of his vulnerability, he struck his human shield with a vicious punch to the shoulder, and he felt the man's arm go slack, reflexively releasing the baton he held. John stepped into the man's torso and turned, once more placing the man directly between him and the youngest team member with the submachine gun. He shoved his unwilling protector with both hands, flinging him backward before he could react.

As the man fell, John reached down to his side and grabbed the cattle prod that had been left there, suspended under his arm. He grabbed it and launched himself forward, rushing toward the submachine gunner, using the tumbling figure of the first man as a diversion.

The young man had been caught off guard, and as his comrade was thrust toward him, he moved to the side to avoid the collision. His right leg slammed into a headstone, and his upper body jerked to the right, threatening to topple him over the grave. He regained his balance at the last moment and swung his gun up toward John's head.

The first attacker fell backward, crashing into another tombstone. The sound of his head striking the hard surface was a sickening *thwap*. He collapsed against the grave marker, unconscious or dead—John didn't care which.

John had sufficiently closed the distance, and as the twenty-something shooter raised his weapon, John reached out and touched the tip of the baton to the barrel of the submachine gun. He pressed the trigger, sending a crackling jolt of low voltage through the black metal.

Designed to stun large farm animals or torture humans, the baton's charge caused the man to scream as white-hot pain shot up his arms into his body. The man stiffened, but when John released the button that served as the baton's trigger, he collapsed to the dry grass below, the gun bouncing off a headstone and coming to rest at its base.

John kicked his downed adversary in the face for good measure, the blow cutting the man's right temple and sending him into oblivion.

He heard a commotion behind him but didn't dare waste a moment to look. He dove toward the submachine gun and landed on his stomach, the breath knocked out of his lungs. Ignoring the discomfort, he swept up the weapon and bounced back to his feet, searching for a target.

What he saw stunned him, and he felt his breath catch at the scene before his eyes.

———

Logan and Cole had reached the rectangular memorial, intent on using the sparse trees surrounding it to mask their movement. The immediate goal had been to reach the fence at the back of the cemetery, scale it, and use the perimeter to flank and ambush the Chinese assault force as the teams tried to leave the grounds. They figured they'd be able to at least take out one of the teams, snatch their weapons, and attack the team that had captured John and David. The plan had changed when they'd spotted two more armed attackers on the dirt sidewalk outside the fence. Their escape was blocked.

Time for plan B, Logan thought.

"Quick! Inside here. We don't have a choice. We really are surrounded," Logan said as he moved toward a roofless building thirty feet long by fifteen feet wide, made of four nine-foot-high stone walls. The only way in or out was a four-foot long entryway covered by a stone arch.

Logan and Cole dashed through the entrance under the arch. Inside, four white stone benches were positioned two by two in the middle of a manicured grass area surrounded by a small walkway. On the walls were names etched in Arabic.

Dead warriors were honored in all civilized cultures. But Logan certainly didn't have plans to join them anytime soon.

The sound of a high-pitched engine—similar to a powerful lawn mower—reached their ears from overhead, and the two men exchanged a quick glance.

"Is that what I think it is?" Cole asked, quickly looking up into the bright morning sky.

"I'm pretty sure it is. The embassy already has eyes-on. Thank God," Logan answered, referring to the UAV both knew was now overhead. "Hopefully, the quick reaction force is nearly here too."

The sounds of shouting grew louder.

"We've got maybe twenty seconds," Logan responded as he moved to the bench closest to the entrance. "Help me flip this over."

They placed the heavy stone bench on its side, revealing a pair of objects underneath it they hadn't seen—two metal urns. Logan smiled at Cole.

"I have an idea," he said. "It probably won't work, but hey, what have we got to lose at this point?"

———

A Special Forces veteran of the Chinese People's Liberation Army, Chief Sergeant Chow Chi-Fong had been hand-selected by Lau Gang, the young major from the PLA's military intelligence unit.

Chi-Fong didn't like surprises, and unfortunately, this mission had already provided plenty. They'd lost one of their best communications officers at the airfield two days before. Gang had acted out of character by gathering all of them together and emphasizing the importance of the mission. He'd assured his men that Chang's sacrifice was for a higher purpose, an endgame that guaranteed their country's future prosperity.

From the briefing, Chi-Fong had the impression that Gang might know who was responsible for Chang's killing, but he hadn't disclosed it. Chi-Fong was sure the major had his reasons, which was good enough for him.

It wasn't his place to question Gang, even though Chi-Fong was at least ten years his senior. He just wanted to get the next few days over with so he could return to the mainland before the international community figured out what was happening.

When the ambush had gone according to plan, he'd been encouraged to hope that there'd be no more digressions from the mission. But then the Americans had somehow escaped the smoking SUV and fled into the cemetery.

Team One had surrounded two of the vehicle's occupants, and Chi-Fong's team and Team Three had converged on the small memorial in the back of the burial ground. The two teams lined up outside the small entrance, with Chi-Fong in front as the operator with the most experience in this type of situation. He looked at Gang for approval, received it with a nod, and moved toward the doorway, a pistol-like Taser held up in front of him.

We have to capture them alive, he thought, recalling a covert operation in Taiwan early in his career when he'd shown mercy to a family member of a target he'd been sent to assassinate. She'd promised never to speak of what had happened to her brother, an enemy of the state and a collaborator with a Western human rights movement. In a moment of weakness, he'd allowed her to live, probably because of her beauty. As he'd left the apartment, his mission seemingly complete, she'd silently snuck up behind him and tried to attack him with a kitchen knife. He'd reacted instinctively, disarming her and plunging the knife into her stomach before he realized what he'd done. Chi-Fong had cursed himself for allowing her to get as close as she did, forcing him to feel momentarily vulnerable. After that mission, mercy was no more. It was always the mission, and always for China.

A sudden thud echoed from inside. *What are they doing? They have to know they're trapped.*

Chi-Fong entered the structure, passing under the stone archway, moving close to the wall. His knees were bent, ready to react. A short passageway opened into the space inside, but it turned around a corner to his right, limiting his vision. Directly in front of him was a stone bench on its side, further obstructing his path. He inched forward and leaned out but still couldn't see anything. *Not good.*

And then he saw it—or rather—*them.* The soles of a pair of dark-brown shoes were sticking out just enough to be visible.

He turned back to the five operatives behind him and pointed at the bench. He used his left hand to signal that he and the man behind him would move toward the bench, and the four men in the rear of the stack would fan out to the right once inside. They nodded in uniform acknowledgment, and he returned his focus to the bench.

Chi-Fong waited a brief moment, listening. Nothing. *They must be hiding, hoping for who knows what.*

Once committed to a course of action, Chi-Fong executed it with precision. He exhaled and stepped quickly past the corner of the inside wall. He took one more step, and then he caught a flash of movement from his right, and he realized his mistake—*the bench was a diversion.*

It was too late. He tried to react as a gold object flashed before him and grew larger as it sailed toward his face. He couldn't see who wielded it, his eyes fixated on the weapon. *Are those flowers?* he thought wildly.

It was all his mind had time to process. There was a loud *crack* as the object collided with his face, and he felt his nose shatter in a bright flash of white pain. The last thing he felt was the Taser being yanked out of his hands. And then, nothing.

―――

The brass urn full of bright purple flowers Logan had spotted at the last moment clattered to the stone pathway. Logan shoved the unconscious man backward as he ripped the Taser from his hands. The unlucky assailant's body crashed into the man behind him.

Logan stepped forward before the nearest operative could react, timing his strike perfectly. As the surprised attacker tried to deflect his friend's dead weight with the police-style baton he wielded, Logan plunged the Taser under his chin and pulled the trigger. The man went rigid and collapsed to the ground. *Two down, four to go.*

As Logan retrieved the baton, he sensed a flurry of activity behind him as Cole entered the fray. They'd achieved a momentary tactical advantage, and he intended to prolong it as long as possible.

Before the engagement commenced, they'd agreed that Logan would disarm the first attacker and use him as a human battering ram to push back whoever was along the outer wall, while Cole would step in behind him to fend off the men along the inner part of the entrance where the passageway turned the corner.

In a conventional urban combat situation, the attacking force usually required a seven-to-one troop ratio in order to dislodge an entrenched enemy. At six on two, the odds favored Logan and Cole, and they'd taken immediate advantage of it. It was paramount that they press their initial momentum and drive the attackers out in order to buy precious time for the QRF to join the fight.

Cole lunged from behind the main wall and rounded the corner, confronting a third man with a Taser aimed at Logan. Cole reached out and grasped his wrists, yanking upward and to the left in a large, sweeping motion.

The Taser discharged into the open air above the memorial.

As the operative's arms slammed into the wall, Cole delivered a precise elbow that struck him in the jaw. Cole followed the strike with two vicious blows to his midsection, doubling the man over. He finished him off by slamming his head into the stone wall, either killing or sending him into a very deep sleep.

Wham!

Pain suddenly exploded in Cole's upper right arm, and he roared in fury as a fourth attacker pulled a heavy steel baton back to strike a second blow. Cole turned to defend himself, even as he sensed another attacker rushing in from his right.

But it was Logan. Cole saw his friend's baton come crashing down onto the Chinese attacker's forearm.

Snap! The man's forearm broke like a dry twig.

He screamed in pain, but his cry was cut short as Logan struck a second blow to the temple. The fourth operative collapsed, adding to the bodies now clogging the entranceway under the memorial's arch.

Ignoring the pain shooting up his arm, Cole leapt over the fallen men toward the final two attackers, the ones armed with submachine guns. Logan was a half step ahead of him to his right, swinging the baton like a short sword.

Cole and Logan had bet their lives that this assault force had orders to take them alive. Their theory was about to be tested as Logan swung the baton and missed.

The gunman in front of him had more than enough time to pull the trigger. He didn't. Instead, he pivoted the submachine gun, striking the baton with the butt of his weapon and knocking Logan's arm to the side.

Even as Logan felt the vibration travel up his arm, he smiled. *Bingo. Got you now, motherfucker.*

Logan dropped the baton and stepped within reach of the armed man. He brought his arm up and slammed it into the back of the gunman's right arm in front of him, pinning the submachine gun against the wall and aimed back toward its owner.

Before the man could react, Logan leaned heavily against him, reached around with his right hand, and located the pistol grip. He inserted his finger into the trigger guard and pulled backward.

Thwack-thwack-thwack! The silenced gun was loud, its three-round burst magnified by the tight quarters. The gunman stood dazed from the shots that screamed past his head, his grip loosening on the weapon.

Logan grabbed the handle of the submachine gun and dug his fingers into the man's right wrist. The hand opened under the intense pressure, and Logan yanked the weapon out of his grasp, stepping backward.

Panic gripped the Chinese operative, and he reached inside his khaki vest for a shoulder holster.

Logan locked his bright-green eyes with the man's dark ones, shook his head, and pulled the trigger.

Thwack-thwack-thwack! Three rounds struck the gun's owner squarely in the chest, and he fell backward through the doorway, landing on the dry grass outside.

Logan turned to see Cole struggling with the last of the operatives. Cole had managed to disarm the man, and the submachine gun lay on the ground between them. Logan watched as Cole broke free of the man's grasp and delivered a front kick that sent his attacker stumbling backward.

We're out of time. We need to get out of here to help John. It's time to end this. With Cole safely out of range, Logan aimed the weapon once more and shot the final man before he could regain his footing. He fell to the ground, landing partially on top of his dead team member.

It was over.

"Thanks," Cole said simply.

"We need to get out of here and help John. There's at least one of them left—their leader, I think. He's got the drop on us, but we already know they won't kill us. Let's go."

Cole picked up the other submachine gun as a black canister sailed in from outside the doorway.

Before they could react, there was a loud *pop* and gray smoke filled the air.

Oh no, Logan thought as he detected a strong, pleasant odor he couldn't quite identify. Then it hit him at the same time as the effects of the gas, a memory of having his wisdom teeth pulled. *It smells like laughing gas.*

"Move!" he screamed and pulled Cole toward the doorway, even as he felt his body become sluggish, his limbs suddenly heavy. He took a step toward the opening, but the effects of the incapacitant were almost instantaneous. He stumbled forward onto the stone walkway, rolling onto his side.

Cole landed on the ground next to him, staring at him in dawning understanding. He managed to utter, "At least we tried," and then passed out as the gas overtook him.

This can't be how it ends! Logan's mind screamed. He struggled to lift his head and look outside as a loud roaring sensation filled his ears. He saw black boots quickly approach but soon lost focus. As hard as he resisted, his eyes closed, and he drifted into unconsciousness.

Gang was in a state of disbelief—an emotion he rarely experienced. Even as the situation rapidly spiraled out of control, each of his actions was calculated for maximum tactical benefit. No matter what else occurred, he'd achieve his objective in the next two minutes.

He was certain he already had his answer—these men *had* to be intelligence operatives, and experienced ones at that. There was no other explanation for their escape and evasion from his small assault force.

Once they'd entered the cemetery—a contingency he'd planned for—he'd maintained a visual on the four Americans until they'd been forced to split up when the one carrying the embassy driver had fallen. Gang had chosen to pursue the two men fleeing toward the rectangular memorial.

He knew the US Embassy would send a response team to rescue their personnel. What he didn't know was how long he had before they arrived, and he'd made the call for a quick extract, even as he directed his men's next moves.

He'd seen his team surround the fallen Americans, confident his prey would be subdued in seconds. He'd been almost as confident that his six men who'd entered the memorial would meet little resistance. Apparently, he'd been wrong on both counts.

He'd heard the struggle inside but had assumed it was his team overpowering the two targets. Gang only realized how much he'd underestimated his enemy when he saw Corporal Feng's body fall, bullet-ridden, through the memorial's entrance.

He had to end this confrontation, which was why he'd thrown the black canister.

It contained a fentanyl-derived chemical agent, the same substance used by Russian commandos to incapacitate Chechen terrorists in the Moscow theater crisis in 2002. Unfortunately, the gas had also killed 117 of the hostages as a result of overexposure. The Russians had shared the technology as part of a military agreement between his unit and the Russian Federal Security Service. The Chinese military had tailored it for close-quarters tactical use.

Now, as he waited for the gas to take effect—a matter of seconds—he radioed the team leader who'd surrounded the other two Americans.

"Do you have the two men? Extract inbound. ETA, sixty seconds."

No answer. He repeated the question as a loud thrumming began to shake the ground. *We're almost out of time. We can't wait.*

Suddenly, another one of Gang's white SUVs crashed through the nearest iron fence, knocking it over and tearing up the cemetery in large clumps of dirt and sod. The SUV stopped beside the memorial, and Gang motioned for the driver to assist him.

The driver jumped out of the vehicle and approached Gang.

"They should be unconscious. Get them out of there now! We have to leave."

"What about our men?" the young sergeant asked.

"We don't have time to retrieve them," he said, starting to raise his voice. "Look!"

He turned around and saw what he'd been expecting—a Russian

Hind Mi-24 attack and transport helicopter approaching low on the horizon.

"I'll arrange a cleanup crew with the Sudanese. Now go. I'm going to get you some help to move the Americans," Gang shouted over the increasing roar of the rotors. He turned away from his driver and ran to meet the Hind as it descended into the fray.

CHAPTER 24

After disarming and rendering unconscious the closest two Chinese operatives, John retrieved the second attacker's submachine gun and regained his footing. He turned to face the sound of the commotion he'd heard in the middle of his own struggle.

Standing before him was a lithe, light-skinned African woman with pale blue eyes. *Gunslinger eyes,* John thought, the initial shock of this woman's sudden appearance fading away. *This day is full of surprises.*

At her feet lay the two bodies of the Chinese attackers John had ignored as he dealt with the two closest to him. They were no threat now. Blood slowly leaked from their lifeless bodies into the hallowed ground below.

A bright, multicolored scarf was tightly wrapped around her upper body, revealing two scabbards for the dual stilettos she held, blood staining each. And then he realized the truth—*she's LEGION. A beautiful, trained killer.*

"Who are you? I know you're not contractors," she said in a calm, controlled voice. "Any idea why these men attacked you?"

John's reply was interrupted as he and his savior looked skyward, their attention caught by the sound of rotors from an approaching helicopter. *What now?*

Gunfire erupted in the back of the cemetery, followed by a smaller *pop.* Moments later, a white SUV crashed through the iron gate and pulled alongside the small, stone building. He heard the helicopter grow closer and saw it rise up like a large, ancient bird from behind a five-story building next to the cemetery.

"My name's John, but I don't have time to explain. We need to help my friends, although it sounds like they're doing okay for themselves." He nodded toward the memorial in the back of the burial ground. "You must be LEGION. We know all about it," he said, cutting her off before she could interrupt him, surprise written on her face at the mention of one of the most closely guarded programs in the US government. "Do you want to grab the submachine gun, or do you prefer the blades? Either way, let's move."

"My name's Amira—my real first name, that is. Let's go help your friends. We'll talk later," she said matter-of-factly.

She sheathed her weapons so quickly John almost missed it. *She may move more smoothly than anyone I've ever seen. Will wonders never cease?* She bent down and retrieved a Type 05 submachine gun as John broke into a run.

The helicopter descended rapidly, its landing gear lightly touching the pavement as the flying beast settled.

John and Amira were halfway to the memorial when gunfire erupted from the direction of the SUV. Bullets kicked up grass and dirt in front of them, and they dove behind two headstones.

"Goddamnit!" John muttered. Bullets tore chunks out of the white marble. "I swear I'm going to kill these motherfuckers!"

"Not if you hide behind that tombstone, you're not!" Amira said, darting around the marker and moving up to the next row.

She's fearless, too.

There was a brief pause in the gunfire, and John joined Amira. He glanced over the nearest headstone. They were still fifty feet from the SUV, and he saw movement beyond it, figures moving toward the helicopter.

Bullets pockmarked their cover again, strafing relentlessly back and forth.

Finally, the gunfire ceased, and John peeked over the headstone. There was no one near the SUV, which meant only one thing. *They're getting away, and they've got Logan and Cole.*

"Let's go!" John said, and jumped over the tombstone, sprinting toward the SUV, using it to partially block his movement. Amira was close beside him.

They reached the SUV just in time to see three Chinese men load Logan and Cole's bodies into the open compartment of the helicopter.

John aimed at the rotors and opened fire with the submachine gun. Bullets peppered the Hind's blades but had no discernible impact on their power.

Amira followed suit, but a young Chinese man with a short haircut turned toward them, drew his pistol, and returned fire as the helicopter lifted off the ground.

Holes appeared in the windshield and passenger window, driving John and Amira behind the SUV's cover once more.

John controlled the rage that seethed through his body. He focused on his breathing and shut his eyes. The gunfire ended, and he and Amira stood up as the helicopter banked upward and away, moving west.

Automatic gunfire erupted from the back of the helicopter. *What the hell are they shooting at now?*

His question was answered when a small explosion echoed across the sky several hundred feet above him as bullets tore apart the embassy's UAV.

"Motherfuckers," John said again, gritting his teeth as he wrestled with his emotions. "Excuse my French," he said to Amira, almost as an afterthought, his quips on autopilot again as the adrenaline in his system subsided.

"No apology necessary. I've killed four of these bastards already,"

Amira responded coldly. "I'll be happy to increase the body count."

"A woman after my own heart," he said, the comment leaping out of his mouth before he could contain it. "Wait a minute. Four? I only counted two back there."

"It's a long story. I'll tell you later, but it looks like the cavalry just arrived." She nodded toward the entrance to the cemetery.

Two armored vehicles with US flags and State Department insignia on the doors had pulled up to the fence. Eight men in tactical clothes fanned out across the cemetery, two of them making a direct path toward David Cross, who now sat up.

"We need to get out of here before the Sudanese show up. They're not exactly understanding, especially toward Westerners," Amira said.

As they jogged toward the security teams, John vowed to recover his friend and his new ally, burning the country to the ground, if that's what was required. *We'll find you, Logan. Just stay alive long enough to give us a chance.*

"What are you smiling at?" Amira asked.

John didn't realize he was, but he answered her directly. "They have no idea who they captured. If they don't kill Logan, they're probably going to wish they had before this is all over," he said, grinning openly now.

Who was this man? she wondered as she ran alongside him, feeling a growing appreciation for someone who lived life the way she did— all in, all the time.

A fit, middle-aged man with short gray hair was waving them over to where David Cross was being attended to by one of the security force members.

"I believe you're looking for us," John said to the man as he and Amira reached him. John looked at David, who still seemed woozy. "How's he doing?"

David managed to look up and smiled faintly at the sight of John. "Where are your friends?"

"Captured," John replied flatly.

"Sonofabitch," David muttered. He stared at the beautiful woman holding a submachine gun. Recognition crossed his face. "I've seen you at the embassy, haven't I?"

"She's with us. We can explain when we get you out of here. We're already losing ground and falling behind these guys. We need to go—*now*."

"Mr. Greco," David said, turning his attention to the man tending to him, "can you please get us out of this cemetery?"

The man nodded, stood up, and turned to John, sticking out his hand. "I'm Tim Greco, the embassy's RSO. Let's get the hell out of here before company arrives."

"What about these men?" Amira said, gesturing to the bodies strewn around them. "We need to know who they are, why they attacked, and most importantly, how they knew you were coming. We have to take one of them with us."

"Ma'am, my mission is to get you all back to the embassy in one piece," Tim responded. "We only have minutes before the Sudanese police get here, and God knows what those guys will do. We need to leave now."

"She's right though, Tim," David said. "Get one of them, and let's get the hell out of here."

"Sir, it's your call, but I'm advising against it. The Chinese will probably file a grievance with the US for kidnapping one of their citizens."

"No. They won't," John said. "These guys are either Chinese special ops or spooks. After what they just pulled and how royally they fucked up, the Chinese government won't acknowledge their existence. I guarantee these guys are on their own as of right now."

"Like I said, I'm advising against this," Tim said.

"Understood," David said.

"This is the one we want," John said as he stood over the unconscious form of the young Chinese gunman who'd first let his guard down. "I know he speaks English, and I'm sure he'll be happy to see me when he wakes up."

He bent over, grabbed the young man, and hauled him over his shoulder. "Now can we please get the hell out of here? I'm tired of carrying bodies around."

CHAPTER 25

The American had come through yet again, providing invaluable intelligence that had been one hundred percent accurate and reliable.

Lau Gang averted his gaze from his unconscious passengers and checked the time. It'd been more than two hours since they'd escaped the battle. They'd be on the ground in minutes to deliver these two spies to their temporary new home. Gang planned then to return to his new base to execute the next phase. They'd abandoned the airfield before conducting the ambush at the cemetery.

There was no time for an interrogation, sadly—he'd been hoping to make these two suffer for what they'd done to his men. Regardless, he'd removed two of the three Americans from the playing field, virtually ensuring there was no way to stop what was coming next. All three would have been better, but Gang knew the US would now be scrambling to recover their operatives. And that meant that they wouldn't be focusing on the ONERING.

Gang had planned to use it tomorrow, one day before zero hour. But with confirmation that the Americans were closing in, the sooner they could exercise the power they now wielded, the sooner an agreement would be signed between China and Sudan. That was all that mattered.

His thoughts turned toward the men he'd lost. His superiors in Beijing would not be pleased, even if they had successfully accomplished their mission. The three senior ranking officers involved in the planning of this mission were not known for their tolerance and understanding.

His satellite phone vibrated, the tone drowned out by the rotors of the helicopter. *What now, Namir?* He inserted a Bluetooth earpiece and answered the phone.

"Yes," he said, and waited.

"My security personnel recovered all of your men except one. Four are dead. We're treating the rest."

"Who is missing?" Gang asked.

"Henry Cho," Namir answered. "A young team member, according to your people. We have to assume the Americans have him. This whole operation could be compromised."

How could this be happening? We have to move faster.

"When are you planning to call your president?" Gang asked, changing topics.

"I'm going to wait a little bit until after you use the device, and then I'll brief the president. He'll have enough information to act at that point. Why?" Namir asked.

"I'm almost at our destination. As soon as I drop these two off, I'll be back to the base within seventy-five minutes. We'll do it then. Waiting until tomorrow will only further jeopardize the mission."

"Once you initiate the attack, you have to relocate again, in case your man breaks," Namir said.

"He'll hold out as long as he can," Gang said, although he knew that eventually, everyone broke. "However, we'll move as soon as it's done."

"Okay. Good luck. Text me when it's done," Namir said, and hung up.

The helicopter started to bank to the right, and Gang looked out the window. A large, three-story, concrete building rose up to meet them as they descended. Gang noted the concertina wire that lined the perimeter of the roof.

What else could go wrong today? He couldn't quiet his racing mind. *Stop it,* his father's voice suddenly demanded inside his head. *You're being weak. Stay focused.*

He breathed slowly and deeply as the helicopter landed on a gravel road outside the main entrance of the building.

"Welcome to your new quarters," he said quietly to his captives.

The front doors opened and four armed Sudanese men in dark-blue fatigues and aviator sunglasses under maroon berets—a uniform unique to this location—stepped into the hot sun. They marched down the steps toward the waiting helicopter.

I really wish I could stay here to watch this, Gang thought sadistically. *Maybe when we've activated the device, I'll come back and take care of you myself.*

PART IV

PROVOCATION

CHAPTER 26

Satellite Operations Center 11, Schriever Air
Force Base, Colorado Springs
0700 MST

Major Scott Winters's gaze was fixed on three rows of monitors arranged around his workstation. The twelve screens provided him with updated satellite telemetry data from the space vehicle missions he was assigned. His shift had started an hour ago, and he was still combing through the overnight logbook. As the assistant senior watch officer, it was his responsibility to review the log each morning for the senior watch officer, Lieutenant Colonel Tommy Bancroft. He'd learned to be thorough and meticulous in his daily reports, since Lieutenant Colonel Bancroft expected him to know as much as—if not more than—he did.

Unlike the majority of Americans, Major Winters knew the real capabilities of the US government's satellite network, made up of both classified and unclassified Department of Defense and Intelligence Community satellites. Hollywood and popular culture continuously glorified the overhead constellation network, but no one in the business itself would ever confirm or deny the real capabilities portrayed. He'd recently watched a rerun of *Enemy of the State*, starring Will Smith and Gene Hackman, an excellent movie for the pure entertainment value. He'd lost count of how many times Will Smith had saved the world over the years.

He was almost finished with the logbook—a lime-green, hard-cover journal, the kind only utilized by the US government—when he noticed a red light flashing on the right middle screen, the one he monitored for alerts from classified spacecraft.

What the hell? He stared at the screen, momentarily stunned. *That's impossible.* He maximized the size of the window, and the alert screen filled the monitor, providing him with the telemetry data from Mission 2324, one of the highly classified CIA satellites.

He watched in dawning horror as the orbital data changed on the geosynchronous satellite. The spacecraft, a SIGINT satellite currently assigned to the African continent, was being moved, but he had no idea by whom. He stared at the screen, quickly scanning the mission data, dread creeping into his gut. Cold sweat broke out across his forehead as he saw it. It wasn't the SIGINT system that was important on this mission—it was the sensitive payload the satellite carried.

Suddenly, a second red alert window popped up on the same screen. He clicked it and read the message. His heart rate accelerated, and he fought to control the full-fledged panic threatening to overtake him. *Oh my God.*

The major, known by members of his squadron as a quiet, reserved family man, suddenly stood, turned to Lieutenant Colonel Bancroft at the senior watch officer desk ten feet away and said, "Sir, someone just activated THOR'S HAMMER, and I don't have a fucking clue who."

The senior watch officer, temporarily dumbstruck at the information, just stared back at the major.

"Sir, what the hell do we do? This has never happened before."

As the seconds ticked by, and he waited for his boss to process the information, a third window popped up. He saw it, closed his eyes, and prayed. It had just become the worst day in the watch center—ever.

South of the Nuba Mountains, Near the Border of Sudan and South Sudan

Shao Xiang followed the Nile as it cut a large swath through the green, undulating plains that passed below the helicopter. He averted his gaze to the horizon, the barren, distant mountains a geographic reminder of the paradoxical nature of Sudan. As beneficial as the Nile was to the people near its flowing waters, most of Sudan was arid desert and mountainous terrain, hostile to those foreign to the region.

Nestled between the Nile River and the Nuba Mountains fifty miles to the north, the Chinese National Petroleum Corporation exploration site was on the verge of becoming a fully operational oil field.

While the other, older executives of the CNPC had focused their efforts along the Sudan–South Sudan border further west, Xiang, still in his midthirties, had applied the scientific method in his search, utilizing hyperspectral satellite remote sensing.

Using high-power computers to scan Chinese satellite images, his research team had identified an area abundant with tiny hydrocarbon leaks that had changed the chemical nature of the plants and soil. Those subtle changes had provided a precise location on which to build their exploratory drilling site.

The site had been functional for the past six months, but it had only taken a week to elevate his status in the eyes of the CNPC board members for one simple reason—his team had discovered the largest underground oil field on the African continent. The numbers were staggering, and when his team had told him the prospective figures, he'd literally needed to sit down. He'd known in that moment that his future—and that of China's—had changed.

Larger than Saudi Arabia's Ghawar Field, which produced five million barrels a day from its eighty-billion barrel reserve, Xiang's field was estimated to hold more than one hundred billion barrels of oil, more than enough to meet his country's exponentially increasing demand.

Once the initial shock of his success had subsided, he'd already begun to solve the next problem—how to get the oil safely to Port Sudan. The main pipeline ran from the port to Khartoum, where it branched off into two pipelines that ended in South Sudan and the oil fields that overlapped both countries. Unfortunately for Xiang, his discovery was tens of miles from each line, directly in between. The oil field required a new pipeline, which was the subject of his meeting yesterday in Khartoum with the minister of oil.

Xiang expected approval at any time, and he'd been informed it was imminent, especially since Sudan's Independence Referendum loomed in the near future. He was certain the south would vote to break away. History dictated the pattern. Too much blood had been spilled for independence *not* to occur. He viewed it as just another obstacle to overcome, and once he had Khartoum's lease, he planned to obtain a similar agreement with the south. It was just a matter of time, after he was able to remove the last barrier—the Americans.

Before Xiang's arrival, the North American Oil Company had established its own exploration site fifteen miles west of his camp. Somehow, the Americans had learned of his discovery, and they were lobbying Khartoum for shared rights to the oil field, claiming they had been there first. Their meddling had stalled his timetable, and it infuriated him.

It was outrageous, and the mere thought of sharing his find with the Americans sickened him. He'd briefed Beijing as soon as he'd learned of the ploy, and he'd been assured that all diplomatic efforts—

including heavy financial pressure—were being applied. He just had to be patient.

The helicopter slowed as it reached its destination. Xiang glanced down at his facility, the multiple buildings, four oil rigs, and assorted vehicles that constituted his personal outpost in Sudan's embattled frontier.

Almost dinner time. I'll brief the team then, he thought as the helicopter descended below three hundred feet.

BOOM!

Even inside the luxury business helicopter China had shipped to Sudan for his personal use, the explosion was tremendous.

Panic gripped Xiang as he frantically whipped his head around, searching for the source of the blast. *An accident? Had one of the rigs blown?*

He saw no evidence of smoke or fire on the ground, and for a moment he breathed a sigh of relief as his mind processed the fact that he was still alive. *What the hell was that? Doesn't matter. You're okay.*

Xiang relaxed slightly, until the sound of alarms shrieking reignited his fear. The helicopter suddenly lurched to the side as the rotors lost power. The door to the cabin slammed backward against the bulkhead, and Xiang glimpsed the cockpit's instrument panel. All the screens were blank.

We've lost power. How is that possible? It was his last thought as the helicopter plunged to the ground, a falling aluminum coffin. The aircraft rolled to the left, and Xiang was thrown against the window, just in time to watch in horror as the ground rushed up to seal his fate.

The helicopter crashed next to one of the oil rigs and exploded in spectacular fashion, blowing apart in large metallic chunks. The concussion wave and rotors tore into the rig's tower, severing the upper half that contained the top drive, the powerful motor that turned the shaft and drill string. The apparatus crumpled to the structure below, sparks and flame shooting out of the shaft.

Whoosh! Thud!

The rig ignited in an immense explosion that set off a chain re-action. Within seconds, the entire site was engulfed in one massive fireball, a conflagration of burning fuel and gas that consumed every-thing in its fiery path.

Shao Xiang's fortune—like his life—was no more.

CHAPTER 27

Defense Special Missile and Aerospace Center (DEFSMAC),
National Security Agency (NSA), Fort Meade, Maryland

Luther Corbitt, the Senior Mission Director on shift in DEFSMAC's Operations Area Watch Center, was bored. A senior General Schedule 15, he was used to the fast-paced operational tempo that the early 2000s had provided. With multiple military operations under way in both Iraq and Afghanistan, it had been an insanely hectic time, a time he longed for once again.

Hell, I'd settle for the Cold War days of Soviet ballistic missile testing, he thought. If nothing else, he hoped that his time as the SMD in charge of the watch center positioned him well for senior executive, the next and final step in his long career.

DEFSMAC was a joint NSA, Defense Intelligence Agency, and National Geospatial-Intelligence Agency venture. Its mission was to collect intelligence on foreign missiles and satellites from the ground, sea, and space. Its existence was not widely publicized, although it had provided some of the most critical intelligence on the Soviet missile and space programs over the past several decades.

Luther stared at the huge bank of screens that monitored the world for launch and space events. Finally, he made a decision and

189

pushed his rolling chair back, standing to his full height of five feet nine inches.

"Steve, I'm going for some chips." It was midmorning, not even halfway through his shift, and he was hungry.

"Roger," Steve, a former enlisted Air Force master sergeant and his Assistant Mission Director, replied. "Pick me up a Snickers bar. Got money?"

"I gotcha covered. Back in a few," Luther said, and shuffled off the slightly elevated platform that served as the watch center's hub.

He walked toward the back corner of the enormous space as his eyes moved across the 1980s furniture, another staple of a bureaucratic government institution.

For some reason, it was always the same—white floor panels that concealed all the fiber optic cables and electrical wiring, cream-colored desks, and gray cubicle dividers. He'd heard renovations were being planned in the next few years, but he'd believe it the day that someone walked in and told them to pack their stuff, and not one moment before.

He reached the community snack fund—which someone had wittily nicknamed DEFsnack—grabbed his chips and a Snickers bar, and began the trek back to his desk.

"Luther, you better move faster than that!" Steve shouted across the watch floor.

That's never a good thing, Luther thought as he hurried back to the hub. "What's going on?"

"You're not going to believe this, but one of our space-based infra-red satellites just detected a large explosion along the Sudan–South Sudan border near the Nuba Mountains," Steve said.

"What's the big deal about that? They've been fighting along that border for a while now. It's not the first time we've picked up an explosion in that country," Luther said, looking at his AMD quizzically.

"I know, but this explosion had *two* distinct signatures," Steve replied, smiling grimly at his boss.

"Huh? How's that possible?" Luther asked, concern creeping into his voice. It was common knowledge that the Defense Support Program satellites could detect even the smallest explosion from space via infrared sensors, but two components to an explosion only meant one thing, and it wasn't good.

"Right now, it looks like a massive explosion, but it *started* with a large electromagnetic burst, as if someone detonated a bomb," Steve said, the smile now gone.

Possibilities raced through Luther's mind. *You got what you asked for, jackass,* Luther thought, now wishing he hadn't been pining away for the good ol' days of the Cold War.

"Get the NGA guys to find out from their imagery what's at that location. Prepare a CRITIC message immediately," Luther said, referring to the years-old Criticom message system that was triggered when a crisis or event occurred, one that hadn't already been broadcast across the world news agencies. A message would be issued via FLASH traffic at the highest priority and reach the entire Intelligence Community and the White House within minutes. "I'm calling the SOO at NSOC," he finished, wondering how the Senior Operations Officer in charge of the National Security Operations Center—who also served as the after-hours director of NSA—would respond to this one.

Hope he's having a slow day so far, because it's about to get frickin' busy, he thought, and picked up the classified phone at his desk.

———

White House Situation Room

Christopher Moran, the Assistant National Security Advisor, stared at the message he'd just been handed, the words "electromagnetic attack" and "secondary, massive explosion at a Chinese drill site" in bold, accusing letters.

One of the CIA's many sensitive special access programs, THOR'S HAMMER was a space-based, electromagnetic bomb that used a maneuverable reentry vehicle to puncture the earth's atmosphere upon release from its satellite. Once deployed, a GPS guidance system locked on to its target, and the bomb glided to its location, detonating a few hundred meters above the earth. The explosion produced an electromagnetic field that disabled most electronics within the target area, from a few hundred meters to a kilometer, depending on the size of the conventional warhead. Compared to detonating a nuclear warhead tens of kilometers above the earth, which could create an electromagnetic pulse to black out an entire city, an electromagnetic bomb was a precision weapon.

What started as a normal Tuesday had just turned into a national security crisis that was spiraling out of control by the minute. Christopher was still holding the email notification from the CIA about the activation of THOR'S HAMMER. He hadn't even had time to head upstairs to brief his boss, Jonathan Sommers, who was himself occupied with the hunt for the stolen DARPA technology. Things had just taken a turn for the worse less than two hours ago when the Americans sent into Sudan had been ambushed, and two of them had been captured. To throw gasoline on the fire, it was the missing ONERING that apparently had just been used to activate THOR'S HAMMER to attack one of the US's largest adversaries. Someone was orchestrating a very dangerous global maneuver.

Christopher turned to a Marine Corps major, who served as one of the communications officers, and handed him the notifications. "Major Turner, please get my boss down here and prepare the secure connection to the president, but don't activate it until Mr. Sommers gets here. Also, we need to reach our ambassador to the UN. This is going to get very ugly, very fast."

Christopher knew the Chinese would be clamoring to get in front of the UN Security Council as soon as they figured out what had happened. The US needed to be prepared to respond, which meant the president and all his principals had to be briefed as soon as possible.

As much as he loved his job, it was on days like this that his thoughts turned to his former life. A University of Michigan law school graduate at the top of his class and former partner at one of DC's most prominent law firms, he'd given up a seven-figure salary for longer hours, less pay, and what amounted to absolutely no social life outside the White House.

Oh well, the price of glory, he thought sardonically as he waited for the arrival of his boss.

McCarran International Airport, Las Vegas, Nevada

Deputy Director Mike Benson was still stunned as he stepped off the lowered ramp that extended from the back of the military C-17 transport jet. He was struggling to process the fact that Logan West and Cole Matthews had been ambushed and captured moments after he'd hung up with them.

The reality that Logan West, one of the most fearsome warriors Mike had ever known, could be taken alive by anyone was deeply unsettling. It told him that whoever their adversary was, they had resources Mike and his FBI task force didn't. It also told him that there was a traitorous mole in the US government. At what exact level, he didn't know—although it had to be very senior—but someone was feeding the enemy information that had resulted in Logan's capture.

Mike felt helpless. Part of him—not a small one—wanted to drop the Vegas lead, reboard the C-17, and fly to Sudan like a bat out of hell to help find his friend. He knew it was irrational, but his loyalty to his brother in arms was a nearly tangible thing.

Fortunately, John Quick was in Khartoum with the full support of both the US Embassy and the entire American Intelligence Community. As a result, Mike had faith that his friend would soon be found. It was only a matter of time.

Logan would've understood perfectly well that Mike had a duty to perform—no pun intended—in Las Vegas. His instincts were screaming at him that somehow all of it was connected—Alaska, Spain, the North Korean cargo ship, and now Sudan.

While he didn't possess Logan's ferocity, he did have a dogged determination that had served him well throughout his entire career. Above all else, he favored a thorough and methodical investigative approach. He'd leave no stone unturned, and before this was over, he'd have the truth.

But first, he needed to get his team and equipment to the Las Vegas FBI field office, north of the city. He'd call his uncle Jake, the current director of the FBI, and find out what the hell was going on in DC. There was a leak at the highest levels of the Intelligence Community, and it needed to be plugged quickly.

CHAPTER 28

US Embassy, Khartoum

The windowless room had four occupants, but only three were conscious. They stared at the wet body of the young Chinese intelligence operative with an uncomfortable combination of anger and respect. The man had endured nearly two hours of relentless interrogation by both Amira and John, but neither had been able to break him. He'd repeated the same sentence in Chinese over and over, until he had finally passed out after the last round of extended waterboarding.

Since the room had microphones and HD video cameras that fed the observation area outside, John had exited early on to find out what the young man was saying from a CIA officer who spoke Chinese and was observing the interrogation.

"Stupid fucking kid," the officer had said and shook his head as John entered the room. All the prisoner had said was one phrase that he kept repeating—"Your friends are not coming back, and I won't tell you anything, no matter what you do to me."

John had rejoined Amira and Cole inside the interrogation room, and it was clear by now it would take more than a little water to break their prisoner. "This is getting us nowhere," John said. "I have to give it to this guy. I never thought he'd last this long. What do we do now?

Every minute that passes is another minute that puts Logan and Cole further away from us."

"I can take a different tactic with him," Amira said coldly, "but I have to tell you, it can get messy."

"What exactly does that mean?" Wendell Sharp, the room's third conscious occupant, asked hesitantly. He had no problem with methods that had been approved in the past—however controversial they may have been—but he sensed that the female assassin had something more primitive in mind. "We're not barbarians."

He was still coming to terms with the fact that he had an operative working in his region he hadn't known existed. A short conversation with the director had sorted it out for him, and he'd been ordered to provide "any and all assistance" to his guests.

"Mr. Sharp, I appreciate the concern you have, and I realize that this is putting you way outside your comfort zone," John said, "but honestly, I don't care. If this woman thinks she can get him to give up their location, then I'm all for it, as *unpleasant* as it may be. You seem like a decent man, but to be blunt, decency is not what this calls for right now. We have an obligation to do *everything* in our power to solve this, no matter how distasteful or morally repugnant it might seem." He turned to Amira and asked, "What do you have in mind?"

"We take his fingers, one by one," Amira replied calmly.

John looked at her for a moment, saw the expression of disgust on the station chief's face, and nodded. "I admit I don't like it, but at this point it's worth a shot."

"You've got to be kidding me. You're going to cut off his fingers?" Wendell asked incredulously.

"Yes," Amira replied flatly. "It will likely only take one or two to get him to talk." She looked at him directly as she continued, her pale-blue killer's eyes penetrating his very soul. "It's not the pain that breaks them. It's the permanent *loss,* the fact that I'm going to take something that can't be replaced or heal on its own. It's the fear that gets them, Mr. Sharp. I've never had to go more than three, and I always start with the pinky, just in case they decide to talk immediately. I figure it's only fair to start with the least-used finger."

She's amazing, John thought. *A female version of Logan, but possibly with less remorse and mercy. Definitely my kind of gal.* The last thought surprised him, but it wasn't a total shock. He was self-aware enough to realize he'd been attracted to her immediately, even in the middle of the bloody chaos. She was impressive, pure and simple, and he wasn't easily impressed by anyone or anything after all of the adventures in which he and Logan had both survived and prevailed.

"What do you need?" John asked.

"Just my stilettos, which I left outside in the observation area. I don't like to bring weapons into an interrogation, just on the off chance that the subject breaks free," Amira said.

"Has that ever happened before?" John said.

"Once. On the second person I ever interrogated. I made the mistake of leaving one of the zip ties loose. He managed to get his right arm free from the chair," she said.

"What did you do?" John asked, mesmerized by her calm demeanor.

"I broke his arm and then resecured him to the chair. After that, I always double-check my bindings," she said. Suddenly, she flashed him a smile. "A girl can never be too sure," she said, and walked out of the room.

"I'll bet," John said, staring at the open doorway.

"You're seriously going along with this?" Wendell asked him.

John studied their captive before meeting Wendell Sharp's accusatory gaze. "Mr. Sharp, this operative ambushed us before we even had a chance to react. I get it that it was his job, his *mission*. I don't take that part of it personally. It comes with the territory. It's not the first time someone's tried to kill me, and I'm sure the way this week is going, it won't be the last." His voice grew steadily stronger. "But what I will *not do* is let him just sit here while the best man I've ever known lies in captivity. I vowed that I'd do whatever it takes to find

Logan." He paused for a moment, his conviction apparent. "And I do mean *whatever it takes.* If we have to take this sonofabitch apart piece by piece, so help me God, we'll do it, because in the end, I'll get what I want from him, and I *will* find my friend."

"Mr. Sharp," Amira added as she reentered the room, "I'm not bound by the same laws you are. The agency may have stopped enhanced interrogation techniques last year, but I have full discretion backed by documentation I can't reveal to you. That's the truth. Confirm it with Langley, if you must. Just make sure you go straight to the director's office."

Wendell Sharp was smart enough to know when someone was bluffing. She wasn't. He only nodded, accepting the inevitability of what was coming. *God help whoever has this man's friend,* he thought.

"One thing that should have you more concerned than what she's about to do is this—how the hell did they know we were here? It was only last night we even knew about this lead. Now that Amira's told us how she was tipped off by Langley, I'm concerned it's the same high-level mole who's had us chasing our tails in circles. Whoever it is had access to LEGION intelligence, and *that* is most definitely not a good thing," John said.

Wendell had already considered the possibility, and the thought disturbed him, maybe even more than removing their captive's fingers. The Intelligence Community had a long history of traitors, and each one had a body count associated with him or her.

Before he had a chance to speak, a single double-edged stiletto appeared in Amira's hand.

"It's time," she said. "Wake him up."

John walked over to the unconscious man, who lay on a metal table that was positioned on a decline, his feet at the top. John stood behind his head at the bottom and prepared himself for what he had to do next.

A loud *smack* echoed off the room's concrete walls as John's open palm connected with the man's face.

Eyelids momentarily fluttered, and he shook his head, as if in a dream.

Come on. Time's wasting, John thought, and hit him again.

Smack!

The eyes popped open, struggling to focus on the upside-down face of John Quick.

"Listen, I know you understand us. So I'm not going to bullshit you right now. I'm going to be as brutally honest as I know how to be."

John bent down and raised the bottom of the metal table until the man was in a standing position. He pressed a lever and locked it into place.

"There you go," he said, stepping around the apparatus to look at the young man. "Now that we see eye to eye, so to speak, let me lay it out for you—although you're already kind of laid out, vertically, that is."

"You see that beautiful woman right there?" John said, putting one hand on the man's shoulder and pointing to Amira, who stood still several feet away in front of the door. "We're out of time, and we need to know where our friends are, but you don't want to tell us. I respect that. I really do. You're tougher than I expected, especially after you let me goad you like that back at the cemetery."

John felt the man stiffen on the table, the reminder of his humiliation obviously affecting him. *Good. Maybe you'll save yourself some pain.*

"So I'm going to give you one last chance to tell us what we want to know. And if you don't answer after the first time I ask, that woman is going to start cutting off your fingers until you either tell us what we want or you have two bloody stumps for hands. I don't want to do that, and this man here," John said, motioning to Wendell, "he really doesn't want me to do it. But you've left me no choice because I need that information, and I'm willing to do *anything* to get it. It's totally up to you."

John looked into his eyes to allow his words to sink in. He saw comprehension spread across the man's face, another good sign that he was taking the threat seriously.

"Okay, then. Let's begin. We're going to start with an easy one. What's your name?" John asked.

There was a long pause, until Amira broke the silence of the moment and stepped toward the metal table.

"Cho. Cho Feng, but I go by Henry," the young intelligence operative said quietly in crisp English.

"See? Now that wasn't so hard," John said, "but this is where you're really going to have to work for it." He paused for effect, and said, "Now tell us where your base is and where my friends are."

Henry stared at him for a moment, and John could see his internal struggle. *Come on, Henry. Don't make us do this.* Just as quickly, he saw the struggle end, and Henry lifted his head in acceptance. *Good. That's twice today,* John thought, thinking he'd won.

"Go fuck yourself and your arrogance. You really are a typical American. I'm not telling you anything, no matter what you do to me. I'd rather have my honor than my life," Henry spat out.

I guess I was wrong, John thought.

Before he could open his mouth to respond, Amira appeared to slide across the floor toward the vertical table. With one swift motion, she raised the stiletto with her right hand, grabbed his left pinky finger, and quickly drew the blade across it, pressing hard.

"*Agghhhhh!*" Henry shrieked, his cry of pain falling on deaf ears.

Amira let go of his finger, and it dropped to the floor of the interrogation room, red droplets splattering across the linoleum. Blood pumped down the metal table, glistening in streaks as it raced toward the floor.

Henry muffled a cry, trying to control the throbbing pain from the wound. He shook his head from side to side in agony, breathing hard in between choked sobs.

"Henry," John said. No response. He grabbed his chin in his

hand and forced the man to look at him. "Henry, I told you I wasn't playing around. You should've believed me. Please save yourself more pain and tell us what we need to know. *Please.*" The last word was spoken imploringly.

There were tears in Henry's eyes, but John couldn't tell if they were from pain, anger, or both. It didn't matter.

"For a second time—and now we're on to your ring finger; hope you're not married—where are our friends? Where are you operating out of?"

Henry looked at him, opening his mouth to speak, but then reconsidered at the last moment. He closed his eyes and shook his head in a defiant and silent *no*.

"Do it," John said to Amira, staring at Henry with pitiless exasperation.

Once again, Amira stepped up to the table and lifted the blade.

Thud! Thud! Thud!

The door opened slightly, and Amira paused, turning toward the entrance, the blade inches away from Henry's finger. She watched Wendell lean out the door for a moment and quickly return.

"We have a location. We need to go," Wendell said.

Just as quickly, Amira stepped away from the table and exited the room.

"What about him?" Wendell asked.

John looked at Henry, still in excruciating pain, throbbing heat radiating into the whole hand.

"Looks like you were just saved by the proverbial bell, Henry," John said, and stepped away to leave. As he walked past Wendell, he said, "Treat his wound, put the finger on ice, and see if you can find a doctor who can reattach it here. No matter what, he doesn't leave this embassy. Now let's find out what the hell is going on," John said, and walked out the door.

Wendell stared at the finger and blood on the floor. *This is definitely not in the interrogation section of the CIA handbook.*

CHAPTER 29

It was always the donkey and the wheelbarrow.

It wasn't his first time running a convoy through Ramadi, but it was the first time he'd been asked to escort General Longstreet, the commanding general of the Multi-National Forces–West in Al Anbar Province, Iraq.

"Sir, we're only a click out from the Government Center," said a voice from behind him.

Why do I know that voice? *He looked around and was confronted with a younger version of John Quick staring at him from the backseat of the up-armored Humvee.*

"I don't like this idea at all, sir," said young John. "We shouldn't be here. This is insurgent territory."

Why were they here? He struggled to remember, grasping for a brass ring just out of reach as the carousel in his head went round and round.

"I don't trust these tribal leaders. They've allowed the insurgents to gain a foothold in this province," John said. Suddenly, Logan realized that although every word was clear, John's lips weren't moving.

As if a dark sky were breaking apart to let the sun shine through, he remembered. General Longstreet had reached out to the local Sunni leaders to discuss the endless cycle of violence that gripped the province.

But Logan didn't get a chance to respond. The driver suddenly slammed on the brakes, and the Humvee skidded to a halt. He heard the three vehicles behind him grind to a stop, and he turned back to look out the windshield.

A teenage boy stood in the road ten feet away, blocking the path of the Humvee. The boy—who looked no older than fourteen—stared at him through the two-inch-thick bulletproof windshield. He wore a traditional white dishdasha robe, which nearly reached his sandaled feet. His arms hung at his sides. He was a motionless figure in the desolate street.

But it was the eyes that Logan always remembered. They were angry, burning with hatred, accusing him of things he hadn't done yet—and never would. For some reason, regardless of details that changed from time to time, he knew this part was real. The same boy. The same hateful eyes. It never changed.

Next to the boy was an old battered wheelbarrow, hitched to a gray donkey that looked as tired and beaten as the cart it pulled by leather straps. It too stood still, its long forlorn face looking at him through the glass.

A wave of overwhelming sorrow engulfed Logan. An uncontrollable grief from the never-ending tragedy of horrors racing through the country threatened to send burning tears streaking down his cheeks. There was no innocence left in Iraq—only death, extremism, and hatred. It was the loss of hope that hurt and paralyzed him. He knew that without hope, there could be no change, and Iraq would die.

He closed his eyes and wished he were somewhere else. He knew what came next, and the familiar dread gripped him, cruelly propelling him forward to witness the horror one more time.

He opened his eyes in time to see the boy, his right arm extended toward the Humvee, pointing at him in accusation.

The IED hidden under the burlap cover in the wheelbarrow exploded, and his grief turned to suffocating panic.

BOOM!

The explosion tore the donkey and the boy to pieces, scattering large chunks of body parts across the dusty street. The boy's head slammed against the windshield with a loud, wet thwack! and for a brief moment, Logan looked into his lifeless eyes. Suspended against the glass, the eyelids blinked reflexively, and then the head fell to the hood of the Humvee, bounced once, and rolled off and out of sight.

He couldn't breathe.

More explosions from behind, and he realized—all over again as if for the first time—the boy had triggered an ambush.

"You may want to do something, Logan, or your men will die," said the eerily calm young John.

He looked once again into the backseat, but no one was there.

"That's right, Logan," said a disembodied voice. "We're gone already. You're the last one left. Why does everyone always have to die around you? Do you know how selfish that is?"

"It's not my fault, John. You know that," Logan tried to explain.

Silence, mocking him in its unique way, torturing him with guilt he couldn't avoid.

"John? John! JOHN!" Logan screamed.

The Humvee trembled, as if being struck by gunfire. He looked out the window, but all he saw was a dark, amorphous gray. Smoke surrounded the vehicle, eager to suffocate him.

The trembling built in crescendo until the Humvee was knocked back and forth, violently jerked from side to side.

"Logan," said the disembodied voice.

He tried to open his mouth to speak, but his lips were sealed shut. He touched his face and discovered his mouth and nose had been duct-taped closed. He tried to pry the thick adhesive from his skin, but it wouldn't budge. Panic gripped him as he fought for breath.

"Logan! Logan!" shouted the voice. Other sounds invaded his ears. More screams of outrage . . .

It would all be over soon. He squeezed his eyes shut, trying to block out the symphony of horror, and finally gave in to the pain, accepting it with its guilty burden. He opened his eyes . . .

And looked up into the face of Cole Matthews, who was studying him with obvious concern.

———

"Logan, are you okay? You were mumbling and screaming, but I couldn't understand you," Cole said. "I need you with me." There was a pause. "We're in a bit of a bind."

Logan sat up, his back propped up against a rough concrete wall. He looked around and realized they were in a small prison cell, complete with iron bars and a door that was ajar. *Someone forgot to lock us in? Why would they be so careless? Unless there's nowhere to go . . .*

His senses were suddenly assaulted. The fetid stench of human waste rushed at him from all around. There was a steady roar of unintelligible screams. For a moment, he almost wished he were back in the recurring nightmare from Ramadi. At least it was familiar to him.

"Why do I have a sinking feeling that that's going to be the understatement of the year?" Logan finally said, placing his hands on his bent knees and forcing himself to stand up. A wave of dizziness hit him. *Aftereffects of the gas and whatever else they drugged us with. Fun times.*

"Any idea where we are or how long we've been out?" Logan asked, bending over to steady himself.

"It's still light outside. So I'm guessing a couple of hours, maybe. As to where we are, I have no idea, but I can tell you one thing—it's definitely not Paradise Island," Cole said sarcastically. "I'm pretty sure it's some kind of prison."

"How long have you been awake?" Logan asked.

"Ten minutes or so." Cole examined Logan. "Don't worry. The effects should wear off in a couple of minutes. The first few were the worst."

More cries of pain emanated from deep inside the building. Voices carried into their cell, suddenly accompanied by footsteps.

Cole stuck his head through the open iron-bar door and located the source of the footfalls. Their cell was positioned in the middle of a cement passageway lit with exposed lightbulbs connected by free-hanging wire. It extended about eighty feet in both directions, ending at a right-turning corner junction at the left end. Cells lined both sides, and he saw hands and bare feet sticking out between the bars. To his right, the corridor ended in a single metal door, but his view was partially obstructed by six men, dark-skinned Africans in an assortment of ragtag clothing purposefully striding down the filthy passageway.

"We've got a problem. Six men. No weapons. I think it's our welcome wagon. We need to buy time," Cole said urgently, looking back at Logan. "Before you woke up, I activated a personal locator beacon I had hidden on me. It's on the sill in that tiny window above you. Hopefully, there's enough clearance to transmit the signal. If so, the agency will already be figuring out a way to reach us. We just have to stay alive long enough for the rescue team to find us."

The voices grew louder, angry, shouting now in an African dialect Logan didn't recognize.

"For how long?" Logan asked, preparing for a fight he knew was coming.

"Four to six hours, depending on how close the nearest team is," Cole said. The footsteps were right outside the door.

"This should be interesting," Logan said, having regained most of his bearings. "Let's play nice-nice and see what they want. Fight if you have no other choice."

The presence of the greeting party had agitated their fellow prisoners in the surrounding cells. Screams and the banging of metal filled the corridor. *It's like a goddamned prison riot,* Logan thought.

"Okay," Cole agreed. "Here we go." He moved to the back of the cell and raised his arms, following Logan's lead.

The first man appeared in front of the door.

He stopped outside their cell and stared at them, assessing them with open hostility and contempt. The man wore a tattered brown tank top and green cargo shorts. His head was shaved and revealed a dent in the left side of his skull that ran from the top of his head to the top of his left eye, which was a dead, milky white.

He smiled, revealing crooked yellow teeth, and Logan swore he could smell the man's stench from the back of the cell. *He's half-crazed, probably on khat,* thinking of the leaves that were chewed in this part of the world for an amphetamine-like high.

The man crossed his wiry, muscular arms in front of his chest as the rest of his greeting party stepped into view. Five more African men, all in similar attire, stood quietly and stared at them.

"Why are you here?" the dead-eyed man finally asked, speaking in broken English with a thick accent. He said nothing else, waiting for a response.

"Actually," Logan replied in a clear and steady voice, "we thought you might be able to help with that. Why are we here? And where exactly is here?"

Deadeye nodded, as if the question made complete sense. He smiled and stepped aside, providing enough room for two of his henchmen to enter the cell.

The two men quickly approached Logan and Cole—arms still raised over their heads—and struck both of them in the stomach. Both men doubled over and fell to the grimy floor, unprepared for the blows.

Two more men entered the cell, and within moments, Logan and Cole were being dragged down the passageway toward the lone metal door.

I guess that was the wrong answer, Logan thought, as he let himself be carried to whatever surprise awaited them next.

CHAPTER 30

CIA Operations Center, Langley, Virginia

Lieutenant Commander Rob Stricker hung up the classified phone to JSOC—the Joint Special Operations Command—headquarters in Fort Bragg and walked to the senior watch officer's position in the center of the operations floor.

A former Navy SEAL platoon commander for SEAL Team 4 and the executive officer of SEAL Delivery Vehicle Team 2, based in Little Creek, Virginia, he loathed the Beltway lifestyle, especially the tailored suit that covered his athletic frame. Unfortunately, it was those years of tactical experience in Iraq, Afghanistan, and off the coast of multiple African countries that highly qualified him for his current assignment—JSOC liaison officer to CIA headquarters.

His job involved coordinating activities all over the world to provide Human Intelligence—simply referred to as HUMINT—in support of JSOC operations and JSOC tactical support to CIA covert and clandestine operations. As much as he despised staff work, it was a critical function, and he excelled in the daily, fast-paced operational environment. It also guaranteed his promotion to Navy commander, although his selection wouldn't be official until next month's promotion board.

"Sir, we've got a team on standby at Camp Lemonnier in Djibouti.

They can be wheels-up in forty-five minutes and over the target in two hours. They've got a C-17 on standby," Lieutenant Commander Stricker said to the senior watch officer, Glenn Saxton, a senior executive, former case officer, and one-time station chief.

Camp Lemonnier was the US base in the Horn of Africa, established in the months after 9/11, when the headquarters element of the 2nd Marine Division officially transformed into the headquarters element for the new Combined Joint Task Force–Horn of Africa, CJTF–HOA. It was strategically positioned, accessible by ship at the port city of Djibouti and by aircraft at the Djibouti International Airport, directly adjacent to the camp.

Lieutenant Commander Stricker had done a deployment at Camp Lemonnier in the early days of the Global War on Terror, referred to as the "GWOT." Djibouti was hot, humid, and so oppressive it made Iraq seem like a cool breeze. He still recalled sitting outside his operations center on one extremely hellish day when two black birds had dropped dead out of the sky from the heat, nose-diving into the gravel next to his boots. Out of all the strange, surreal, and horrifying things he'd seen during his combat tours, it was the dead black birds that epitomized Africa for him. *So forsaken even the birds couldn't survive . . . fucking Africa . . .*

"What do we know about the location, sir? I need as much intel—imagery, SIGINT, whatever you have—that you can get before we launch them," Lieutenant Commander Stricker said.

The personal locator beacon had been activated more than fifteen minutes ago, and all rescue options were being explored. Due to the individual assigned to the beacon, it was no-holds-barred.

An arrangement between the CIA and the International Cospas-Sarsat Programme—a satellite-based search and rescue distress alert detection and information distribution system—provided the monitoring of a sensitive list of beacons in the event they were activated.

The initial 406-MHz signal had been detected by the mission control center in Abuja, Nigeria, which had then fed the information to the main US mission control center operated by NOAA and co-located with its Satellite Operations Control Center in Suitland, Maryland. A call had been immediately placed over a secure line to the CIA's operations center, and all data associated with the signal was now being fed live to a local user terminal inside the operations center.

"Our NGA folks are looking for stored imagery for that location, and they're tasking the nearest satellites to start snapping pictures during the next passes. I've already contacted NSOC, and NSA is searching through its databases for any SIGINT reporting. And any HUMINT reporting we have on that area you'll have within the next thirty minutes," Glenn said. "What else do you need?"

"That should cover it, sir," Lieutenant Commander Stricker replied. "You calling the White House next? As you know, something like this requires either SECDEF or presidential approval. Once JSOC has it, it's a 'go,' for all intents and purposes."

"What if we get the approval but still don't have all the intel for you?" Glenn asked, considering the negative ramifications for the operation. He wanted to know what could go wrong and how bad it could be if they went in blind. Calculating all aspects of an operation was a habit he'd formed early in his career.

Lieutenant Commander Stricker smiled. The question underscored the difference between the civilian and military mindsets. It wasn't the first time he'd noticed it, and as long as civilians controlled the power of the military, it wouldn't be the last.

"Sir, they'll go no matter what, especially in a situation like this. It's what *we do*," he responded confidently. "It's who *we are*."

CHAPTER 31

They were led to the end of the cellblock, through a solid metal door, and into a covered enclosure that served as the main entrance for the prison's vehicles. The small tunnel was secured at both ends by fabricated, sheet-metal doors set on rails. An old, topless jeep sat parked in the middle, while a seven-ton cargo truck with a canvas cargo area was positioned behind it. The entrance to their right had an extra set of iron doors on hinges, secured by a padlock. *Must be what passes for high-tech security in this part of the world,* Logan thought.

Logan and Cole were pushed toward a gap where a small area of light invaded the darkness under the raised door at the left end of the tunnel. Voices, cries of pain, and—most surprisingly of all—*cheers* emanated from the opening.

As they neared the raised door, their captors shoved them hard, knocking them to the ground into the hot African sun.

Logan stood up, his eyes sweeping the landscape of the enormous interior prison courtyard. *Oh boy. This makes Alcatraz look like day camp.*

He'd read about horrible conditions in Third-World prisons—starvation, torture, overcrowding—but he never thought he'd experience them in the flesh. The *idea* of the existence of such places of human misery and suffering where unspeakable horrors were endured on a daily, relentless basis was much different than viewing it up close and personal.

Logan felt the weight of it immediately and let out a long, slow breath to steady himself. He heard Cole's similar response to the hellish scene before them.

They were in a barren rectangular dirt courtyard. Their vantage point revealed that the prison was only three stories tall, constructed of dark-gray concrete, with iron-bar windows on all four sides. Logan thought he saw dark faces peering out from behind several of them.

In each corner of the roof was a wooden, open-air guard shack that provided a view of the courtyard. Two guards were positioned at each ramshackle tower, AK-47s slung across their chests to provide quick access. *Not exactly a marksman's weapon, which means they don't care how many inmates they kill if there's a problem.*

In addition to the guard shacks, a large area of darkened glass at least thirty feet wide was built into the leftmost wall on the third floor of the prison. *Must be the control room.*

To Logan's right was a small, single-story square garage. It had a roof and one wall, but the side facing him was open, revealing multiple jeeps and an ambulance that looked like a relic of WWII. *Doubt that gets much use,* Logan thought. A barbed-wire fence with a padlocked gate surrounded the makeshift vehicle bay.

In the opposite corner of the courtyard, three wooden poles stuck up out of the ground, fixed in place with bases of concrete, but it was what was on them that grabbed his attention.

Unfortunate souls whose hands were secured above their heads so their arms were strained awkwardly had been tied to two of the poles. The position prevented the prisoners from sitting down or easing the tension in their arms. Logan knew how brutal that kind of torture could be after several hours without moving. When it was over, the relief of movement was almost as excruciating as the position itself.

The middle pole was vacant, but even from afar, Logan saw it was stained with large, dark splotches of what could only be blood. He didn't want to fathom how many men had suffered agonizing deaths on the wooden posts.

As disgusted as he was at the torture, it wasn't the worst part of the courtyard. It was the event under way, a display of medieval human savagery, that told Logan all he needed to know about the prison—there was no value placed on human life. The guards were using the inmates as sport, both for their own sadistic personal amusement and as a way to manage the behavior of the prisoners, hoping to provide a psychological release that made them easier to control. Unfortunately to Logan, it looked like the prisoners, with no alternative choice, had become participants in the human degradation.

In the center of the courtyard, surrounded by cheering and shouting inmates, was an Everlast boxing ring, complete with a black base, black-and-white corner posts, and white ropes. It glistened in comparison to its environment, a modern creation in stark contrast to the abject depravity and surrounding degradation. Inside, two men battled, although to call it any kind of fair fight was a gross misrepresentation.

A gigantic Sudanese man with a beard and short hair that stood out in wild tufts on his enormous head wielded a machete and an old bat adorned with ugly, metal spikes on one side. His face was covered in dark markings, but Logan couldn't tell if they were scars or tattoos. He stood more than six and a half feet tall but moved gracefully for a man of his size and girth. The only article of clothing on his body was a worn pair of jungle-pattern camouflage pants, over which hung a loose layer of fat.

Thud!

The spiked bat slammed into the ring, sending a tremor through the surface.

His opponent, a shorter, younger, and much skinnier man, backed away from the attack. He held a bat in his right hand, but it was obvious he didn't know how to use it. Eyes wide with horror and fear, he looked around, pleading for help. None was offered—only more shouts in Arabic and other languages Logan didn't recognize. *This isn't going to last much longer, and there's nothing I can do about it,* Logan thought helplessly.

The giant stepped forward, holding the machete and bat at his sides like extensions of his limbs.

In a moment Logan recognized as acceptance, the young man's fear turned into resolution, and rather than die cowering, he chose to act. He pulled the bat backward and then swung with all the might he could muster, targeting the giant's left side.

The giant smiled—a malevolent, cruel grimace—and Logan knew the end was near.

Amazingly light on his feet, the giant stepped aside and back, and the smaller man's bat sailed harmlessly in front of him. The crowd roared in primal pleasure, sensing the coming kill. He whipped the bat around with his right arm, aiming under the young man's failed strike.

A sickening *smack* was heard as the spikes drove into the man's rib cage, impaling him. He screamed in agony and dropped the bat, blood trickling from the puncture wounds in his side. He bent forward from the pain, but the giant raised his arm, standing him up with his brute strength.

Defeated and knowing his death was near, the man looked up into the face of his killer. The executioner's grin broadened, amplifying the evil glee on his face. The man let his head fall, and Logan saw him begin to mouth something. Logan realized what it was, and the knowledge sent a wave of empathy and pity coursing through him. *He's praying before he dies.*

The defiant act outraged the giant, and he swung the machete over his left shoulder, all the while holding his prey up like a butcher with a skewered piece of meat. The blade flashed through the air toward the back of the man's bare neck.

Thwack!

The machete plunged into the man's flesh, severing his spinal column at the base of his neck. Blood poured from the grievous injury, and his body began to spasm in its death throes. Yet somehow the giant held his kill up, withdrawing the machete quickly and pulling it back for a second blow. Blood splashed in buckets to the black canvas, and portions of the crowd went wild with approval.

But not all, Logan thought. *Some of these prisoners have some humanity left . . . somehow.*

The giant unleashed a primal scream and struck a second blow, the machete severing the man's head, which fell to the canvas and rolled, ending facedown when it finally stopped. Blood sprayed into the air, and a red mist covered the ring, his killer, and several inmates who stood next to the ring, hands banging on the canvas floor.

You don't get that kind of ringside experience in Vegas, Logan thought, his sarcasm alive and well, even in the face of pure evil. His wit kept him from the edge of insanity as he was faced with the incomprehensible human suffering.

The killer yanked the bat from the side of the body, and the corpse fell to the floor, blood quickly pooling around it. The giant stood in the middle of the ring and raised the weapons over his head, turning and posing in victory for the wild crowd.

Logan realized that whoever these inmates had been before their imprisonment, those lives were gone. A large percentage of the population had acclimated to their environment so well that they *enthusiastically* participated as cheering fans. This monster was truly their champion.

"Jesus . . . fucking . . . Christ," Cole said from beside him.

"I don't think he's around right now," Logan said drily. "And I don't think this is going to be a very fun visit."

When the cheering faded, the giant stepped out of the ring, and a six-man inmate crew leapt onto the apron with several buckets, towels, and mops. Two of the men grabbed the headless corpse by the arms and dragged it to the edge of the ring, callously pushing it under the ropes until it dropped out of sight onto the dirt.

At that moment, Logan spotted a Chinese man studying him,

gazing at him across the blood and gore in the ring. No older than Logan, he stood motionless, his demeanor screaming military. *He's part of the operation that captured us, although he wasn't at the cemetery. He must work for the young leader I saw barking orders. Has to be. It's not a coincidence.*

"You see him?" Logan asked quietly amid the chaos. "He's the one we want."

"Or who wants us," Cole replied.

"Shut mouths!" one of their captors yelled, striking Logan in the back with a black baton.

Logan staggered forward but maintained his balance, his eyes locked on to the Chinese man, his face set in stone. The man finally broke the stare and leaned in to whisper to a prison guard in dark fatigues next to him.

Logan didn't know what was said, but it didn't matter. The end result was the same—the guard approached them. *Here we go.*

"Get ready," Logan muttered to Cole.

"For what?" Cole asked.

"Absolutely anything," Logan replied as the guard reached where they stood and issued quick instructions in Arabic to the man who'd led them from their cell.

The inmates surrounding the ring hadn't left, an ominous sign that the day's entertainment was only at an intermission. They cleared a path as Logan and Cole were shoved to the other side of the ring, a short trip that ended in front of their newfound admirer.

Logan and Cole remained silent, waiting for their captor to initiate the conversation.

The moment stretched before them, magnified by the chaos and bombardment of sound. They were in the center of a storm, and the Chinese man was the only port in sight.

"Mr. West, it's a pleasure to make your acquaintance. Your scar gives you away," the man said in nearly perfect English. He looked at Cole momentarily. "Mr. Matthews, I don't know a lot about you, but it doesn't matter. I have only two questions, both of which I encourage you to answer honestly, the *first* time," the man said. "What are you doing here? And what do you know about us?"

Logan considered the questions, his green eyes revealing nothing, including the alarm he now felt. *How the hell does he know my name? Someone sold us out. We're screwed.* He had no options, no proverbial cards to play. The only commodity that mattered for their survival was time, and he needed to buy some.

"We were hoping you could tell us, since you apparently know more than we do," Logan replied. He looked at Cole and turned back to their inquisitor. "I'm afraid we're at a loss."

"I thought that might be the case. You remember when I told you that what I know about Mr. Matthews didn't matter?" the man asked.

"How could I forget? It was only seconds ago," Logan replied sarcastically.

"Well, that's because he's about to die. We only need one of you, and sacrificing Mr. Matthews to the ring satisfies the thirst for blood these men have. Watching others die in combat provides them a temporary escape from the crushing sense of imprisonment and makes them less"—he paused, searching for the right word—"*confrontational*, at least with the guards," the man said icily, and nodded.

Before he could react, several pairs of hands gripped Logan and held him in place, his arms bent behind his back. More hands grabbed Cole, and he was violently shoved forward toward the ring. The crowd reacted enthusiastically, a low roar of encouragement growing in intensity.

Cole was spun around and slammed into the ring's apron, sending a bolt of pain up his back. A gun appeared in the guard's hand, and he aimed it point-blank at Cole's head, nodding for him to step into the ring.

"No need to play rough," Cole said calmly. "I get the idea."

As he hoisted himself up onto the apron, still facing the crowd and Logan, he said, "I hope you have a plan."

He stepped between the ropes into the makeshift gladiator ring, and the din of the crowd boiled over into a roar of uncontainable excitement. The main event was about to begin.

"Yeah. Don't die," Logan said calmly, disguising his roiling emotions beneath.

"Thanks for the pep talk," Cole said, shook his head, and stood to face his fate.

CHAPTER 32

US Embassy, Khartoum

"We've actually got *two* locations," Wendell Sharp said as he hung up his classified voice-over IP telephone and turned to the assembled group, which now included Tim Greco.

"What does that mean?" John asked.

"It means that we know where both the ONERING *and* Logan and Cole are being held, but there's a problem. They're not in the same place," Wendell said.

"Where are our friends?" John asked.

"They're being held at some kind of off-the-books Sudanese prison. We didn't know it existed until Cole triggered a miniature personnel locator beacon. Due to its size, the device only stays active for one minute every half hour until its battery dies."

He grabbed a map from the cabinet behind him and placed it on his desk. Khartoum was figured prominently in the center. He pointed to a bend in the White Nile a little more than a hundred miles south of the city.

"Here. Langley is sending me a file that has details, satellite imagery, and anything else they have, but it's limited since we didn't know about the place. God knows what they do or who they keep there, but it can't be good," he said.

"How do you know?" John asked.

"Because the prisons that we do know about are completely inhumane, with conditions that make one of our maximum security facilities look like a spa resort," Amira said, looking at John. "Trust me. I've been in them," she said, recalling flashes from a previous assignment in Uganda.

"Seriously?" John asked, unable to contain his amazement.

"John," she said, pointedly using his first name, amused at his reaction, "have I struck you as someone who would make up something like that?"

"Of course not," John said, pausing. "I've seen you in action. Sorry. No offense intended."

"None taken," Amira said, and smiled, her blue eyes sparkling at him.

She's beautiful—and deadly. Don't forget it. And stop acting like you're in fucking high school! his inner voice screamed. *Now is not the time for a boyhood romance. Then again, was there ever really a good time, especially in this line of work?*

"So they're in some sort of god-awful, black-site prison, being subjected to God knows what." John turned back to the station chief. "So when do we go? I assume that's why Tim's here now, to help with a rescue mission."

"We don't," Wendell said, responding immediately since he knew John wasn't going to like the answer. In his experiences in dealing with men like John Quick, the brutal, honest truth was always the best course of action.

"What are you talking about?" John said, closing his eyes and clenching his hands to control the rising tide of anger.

"It's not our mission. I'm sorry. There's already an operation under way to get them, but it's not going to be ours. We have a different task, one that comes straight from the president through the director," Wendell said, giving them a moment to absorb the last statement.

"Of course," John said, hanging his head and already knowing what it was. "The ONERING. Where is it?"

"Tuti Island, which is why we have it," Wendell said, and pointed once more, this time to a half-moon-shaped island at the center of where the White and Blue Niles converged to form the main Nile River that flowed north.

"You're kidding me! How did we confirm it?" John said.

"The engineers at DARPA built a fail-safe into the device. Since this thing is so dangerous *and* portable, they wanted to be able to track it. It was activated a little while ago, and when it went live, it initiated a satellite GPS chip embedded into the main system. I was also informed it's not detectable to the users."

"Thank God," John said, remembering the DARPA director telling them about the GPS device. Then the obvious implication of the ONERING's activation hit him. "What did the bastards use it for?"

"To hijack one of our space-based weapons to attack a Chinese oil site near the South Sudan border," Wendell said flatly.

"Why would Chinese operatives be trying to start a war between us and the Chinese?" John said to no one in particular. "That's insane. It makes no sense."

"I know, which is why it's all the more urgent that we get this back before they can do more damage with it," Wendell said.

"No kidding," John replied, and turned back to Tim Greco. "So what do we know about this island?"

"That it's a very good place to hide things you don't want discovered," Tim said. "The island is only three square miles and has one village, whose residents are farmers that produce most of Khartoum's fruits and vegetables. Most of the island is covered with citrus orchards and farmland. There are plenty of places to set up a small camp and remain undetected, especially from commercial or spy satellites."

"Have you been there?" John asked.

"As the RSO, I like to know my environment," Tim said, smiling. "It comes with the territory, so to speak. I'd heard about this 'jewel of the Nile' island that was supposedly an oasis from the chaos and congestion of Khartoum. So I took a day trip there on my own. You used to have to take a ferry to get to it, but in 2008 they finished the suspension bridge that connects to the mainland. The good thing for us is that the single-story homes and buildings are concentrated in the center of the island. If they've set up camp on the island and want to remain away from prying eyes, they'll be near the water in the outskirts, where the crops and orchards are. But there's one problem—the river. It makes this tricky because if they see us coming, they can use either the bridge or the water as escape routes."

"The agency provided what they think is the camp's location, and we'll get the other UAV up to confirm it," Wendell said.

"Do we have an assault time?" Tim asked, knowing if another operation were under way against the prison, theirs would be launched simultaneously in order to minimize the possibility of one location tipping off the other. The fact that the Sudanese government was clearly working with the Chinese only complicated matters.

"We do," Wendell replied. "A SEAL team out of Camp Lemonnier in Djibouti is going to do a high-altitude, low-opening insert at twenty hundred local time to hit the prison." He looked at his watch. "Which is a little less than three hours from now."

John knew getting the ONERING was the right decision, but his loyalty to his friend pulled him at a gut level. Yet he knew that if Logan were in his place faced with this decision, he'd make the right call. Logan was unlike any other human being he'd encountered— merciless, moral, and singular in purpose. In the Marine Corps, it was always mission accomplishment first, troop welfare second. At the end of the day, everything they'd done was for one objective—to retrieve the ONERING and protect the national security of the United States and its citizens.

Fuck it. Let the frogmen get him. They're almost as crazy as Logan and might try to adopt him like a lost puppy.

"Okay then," John said. "What's our plan?"

CHAPTER 33

"Okay then, boys. If you insist," Cole muttered under his breath as he faced off against his would-be killers inside the ring.

Two men stood before him, including the pack leader with the dented skull who'd escorted them from their cell. The man had removed his dirty tank top, revealing taut muscles designed for this kind of combat. The dead eye darted about the ring. *Can he see with that thing? I guess I'll find out,* Cole thought.

The second opponent was the same size as his leader, although he moved with a slight limp that made him appear as if he were rolling from side to side rather than stepping, a human buoy on a canvas sea. He wore his hair in braids that whipped about his head, reminding Cole of the mythological Medusa. Both wielded rusty machetes, the edges gleaming in the waning daylight in stark contrast to their overall condition. *If they don't kill me, I'll probably get tetanus.*

They'd forced him into the ring unarmed. *I guess it's going to be that kind of fight. That's fine. I can play dirty,* he thought.

A skilled practitioner in multiple martial arts, Cole had taken a particular interest in Krav Maga when he'd spent eight months with the Israeli Shin Bet in Jerusalem while hunting down a notorious Lebanese terrorist who had posed a significant threat to the CIA's Israeli partner. A fighting style developed by the Israeli military for very real and ruthless hand-to-hand combat scenarios, Krav Maga focused on aggressively countering an enemy's attack in order to quickly neutralize the threat, often with lethal force.

When everyone around you wants you dead, you better know how to handle yourself, Cole thought, momentarily reflecting on the fact that Israel was surrounded by its enemies. *Seems apropos right about now.*

Deadeye and Medusa moved apart and slowly closed the distance. Cole knew they would come at him from different directions, trying to overwhelm him as quickly as possible.

The crowd sensed the coming attack, having seen this tactic before, and the shouts intensified. The courtyard of the prison had turned into a Sudanese version of the Colosseum, and bloodlust was in the air.

Cole knew he'd have to act quickly to shut this confrontation down. He knew the moment was almost at hand when Deadeye stopped a little less than six feet in front of him and Medusa continued to circle to his left.

Cole's back was near one of the corner posts. The canvas shook from the pounding of the inmates' hands on the apron. He took a deep breath and exhaled, a sense of battle calm enveloping him, not for the first time. *Wait for it. Wait for it. Wait for it.*

Even as Deadeye stepped forward and swung the machete laterally toward him, Cole was already timing his counterattack. He planted his right foot forward and spun one hundred and eighty degrees to his left inside the arc of the machete. He delivered a vicious and precise elbow to Deadeye's left temple, hoping to enlarge the dent in his head. He grabbed the man's wrist with his other hand, digging his fingers into the nerve bundle at the base.

There was a pause in the cheering, a shocked intake of breath, as the prisoners processed what they were witnessing.

Cole sensed Medusa reacting, but he pressed the attack, knowing if he didn't finish Deadeye, he'd lose the tactical advantage he'd just gained.

As Deadeye loosened his grip, the machete appeared in Cole's right hand so quickly it could have been sleight of hand, and he spun another one hundred and eighty degrees, extending his right arm forward as he completed the circle. The razor-sharp blade slid into Deadeye's abdomen, just below the sternum.

Cole looked into his face momentarily, the maniacal grin gone, replaced with a mask of pain. He noticed the man's milky eye open wider. *Guess you can see out of it—if only for a few more seconds.*

He turned to his left and caught Medusa's movement in his peripheral vision. The man had let out a primal scream of fury when he saw his partner impaled. *Amateur. Thanks for telling me where you are.*

Medusa was almost upon him, his scream reaching a fevered pitch as he held the machete over his head, enraged at the sudden turn of events. Cole didn't notice the total silence that had fallen over the prison yard or the shocked expressions of amazement on the inmates' faces. He was completely engaged and focused on his next move. He saw the machete begin to fall, the blade of death searching for his flesh.

Cole smoothly stepped aside, using both arms to push Deadeye's weight to his left. Unable to stop its momentum, Medusa slammed the heavy blade into his tag teammate's collarbone.

The weapon buried itself into the still-breathing man until the top of it disappeared, stuck in the thick bundle of his trapezius muscle. Blood poured from the wound down the man's chest, but Cole hardly noticed.

Medusa stared in shock as he realized what he'd done, his hands frozen to the machete's hilt.

Cole withdrew the bloodied machete from Deadeye's stomach— the man's eyes had rolled up into his head; he was fairly certain he'd just earned his nickname—and moved around the man's corpse with ghostly speed.

Deadeye's body began to fall to the canvas, a knockout from

which he would never recover. His momentum pulled Medusa forward, knocking the man off balance, his grip still tight on the machete buried in his friend.

No mercy, Cole told himself. *It's them or you.*

Cole brought the blade up and down so fluidly the move appeared almost casual.

A loud gasp escaped the crowd. Cole was a statue, staring at the second attacker, the machete held down in both hands, waiting to be used again, even as his opponent bled out through the stumps of both arms, severed now below the elbow.

The mortally wounded man looked around the ring, shock shutting down his nervous system as his lifeblood spewed onto the canvas in geysers. He gazed into Cole's eyes—cold and unforgiving—and then his vision darkened at the edges. He fell backward onto the canvas and through it into oblivion.

Silence. Cole waited for the next moments to play out, knowing they would determine his fate. He remained motionless, a gladiator soaked in blood. The inmates' disbelieving reverie broke, and a tidal wave of applause and cheers roared through the prison's inner sanctum, crashing against the walls in a crescendo.

Logan looked around, only to see that the Chinese man who'd issued the instructions was now standing next to him.

"Hey," Logan said calmly. "Maybe you should've tried three guys."

The man stiffened and met Logan's gaze, his eyes dancing with a combination of amusement and frustration. He smiled, and Logan felt a creeping dread insert itself into the back of his mind.

"Don't worry. We're not done yet," the man said, and walked away, nodding at the Sudanese guards surrounding the ring.

The crowd continued to cheer as two guards leapt into the ring and pulled black pistols from shoulder holsters. They aimed them at Cole, but he didn't need the encouragement. He'd already dropped the bloody machete.

He exited the ring and dropped down to the dirt, the guards

pushing him toward Logan. Prisoners slapped him on the back in congratulations, a victorious prizefighter leaving the ring of battle.

Logan watched Cole approach, but then he spotted someone across the ring staring at him, seeming to soak him up with hatred-filled eyes. It was the giant, and he wasn't basking in the glow of Cole's victory. *Uh-oh. I don't think the champ's too happy.*

Unable to contain himself, he waved and smiled at the towering killer. The man scowled and turned away.

"What was that all about?" Cole asked as he reached Logan.

"I don't think your new popularity made the people's choice too happy. I think he's pouting," Logan said.

"Great. Just what I need—a jealous maniac," Cole said.

"I know," Logan said, looking at Cole and smiling. "Isn't Sudan wonderful?"

"Yeah. It's a fucking laugh riot," Cole said, wiping blood off the backs of both hands.

Logan sensed the man's mood darken. "Hey, you did what you had to do. It was pretty impressive. I'm glad it's them and not you." He paused, and said, "If it makes you feel any better, I think the next match is for me."

Suddenly, hands roughly grabbed them from behind and shoved them away from the ring toward an opening in the crowd. Through it, Logan saw the door from which they'd entered earlier.

"I guess it's back to our cell for some rest and relaxation," Logan said.

"And maybe I can get a massage. I'm a little sore from that workout," Cole said.

"Sure. I bet they'd even throw in a pedicure—with a rusty machete," Logan said, and grinned as he was shoved toward the opening.

CHAPTER 34

FBI Las Vegas Division, Nevada

Almost twelve hundred here, which means it's nineteen hundred in Sudan. Time is passing too quickly, Mike thought. It'd been more than seven hours since Logan and Cole Matthews had been captured. *You better be alive, Logan, or I'll kill you myself.*

The waiting was agonizing, and his investigation into Mrs. Natalie Chambers's murder was progressing just as slowly. The pictures of the Chinese suspects had been disseminated all over town, and the local news channels were doing an excellent job of running hourly updates. But still, nothing new had come in, the lack of actionable information taunting him with each passing hour.

Things were just as bad—if not worse—on the Sudanese front. In addition to Logan and Cole's abduction, his uncle had just informed him about the activation of the ONERING to attack a Chinese oil site. *More Chinese connections. It's starting to feel like the world's worst buffet, with a little death and destruction here, a little kidnapping there, and an act of war on the side.*

The HRT had set up shop in the FBI office's vehicle bay, running their encrypted fiber-optic cables to mobile satellite dishes erected outside. The team was led by Special Agent Lance Foster, a fellow veteran of Mike, John, and Logan's escapade in northern Mexico at the Los Toros cartel compound two years ago. Foster's team was still the best, which made them exactly what Mike needed right now.

Mike stood in the doorway of Special Agent Amanda Hunt's office, watching the organized bedlam on the floor of the field office's operations center. The investigation was in full swing, even if it was progressing slower than Mike preferred.

Young agents were making phone calls to other federal agencies, taking call-in tips, looking through financial records, and trying to piece together a time line for the Chang brothers since they'd arrived in Vegas. He smiled inwardly, slightly nostalgic for the adrenaline rush he knew the agents were experiencing.

A major case, the threat of a possible attack on the homeland, the hope that they would be the ones to save the day—these were the dark and exhilarating vices of all young agents, Mike thought. *Let's see how they feel in twenty-four hours, when they haven't slept and real fatigue sets in for the first time.*

He shook his head nearly imperceptibly, remembering that it was moments like these that had led to his failed marriage—his first and last. His ex-wife, Corey—a botanist of all things—had understood the extreme demands of his job, especially as a junior, African-American agent eager to prove himself. She'd initially supported him through all of it. They'd entered the marriage together with eyes wide open, but after the first few years, they both realized it was untenable. Ironically, it was his success and the prospect of children that ultimately led to their divorce.

Mike had known dozens of senior executives and midlevel agents throughout his career. Many had children and families whom they loved dearly, but at the end of the day, there were only so many hours in each one.

Love was one thing, the foundation of a bond, the bedrock of a family. But time? Well, time was an entirely different animal. All the love in the world didn't make up for all the lost time. It was always the same regret—not enough time with those who mattered most.

Fortunately, he and Corey had recognized it, and they'd made a choice together. It hadn't been his alone, and he was still grateful to her for it. She'd known who he was at his core, and she'd been the one to force him to look inward, to see who he truly was, and more importantly, what he wanted. For them, a divorce had been the right decision.

His career had accelerated upward, his success secondary to the satisfaction he'd derived from protecting his country from the evils that plagued it and the world. Corey had rebounded and remarried, happily, and had two children now in their teens. Now that they were both in their midforties, they didn't talk often, but Mike knew from their last correspondence that she was content, at least as much as anyone could be in a world like this.

"I know this is an imposition and that our presence has thrown everyone into a frenzy. I sincerely appreciate the hospitality," Mike said, turning to face the division's special agent in charge.

"It's really no problem, sir," Special Agent Hunt said, revealing an attractive smile that brightened a face lined by age and experience. "This is what we do, as you well know, and we're happy to have you."

"Excuse me, sir," said a voice behind Mike, who turned to face a young female agent looking up at him expectantly. "I have something for Special Agent Hunt, although I doubt it's related to the Chambers investigation and the current threat."

"Don't let me stand in the way," Mike said self-deprecatingly.

"Never, sir," the young agent said, a grin splitting her chiseled and pretty young face.

Jesus. These kids sure are confident these days, Mike thought. *Makes me feel like a dinosaur.*

"Come on in, Special Agent Marcus. What do you have?" asked her boss.

"Like I said, it's probably nothing, but I thought you should know about the trucks that were reported stolen this morning," Special Agent Marcus said.

The skin on the back of Mike's neck prickled, and he looked at

Special Agent Hunt. Her reaction told him she was already thinking the same thing. Trucks were stolen for usually two reasons—to be used in a heist or as the casing for a large vehicular explosive. Because of the direction in which this case was heading, Mike feared the latter. *Not another Oklahoma City bombing. Please let us catch this in time.*

——————

MGM Grand Casino

Crawford Stubbins had a problem. His three-day, self-described "end-of-the-line" trip to Las Vegas wasn't working out as planned. An electrician from Baton Rouge, he had two expectations—get out of the hole he was in with the union boys back home and get his relentlessly nagging wife off his back. Neither one looked like it was going to happen. He'd lost more than three thousand dollars in the casino's sports book over the past forty-eight hours, and he knew the moment he told his wife, he'd never hear the end of it.

A longtime low-limit gambler, he'd been careful always to stay even or just ahead. Somehow, the college football season had wiped him out. He'd had a string of bad luck—that's what he knew it was—with a series of losses, almost all of them by only a few points. If they'd gone the other way, he'd have been way ahead for the year. Instead, Rayleen's haranguing had forced him to make a resentful promise to her—he'd go to Vegas, get up a few thousand dollars, and then quit.

His American Express still had two thousand dollars left in cash advances. *I just need one winner to turn it around. I know it's going to happen.*

Forty pounds overweight with thinning black hair, and in his early fifties, he was smart enough to know if he lost his wife—epic pain in the ass that she was—he wasn't likely to find a second one. He wasn't exactly a keeper, and his bachelor days were long gone. *Don't fuck it up anymore, Crawdaddy. Just one more bet for the day and then take a break.*

He needed fresh air. The stale odor and overpowering smoke of the casino dwellers was getting to his head.

He pushed back from the slot machine in which he'd lost another hundred and walked past the lion exhibit where some young trainer working her way through college threw a blue ball at three lions that looked as bored and desperate as he felt. *At least you don't have bills,* he silently told the big cats.

He fought his way through the haze toward the main lobby and stopped at the gold MGM lion. *They sure like these things around here.*

He grabbed his cell phone from inside his worn blue sport coat and saw a missed call from his wife. *Guess I should call her back.*

BAM! BAM! BAM!

What idiot set off firecrackers in the lobby? Crawford thought, but then he saw the red droplets on the golden lion. *What the hell?*

A solitary scream rose above the echoes of the loud noises.

Crawford suddenly felt weak, and wet warmth spread across his white cotton polo. *This isn't real. I'm drunk somewhere in the casino, having a really bad day.* But then he turned and slumped to the floor, his rear end slamming onto the ground. Even though the impact was hard enough to shatter his reality, what he saw heightened the panic that suddenly gripped him.

Four men in dark brown camouflage fatigues moved from the glass doors of the main entrance toward the floor of the casino. Crimson scarves were loosely tied around their throats, covering their mouths. Only their eyes were visible under the black wool hats pulled over their dark hair.

More shots rang out through the lobby, and the solitary scream he'd heard turned into a symphony of terror as men, women, and children joined in the panic.

This can't be happening, he thought, but he knew it was. He felt himself slipping away, and he fumbled for his phone inside his jacket. He realized with brutal clarity he was dying, but he hoped he had enough time to send Rayleen a text message telling her that he loved her.

The phone clattered next to his hand, and he picked it up, noticing the blood on the shiny tiled floor. He struggled to punch in his message in the text screen, the panic slowly ebbing away with his life.

A pair of black boots appeared in his vision. He felt compelled to look into the face of his killer, but he forced himself to finish what he'd started. *At least I can do that right . . .*

Crawford heard the man shouting in some language—*Chinese? Japenese?*—but he ignored him. *One more moment . . . there!* He hit the send button with his thumb, and the phone dropped from his hand onto the floor. He was fading fast now. *Time to go, Crawford.*

His head felt like the weight of the world was on it, but he finally lifted it enough to stare into the face of his killer.

A young man with olive skin looked down at him, holding a black automatic rifle pointed at his chest. *He can't be older than twenty-five.* But then he saw the eyes, and he realized age didn't matter. The ends of his eyes sloped upwards—*he's definitely Asian*—but the black pools stared down at him with a calculated coolness, and Crawford realized he only had a moment left in this lifetime.

How can he be so cruel? How can he carry the weight of being a cold-blooded murderer? He suddenly felt compassion for his killer, the rational part of his mind clinging to life, telling him to let go, but to go with peace. So he closed his eyes and thought of Rayleen, summoning an image of her from their wedding day, her red hair blowing in the warm Louisiana breeze from the Gulf. He felt a strange sensation as he was pulled away toward the breeze, and he realized he was smiling.

Crawford Stubbins never felt the bullet fired point-blank into his chest, intended to finish the job the first shot had started. He was already gone.

"What kind of trucks?" Special Agent Hunt asked, the levity gone from her voice.

"Two laundry trucks were stolen from a Laundromat in Eastland Heights last night. The police took the report this morning, and they just forwarded us a copy since we have that standing request for information about any large stolen vehicles," Agent Marcus said, sensing the tension in the room rise exponentially.

Mike's mind processed the information in overdrive, and he was the first one to ask the question, even as Special Agent Hunt opened her mouth. "Who owns the Laundromat?" *Please let me be wrong,* Mike thought, dreading the answer.

"Hold on," Special Agent Marcus said, scanning the three-page police report, finding the information halfway down the first sheet. "Looks like a Chinese family . . . the Yee family. It's a mom-and-pop place. Their two daughters work there as well."

"Shit," Special Agent Hunt said.

"Yup," Mike added. "Bet you my badge our four Chinese suspects were working there." *It's happening soon, if not today.*

"Special Agent Hunt, I need you to get all your folks together on the floor. We need to find these trucks." Mike turned to Special Agent Marcus and said, "We also need a list of places they service. It might help determine a target, unless whoever has them just plans to use them as truck bombs."

"I already did, sir. It was easy since they only service one company—American Elemental, a rare earth elements mining corporation about an hour north of here. They're one of two companies in the United States that mine and process rare earth elements for the US government. The other one has been shut down for the past decade and is in the process of obtaining approval to start up again. American Elemental was built two years ago, but they don't go fully operational for another month."

"Which means American Elemental is the *only* US company that produces rare earth elements for our government," Mike said definitively. "That's the target."

"How do you figure, sir?" Special Agent Hunt asked.

"China has been behind this all along. They only used the Russians as proxies to obtain the ONERING," Mike said quickly, his words trying to keep up with his racing thoughts, which were already anticipating the next moves. "Now that it's been used in Sudan to attack an oil exploration site—one of their own—American Elemental has to be the next target. It's all about natural resources. The Chinese government has a global monopoly on rare earth elements. In fact, most of them are mined in China. Last year, we investigated a Chinese corporation that was conducting cyberattacks against several US companies. This Chinese company was the largest supplier of satellite technology, but in addition to that, they also owned several of the largest rare earth element mines in China. Rare earth elements are key components for all satellites, from batteries to heat shields. I had no idea how dependent we were on China for these things until these cyberattacks happened."

"Jesus Christ," Special Agent Marcus said.

"My sentiments exactly," Mike replied. "The Chinese government has to be behind this whole thing. And somehow, Sudan fits into this plot. Regardless, by eliminating our source of rare earth elements, it gives them a complete monopoly and makes us even more dependent on their resources. And after this, they're under no obligation to provide us with anything, leaving our satellite technology to fall behind as the Chinese keep on building and advancing their own satellites. I'd be willing to bet this is just the opening salvo in a new type of cold war."

"Sir, that sounds incredibly scary," Special Agent Marcus said.

"It is," Mike said. "It's a brave new world, with new enemies that masquerade as benevolent friends." He turned to Special Agent Hunt. "I need a secure line. I have to call the director and let—" was all he had time to finish as an audible gasp came from the operations floor behind him.

With a growing sense of dread, Mike turned his head toward the source of the outcry. A tall male agent stood in front of the bank of

HDTVs the field office used to monitor local and national news. All six monitors now played the same footage.

The video was hard to follow because of the jittery camerawork, but Mike caught glimpses of at least three gunmen wielding automatic weapons. Three bodies lay on the ground, and when the cameramen zoomed out, he didn't need the caption to know where the violence was unfolding. *We're too late. It's already begun.*

"Terrorists Attack the MGM Grand Casino Hotel," read the main caption as the video played.

Mike grabbed his secure cell from his suit coat pocket and sent a text. He looked up at Special Agent Hunt and said, "I need you to mobilize your HRT guys to support the team I brought with me. If there are hostages at the MGM Grand, you're going to want my guys. They're the best shooters in the Bureau. Also, I'll be borrowing Special Agent Marcus here. She and I have a different location to investigate."

"Sir?" Special Agent Marcus said questioningly.

"You and I and a small team are heading to American Elemental. You told us about the trucks, so I assumed you'd want to check it out." Mike raised his eyebrows. "Correct?"

"Absolutely, sir," Special Agent Marcus said enthusiastically.

"I thought so," Mike said. He turned to Special Agent Hunt. "I need you to send a team of agents to the Laundromat and see what they can find out about this robbery. I'm heading downstairs to meet Special Agent Foster in the motor pool. We're out of here in ten mikes. I'll call my uncle on the way. You have my cell. I trust you to make the operational decisions for HRT, but Special Agent Foster's second in command, Danny Palmer, will run tactical once on site. He's as good as his boss. Call me if you need anything."

"Got it, sir. Good luck. Be safe," Special Agent Hunt said. "Once I brief the floor on what your plan is, I'll get HRT and myself to the MGM."

"Sounds good. One more thing—don't hesitate to kill these monsters. Whoever they are, they don't care about negotiations. If you can take one alive, great; if not, kill 'em all and call it a day. Bring everyone home safely. Understand?"

Special Agent Marcus heard the conviction in the deputy director's voice, and it sent a chill through her small frame. She knew his background. It was legendary. *He knows exactly what needs to be done. He's been face-to-face with evil before. He might be the deputy director of the FBI, beholden to the Constitution and the laws of our land, but he's a man on fire. More importantly, he's one of the good guys.*

"Absolutely, sir. I've got it," Special Agent Hunt replied.

"Good." Mike turned to Special Agent Marcus and said, "Let's go."

"Anywhere you want, sir," Special Agent Marcus replied with growing admiration, reacting instinctively to his natural leadership.

Had she known where that would be, she might've reconsidered.

PART V

BLOOD AND GLORY

THE BLACK HOLE

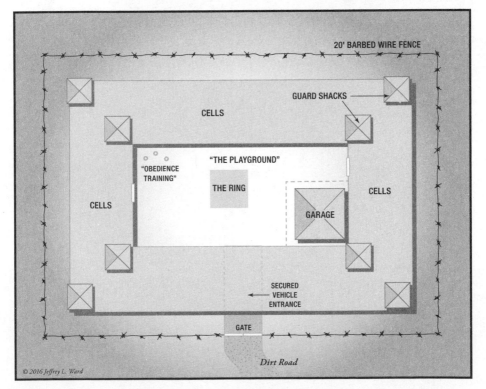

20' BARBED WIRE FENCE

GUARD SHACKS

CELLS

"THE PLAYGROUND"

"OBEDIENCE
TRAINING"

THE RING

CELLS

CELLS

GARAGE

SECURED
VEHICLE
ENTRANCE

GATE

Dirt Road

CHAPTER 35

Republican Palace, Khartoum, Sudan

The twinkling lights from the small vessels flickered across the water of the Nile like luminescent guides, begging to be followed into the black horizon of the African wilderness beyond the outskirts of Khartoum. Namir wouldn't be fooled. He knew what lay in those lands. He'd survived them as a child. Even though they were his origin, the clay that had molded him, Khartoum was now his home.

For the first time since the operation had begun, Namir was calm and content, though not happy. He wasn't sure he was capable of such a mundane emotion. He'd just left an emergency cabinet meeting that his president had convened regarding the attack on the Chinese drill site.

Namir had provided carefully crafted intelligence to the cabinet, explaining that initial indications were that an American space weapon of some kind had attacked the Chinese exploration site. The Americans were, of course, denying it, but the evidence was overwhelming. *Mainly, because it actually* was *their satellite,* he'd thought as he'd lied to the most senior leaders of his country. *But the question of who actually fired the weapon that attacked their oil site was a different matter entirely.*

The president planned to file a complaint with the UN Security

Council within the next hour. But before he did, he would place a call to the president of China to convey his condolences and assure him that China would be given anything it needed during its operation to recover those killed. At Namir's urging—backed by the minister of oil—he planned to conclude the conversation by promising that the contract for Xiang's field would be drafted immediately. Once the initial agreement was signed, China would have the sole rights to the world's largest oil reserve.

The financial future of Sudan had been secured, exactly as Namir had planned. The prime minister and president might never know the direct role they'd played, but—praise Allah—he himself knew, which was all that mattered.

Namir's sense of accomplishment had been magnified when the president had issued an order to the minister of oil to immediately rescind all of North American Oil's drilling rights. He'd anticipated that move, but to see it unfold in exactly the way he envisioned? He'd thoroughly enjoyed adding insult to American injury.

He looked at his watch. It was nearly seven thirty p.m., and he needed to check in with Gang. Even though Namir had been certain that the fierce leader, his men, and the ONERING were secure on Tuti Island, Gang had decided it was safer to relocate to an abandoned factory southeast of Khartoum. He'd planned to do it this evening, but events concerning their two captives had altered his plan. Now that the ONERING had been used, Gang wanted to return to the Black Hole this very night.

Namir's name for the prison was fitting—it was where rebels from Darfur and others opposed to his government vanished from the heart of Africa. Gang wanted to personally question the American prisoners, if they were both still alive. Namir almost pitied them.

Namir still wasn't sure how Gang had known about the Americans' presence in Sudan. He assumed it was Gang's Chinese Ministry of State Security that had fed him the information. Gang had even obtained pictures, which was why it'd been so easy to identify them as they left the airport.

Namir dialed Gang's cell. It rang four times before automatically disconnecting. Gang didn't use voice mail. He'd told Namir that even though he was confident his phone was secure thanks to the advanced encryption software developed by his government, he wanted to minimize the amount of time his phone was active. Gang had told him that even the time it took to listen to a thirty-second message established an accurate "handshake" between a handset and the nearest tower, allowing the phone's user to be all-too-easily located.

He's a very smart, resourceful young man. No wonder his government sent him.

Namir hung up the phone and returned to his desk to check his computer. An AP story questioned the moral authority of the US, asking, "How does the largest superpower in the world justify attacking another nation engaged in capitalism, the very economic principle that drives the US economy and underpins its moral imperative to spread freedom to the rest of the world?"

Namir smiled at the drivel. The American media reveled in pointing out the flaws of its own government. He didn't understand it, but he was grateful for the propaganda.

Soon they'd have tied up the loose ends that their American captives represented, their graves serving as unmarked capstones to the success of the operation. And his adult ambition would be fulfilled—to further and protect the interests of his beloved Sudan.

CHAPTER 36

Darkness had settled over the prison compound.

Logan and Cole had been led back to their cell after Cole's bloody victory, and now they waited for the next evolution of their prison stay. Neither of them had been asked any more questions, which worried Logan more than a beating or the threat of torture.

"I'm a bit concerned that our hosts haven't been down here to chat with us," Logan said. "You know what that means?"

"Unfortunately, I do," Cole responded, looking solemnly at Logan. "They don't really care what we know or don't know, and that makes us expendable."

"Or at least worthy of another round in the world's worst version of Medieval Times," Logan said. "I think I'm the next contestant on *The Price Is Most Definitely Fucking Wrong*."

"Maybe they'll have a bonus wheel for yours, although in this place, they'd probably nail you to it before they spin," Cole said.

"It doesn't matter," Logan said. "We always said in the Marine Corps, 'Hope is not a course of action,' but I really hope your signal was picked up or we're going to have to start figuring out what plan B is."

"What's plan A again?" Cole asked.

"Survive," Logan said seriously, and then added with a grin, "Do you need me to write it down?"

"Thanks. I think I got it," Cole said wryly.

The sound of a door slamming echoed through the corridor, followed by the deliberate footfall of several pairs of boots.

"Showtime," Logan said, and looked at Cole. "If something happens to me, hold out for as long as you can, and if you get out of here, make sure you let John and Mike know I went out on my shield." Logan paused for a moment and looked at the ground, his voice changing to a hushed tone of regret. "Most importantly, you tell my wife that the last two years have been the clearest, most rewarding years of my life. Make sure she knows how much I love her." He looked up at Cole and said, "You got that?"

The footsteps were halfway to their cell.

"Nothing's going to happen to you, Logan," Cole said, a sense of foreboding sending chills down the nape of his neck and forearms. "I've seen you in action. They haven't."

"I know, but they've seen *you* in action, which means they'll be better prepared," Logan said.

Four Sudanese guards appeared outside the iron bars. Three of them held AK-47s at an angle across their chests; the fourth was unarmed.

Or not, Logan suddenly thought, realizing these guards had grown complacent, even in the light of the daily violence and chaos. And it hit him like a slap to the face—they didn't fear the prisoners. *Fools. In this place, all the guards should be armed.*

He'd learned a long time ago to stop questioning the often insane and irresponsible decisions he'd witnessed in foreign countries. There was no point in trying to rationalize *why* things were done differently in Third World nations. Logan chalked it up to a lack of training and experience. Either way, it was to his and Cole's advantage.

The cellblock had suddenly grown quiet, a hushed anticipation overwhelming in its silence. The other prisoners' excitement was palpable, an electricity created by the prospect of more violent entertainment.

"Back!" the unarmed lead guard barked as he inserted a key into the lock and swung the cell's door inward.

They obeyed, moving against the back wall and placing their hands above them in submission.

"Out!" the guard yelled as the four guards moved apart, motioning for Logan and Cole to step into the gap.

You've got to be fucking kidding me, Logan thought, the engine of his mind accelerating from idle to autobahn. *Why wait for primetime when we can act now?*

With his hands still raised, Logan stepped in front of Cole and said, "Remember the cemetery?"

"Uh-huh," Cole said cautiously.

"Good. Same thing, except two less."

"Got it," Cole said, emotionless as he stepped behind Logan in the dank passageway.

Logan and Cole now stood between the guards as inmates lined up at their cell bars to watch the six-man procession bound for the arena.

Good. Then let's get this show on the road.

Logan sprang into action, grabbed the head of the guard directly in front of him—the one with the keys—and slammed it into the iron bars with a rewarding *crunch.* The man went limp, and Logan released him to focus on the second guard, the one holding an AK-47.

Shouts erupted up and down the cellblock, the sudden violence sending the inmates into a frenzy like a blood-hungry school of sharks.

The guard just ahead of Logan managed to turn halfway in the confined quarters, but the barrel of his weapon caught between the bars of the cell across from theirs. As the first guard's body slumped to the concrete floor, Logan stepped around the unfortunate man's now-still form. The second guard's panicked eyes darted back and forth from his useless weapon to Logan's determined face. *Tough luck, idiot,* Logan thought, and brought both arms down in a hammer fist on the guard's forearms.

"Aggghhh!" the guard screamed in pain, dropping the rifle to the floor.

Just as quickly as he'd brought them down, Logan lifted his two arms, stepped forward to gain leverage, and slammed his fists into the side of the guard's head, flinging him face first into the bars of the cell.

Logan was rewarded with a second *crunch* as the guard's nose exploded in a shower of red, blood splattering onto the floor and dripping down the bars.

Logan bent, retrieved the AK-47, and slammed the stock of the rifle into the back of the second guard's head. He fell on top of the first guard. Logan whirled, the AK-47 raised and the safety off, searching for more targets. It was unnecessary, as he'd expected.

Cole had not been as shocked by the lackadaisical attitude of the guards. *They're accustomed to ruling by fear here. They're not used to resistance.*

When Logan acted, Cole spun to face his first threat so quickly that he'd completely taken him by surprise. He reached out, grabbled the AK-47 still gripped in the man's hands, and jerked the barrel of the weapon up and over in a semicircle, pulling the guard off balance and tangling his arms.

The guard released the weapon as he was knocked over, his hands touching the floor of the corridor. As he tried to regain his balance, he looked up—just in time to see the butt of the rifle come crashing down onto his face, driving him into unconsciousness.

The second guard was quicker than the first.

As Cole turned toward him, he came face-to-face with the muzzle of the AK-47, now pointed directly at his head. *Damn, wasn't fast enough for both,* he thought as he watched the guard pull the trigger, wondering if he'd feel the bullet before his life ended.

Click.

Cole's heart skipped a beat as he realized he was still alive, just as he met the second guard's eyes, now full of fear. *Rookie forgot to chamber a round.*

Cole didn't wait to give him a second chance. He slammed the barrel of his AK-47 against the other man's rifle, knocking it aside. The guard tried to recover, but Cole swiveled his arms and the butt of the weapon, striking the man on the jaw with the wooden stock.

He heard a *crack* as the bones shattered, sending a shock impulse to the guard's brain that shut him down immediately. His eyes rolled upward into his head, but Cole hit him again in the temple as he fell to ensure he stayed down.

"Nice play," Cole said as he kicked the second AK-47 away and bent over to retrieve two extra magazines from each guard. He looked back at Logan, who was doing the same.

"It just sort of came to me," Logan said, and looked down the corridor from end to end. "I figured we had a better chance against only four guards, rather than having the odds stacked against us outside in the yard."

"Good call," Cole said.

"Thanks, but that was the easy part," Logan said, and grabbed a large, round key ring—he noted nine worn keys and a single, shiny new one—from the belt loop of the unconscious guard who'd ordered them out. "Now we have to figure out how the hell to get out of here. They'll send reinforcements in the next few minutes when we don't show up outside."

"We only have one option," Cole said, nodding behind him. "If we go through the tunnel, we'll run right into them—so we go the other way."

"Right behind you," Logan said.

They sprinted to the end of the corridor, past screaming inmates pounding on the bars for help, until they reached a solid-metal door with a heavy handle and a single keyhole above it.

"Here goes nothing," Logan said and inserted the same key he'd seen the guard use on their cell door. He turned the key.

Click. The lock released, and he lifted the handle, pulling the door open to reveal a dark stairwell.

Logan and Cole raced up the steps. They heard shouting from below, but as they climbed, it grew dimmer. *Maybe they haven't discovered we're missing. So far, so good.*

They reached the top of the stairs and faced another door, which Logan suspected led to the control room—or whatever passed for one in this place. Once again, Logan tried the keys from the unarmed guard he'd subdued. The first two didn't work, but the third one resulted in another audible *click.*

"Third time's a charm," Logan said, and pulled the handle. The door swung toward them, and they stepped quickly through . . .

. . . To find themselves in another empty corridor. Dark gray painted walls ran the length of the hallway. Fluorescent lights lined the ceiling. The corridor ended in a newer, smoother, stainless steel door.

"Bingo," Cole said as he and Logan moved into the corridor.

When they reached the door, Logan inserted the only key on the ring that looked new enough to match the lock. A tiny *beep* sounded, and the door automatically popped open a few inches inward.

The sound of voices speaking in Arabic trickled through the narrow opening. Logan looked through the slit in the doorway, trying to get a feel for the inside layout.

The control room was formed by two large areas divided by a large glass door. Banks of servers lined the back wall of the room, while individual workstations were installed along the glass. Two guards sat at separate terminals in the area immediately inside the door, but from his vantage point, Logan couldn't quite see into the other room.

Logan turned to Cole and said, "Two large spaces divided by a glass partition. I've got two guards approximately fifteen feet away on this side at workstations near the window. I can't see much else. Let's try to take them quietly. You ready?"

"As I'll ever be."

"Good. Guns up," Logan said, and pushed the doorway fully open.

Logan entered the room first, his AK-47 trained on the back of the head of the man closest to him. He felt more than heard Cole enter behind him, and he crept quietly across the smooth-tiled floor. *Please don't turn around. Just a little more luck . . .*

The second man—Cole's target—suddenly turned in their direction, and Cole saw he was on the phone. The man's eyes went wide the moment he spotted them, and Cole tilted his head and raised the weapon slightly, as if to say, *Don't make me do it.* Unfortunately, the young guard didn't get the message—he reached toward his console, dropping the handset. *You idiot,* Cole thought, and quickly pulled the AK's trigger.

Boom! Boom!

The AK exploded in his hands—he'd set the fire selector to semi-auto for precision—and two 7.62mm bullets struck the guard in the head, showering the inside of the window with blood, brain matter, and skull fragments.

Logan's target panicked at the shots, and he reached for a pistol resting on the desk in front of him. Logan shot him once in the back of the head, and the dead guard's face slammed forward onto his keyboard, blood trickling down the monitor in front of him and in between the keys.

"We've only got seconds. What's next?" Cole asked quickly.

Logan saw that the second area was clear of guards, and he stepped over to the window to assess the situation.

Spotlights from the four guard shacks in the corners of the courtyard illuminated the battle ring, revealing preparations for the evening's main event. It appeared relatively calm in the immediate wake of the two shots they'd just fired, although dozens of prisoners who'd been escorted outside now looked up toward the control room. Logan saw a half dozen prison guards, as well as the Chinese man he'd seen earlier, milling around the ring. The gigantic killer stood next to the canvas slaughterhouse, looking angry and impatient. *Sorry, buddy. No time to play.*

"We can't leave through the yard. There's too many—" was all Logan had a chance to say. A spotlight from the guard shack across the prison courtyard swiveled toward them and silhouetted them in its beam.

Simultaneously, the door to the second room burst open, and guards in black uniforms poured in, looking for the source of the gunfire.

As the Americans were spotted, shots rang out, and two guards unleashed a fusillade of bullets their way. The glass partition to the room shattered, computers exploded, and glass blew across the inside of the room.

Logan and Cole returned fire with tactical precision before crouching behind two desks in the middle of the room.

"Goddamnit!" Logan shouted above the din. "We're trapped."

"I noticed!" Cole screamed, as the other guards opened fire on their illuminated position. He leaned around the corner, spotted a guard in the open, and fired. The guard's AK-47 went silent, which was as much as he could hope for, given the situation.

Logan knew there had to be a way out, but he couldn't see it. All options led to the same result—death.

Suddenly, the room darkened once again, the spotlight gone. *What the hell?*

Logan glanced outside just as the other three spotlights went dark. Screams echoed from outside, and he instantly put the pieces together. A smile appeared on his face.

"What the hell is going on?" Cole asked.

Logan answered by leaning back—still covered by the desk—and shooting out all the lights he could see in their area, as well as the ones he could safely target in the next. He and Cole were shrouded in darkness once more.

"On three, change magazines, empty one in their direction, and then follow me," Logan said as he reloaded and Cole emptied the remaining rounds in his AK-47. "Trust me," Logan said. "The cavalry's here."

"Roger," Cole said, and inserted a fresh magazine.

In a seamless motion, Logan raised himself high enough to see over the workstation at the window and unloaded an entire magazine at point-blank range into the still-intact glass.

Cole opened fire toward the guards, sending the disorganized men diving for cover.

"I'm almost out!" Cole shouted, turning just in time to see Logan dive through the shattered window of the third-story control room.

Oh Christ! He's fucking crazy! Cole's mind screamed. Then he realized he'd better follow unless he wanted to be torn apart by gunfire as soon as the guards regained their courage.

If I don't die, I'm going to kill him, he thought, and scrambled to his feet, sprinting toward the window. He launched himself over the workstation and sailed through the opening into the now-dark courtyard as bullets struck the desks behind him.

CHAPTER 37

Tuti Island, Khartoum

Yin Liu walked through the camp. He'd been with Gang's team since the young officer had been selected to lead the elite unit. As Gang's second in command, his relationship with his commanding officer was complicated and personal.

A thirty-year veteran of the Ministry of State Security, he'd spent his career conducting operations in Europe and the Mediterranean. It was how he'd met Gang's father and how he'd come to the attention of the MSS for this highly selective assignment. Lau Han had saved him from an ambush in a cobblestone walkway in Malta's shopping district. The entire affair had been orchestrated by the CIA and was intended to draw Liu out of the shadows. Han had killed one of the CIA operatives, allowing Liu to defend himself in a fair fight, unfortunately for the second American.

Malta had changed everything. Liu owed Lau Han his life, and he'd pledged his loyalty to him. They became close friends, as well as an excellent tandem covert team. When Han had asked Liu to be his son's second in command, it had been a formality. Beijing had already organized it, and Liu had enthusiastically jumped at the chance to help pay back a debt and protect his friend's son.

Now that the American device had been activated, they were relocating the camp off the island and moving to a cluster of isolated, ancient ruins an hour east of Khartoum. Gang had told the Sudanese they were going to an abandoned textile factory, but he'd decided to keep their true destination secret. The risks were too high at this juncture. Gang had departed for the prison an hour ago, ordering Liu to be ready to move by midnight when he returned.

He was ahead of schedule, awaiting Gang's return. The trucks were lined up and ready to go. The American equipment that was central to their mission was safely packed away.

He listened to the background noises in the quiet blackness of the Sudanese night, the soft sounds of the rushing Nile a contrast to the violent struggle in which they were engaged.

Convincing the Sudanese and Chinese that the Americans had attacked the Chinese oil site, guaranteeing them the contract to the world's largest undeveloped oil field, had been a success.

Liu was also the only other member of Gang's team that knew about the operation unfolding on American soil. Now that they'd achieved their first tactical success, the plan was moving forward once again—Sudan today, the US tomorrow, depending on how Las Vegas ended. As that classy American singer Sinatra once sang, "The best is yet to come."

But not for the superpowers destroying the world, Liu thought. *Your best is over.*

One generator still powered the floodlights they'd erected around the camp, also charging their personal smartphones and providing his men the opportunity to check email from their families in China on untraceable accounts.

They'd gone dark since they'd entered the country three weeks ago, and the phones had been locked in a small container to which only Liu had the key. But since the operation was almost over, he'd decided to lift the ban, hoping the small privilege would lift the morale of his men. They'd lost their fair share of human assets, and even though they didn't show it, he knew they had to have their doubts.

Even though the entire unit was as elite as it was lethal, its members were still human.

Liu hoped Gang wrapped up the inquisition at the prison early. He wanted to be gone from the island sooner rather than later. Even though waiting was a part of the business, he'd never quite grown accustomed to it. Boredom made him restless.

He looked at his satellite-enabled laptop and scanned the international headlines. The attack on Sudan's soil had exploded onto the UN's radar, and the Security Council—notorious for inaction—was convening a meeting to discuss the situation. Liu knew the truth didn't matter, not with those political devils. They only cared about their personal gain, not the welfare of the countries they served. Their superiors had counted on it and knew that the "truth" was a matter of interpretation.

"I'll be back. I'm going to do one last sweep," Liu said to a sergeant they'd recruited from the PLA's Special Reconnaissance Chengdu Region, known as the Falcons of the Southwest.

The thirty-year-old warrior looked up from his handheld device and nodded, swiftly returning his attention to the tiny screen.

Can't really blame him, Liu thought. *Anything beats this standing around.*

———

The current was a steady pull but navigable this close to the island. John's face was covered with black camouflage paint, his head the only part of his body visible as he breaststroked his way through the warm, dark waters. Three ghostly shapes moved in unison with him.

The UAV had confirmed the location of the camp that the Chinese team had constructed inside an orchard. It consisted of four large tents, two satellite dishes, multiple generators, two large trucks, and two SUVs. They'd seen a flurry of activity, indicators that the small force was breaking down the camp in order to move.

If they didn't act quickly, they'd lose their window.

The plan was simple—at least as simple as a tactical assault against an enemy position could be. John would lead a four-man team across the quarter mile of open water; Amira and Tim Greco would drive onto the island from the mainland. The two teams would converge on the location and synchronize a diversion and the assault. The objective was clear—secure the ONERING at all costs and return to the embassy. All personnel on site were considered enemy combatants, which made the rules of engagement easy to understand—shoot everyone unless they surrender.

Uh-huh, John thought as he swam steadily through the current. *Until first contact. Then it all goes to hell like any best-laid plan.*

The dark island grew closer, the shoreline less than ten meters away. At this short distance from the sprawling mess of Khartoum, the chaotic mayhem of the city seemed quieter, a deceptively slumbering metropolis. The river had an isolating effect, and it afforded him the opportunity to sharpen his mind into a heightened state of awareness.

Suddenly, he felt the soft bed of the river beneath his feet, and he trudged forward, careful not to disturb the surface as he worked his way through the muck below.

Four dark specters emerged silently from the river, appearing to glide across the last few feet of water.

Once on solid ground, he moved ten feet inland and dropped to a knee, listening for any signs they'd been detected. The team followed suit, awaiting instructions. A faint glow emanated through the trees, and he heard the mechanical grind of generators.

We're good so far, he thought, and removed the black waterproof backpack he'd been carrying. He nodded to the others, and the three members of the embassy's security team did the same.

John smiled in the dark as he removed his gear. It was common to carry more than a hundred pounds of equipment on an operation. The movies always made it look so easy, with Special Forces or paramilitary heroes moving with speed and stealth, avoiding the enemy and killing at will. The reality was a bit more cumbersome, usually due to the weight of tactical communications equipment, weapons, ammunition, food, and water, the last weighing eight pounds per gallon—none of it was light.

But in this case, they were on a raid, which meant they kept the tools of the trade to a bare minimum, and John's aging back appreciated it, regardless of his level of fitness. *You're not some young grunt anymore,* his body told him.

He pulled out a sound-suppressed H&K MP5SD-N, specially designed for the US Navy for close-quarters combat in wet environments, and slung it across his chest. His Colt M1911 .45-caliber pistol went into a holster on his right thigh; the KA-BAR fighting knife into a sheath behind the pistol. Finally, he removed a small, encrypted radio and secured it to the tactical harness he wore over his black fatigues. He placed the earpiece in his left ear, secured the tactical throat microphone around his neck, and plugged the end into the handset.

Now for the real test—establishing comms, he thought, knowing that no matter how much preparation went into an operation, communications were paramount. He'd seen more than one tactical masterpiece end in death and destruction because communications equipment had failed, either from technical or environmental reasons.

"Alpha, this is Bravo Actual. Comms check," John said softly.

"Bravo Actual, this is Alpha Actual," the clear voice of Tim Greco responded. "Read you loud and clear."

"We're on the island and ready to move into position. Once we're on target, I'll initiate the assault. How copy?" John asked.

"Roger all, Bravo. We're in position and ready when you are. No issues getting here. Good luck." Tim said.

"Roger. Going radio silent now. Out."

He turned to the rest of the team, who'd overheard the quiet exchange, and said, "Okay. Let's move out. The target must be that glow coming from the trees. When we get closer, I'll stop us at the final assault point and radio Alpha team. Any questions?"

Silent shakes of the head answered his query. *As I expected,* he thought. The three members of the embassy's DSS team were all former military with combat experience. *Exactly the kind of guys I can work with. Now let's get the show on the road.*

He began to stalk across the dark, grassy earth of Tuti Island. Moving quickly, they covered the remaining distance within minutes, until the four shadows stopped at the outer perimeter of the camp.

John crouched motionless behind the hedgerow of bushes, his assault team arrayed in a line beside him, waiting for the order. Their objective was less than forty meters directly ahead, illuminated by four sets of portable floodlights. *This can't be this easy,* he thought, unconsciously shaking his head.

Four vehicles—two SUVs and two canvas-covered cargo trucks—were parked in the middle of the clearing and pointed toward the dirt-road entrance to the orchard. Eight Chinese men, wearing Western clothing and dark military boots, casually milled around the right side of the trucks and were exposed to John and his team. What shocked John the most was the fact that these elite soldiers' weapons were holstered or lay across the hoods of the vehicles. Some of the men were checking smartphones, while others were engaged in conversation. One of the Chinese team even appeared to be dozing in the cab of the front truck.

I feel for you, pal, John thought, remembering his operational days when exhaustion became a physical weight and any brief respite was a welcome gift.

But it was a scene of total complacency, and as John knew from his multiple tours in Iraq, complacency killed.

John grabbed his handset and deliberately pressed the button three times, each one issuing an electronic *click.* He looked at the three members of his team and nodded.

Good. This is going to be fast, he thought. He gripped his suppressed MP5SD submachine gun and waited. It didn't take long.

A vehicle's engine sounded on the audible horizon, growing louder by the second. The posture of the men in the orchard changed instantly, just as John had expected. Suddenly alert, those sitting stood and placed their hands on their pistol holsters or grabbed black submachine guns from the hoods of the trucks. They faced the entrance to the orchard almost in unison.

John exhaled and felt his familiar battle focus sharpen one last time. He never tired of the sensation, a calming sense of power and confidence, strengths required for the violent work that lay before him. The battle focus reinforced for him that what he was about to do was necessary, a sacrifice at the altar of the greater good.

A black SUV emerged into the clearing and stopped just inside the tree line, thirty meters away from the lead cargo truck. Its engine idled, as if waiting for permission to join the party.

The men stared at the vehicle, but no one reacted impulsively. *They're trained and patient, waiting to see who's in it.*

Finally, a young man in his late twenties approached the vehicle, shouting as he moved closer. The SUV remained stationary, unmoved by the man's orders, taunting him with its pitilessly bright headlights.

The remaining men all stepped toward the SUV in unison, like moths drawn to a flame. The combination of Chinese shouts, the running generator, and the idling diesel SUV masked the short movement of John's team. *That's our cue,* John thought, and exhaled one last time, initiating the assault.

At the far right of the assault line and closest to the SUV, John took two steps forward and achieved a clear sight picture with the red-dot reflex scope of the MP5. For him, the scope allowed him to rapidly move from one target to the next much faster than with iron sights. He focused on the man closest to the SUV, exhaled, and gently squeezed the trigger.

Thwack!

A single bullet tore into the right side of the man's head. He dropped straight down in a crumpled heap, dead in the glow of the SUV's headlamps.

John shifted the weapon to the next target as he heard three more shots so closely fired together they made a loud, singular sound.

Three more men fell, struck down by gunfire less than a second after his first shot.

The remaining men reacted, spinning to their right to face the danger head-on. They fired blindly into the underbrush, the flood-lights' glare concealing the darkness beyond, from where John and his team fired with lethal precision.

John pulled the trigger on the MP5 one more time and executed a flawless failure-to-stop drill on his target. The first two bullets struck the man in the chest, and he fell backward against the lead truck. The third round struck him in the middle of the forehead, snapping his head back.

Three left, he thought and smoothly shifted the weapon one more time, searching for a target. He was too late—there were no more to be had. The three members of his team had dropped the remaining targets where they stood. The entire ordeal had lasted less than three seconds.

It's always so fast, a detached part of his brain thought.

Eight men, members of an elite Chinese unit, lay on the ground, their death poses spotlighted on a dirt stage by the lighting they'd erected themselves.

None of the bodies moved. *Good.*

John stepped forward, and his men followed. They appeared out of the blackness, four wraiths materializing into the light of the inner circle. The three other shooters broke off from him and checked the bodies to remove weapons and ensure they were dead.

As John glanced across the carnage, he briefly wondered if any of these men had participated in the ambush at the cemetery. He didn't know if there were more men at other locations, but it didn't matter.

They were engaged in a shadow war with this unknown Chinese force, and they'd won this round.

The doors on the SUV finally opened, and Tim Greco stepped out from behind the steering wheel, quickly followed by Amira from the passenger side.

Even at this distance, the low level of illumination only accentuated her beauty, transforming her into some otherworldly creature John longed to be near. *She's gorgeous.* It was the discipline and dedication she personified that awed him. She was special, although he sensed she tried to diminish it by withdrawing inward, refusing to let anyone inside the protective, steely exterior their work demanded.

John waved at them, and Tim nodded. Amira smiled, and John felt his face flush under the layer of black paint. *Thank God she can't see me blush. What are you? In fucking high school? Get a grip, old man. She's too young for you.*

He'd thought—hoped—that he'd seen her looking at him strangely earlier at the embassy, secretly assessing and analyzing him, like a puzzle she was trying to solve. *Or wondering what the hell was wrong with you, more likely.* But it seemed like it had been more than casual interest.

Tim, Amira, and two men from the embassy's security team who had exited the SUV stepped toward the truck, bringing him back to the ONERING and the task at hand.

"I'll check the lead one," John said. "Brad, take the second truck."

"Roger," Brad, a former Army Ranger, said. "I've got it."

John was halfway to the truck, hoping the DARPA system was in the back of it, when he heard, "What the—"

He turned to his left just as a single gunshot boomed from behind the second truck.

Brad fell backward, landing on his side and lying still.

Oh God, no, John thought as more gunshots echoed through the small orchard. He searched for the shooter, but he didn't see anything.

Terry, a former Navy SEAL, returned fire toward the back of the second truck as Frank, the third member of the team, ran over to his fellow Ranger's fallen body.

A black canister sailed through the air and landed next to Brad's motionless form.

"*Grenade!*" Frank shouted, and dove to the ground, landing on top of Brad to shield him from the blast.

John dove to the earth, his back to the grenade, and waited.

BOOM!

The flashbang grenade exploded, sending a concussive roar and blinding light across the space.

For a brief moment, the world inside John Quick's head went silent. All he could see was a white blur, but he knew the effect wouldn't last long. The ground quickly came back into focus, and he forced himself to his hands and knees.

His training propelled him into action. If the shooter was still there, it was either move or die.

Sound rushed in next, and he thought he heard echoes. But then the ground vibrated under his fingertips. *That isn't good.*

The Chinese cargo truck lurched forward in the clearing, accelerating toward the American SUV and the freedom beyond, intent on destroying everything in its path—including Amira and Tim.

CHAPTER 38

As Cole soared through the air, he thought, *This is it. I'm dead. This maniac got me killed.* But then he landed on top of a flat tin roof with a *crunch* and rolled into a kneeling position with a ringside view of the chaos unfolding in the courtyard below.

The landscape was cloaked in dark shades of gray, the dim glow from various windows inside the prison creating distorted macabre shadows that danced across the walls and ground. The prisoners had scattered in all directions at the first sound of gunfire, and the darkness only heightened their panic. Cole saw several men crouched in corners against the walls, as if waiting for someone to save them. *You guys need to save yourselves, or you're never getting out of here,* he thought sympathetically.

"We need to move and get off this roof," Logan said as gunshots and muzzle flashes lit up the courtyard like cameras at a rock concert. "We're sitting ducks up here. Cover me."

Before Cole could respond, Logan slung the AK-47 over his shoulder and slid off the edge of the roof. He hung momentarily and then dropped out of sight.

Cole heard him hit the ground, followed immediately by, "Your turn!"

He scampered to the edge, slung the rifle across his back, and slid his legs out into the open air, allowing gravity to take control.

Bam-bam-bam!

Below him Logan fired three quick shots, and Cole heard a scream of pain mix with the chaotic shouts of confusion and fear. His arms fully extended, Cole released his grip on the metal roof and plummeted to the ground.

The shock of his landing sent a deep vibration through his body, but he reacted quickly, bending his knees and allowing himself to roll backward to absorb the energy of the fall. He scrambled to his feet and stood next to Logan.

"What now?" Cole asked, glancing at Logan, who was staring at the northwest corner of the courtyard in the direction of the telephone poles of death, where inmates had been crucified in the blazing heat and sun.

"Follow me," Logan said, and moved into a crouching run.

Cole sprinted to catch up and then slowed himself to Logan's pace once he reached his partner's side. He spotted what Logan had already seen and was overcome with relief. *It's about time.*

Two figures in black fatigues were rappelling from the guard tower, while two men still in the guard shack on the roof covered them with automatic weapons fire from suppressed submachine guns.

Cole heard their distinctive bursts and realized they were coming from all directions. At the courtyard's northeast corner, even more black-clad men fast-roped down the prison's walls.

"Looks like that little receiver of yours worked," Logan said, scanning their surroundings for any threats.

"It was a transmitter, not a receiver," Cole said.

Logan smiled to himself. "We can discuss the nuances of satellite communications some other time."

The two men dashed across the courtyard, closing the distance to the nearest team of commandos. The first of the commandos landed on the ground and released the rope, spinning on his heels to assess the situation.

The commando whirled his submachine gun at Logan and Cole, who both stopped in their tracks and lowered their weapons.

"Don't shoot! We're Americans, and I assume you're here for us," Logan said quickly, looking into a serious face covered in black camouflage paint.

"Come closer, but no sudden moves. Understand?" the man said as the second commando landed on the ground behind him and released the rope.

The man's steady eyes studied Logan's face. "You must be Logan West." He nodded at Cole and said, "Mr. Matthews."

"What gave it away?" Logan asked.

"Your scar. We were briefed on your physical appearance before we took off. I'm Chief Sorenson, SEAL Team Six." Sounds of more suppressed automatic weapons fire carried across the battleground. "And we need to get you two out of here as soon as possible. We've got rotary support on standby, but I don't think we want to bring it in here. God knows how many guards are scrambling toward us now, and we don't need to lose a bird. We need to get through this building and get some distance between us and this place."

"Chief, I know how we can get out of here, and we won't have to walk anywhere," Cole said. "When they dragged us in here, we came through a tunnel behind that corrugated metal door," he said, pointing to the tunnel. "It leads to the front of the prison, but more importantly, there's a jeep and a cargo truck inside."

"Exactly. Why walk when you can drive?" Logan added.

Logan watched Chief Sorenson quickly calculate his options. He spoke into a throat microphone, "Serpent Actual, this is Serpent Bravo. We have both packages alive and well. There's a tunnel behind the metal door in the center of the south wall. They say there are vehicles there. Recommend we rendezvous at the door, breech, and get the hell out of here. Recommend overwatch teams go down the outside and meet us at the entrance. How copy?"

There was a pause as the chief waited for a response. The second SEAL in Chief Sorenson's team suddenly opened fire and dropped a guard with a machete who must have thought he was invisible. Two bullets from the SEAL's submachine gun ended his not-so-stealthy approach.

"Roger, Actual. See you there," Chief Sorenson said, and nodded. He looked at Logan, unexpectedly grinned, and said, "How does it feel for a Marine to be rescued by the Navy?"

"Hey, I thought you just came to give me a ride," Logan quipped back. "Isn't that what you guys do anyway? Take Marines to the fight?"

"And use them as sex slaves on ship. Don't forget about that," the SEAL said. "But we can discuss male bondage later. Let's just get you the hell out of here."

"You guys are all fucking crazy. You know that, right?" Cole asked Logan.

"Hey! Don't look at me. He started it," Logan said.

"Guns up, gentlemen. Let's go," Chief Sorenson said, serious once more as he took point. He and the second SEAL led the way out of the corner, moving directly toward the garage door across the open courtyard.

Gunfire erupted from the shattered windows of the control tower, and bullets struck the dirt to their right. Logan heard a scream as either a guard or a prisoner was hit, and he looked over to see a form writhing on the ground in pain. *Indiscriminate fire. Nice, assholes.*

Several suppressed weapons returned fire, and the guard's weapon ceased chattering. *These guys do know how to shoot,* he thought, knowing in truth that SEAL Team Six—now renamed the United States Naval Special Warfare Development Group, DEVGRU for short, although it was still referred to by the outdated moniker—had some of the best shooters in the world.

An eerie silence had fallen over the entire scene. The guards had either fled or were in hiding in the shadows of the courtyard from the assault force. The prisoners who'd assembled as fight fans had scattered throughout the confined space, and Logan heard rapid conversations in Arabic and other languages. The initial panic was over, and now everyone inside—including Logan—waited to see how the incursion would end.

They passed the Everlast ring to their left, weapons up and searching for threats.

"Yeeeaaaagghhhh!!!"

Logan sensed movement to his left, and his lightning-quick reflexes reacted. He dove to his right as his peripheral vision detected an enormous shape. Logan aimed the AK-47 in the general direction of his attacker and fired.

Crack!

As the single shot rang out, Logan realized who it was—the giant.

The killer's spiked bat smashed into the barrel of Logan's AK-47, knocking it out of his hands and rendering the weapon useless.

Fucker almost got me.

The giant stood in front of him momentarily, illuminated by the faint, increasing glow from inside the building as more lights were turned on in response to the ongoing battle. He scowled with obvious contempt and stepped toward Logan—and faltered. He looked down at his stomach and then back up.

Something's wrong, Logan realized, squinting through the darkness. Light flashed off a slick surface on the giant's torso. *Blood.*

Logan's shot had hit the mark, even as he had evaded the giant's attack. *Tough luck, motherfucker. It's time to end your reign of terror.*

"Knife *now!*" Logan shouted instinctively.

"Catch!" came a voice from his left. Logan redirected his eyes, keeping the giant in his line of sight, as an elongated object sailed toward him. The giant stared at the object as it flew through the air past him.

A look of fury appeared on his face as he recognized what it was, and he stepped forward to attack—only to collapse to his knees in the dark dirt. He grunted as the black patch of blood spread across his entire torso.

Logan snatched the object out of the air and looked down to see the black handle of a combat knife with a four-inch tanto blade, now held in his right hand with the angled tip pointed forward.

"Not the people's champion after all, are you?" Logan spat out.

The giant knelt in front of him, motionless, still holding the spiked bat in his right hand. His breathing was labored, and he hung his head, the beard touching his chest.

The bullet must've punctured a lung, Logan thought.

A loud cheer roared through the assembled spectators at the sacrifice about to be made at their twisted altar of violence.

Logan stepped around the fallen giant and pressed his legs into the giant's back, placing his hand on top of the killer's head. He leaned over and said, "This is for that poor SOB you killed earlier today, as well as for all the others you've butchered." The giant moaned, which was acknowledgment enough for Logan.

Logan plunged the blade into the right side of the giant's neck and twisted his wrist, opening the deep gash for maximum effect. Warm blood sprayed across his hand and shot several feet into the air in a dark, spectral mist. Logan withdrew the blade, and the blood pumped out of the man's neck onto the dirt.

There was a hushed silence as the giant who'd tormented and killed the inmates of the Black Hole bled out in spectacular, horrific fashion. After a few moments of suspended gore, he fell facedown, his hands still at his sides, dead.

The first two prisoners who'd approached the two combatants stared at Logan in dumbstruck amazement. Logan even spotted a guard looking at him in disbelief. The guard felt the rage in Logan's gaze and averted his eyes, hands raised in front of him as if pleading for mercy.

Before anyone could react, Logan raised his voice and declared, "I don't know if you understand me, but this monster can't torment you anymore. We're getting out of this place, and I suggest you do the same."

Logan wiped the blade on his pants, removing most of the blood, and turned to Chief Sorenson, offering the blade back to its owner.

Chief Sorenson stared at him with respect and admiration.

"No. You keep it," he said. "You earned it."

"Thanks. Now let's get the hell out of here. I don't think we'll have any more resistance."

"You think?" Cole said. "After that display, I'm pretty sure no one's going to try and stop us."

"I agree," Chief Sorenson said. "Now let's go find those vehicles and get the hell out of here, once and for all."

They set off again for the tunnel, this time without gunfire or random, potshot attacks. As they crossed the remaining distance, the prisoners cheered them on, shouting praises and clapping. Logan had won freedom, not only for himself, but also for all of them. He was their champion now, even if only for a short time, and they intended to shower him with the respect he'd earned through blood and glory.

CHAPTER 39

Tuti Island

John heard the cargo truck slam into the embassy's Range Rover, but his view of the crash was obstructed by the truck itself, as it plowed forward, gaining momentum and disappearing into the island's underbrush.

Tim had already recovered after dodging out of the way and was jogging toward John. Amira was motionless on the ground to the left of the entrance.

Please, no, John thought, and breathed in a gasp of relief when she jumped up and brushed herself off, looking at the ruined SUV. "We need to go after him."

"Tim, secure the scene here," John said, quickly gathering himself together. "Do a quick sweep for intel, laptops, cell phones, whatever. Leave the bodies. Hide them in the brush, but hurry and take the second truck and the SUV back to the embassy. The device has to be on that truck, and I plan to get it."

"Go," Tim said. "I've got it covered here."

"Good," John said, and turned to Amira. "Come on. Let's check on Brad."

John ran over to Brad's fallen form. Terry and Frank were at their friend's side, and his black camouflage blouse was open, revealing a small Kevlar vest.

"What the hell happened?" Brad asked, groggy from the gunshot and explosion. "I blacked out."

"More like you got shot and knocked out by a flashbang grenade," Terry said. "You seriously brought your vest? You carried it on the swim in your pack? Good on you, man. It saved your life."

"It's an old habit. It saved my life once before, and I *always* use it, no matter how much of a pain in the ass it is," Brad said, feeling the sore spot on his chest that would soon turn greenish blue.

"No kidding," John said, nodding in obvious relief. "Glad to see you're still with us. We're going after that bastard. These guys will get you back to the embassy. See you there."

John ran to the driver's side of the Mercedes SUV and yanked open the door, grateful the keys were in the ignition.

"Why do you get to drive?" Amira asked.

"Because I may ask you to do something borderline suicidal, and you can probably do it better than I can," John replied.

"I can probably do a lot of things better than you," she said drily, as she slid into the passenger seat.

John looked at her, tried to give her his *Don't-fuck-with-me* stare as he started the engine, and laughed. "You, my dear, are probably right," he said. He slammed the SUV's gearshift into drive and pushed the accelerator all the way to the floor. Before he could catch himself, he added, "And when this is over, I may just ask you out to see a few of them. God knows what skills the CIA has taught you."

She looked at him, silent. Then her face turned deadly as she focused on the road in front of them.

Can't take it back now, jackass. At least she knows how you feel, especially if you get yourself killed.

He navigated a turn at high speed, and the tires slid on the dirt as he entered the curve. He let up on the pedal, turned slightly into the slide, and allowed the tires to regain their traction. Once they did, he rocketed forward, pursuing the fleeing cargo truck.

The command center was on the far northern tip of the island, and the only escape route was over the Tuti Island Suspension Bridge at the southern end. The driver had a minute's head start, and John estimated they'd catch up to him halfway to the bridge, in the center of the island where most of the inhabitants lived.

Thank God it's nighttime, he thought—there'd be a lesser chance of civilian casualties.

The overgrowth of the orchards suddenly vanished, revealing the congested residential center less than one hundred meters in front of them. It was densely packed with single- and two-story tan brick buildings of varying heights and sizes. The road narrowed as it entered the village, and John was forced to slow down.

"Definitely no building codes here," John remarked absently.

The road veered to the right at an angle, continuing its trek to the south. John maintained his speed, and as they emerged around the bend, they spotted the cargo truck's reckless getaway through the populated area.

"The bastard's going to kill someone before we can get to him," John said.

"Then drive faster," Amira responded, as straightforward as ever.

"Yes, ma'am," John said. Regardless of his attraction to her, in her current state of focus, she reminded him of Logan. He immediately dismissed the thought of his friend, not wanting to jeopardize his current mind-set. He just prayed the SEAL team was doing its job.

The SUV surged forward, and buildings flashed by the windows in a blur. The cargo truck grew closer.

Forty yards . . . thirty yards . . .

The lights of the suspension bridge loomed ahead, less than a mile away. John reached sixty miles per hour and desperately hoped that no innocent soul stepped out of one of the houses.

Twenty yards . . . ten yards . . .

The cargo truck slammed on its brakes, its red taillights sending a moment of panic through John.

"What the hell is he doing?" Amira said as John locked up the brakes, sending the SUV sliding across the pavement. In seconds, the rear of the cargo truck increased in size until it filled the entire windshield.

"Hold on. This is going to be close," John said through gritted teeth.

The SUV ground to a halt, angling past the rear of the truck. John looked up into the driver's side mirror of the truck and was greeted by an older Chinese man looking at him with a mixture of contempt and amusement, his arm extended out the window.

What the hell is he up to? was all John had time to think before he heard an ominous *thud.*

A round object landed on the hood of the Mercedes. As John processed what it was, Amira shouted, "Back up! Back up!"

The cargo truck pulled away, leaving its lethal package behind.

It suddenly occurred to John why the driver had used a flashbang grenade at the campsite—he didn't want to damage the cargo truck or its contents. That meant only thing—the ONERING was definitely in the back.

John reversed the SUV and floored the pedal, hoping the sudden motion would fling the grenade off the hood.

Amira unbuckled herself from the passenger seat in one agile movement and extended herself halfway out the window, reaching for the rolling grenade in the middle of the hood. It was just out of reach, and the backward momentum pushed it farther . . . but not far enough.

Realizing she only had another second or two at most before the grenade—*not* a flashbang, but the real thing—detonated, Amira flung herself out the window onto the hood, lengthening her slim body for maximum effect. She reached her arm out as she rolled to her left, her body a living corkscrew. *Another few inches—got it!* Amira grabbed the grenade and rolled one more time, launching herself off the hood and into the air. As she fell, she threw the grenade with all the strength she had, using her momentum to fling it into an alleyway to the right of the SUV.

She disappeared below the hood, and John slammed on the brakes as the grenade detonated.

BOOM!

Shrapnel and fragments of stone and mortar harmlessly showered them as the buildings absorbed the force of the blast.

John gaped at Amira in wonder. She stood, brushed the dust off her black, form-fitting combat fatigues, and smiled at him through the windshield as casually as if she'd been waiting for him all night. *That might be the sexiest thing I've ever seen.*

She ran back to the SUV, hopped in, and said, "Let's go get that motherfucker. He made me tear my pants."

John looked down at her muscular left thigh and saw a rip three inches long. "Are you going to live?" he asked.

"I am," Amira said matter-of-factly, "but he's not."

John nodded as the SUV shot forward. "Oh, by the way, that's why I drove."

"What do you mean?" Amira said.

"Because there's no way in hell I could've done what you just did," John said, looking at her in wonder.

"Thanks," she said, averting her eyes from the honesty expressed on his face. "But I've seen you fight. You're not too shabby yourself."

"I try."

The SUV raced down the street. The cargo truck was now nearly a quarter mile away. It had reached the end of the island, and the bridge was directly ahead. The truck slowed and turned left, leaning precariously as it raced through the intersection.

"Better try harder. He's heading to the entrance ramp. There's only one way to the bridge," Amira said.

John arrived at the intersection moments later and deftly controlled the SUV as it angled around the corner, reaching the entrance ramp that curved up from the island to the bridge. The cargo truck was moving through the curve as fast as its driver could control it.

Not fast enough, John thought.

The SUV barreled up the ramp, gaining ground with each second. The cargo truck reached the top of the ramp and accelerated on the half-mile stretch of smooth, suspended concrete. The Mercedes rocketed onto the four-lane bridge moments later and pulled alongside the truck, carefully avoiding the foot-high black and yellow divider.

"Gotcha," John said to himself.

At this time of night, traffic was sparse, with only a few random vehicles traveling in either direction, oblivious to the pursuit that had just invaded their tranquil crossing.

"It's now or never," John said, but Amira was already ahead of him. "Try to keep him alive," he said, thinking of the intelligence value their quarry represented.

She aimed the Steyr tactical machine pistol she'd been carrying and opened fire at the moving target, firing in controlled bursts at the rear left tires of the cargo truck.

Brrp-brrp-brrp!

The muzzle flashes danced across the inside of the windshield, mixing with the soft lights of the suspension bridge to create an odd, lonely luminescence. Combined with the deafening fire in the confined space and the ejection of shell casings, which flickered inside the SUV like miniature fireworks, John felt like he was in some hellish version of a rave.

Amira's bullets bombarded the left-rear two wheels of the speeding truck, striking rubber and metal and sending a shower of sparks across the pavement below. The driver glanced out the window and sharply turned the truck to the left, trying to force the Mercedes into the short median wall.

John pulled back as Amira emptied the thirty-round magazine, ejected it, and loaded another. The truck was now directly in front of them, and Amira opened fire again, this time aiming for the right rear tires.

Brrp-brrp-brrp!

Bullets once again hammered the truck in a well-aimed fusillade, striking the tires and the rear axle. The machine pistol went quiet, empty once again.

For a moment, John thought their efforts had been futile, and he wondered what plan B would be. They were now a little less than halfway across the bridge and running out of ground.

Thump! Thump!

Suddenly, the truck's right-rear tires exploded, disintegrating completely as the truck tried to maintain its speed. Pieces of rubber unraveled, discarding themselves along the pavement like dead skin. The truck careened from side to side in large, slow movements, a lumbering beast injured and unsure.

With nothing but the rims remaining, the right rear corner of the truck dropped several inches. Sparks exploded from underneath the truck, the metal rims gouging the surface of the bridge.

"Uh-oh," John said.

"Yeah," Amira said in fascination as she watched the slow-motion destruction unfold.

The driver tried to maintain control, but it was too late. The truck turned lazily to the right and lurched toward the railing of the bridge in a wide arc. The flat front cab of the Chinese truck smashed through the bridge's railing, slowing the vehicle's momentum.

Fortunately for the driver, the engineers had constructed two sets of railings, one for the road itself, and one for the outer walkways on both sides of the bridge.

Twisted chunks of metal punctured the underside of the truck and severed the front axle. The front of the truck's cab smashed down onto the pavement, grinding purposefully toward the second set of railings.

A lone man walking across the bridge had stopped to watch the mayhem, realizing just in time that he was about to become part of the action. As the truck broke through the second set of barriers, he ran for his life, sprinting up the walkway and escaping with mere inches to spare.

The truck ground forward, its cab extending out over the open air eighty feet above the Nile, as it was finally, permanently, crippled.

Parts of the second railing broke away and plummeted into the dark waters below.

"That was close," John said, turning to Amira as he stopped the SUV behind the wreckage of the truck.

"You spoke too soon," Amira said with awe in her voice.

"What?" he asked, and then turned back to the truck.

The wrenching sound of metal being torn and twisted reverberated across the bridge as the death throes of the mechanical monster slowly lifted the rear of the ruined vehicle into the air. The truck, a giant, broken teeter-totter balanced precariously on the edge of the bridge, inched forward, yearning for the watery grave below.

CHAPTER 40

By the time Logan and the SEAL team reached the tunnel, the other half of the assault force was already inside. They'd breached the door and found the keys to both the jeep and the cargo truck hanging on a wooden peg hammered into the wall next to the vehicles.

A SEAL slightly younger than Logan approached him, extended his hand, and said, "Lieutenant Reed, Mr. West. It's nice to meet you. I've heard plenty about you, both officially and unofficially."

Before Logan could respond, Chief Sorenson said, "Sir, you'll have something to add to that laundry list of stories when you hear about what he and Mr. Matthews did inside."

"Is that so?" Lieutenant Reed asked, genuinely interested.

"We just took care of some problems. Nothing more," Logan said.

"If that's what you call it," Chief Sorenson said drily.

"Tell me about it later because we need to get the hell out of here. The guards are either dead or scared, and I don't want to linger long enough to allow anyone to get any bright ideas. Let's load up and go," Lieutenant Reed said.

"Sounds like a plan, Lieutenant," Cole said.

"Chief, I'll take the jeep and three men. You take the rest of the team in the truck. Once we're at least ten miles out at a secure location, I'll call in the extract. Sound good?"

"Roger, sir," Chief Sorenson said, and turned to Logan and Cole. "You want to drive, Mr. West?"

"No thanks, Chief. The last time I drove a seven-ton, I drove it off the top of a dam in Iraq. Didn't go so well."

"I was kidding. No offense, but I'm driving," Chief Sorenson replied.

"I know, but I wasn't," Logan said, a slight grin breaking across his face.

"Why am I not surprised? Are you sure you weren't one of us in a former life?" Chief Sorenson asked as he jogged around the front of the truck and hopped in the driver's seat.

Cole stepped up and slid into the middle of the seat, holding his AK-47 between his legs, the muzzle pointed forward. Logan followed, rolling his window down to allow the barrel of an AK-47 to stick out. He'd picked it up after the giant had destroyed the first one.

Three loud thumps on the back of the cab informed them that the rest of the team was secured and ready to go.

"Here goes nothing," Chief Sorenson said, and turned the key.

The Mercedes-Benz engine turned over immediately, spitting exhaust from its vertical pipe.

"You gotta love German engineering," Chief Sorenson said. "Take away the whole Third Reich–Aryan supremacist–Holocaust thing, and they're not so bad," he added sarcastically.

Chief Sorenson honked the horn once, and the jeep in front of them pulled away. The truck followed, driving through the tunnel entrance and out the front gate without so much as a single shot fired.

"No fanfare? I'm a little surprised," Logan said, thinking of the Chinese man he'd met earlier in the day. He found it hard to believe that he'd let them slip away without a fight. He hadn't seen him during their escape. *Bastard was probably hiding. Maybe he's dead. If so, good.* "Be alert. One of the shot callers in the prison didn't seem like the type to let us go so easily."

"Logan, we're always alert," Chief Sorenson replied seriously. "You know that."

"Good point," Logan said, and then added, "I meant to ask, how did you guys insert and get to the guard towers?"

"We HALO'd in five clicks away and then humped in. Since this place is so remote, it was a fairly easy movement. Once we were in position with a four-man team at each corner, we took out all the guards in each tower, cut through the fence—it wasn't electrified—and scaled the towers. The plan was to gain access to the inside since satellite imagery showed an access panel in each tower and work our way through the prison until we found you. But you literally shot our plan full of holes when you got into a gun battle in the control room."

"It was rather unexpected," Logan said, watching the side-view mirror as the prison disappeared into the night. *Good riddance,* he thought, and shifted his focus to the single-lane dirt road that meandered its way along the Nile River flowing less than thirty meters to the left.

"Two of our teams on the east wall had a better view of it than we did," the chief continued as he navigated the winding road behind the jeep. "The lieutenant thought you could use the cover of darkness. So we took the lights out for you, and when our guys saw you two jump out the window, the lieutenant ordered us to rappel into the courtyard to get you. After that, well, you know the rest."

"I just want to say thank you, Chief," Cole said. "I appreciate the effort. I know it's what you guys do for a living—hell, it's what you live for—but it makes a difference to me."

"Ditto, Chief. That was an excellent piece of work," Logan said sincerely. "Hopefully, we can get back to the US Embassy without further incident."

"It's a little more than eighty miles away, which is why we have a Marine Corps CH-53E staged twenty miles from here. It'll pick us up and take us back to sovereign soil," Chief Sorenson said.

"The embassy had a CH-53 in country?" Logan asked incredulously.

"Negative," Chief Sorenson said. "You don't miss a thing, do you? We got lucky on that count. There are actually *two* here, supporting a USAID mission. The crews are Marines, but they fly in civvies to keep things friendly with the locals. I think they even grew beards and let their hair get out of regs," he said dramatically. It was common knowledge Marines were more stringent about grooming standards than any other branch of the service. "The birds have no weapons on them as part of the agreement between us and the Sudanese government," he finished.

"I had no idea," Logan said.

"We were just as shocked, but we figured we may as well take advantage of it. And the Marines were happy to help, even if they can't talk about it back home after this is all over," the chief added.

"I'm sure they are," Logan said, staring out into the pitch-black night. "How much farther before we're in the clear?"

"Ten minutes or so," Chief Sorenson said, and then spoke into a microphone he wore around his neck. "How's it looking up there, sir?" he asked his commanding officer in the jeep in front of them.

The truck hit a shallow pothole and bounced, the Mercedes's shocks efficiently dispersing the energy from the jolt.

A deep, low rumbling grew in the distance, entering the noisy cab in waves through the open window.

A chill ran across Logan's neck. *Oh no,* he thought. *It can't be.*

"Chief," Logan said, hiding his sudden concern under his ever-present calm facade. "Please tell me your lieutenant already called the helo, and it's on its way."

"Wait one," Chief Sorenson said, and then asked Lieutenant Reed over the radio. "That's a negative. Why?"

"Because we've got an inbound bird. I can hear it in the distance. It's getting closer."

"Great," Cole said. "Just what we need."

"Chief, let your lieutenant and our guys in the back know. Tell him to kill his lights on the jeep. You too. Any of you packing an M79, by chance?" Logan asked, referring to the 40mm grenade launcher that dated back to Vietnam but was still a preferred weapon of the SEALs.

"As a matter of fact, we are," Chief Sorenson answered. "What do you have in mind?"

"It depends," Logan said.

"Roger," the chief said, and informed his commanding officer. He changed channels on the radio and spoke quickly, telling the team members in the back of the truck about the incoming helicopter and to load the M79s.

"Now what?" Chief Sorenson asked, slowing the vehicle in the dark and maintaining a safe distance between himself and the jeep as he kept it visible.

"Now we wait and see if he can find us," Logan said in an eerily calm voice. "I'd be shocked if he doesn't, since I'm sure he's flying with night-vision goggles, but if he does, we knock him the fuck out of the sky."

———

Lau Gang watched the commandeered vehicles through night-vision goggles the copilot had provided him as the two vehicles worked their way northward. The heavily armored Russian Mi-24 Hind helicopter gunship—one of six the Sudanese government had purchased—maintained a standoff distance of two miles, a distance the war bird could easily cover the moment Gang gave the order.

He was furious with himself for letting the situation spiral this out of control, even though the main objective in Sudan had been achieved. He was a man accustomed to controlling all aspects of an operation, and in the last ten minutes, he'd been blindsided on two fronts. Liu had just called him from one of the cargo trucks to inform him that the rest of his team had been slaughtered in an assault at the campsite and that he was trying to get off the island before the Americans captured him. That call had come moments after an earlier call to the prison control room had been interrupted by gunfire. The line—and likely the guard—had gone dead.

Somehow, the Americans and their allies had simultaneously reclaimed their two missing operatives and pinpointed the location of the ONERING. He'd told Liu that he'd be in route as soon as he dealt with the escaping Americans.

It would be so easy to order the pilot to destroy the convoy with the Hind's assortment of rockets, missiles, or its single 23mm twin-barrel cannon.

Gang still wanted at least one or two Americans alive, to interrogate them to see what they knew, even though he knew it was a risk. Logan West and Cole Matthews could be on either the truck or the jeep. There was no way to find out which one. His mind raced through his options.

The two vehicles continued to wind their way along the Nile, seemingly oblivious to the Hind's presence, which wouldn't be the case for much longer.

"Catch up to them and pull alongside the jeep. I want to see all four passengers. Use the river but continue to keep internal and external lights off. They'll hear us coming, but we don't want to make it any easier for them to spot us. And even if they do, what can they really do about it?" Gang said. If he didn't see Logan or Cole, he'd order the pilot to destroy the jeep.

"Roger," the Sudanese Air Force pilot responded. He'd been given explicit orders from the defense minister's office—*Do whatever Mr. Lau asks*. A born pilot, he'd been trained on the Hind since his government had purchased it six years ago, and he loved every second he'd spent with the powerful war machine. He felt invincible, especially against the rebels in Darfur. Some of the aerial assaults he'd been ordered to execute on villages had felt like a video game, albeit one played with real lives. He relived every moment of every raid through the helicopter's FLIR cameras and reveled in the awesome power of the mechanical beast. He would do nothing to jeopardize his assignment, least of all disobey a VIP he was ordered to accommodate.

He twisted the collective control next to his seat with his left hand and pushed the cyclic control stick forward with his right. The Hind tilted forward and increased its speed as it descended from its thousand-foot altitude toward its targets.

Gang stared at the barren alien landscape, accentuated by the lunar illumination. He longed for the lush, green hills of his homeland, but he knew they might be lost to him forever if he didn't fully succeed in Sudan.

The Hind had cut the distance in half when the two vehicles turned their lights off just before they veered right at a bend in the river, suddenly disappearing behind a low berm naturally formed by the sloping land. It didn't matter. They'd be upon the Americans in another thirty seconds, and then he'd take action, ending this cat-and-mouse game. The situation would be easier to control if there were only one vehicle remaining—and fewer American commandos.

"Drop down to the river and use it to make your approach. Don't let them see us coming from above," Gang ordered. He'd exploit any tactical advantage that presented itself, and the berm they'd just turned behind would serve nicely.

———

Logan had been searching for an ambush site from the moment he'd heard the helicopter. Lieutenant Reed and Chief Sorenson had concurred, agreeing an ambush might be their only chance to escape.

With clear fields of fire and concealment provided by the terrain, Logan had realized that inserting themselves in the ditch and surrounding rocks of the berm gave them the best chance they'd have to knock the bird out of the sky.

Lieutenant Reed and Chief Sorenson had stopped the vehicles, and every team member had disembarked from the truck and jeep, taking only their weapons and sprinting into the ditch in a single line that ran parallel to the road and river behind it, establishing a perfect linear ambush kill zone. Logan and Cole were the last ones in place, diving into the ditch seconds before the helicopter appeared like the grim reaper of mechanical death.

The roar of the helicopter shattered the landscape's relative calm. The ground shook as the bird neared their location, and Logan watched ripples appear on the otherwise calm waters of the Nile.

A few more seconds, Logan thought. The plan was simple but risky, and they'd only have a single moment to take advantage of their tactical surprise.

Logan waited, breathing hard as he looked over the sights of his AK-47, aimed toward the river and its banks, only twenty yards behind the parked vehicles.

The reverberation of sound intensified across the water and off the berm with each second.

The SEALs were in position and needed no guidance from him, as Chief Sorenson had pleasantly reminded him. "We got this. Just enjoy the show."

The helicopter appeared from behind the berm and hovered fifteen feet above the flowing Nile, a black phantom with a deafening roar and a raging rotor wash that sent water showering over their parked vehicles. The helicopter maintained its position, exposing its starboard side, as if it were a living, breathing predator assessing its prey before it pounced.

No one had realized they might be facing the most fearsome of attack helicopters, but it wouldn't have changed the plan. From the large silhouette, the weapons hanging off two angled wings, and the bulbous low-profile cockpit that made Soviet pilots unofficially nickname it the "crocodile," Logan identified the last thing he wanted to see—a Russian Mi-24 Hind attack helicopter. *Fuck me.*

Also nicknamed the "flying tank" due to its heavily armored body, Logan knew it only had three vulnerable points—the tail rotor, the air intakes below the main rotor assembly, and an oil tank near the fuselage.

The Hind rotated quickly, its nose now pointed directly at the vehicles, its external lights still off, although Logan could see the faint illumination from the instrument panel inside the cockpit. Once the beast had turned, Logan knew they had only one realistic target.

"Aim just below the rotor assembly!" Logan screamed above the din of the Hind's blades.

From a ditch between the road and the berm behind it, two SEALs opened fire with M79 grenade launchers, while the rest of the SEAL team, along with Logan and Cole, opened fire with their automatic weapons.

Thwump! Thwump!

Two 40mm grenades sailed toward the Hind as the pilot realized a moment too late that he'd flown directly into a trap.

The automatic gunfire from sixteen weapons was almost loud enough to drown out the roar of the rotors, but the gunfire was only a distraction. Logan knew the Hind's armor could stop anything up to a .50-caliber round. Their only chance was in the accuracy of the SEAL grenadiers.

The two SEALs didn't wait for the grenades to hit. They released the barrels and dumped the high-explosive casings before reloading, closing the barrels in unison. They were so proficient that they completed the reload as the first two grenades struck their target.

Two explosions shook the Hind just above the cockpit as the gunner opened fire in return, delivering a barrage of destructive four-barrel 12.7mm cannon fire. Unfortunately for the gunner, the pilot pulled up, and the heavy-caliber rounds chewed up the berm above the SEALs, spraying them with a drizzle of dust and rocks.

The Hind lifted a few feet into the air as the pilot attempted to escape the kill zone.

Thwump! Thwump!

A moment later, two more grenades struck the Hind just below the rotors. The explosions sent shrapnel ricocheting off the pilot's canopy and directly into the starboard intake vent. There was a sudden burst of flame as the engine internally disintegrated, and smoke poured out of the intake's opening.

Logan heard one of the SEALs hollering, taunting the war machine as he and his teammates continued to fire.

The Hind, wounded but not crippled—its port engine now operating at full power to compensate for the lost engine—lifted up and away across the river, leaving a trail of black smoke behind.

The SEALs ceased their fire. Logan heard Lieutenant Reed say, "Not too shabby, Parker. I guess even a city boy from Chicago gets lucky once in a while."

"Fuck you, sir, with all due respect. That wasn't luck," Petty Officer Parker shot back.

"No kidding, sir," the other grenadier said. "We can't both be lucky. We're just that good."

Chief Sorenson laughed. "He's got a point, sir."

"Fine, fine," Lieutenant Reed said, a serious and proud look on his face as he turned to his two SEALs. "That was pretty good. Hopefully, those motherfuckers crash and burn."

"Amen to that, sir," Chief Sorenson said. "Time to load back up, drive north for another ten minutes just to make sure that asshole doesn't return, and then call in our evac. What do you say?"

"I think that's a fine idea, Chief," Lieutenant Reed said, and then turned to Logan and Cole. "How are you two holding up? Having fun yet?"

"Just like old times for me, Lieutenant," Logan said.

"As for me, now I know how the mujahideen in Afghanistan must've felt every time they shot down a Russian helicopter," Cole said. "That was pretty intense and a little crazy."

"That's the way we do things, Mr. Matthews," the lieutenant responded. "A little crazy can often go a long way. Now let's get out of here and finally get you two very important people back to the embassy."

CHAPTER 41

"I'll get the driver. You get the device," Amira said as she scrambled out of the Mercedes. She was two steps away from the SUV before John had cleared his door. *Let's see if he can keep up,* she thought, a wry smile forming on her strikingly beautiful face, blue eyes glinting.

"On it!" he shouted as he dashed across the bridge.

Amira reached the passenger side of the precariously positioned truck, leaving John to find the ONERING. The rear bumper was already elevated to her waist, and she heard the metal frame grinding on the edge of the bridge. *We don't have long.*

She inched alongside the vehicle, careful to avoid making any sound as she stepped over the gnarled remains of the first railing the truck had destroyed. The passenger side-view mirror was visible, but due to the elevated angle, its reflection was impossible to see. She knew she was likely creeping into a trap, but she was focused, ready for whatever surprises the driver had in store for her.

Bang!

Amira flinched slightly at the noise before realizing that it was John opening the rear of the cargo truck. *Don't be so jumpy.*

She reached the passenger door and waited below the open window. More sounds emanated from the truck's bed, but still nothing from the cab. *Maybe he's dead,* she thought. *Or more likely, he's aiming a gun and waiting for you to show your face so he can blow it off.*

She couldn't approach from the driver's side because all he had to do to was lean out and open fire. She'd be a sitting duck. The roof was out of the question because her approach would make too much noise. No. It had to be this way. Hopefully, if the driver were still conscious, he would be distracted by the sounds of John's searching. If not, she'd find out soon enough.

She planted one black boot on the large runner under the door and grabbed the handle with her left hand as she withdrew a compact SIG SAUER 9mm pistol she carried for close-quarters situations. She'd left the Steyr tactical machine pistol in the SUV. She was as lethal with a pistol as she was with her stilettos. Her professional pride and proficiency demanded expertise with all the tools of her unique trade.

It's now or never, she thought, and leaned up to catch a glimpse inside the cab from the mirror.

Blood poured down the face of the man who leaned against the door, a middle-aged Chinese operative who had the look of an experienced veteran. A black pistol was aimed in her direction. Their eyes met, and he opened fire.

BAM! BAM! BAM!

The noise of the shots was magnified by the cab's confines. The bullets struck the metal frame next to the window, sending vibrations shuddering up Amira's arm as she quickly ducked down.

No way to get a clean shot without getting your head blown off. Her subconscious then added, *I don't think John would like that.*

A sudden grinding screech rang out from beneath the vehicle, and the cab lurched forward. Amira leapt onto the runner as the middle of the cab passed through the second railing and into the open night air.

Realizing this might be her only opportunity, she stood and exposed herself as she took aim with the SIG SAUER. She'd guessed correctly—the vehicle's sudden movement had panicked the driver, distracting him from the threat of her attack. He was struggling to free himself from the shoulder seat belt that held him in its grip.

As his momentary panic subsided, Yin Liu looked up at the deadly assassin, her upper body framed in the window like an avenging angel suspended in the air. His pistol lay on the seat next to him, ignored as he struggled with the seat belt. He realized he didn't have a chance to defend himself. He still wanted to live. He did the only thing he could—raised his hands in surrender.

Amira didn't react, the pistol trained on his head never wavering.

"What now?" the man asked in English.

She contemplated a moment before responding. "Toss me your cell phone," she said. "The one on the dashboard."

She didn't ask for my pistol? Maybe I still have a chance, Liu thought. He slowly reached forward and extended his arm to where the glass met the PVC surface of the dashboard. He grabbed the phone and carefully threw it to her. It landed short of her outstretched hand and fell to the passenger seat, sliding forward due to the angle of the cab. It stopped at the edge of the bench seat.

Amira's gaze was steady, and she didn't avert her eyes from his. She carefully switched the pistol to her left hand and leaned further into the cab, her right arm feeling for the phone on the seat. Her hand explored the leather until it touched the cell's hard shell.

The truck tilted forward yet again, and Amira felt the cell phone slide off the edge. *Damnit!*

Taking her eyes off the driver for a split second, she shot her hand out and grabbed the phone as it fell off the seat. But that moment was all he needed.

Yin Liu knew the unexpected movement had this time given him an advantage, as it had given his deadly female attacker the tactical edge a few moments earlier. His hand grasped for the pistol, and once he'd secured it, he raised his eyes to his target as he lifted his arm.

The woman was smiling at him, her lips an all-knowing line that turned up only slightly at the ends, accentuating her beautiful features. *She expected it. She's good, better than me,* he thought right before his world went black.

BAM!

The round struck him in the head above his right eye, sending a spray of blood against the headrest. As the seat belt released, his body slumped forward and slid off the seat, coming to rest as a mere pile of flesh and bone under the steering column.

Tough luck, Amira thought, and holstered her pistol on her right hip. She'd expected him to try something. *I almost would've been disappointed if he hadn't.*

"John!" Amira screamed. She scrambled along the running board toward the rear of the truck, now elevated even higher. "Do you have it? The driver's dead, and we need to get the hell off this thing before we go for a swim."

She reached the surface of the bridge, dropped down, and ran to the back of the vehicle. Staring down at her from the end of the truck several feet above was John Quick, a confident, mischievous grin on his grizzled face. He was holding a black Pelican case the size of a footlocker.

"What took you so long?" he said playfully. "You want to give me a hand with this thing, please?"

"While you were finding the Ark of the Covenant, I was obtaining the driver's cell phone for future intelligence value," she said, smiling back at him before holding up the black phone she'd retrieved.

"Well, unless you're going to phone a friend to help me, can you put it away so I can slide this down to you? Like you said, I don't need to go back in the Nile. I've already been swimming once tonight."

"Quit complaining and give me the case," Amira said, and secured the phone in a pocket on her vest.

John didn't respond but slid the heavy case over the edge of the truck.

Amira grabbed it at shoulder height and secured it against her torso as John released it. She stepped backward and carefully squatted to the ground, setting the case on the pavement.

"That wasn't so—" was all John had time to say before there was a loud crash as the rear chassis broke in half and the tangled railing released its hold on the cargo truck.

The vehicle suddenly slid forward and John launched himself off the back of the truck, sailing through the air. With nothing to break his fall, he landed with a loud smack on the pavement, the wind knocked out of his lungs. Seconds later, a loud splash signaled the final fate of the truck and its dead occupant.

He gasped for breath and rolled over, only to see the beautiful figure of Amira Cerone standing over him, staring down with a look of bemusement.

"You going to lounge around all night? Or can we please get this highly dangerous piece of equipment in our SUV and get the hell off this bridge before God-knows-what authorities get here?" She bent over and offered her hand. "Come on. Get up." She helped pull him up as his lungs struggled to refill their oxygen supply.

"Thanks," he muttered in between short breaths.

She picked up one end of the case by its hard-plastic handle as he hoisted up the other. As they slowly walked the cargo toward the back of the SUV, Amira said, "Nice jump, by the way."

"Thanks, although I usually try to do a flip with my dismounts," he said, grinning at her, his composure regained.

"Uh-huh. Maybe you can practice some more when we get back to the embassy," Amira said as they lifted the case into the SUV and John closed the hatch. "But first, radio the rest of the team and find out where they are. Tell them we're on our way with the package. We'll meet them at the embassy. We also need to call the station chief and let him know what happened. He's going to have to call DC with an update."

As John slid into the driver's seat, he turned to her and said, "Anything else you'd like me to do while I'm at it?"

"I can probably think of something," Amira said slyly, meeting his eyes.

His heart raced at the words. *You're so screwed, John.*

CHAPTER 42

US Embassy, Khartoum

The CH-53E touched down inside the compound on a designated helicopter landing zone behind the main building of the embassy. Under normal circumstances, the HLZ would've been used for loading US personnel and citizens in the event of a noncombatant evacuation operation, or NEO. In this case, it was dropping off two very weary passengers and sixteen satisfied US Navy SEALs.

Logan walked down the ramp of the helicopter and turned left, keeping his head lowered as he'd been taught years ago at the end of Officer Candidate School. "Turn right, and you just might get a haircut you won't recover from, Candidate," the crew chief on his first CH-53E ride had yelled at him. *Some things just stick with you,* he thought.

Cole exited the helicopter right behind him, and they made a beeline for the main building, where David Cross and another man they didn't recognize were waiting.

"Mr. West, Mr. Matthews, I can't tell you how good it is to have you both back with us," David said, a sincere look of relief on his face. He held out his hand and shook Logan's first, followed by Cole's.

"Mr. West, I'm Wendell Sharp," said the second man, an older African American with graying hair.

"I have you to thank for the rescue?" Logan asked.

"We helped coordinate, but that was all JSOC. We had our hands full with something else, which we'll tell you all about inside," Wendell said.

"Mr. Sharp," Cole said curiously, pausing, "by chance, were you in Algiers six years ago?"

Wendell raised his eyes at Cole and said, "As a matter of fact, I was." He paused and then added, "But I don't remember you."

"We hit a target there, a local extremist who'd attacked an oil refinery and kidnapped several hostages, including two Americans. We never met, but your intelligence package was fantastic. My team memorized it, including the locations and details for the hostages. Thank you," Cole said.

"I'm just glad that incident had a positive outcome," Wendell said. "Not all of them do."

"Very true," Cole replied.

"Come on. Let's get inside so we can bring you up to speed. Plus, you have some friends who I'm sure would love to see you," Wendell said.

Logan was about to respond when Lieutenant Reed and Chief Sorenson walked by, making their way to the glass doors.

"Lieutenant Reed, Chief Sorenson, hold up a sec!" Logan said loudly to get their attention over the spinning rotors, which slowed as the pilot powered down the helicopter.

The two SEALs turned toward him, and Chief Sorenson said something to his commanding officer. They changed course, stopping directly in front of Logan.

"Mr. West, what, pray tell, can we do for you now?" Chief Sorenson asked good-naturedly.

"Absolutely nothing, Chief," Logan said. "I just wanted to personally thank you and your team one last time for what you did. Having been in your shoes once upon a lifetime with Force Recon, we appreciate it."

The two SEALs exchanged a glance, and Lieutenant Reed said, "Mr. West, from what I know about you, we should be thanking you—for Iraq, that is. I got my hands on a classified after-action of that Al Anbar operation. That was a slick piece of work."

"More importantly," Chief Sorenson said seriously, "if you had failed, it would've jeopardized us in that part of the world once again, embroiled in a war with God knows how many countries. So it's really we who should be thanking you."

Logan was caught off guard by the sentiment, the fatigue from the painfully long day finally setting in now that his adrenaline had worn off. He just nodded, which was enough to express his appreciation. It was obvious they understood.

"Plus, what you did to that monster earlier? That was worth the price of admission," Chief Sorenson said suddenly with a grin. "I'll be telling that story to the boys back in Dam Neck. You can count on it."

"Nothing like being famous in one of the most covert units in the US military," Logan said jokingly. "So what's next for you guys?"

"We're going to head inside, conduct maintenance on our gear, and then do a quick debrief. Hopefully," the lieutenant said, now looking at Wendell, "there's some place we can get a hot meal before catching some shut-eye. We've got a C-17 flight out of the airport in the morning. State Department set up a 'diplomatic' flight for us," he said, using his hands as quotation marks for emphasis.

"I'll have the chefs find you. It's the least we can do," Wendell said.

"Sounds like a plan, sir. We appreciate it. Mr. West, Mr. Matthews, it's been fun," Lieutenant Reed said.

"Second that," Chief Sorenson said. "Fun, as in escape-from-a-secret-prison-and-win-a-firefight-with-a-Hind-attack-helicopter kind of fun." Once again turning serious, he added, "See you around, but you also know where we are if you need us. Stay safe, gentlemen."

As Chief Sorenson and Lieutenant Reed walked away, the chief abruptly turned around at the glass doors and fired one last parting shot. "I'd normally advise you to stay out of trouble, but I know that's not possible with you Marines."

"Fucking squid," Logan said.

"Fucking jarhead," the chief shot back, and entered the building before Logan could reply.

———

Logan entered the station chief's conference room, and the tension from the day was forgotten at the sight of his closest friend.

Logan West and John Quick had been through more combat together than either cared to recall. They'd seen their Marines die brutally at the hands of insurgents in Iraq, where they'd been indoctrinated into the real horrors of war and the crushing emotional and psychological toll it took. Yet they both had escaped—one spiraling out of control inside a bottle; the other trying to lose himself in the isolation of the Montana wilderness. But fate had other plans for them, and they'd been thrown together again when Cain Frost had launched a personal vendetta against the Iranian government, only to be thwarted by Logan and John at the last minute. Each would lay down his life for the other, and John had displayed that type of love one brother has for another in the cemetery by trying to buy time for Logan and Cole to make their escape. He'd been willing to sacrifice himself, and the bond they shared was closer than any familial bond either knew. Logan felt the full weight of it when he saw his friend, his brother, for the first time since his capture.

John was studying a laptop screen at the large cherrywood table, and when he saw Logan, followed immediately by Cole and the CIA case officers, he stood up and walked over to meet them.

When Logan reached John, he stopped in front of him, appraising him from head to toe. "Am I ever glad to see your ugly mug," Logan said, his voice thick. "Looks like you're still in one piece. I'm just glad you were the one who got away." He grasped John by the arms, unflinching in his affection, green eyes blazing into his friend's battle-hardened face, and said, "What you tried to do for us in the cemetery, that was as selfless as anything I've ever seen." He paused, his voice steady but raw with emotion. "You know I'd do the same for you, without hesitation."

John Quick, normally fast to respond with a razor-edged comment, just nodded, the display of affection suppressing his sarcastic impulses. "I know, brother. I know."

Logan embraced him. "You know I love you, right?"

John smiled and pulled back slightly. "I love you too," he said and then added, "Just don't get any ideas."

"You're not my type," Logan said, and released him, eyeing the newcomer. "So who's your new friend?" he asked, assessing the stunningly beautiful woman who stood silently before him. She possessed gorgeous pale-blue eyes and an African ethnic background Logan couldn't identify. He sensed an inner strength concealed beneath her athletic physique. He realized what it was a moment later. After spending a lifetime around trained killers with extremely strong moral compasses, it was impossible to miss, *She's an operator. Not the Special Forces kind but some other.*

"Logan, allow me to introduce you to Ms. Amira Cerone, this embassy's LEGION operative. She's the reason I made it out of the cemetery. And Logan—this I swear—she's as lethal as you. God's honest truth," John said.

Amira scowled at John for the uninvited praise. "Flattery will get you nowhere." She looked at Logan and said, "He's just being nice."

Logan's curious expression had turned to one of respect at the mention of the clandestine program. He offered his hand. "I highly doubt that. John's a lot of things, but prone to exaggeration, he's not. Regardless, it's a pleasure and an honor to meet you. Thank you for helping him. I won't forget it."

Amira only nodded, unaccustomed to the open appreciation. Due to the level of secrecy her work required, the only thanks she ever received was an occasional innocuous email from one of the deputy directors and the regular GS14 paycheck that was deposited into a bank in Falls Church. Ironically, since she was out of the country so much, she was hardly home enough to enjoy the substantial savings she'd accumulated.

Logan released her hand and looked around the room, his eyes stopping at the black Pelican case on the table. He looked back at John and asked, "Is that what I think it is?"

"It is," John said. "While you were away at Spa Sudan—which you'll have to tell me all about later—we recovered the ONERING. Oh, and we took out all the Chinese mercenaries, or whatever the hell they were."

"Chinese Special Forces and intelligence operatives," Amira injected. "These guys weren't your run-of-the-mill covert unit. They were elite. We just happened to be tactically smarter and caught them off guard, which can happen to even the best."

"Yes. It can," Logan said, vividly recalling the ambush at the insurgent compound in Fallujah in 2004. "But as for getting them all, you're wrong on that count."

"How so?" John asked.

"At the cemetery, there was a guy with short, black hair. Only in his midtwenties, he was the one coordinating the entire thing. I saw him. The way he acted, I have no doubt he was in charge. I'll tell you about him later, but—"

"We may not have to wait until later," Amira said. "We captured one of his team alive at the cemetery. We interrogated him after you two were captured. We were in the process of breaking him, but then we got word from DC they had your location, as well as the ONERING's. So we never followed up. He's recovering in the medical wing from surgery. I have no doubt he'll talk."

"Surgery?" Logan asked. "What did you do to him?"

"I cut off one of his fingers," Amira said flatly.

Logan studied her slack-jawed for a moment, his admiration increasing. John's comment about her lethality echoed in his head.

"Good," Logan finally responded. "As for the cemetery team's leader, we had a run-in with a Hind helicopter during our exfil with the SEALs, and if he's the one calling the shots, I'm betting he was on it. So he's still out there, but God knows where."

"We might be able to help with that too," Amira said. "I recovered a phone from one of the dead guys. We've transferred its contents to Langley for digital forensic analysis, including call chaining and geospatial metadata analysis, and I'm willing to bet your guy's cell comes up. It just depends on how quickly Langley gets back to us."

"That's excellent work, Ms. Cerone," Logan said. "Now I'd like to give Mike a call in Vegas to check in and see how he's progressing on his end."

There was a pause in the room, and Logan felt a shift in the air as John let out a rush of breath.

"What is it, John?" Logan asked. "Spit it out. You know bad news doesn't get better with time."

"There's been an attack at the MGM Grand Casino. Several dozen casualties. The bad guys are dressed in battle fatigues, black masks, and maroon scarves, almost like Islamic extremists, but who knows who they really are with everything else going on," John said.

"Why? These guys would be happy to massacre Americans anywhere they can," Logan said.

"I find it almost impossible to believe that the Chinese or the Russians—especially the Russians, with all of their problems in Chechnya fighting Islamic extremism—would be working with a cell of radical terrorists."

"You're probably right. Makes sense," Logan said.

"Occasionally, I do," John shot back. "My guess is it's a professional crew who's been paid to make it look like a terrorist attack, which leads me to my next point—it has to be part of the larger picture, which we still can't see."

Logan shook his head in disgust. "These bastards have been ahead of us at every turn. We need to start hitting back—and hard."

"At least in Vegas, the FBI HRT—Lance Foster's crew—is on scene. Last we heard on the news was that they were holed up with hostages in a theater that runs one of those Cirque du Soleil shows."

"Wait a second—so where's Mike?" Logan asked.

"I tried to call him earlier. There was no answer on his phone. So I called DC," John said. "They put me through to the director's office."

"You talked to his uncle?" Logan asked.

"No. One of his senior executive assistants. Jake wasn't in the office. But his assistant was instructed to let us know that Mike was investigating a separate lead outside Vegas at a place called American Elemental, a rare earth elements mine."

"Rare earth elements? What the hell does all this have to do with rare earth elements?" Logan asked.

"It gets worse," John said. "You never asked how we located the ONERING. After you were captured, the Chinese activated it, hijacked some supersecret US space-based weapon, and attacked a Chinese oil exploration site near the South Sudan border."

"*What?*" Logan asked incredulously.

"And guess who's getting the blame?" John asked with utter disdain. "The Chinese have requested an emergency UN Security Council meeting to request sanctions against *us*. It's a sham, but we're the only ones who know it, unless we can somehow use the data on the ONERING to prove otherwise."

"I don't even want to touch that thing," Logan said. "It's brought nothing but death and misery to us and our country today. Tolkien would be furious. 'One ring to rule them all,' my ass. More like 'One ring to set off a global calamity.' What a fucking mess. We just need to get it back to DARPA in one piece. Let *them* analyze it."

"So what now?" Wendell Sharp asked. He'd remained silent during the impromptu debriefing, but he needed to know how they wanted to proceed so he could plan accordingly, especially if the truth required a cover story.

Logan considered for a moment before answering. He looked around the room at his friends and new allies, people willing to fight and sacrifice for the right ideals, the right principles.

"The SEAL team has a C-17 under a State Department charter departing in the morning," Logan said. "We accomplished what we came here to do. We take the ONERING and our prisoner and get back to the US, and then we let the State Department and DC deal with the political blowback. Our job is done."

The nods assured him he'd made the right decision. There'd been enough blood shed on Sudanese soil. It was time to go home.

PART VI

A MAGNIFICENT VIEW

AMERICAN ELEMENTAL WILD HORSE MOUNTAIN FACILITY

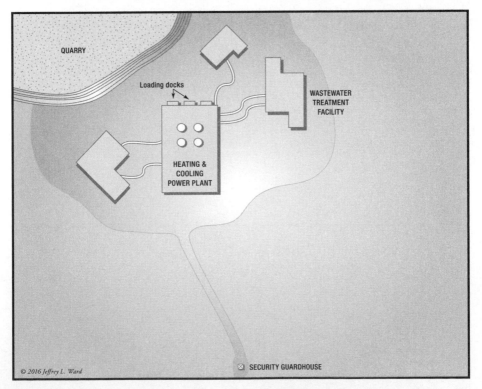

QUARRY

Loading docks

WASTEWATER
TREATMENT
FACILITY

HEATING &
COOLING
POWER PLANT

© 2016 Jeffrey L. Ward

SECURITY GUARDHOUSE

CHAPTER 43

American Elemental, Wild Horse Mountain Facility

Once the black Suburban had fought its way out of the Vegas city limits, the rest of the drive to the rare earth elements production facility had been a smooth ride. It was a thirty-mile straight shot northwest on US Route 95 to the exit that had been built specially for the sprawling complex.

After the conversation he'd had with his uncle about the potential source of the intelligence leak—*actually, a fucking traitor*—Mike Benson had used the time to clear his head and focus his thoughts. The drive also afforded him the opportunity to contact the facility and check with security at Wild Horse. Unfortunately, all calls to the various numbers listed on the company's website ended in the same automated message from the phone carrier—"We're sorry, but your call cannot be completed at this time. Please try your call again later. Thank you and have a nice day."

It'd been a bad omen, but rather than assume the worst, Special Agent Marcus had reached the company's CEO through the field office. He'd assured her that the loss of communications was actually a common occurrence since they'd begun construction of the facility. It was usually due to heavy equipment cutting one of the various large fiber-optic cables that snaked underground all over the facility and exited the premises through one large pipe that led to Indian Springs, thirty miles away.

The CEO promised he'd call Matt Stillman, the head of his small security detail, just to ensure everything was okay. Less than five minutes later, he'd proven true to his word and called back to report nothing out of the ordinary at the facility. Security was aware of the communications outage, and they'd already been assured that a repair crew had been dispatched from Indian Springs and should arrive within the hour. He'd asked Matt to do another walk-through of the major production buildings and report back to him once he was finished.

It all seemed copacetic, but Mike didn't believe in coincidences, not with the attack on the MGM Grand.

"Lance, I still don't like this. I don't care what the CEO says," Mike said as he turned to face the head of the FBI's HRT Red Team, which specialized in counterterrorism and in extremis hostage rescue operations. Lance Foster was an imposing figure, a midfortyish African American in phenomenal shape who wore a sharply defined goatee.

"I know, sir," Lance said, addressing Mike with the professional courtesy due his position, although they'd been close friends for years. "We're still in khakis and you might look like a suit, but we both know we're all ready to rock 'n' roll at a moment's notice," Lance said, smiling.

"Good. That's exactly what I want to hear. Be prepared for anything," Mike said.

"Don't worry, brother. Me and my gang," he said, referring with a thumb over his shoulder to Special Agents Jason Champion, a former Navy SEAL and EOD technician, and Tommy Chaney, a former Delta operator and expert marksman, in the third row of the Suburban, "we've got your back."

The two lethal HRT members leaned in toward one another, smiled, and formally waved at the deputy director of the FBI as if they were queens of England.

"I'm surrounded by children. No offense, Special Agent Marcus," Mike said, and shook his head.

"None taken, sir. They're just like my big brothers," Special Agent Marcus said, showing no intimidation at the playful display of immaturity, yet silently wondering how she'd ended up in the Suburban.

The daughter of a pediatrician and a criminal defense attorney, she'd gravitated toward her father's profession in law by the early age of nine. By the time she was in high school in the suburbs of Chicago, she knew she didn't want to defend criminals; instead, she wanted to put them away, permanently. Her path had become tragically clear when a former associate of one of her father's clients had shot and killed him as he'd left his office one evening. It'd been retribution for her father's not being able to avoid the death penalty for his client, who'd ordered the murder of a Korean family, including two young children.

Special Agent Marcus was driven by her anger—which she'd learned to harness—to earn a spot in the renowned Violent Criminal Apprehension Program. Her plan had been to excel at her field assignment in Las Vegas and then apply to ViCAP at the first opportunity.

Yet now she found herself in an armored Suburban driving the deputy director, the chief of the FBI's HRT Red Team, and two superbly trained shooters. *Definitely didn't see this one coming,* she thought as the Suburban approached an open gate at the end of the dirt road.

A newly constructed guard shack divided the entrance, and she noted the bulletproof glass. A rising arm traffic barrier was lowered across the road. She stopped the black SUV. Beyond the guardhouse lay the expansive sprawl of American Elemental's Wild Horse Mountain Facility. The dirt road gradually sloped downward, affording them a bird's-eye view of the layout.

Several buildings of varying size and shapes, like giant Tetris pieces, stood in close proximity to one another. They resembled ordinary—albeit enormous—warehouses, but Special Agent Marcus recognized their true purposes as components of the rare earth element production process. Multiple exhaust pipes, ventilation systems, and aqueducts ran throughout the compound between buildings.

A complex power station comprised of multiple buildings and towering exhaust stacks several stories tall occupied the center of the compound. Steel girders containing power lines jutted out in several directions, working their way in ninety-degree angles to all buildings in the complex.

It's like an enormous Erector Set, she thought, recalling a long-forgotten toy from her childhood.

And just beyond it all was a vast hole in the earth at least a half mile wide—the ore deposit. Only the first forty feet were visible, exposing a layer of narrow roads carved into the sides of the enormous bowl. The dirt and rock roads spiraled downward and dropped below their line of sight into the high-desert pit.

"Wow," Lance said from the backseat. "That's quite a view, including plenty of potential targets for the bad guys to hit."

"No kidding," Mike said as a young guard wearing a uniform and a Glock 9mm pistol exited the guardhouse and approached the vehicle.

Special Agent Marcus rolled down her window, and the young guard leaned in to speak, only to be interrupted by Mike.

"I'm FBI Deputy Director Mike Benson," Mike said. The young man raised his eyes in surprise at the mention of his title. "I believe you're expecting us. I was told by the CEO to find Matt Stillman, and he'd escort us through the facility."

Chirping from a cell phone erupted in the backseat.

"Yes, sir. We've been waiting for you guys," the college-age guard said. "Mr. Stillman's not back yet, and I've been trying to reach him since I saw you driving down the road. He should've been back by now."

Mike and Special Agent Marcus exchanged glances as Lance Foster answered the call.

"This is Special Agent Foster." A pause as he listened to his second in command. "You're secure, Danny. Go ahead."

"Son, what's your name?" Mike asked.

"It's Eugene Wabash, sir," the guard replied. "Why?" he asked cautiously.

"Well, Eugene. We're going to need your help. When was the last time you spoke to your boss?" Mike asked.

From the back seat, Mike heard, "That's absolutely fantastic, Danny. Outstanding job. I'll let the deputy director know. I'm sure he'll be as relieved as I am."

"About ten minutes ago, sir," Eugene replied. "He'd checked all the main buildings and was proceeding to the power plant. He reported nothing unusual. We've only got a skeleton crew working. They're finishing up production of the wastewater treatment facility. Otherwise, everything else is done. One more thing—landline external communications are still down. No ETA on when they're supposed to be back up."

Mike felt a mounting sense of persistent concern in the back of his mind. It wasn't panic yet, more akin to a dog scratching at the back door to be let in from the cold.

"Copy all, Danny. Let forensics do their thing. Tell Special Agent Hunt we just arrived at the facility—literally, we're at the guard-house—and we'll check in after we get a look around. Again, great job. Next round's on me. Out here," Lance said, and hung up the phone and waited for Mike to finish with the guard before providing his update.

"Eugene, can you point us in the direction of the power plant, although I'm guessing it's the one in the middle with the four tall stacks?" Mike said, pointing through the windshield and down the road.

Eugene nodded.

"You have an extra Motorola handheld we can borrow? I need you to stay here and man the gate, but I need to be able to reach you."

"Yes, sir. Give me one sec," Eugene said, and disappeared from the window.

Mike turned around to meet the smiling face of Lance Foster. *Thank God. It must be good news,* he thought.

"Tell me," he said, hoping his assumption was correct.

"It's over," Lance said. "Danny and his team took out all the bad guys, all four—dead—without any more civilian or friendly casualties. Forensics just arrived and is processing the scene. The civilians wounded in the initial assault are being transferred to Valley Medical and University hospitals."

"How?" Past experience had taught Mike the harsh realities of hostage rescue operations, especially when the hostiles weren't interested in negotiating, which had been the case with these terrorists.

"The bad guys secured the entrances and backstage exits to the theater. But this theater is enormous, seats hundreds, and has a gigantic stage they can manipulate and change during each show. In addition to the stage, there's a catwalk architecture that's used during shows for aerial acrobatics. Danny and his team realized one of the catwalks was right below a major heating and cooling air duct. They inserted four shooters without being detected. He said it was shockingly easy because they never looked up once. Guess they hadn't seen the shows. Too bad for them. The hostages made more than enough noise to conceal any sounds from our guys. Plus, they were almost seventy feet up and in the dark, above the lights. The fuckers never had a chance. Danny gave the order as soon as they were in place, and they took 'em all out at once—clean head shots," Lance said proudly.

"That's fantastic. The best news I've heard since this whole affair started," Mike said, a tsunami of relief washing over him.

"No kidding," Lance said, sharing the brief moment of victory. And then he laughed. "It initially traumatized the civilians, seeing the terrorists drop dead from bullet wounds to the head, Danny said. But they were able to breach the entrances immediately and evacuate them. By the time it was over, they were just grateful to be alive."

"I'm sure," Mike said. "Do they have any idea who the bastards were?"

"Negative, but they definitely were *not* Islamic terrorists," Lance said. "Once they cleared the theater of civilians, they removed the dead guys' masks. Danny said they looked more Asian than Middle Eastern. They'll be running their prints and DNA through every international database as soon as they can."

"Let's hope this goes as smoothly," Mike said as Eugene approached the vehicle, a black radio in hand.

"Sir, here you go," the guard said, and handed the radio to Special Agent Marcus. "I've set it on channel three, and it's good to go."

Mike's ears perked up. "What did you say, Eugene?"

"I said you're good to go, sir," Eugene answered cautiously.

"Which branch of the service, although I think I can guess?" Mike said, his eyes raised in amusement.

"The only one that matters, sir. The Marine Corps, of course," the guard said proudly, grinning for the first time.

"What the *fuck* did he just say?" one of the two HRT operators in the third row shouted in mock outrage.

Eugene's grin faltered, and Mike laughed. "Son, I've got a former SEAL and a Delta boy back there. I think you hurt their feelings."

Eugene's eyes widened, but he stood his ground. "Those are some tough bastards. I did a tour in Afghanistan and crossed paths with the SEALs a time or two. Didn't see much of Delta, but we heard about their exploits."

He stuck his head partially through the window—making Special Agent Marcus slightly uncomfortable from the close proximity of his grinning face—and said, "No offense intended. I just love the Marine Corps."

Jason Champion and Tommy Chaney exchanged a glance. Jason, the older of the two veterans, said, "None taken. It's a pleasure to meet someone who served in the mountains." He nodded and touched an invisible cap.

Eugene nodded in return and stepped away from the vehicle.

"Now that the lovefest is over, one last question." Mike said. "Eugene, did your laundry trucks arrive today?"

"Yes. About thirty minutes ago. Both of them. Why?" Eugene asked, thinking the question odd.

"You notice anything strange about them? Different drivers, perhaps?"

"As a matter of fact, both drivers were new. I asked them about it, and they said there'd been an illness at the Laundromat," Eugene said.

"Did they have anyone else with them?" Mike asked.

"Negative, sir. Not that I could see, but then again, I didn't check the backs of the trucks. We've been using the same place since we began construction a few years back."

"Thanks, Eugene. And stay available. Let us know if you get comms up," Mike said and turned to Special Agent Marcus. "We need to go. *Now*."

CHAPTER 44

"In front or around back, sir?" Special Agent Marcus asked as she directed the Suburban toward the power plant.

Mike quickly studied the building and turned to Lance in the backseat. "My guess is there's a loading dock out back. If these guys are here, we want to surprise 'em. I say we split up. Who's your best shooter?"

"Chaney," Lance said without hesitation. "Sorry, Champion. It's true, but only slightly."

"No worries, boss," Special Agent Champion said, "but I got him on the demolitions."

Mike nodded. "Special Agent Marcus, Chaney, and I are going in the front. You and Champion take the back." He looked at Lance directly and said, "As good as they are, I know you're better. This balances the teams out."

"You always were a smart bastard," Lance said.

"Maybe. Or maybe I just fooled 'em all into making me deputy director," Mike said, smiling subtly.

"Uh-huh," Lance responded as the vehicle stopped in front of the enormous building.

It was several hundred feet long, four stories tall, and had no windows that Mike could see. A lone set of solid metal double doors stood sentry at this end. *It's just a giant rectangular box with aluminum siding,* Mike thought.

They exited and rallied at the back of the large SUV, weapons drawn. All wore bulletproof vests that announced FBI in large yellow letters.

"Here's the deal. Unless there's some other laundry service we don't know about, whoever stole those vehicles is already inside. We have to assume we have at least two—maybe four—bad guys, possibly with bombs. Treat them as hostile. Take no chances," Mike said, looking at each member of his ad hoc assault team.

The relief at the resolution of the hostage situation at the MGM Grand Casino had dissipated. Even the young Special Agent Marcus looked fiercely determined. *She's going to be one to reckon with as her career progresses,* Mike thought.

"Good. Let's do this. Radio silent. We link up inside." He didn't need to warn them to watch for friendly fire—their level of training would prevent it.

As the team split up, Lance smiled and said, "See you on the back side, brother."

"Not if I see you first, hombre. Now go," Mike shot back as Special Agent Lance Foster and Special Agent Jason Champion disappeared around the southeast corner of the building.

———

This is going to be a lot harder than I thought, Mike realized as soon as they passed through the double doors.

The inside of the facility was cavernous, at least the size of a football field. To complicate matters, the power and heating plant was crammed with enormous equipment chained together as part of the power and steam production process. A mechanical amalgamation, it rose toward the ceiling like a group of fettered animals trying to break free through the roof above.

Directly in front of them were two gigantic rectangular machines that obstructed their view of the rest of the plant. At least thirty feet above them, four large cylindrical exhaust stacks pierced the ceiling.

His Glock raised, Mike turned to his team. "Chaney, take point with the M4. Let's work our way along the exterior wall and avoid this mechanical mess. Use hand signals if you spot anything. Marcus, cover our six."

"On it, sir," Special Agent Chaney said, and quickly assumed the lead position.

They moved silently along the wall, working their way toward the rear of the facility. Since the plant wasn't fully functional, the heavy machinery was operating at a lower capacity, although the hum of turbines still drowned out their every step.

Halfway to the rear of the facility and next to two gigantic flat, cylindrical shapes that looked like enormous, thick flat circles standing on their rims, Special Agent Chaney suddenly stopped and raised his fist in the universal *freeze* gesture. Mike and Special Agent Marcus halted behind him.

Chaney's gaze was directed inward and toward the back of the building. With the M4 locked in his shoulder, his eyes forward, and his right hand on the pistol grip, he used his left hand to beckon Mike to him.

The tension escalating, Mike shuffled quietly until he was within breathing space of Special Agent Chaney, who pointed with his free hand.

"Jackpot," he said quietly.

Mike looked in the direction he indicated, but initially, all he saw was more ductwork and equipment. *What the hell does he see?*

As if reading his mind, Chaney said in a hushed voice, "Look *through* it all, about eighty feet away. You'll see them."

Mike squinted his eyes, and after a few moments, spotted it. Like a painted optical illusion revealing its hidden picture, the scene materialized before him, the gravity of the situation growing by the second.

Through the tangled metal mess of coils and oddly shaped equipment, two figures in white overalls stood behind two laundry trucks speaking so quietly that their words faded into the machines' constant hum. The rear doors of one of the trucks were open, and Mike glimpsed several large oil drums—both blue and yellow—packed into the back of the truck. *Oh no. It's Oklahoma City all over again. Probably some kind of fertilizer/fuel combination. That'll take this whole place down.*

As if that weren't horrifying enough, he spotted a pair of legs attached to a prostrate body, facedown on the industrial floor. *Motherfuckers,* Mike thought. *That has to be Matt Stillman.*

The sense of purposeful righteousness that had fueled his career coursed through his veins, and in a split second, his decision-making process switched. As much as he wanted to take one of these bastards alive for information—and he still would if they surrendered—what he wanted even more was justice, swift and violent, for the unforgivable act these men had committed. It was simple—they didn't deserve to live. They'd forfeited their rights to life the second they'd taken Matt Stillman's.

Mike looked at Tommy Chaney and saw the same fury he felt displayed on the former SEAL's face. There was only one possible course of action that would satisfy them both.

"Okay, then. We take 'em out. No warnings. I'll let Marcus know," Mike said.

"Good," was all Chaney said.

Mike turned around to tell Special Agent Marcus the plan, only to discover a Chinese man in white overalls twenty feet away pointing a black pistol at the back of her head. He realized his fatal oversight. *There were more than two of them, and they sent at least one to maintain security. Fucker must've been hiding in all the machinery, and we walked right past him.* Mike's mind raced, and he reacted in the next split second, pulling Special Agent Marcus down and to the left as he tried to raise his Glock. As good as Mike was, he wasn't fast enough.

Bam!

The echoing shot shattered the silence, accelerating events into overdrive.

The bullet missed Special Agent Marcus as she tumbled to the floor, but Mike felt a searing pain under his right arm as he pulled the trigger on his own weapon.

Bam! Bam!

Special Agent Marcus spun on the floor into a sitting position, her Glock locking on to her would-be killer as she fired.

Red blossoms from both FBI agents' bullets appeared on the man's overalls, and he dropped to his knees, the black pistol clattering to the floor.

The look of contempt on the operative's face was replaced by one of surprised amusement, as if the reality that he'd been shot was somehow funny.

Behind Mike, Special Agent Chaney whirled and his M4 added to the drumbeat of gunfire.

Bam-bam-bam!

Three well-placed bullets took the Chinese shooter's life—as well as his nose and the back of his head. He fell forward with a sickening wet smack.

"Go!" Mike tried to yell, but he dropped to a knee, the pain in his right side nearly paralyzing him. He felt under his arm with his left hand and discovered the bullet had torn the top edge of the bullet-proof vest before entering his body. *An inch lower, and I'd have been okay.*

"Oh shit!" Chaney said as he realized Mike had been hit. He scrambled over, looking for the wound. "How bad is it?"

"I'll be fine," Mike said, gritting the words out through the pain, although he wasn't so sure. His side was wet and warm with blood.

"He got me in the side, above the vest, right as I aimed. Dumb fucking luck."

Shouts in Chinese erupted from the direction of their objective.

"Go now, because I guarantee all hell's about to break loose," Mike said. As if on cue, gunfire erupted from the rear of the power plant.

"Special Agent Marcus will help me, and we'll be right behind you. Now go!"

CHAPTER 45

Special agents Lance Foster and Jason Champion had infiltrated the far side of the power plant without incident. A large loading area that could accommodate several tractor-trailers sloped up to the back of the building. The dock was so wide that three rectangular corrugated doors guarded the entrance; two were lowered shut, but the middle one was raised and provided a glimpse into the darkness.

Rather than risk exposure, they'd found an unlocked corner door and used it to enter the power plant. They paused in the shadows next to a large cylindrical piece of equipment at least thirty feet long and fifteen feet wide.

From their vantage point, they'd seen the two laundry trucks and heard hushed voices behind them. The plan had been simple—quietly gain a better line of sight and determine the level of the threat before neutralizing it as quickly as possible. But then the shooting had started in the middle of the building, and like any good plan, it hadn't survived first contact.

Using the commotion to react quickly, Lance weaved his way along the perimeter of the power plant, looking for an opening to provide a direct pathway to the back of the trucks. He suddenly spotted a gap in the machinery. He stepped into it and scanned the cramped space with his M4.

Bingo.

Thirty feet in front of him stood two Chinese men in white overalls. He wondered whom they were shouting to, and then the realization hit him—*they have more men in here with us.*

Lance turned around to warn Special Agent Champion, who stood crouched just outside the gap. He didn't get the chance.

Two shots rang out—*bam! bam!*—and Lance watched as a hole suddenly appeared in Champion's upper left leg. The wounded HRT shooter fell to the floor in pain and tried to aim his assault rifle toward the source of the gunfire.

Lance dropped to his knee and spotted movement through his red dot reflex scope fifteen feet away on the other side of several large pipes and tubes. He opened fire and hoped several of the bullets would find their way through the metal maze.

He thought he saw the shadowy figure fall, but he wasn't sure until Jason said, "You got the sonofabitch, boss, but I think my leg's fucked."

Lance stepped toward his wounded operator when a loud slam echoed throughout the surrounding equipment. He wheeled around and saw that the doors had been closed on the rear of the truck closest to him—*that can't be good*—and both men had disappeared. *That's* definitely *not good.*

Goddamnit! He had a horrible choice to make, but fortunately, Special Agent Champion made it easy for him.

"Go get those fuckers," Special Agent Champion urged him. "I'll keep pressure on my leg until you get back."

"Shoot anyone who doesn't look like us," Lance said.

"You mean FBI and pissed off?" Special Agent Champion tried to joke through the pain.

"Exactly," Lance said, and turned around, sprinting away through the opening toward the trucks.

———

Mike held his Glock in his left hand, his right arm slung across the shoulders of Special Agent Marcus, who used all the strength she could muster to keep him standing as they shuffled quickly toward the trucks.

Mike heard a small, faraway voice, and he realized it emanated from the handheld Motorola Eugene had given him earlier. *Yes, Eugene. That's gunfire you're hearing. I'll be with you shortly.*

Special Agent Chaney led the way, clearing every nook and dark cranny as he scouted ahead toward the trucks. He reached the last piece of machinery when a loud engine roared to life.

"Oh shit!" Mike said through gritted teeth. "Stop them if you can!"

Special Agent Chaney rounded the corner of the enormous piece of equipment as Lance Foster emerged from a small space thirty feet to his right. The two HRT operators momentarily locked eyes before opening fire.

Bam-bam-bam-bam-bam-bam!

Bullets tore into the metal skin of the truck, which lurched forward. It gained momentum, oblivious to the superficial damage the rounds had caused, and shot down the ramp through the raised doorway. More bullets followed it out to no avail.

The two HRT operators ceased firing and converged on the remaining truck, which had been ominously left behind.

"I don't like this," Special Agent Chaney said. "The deputy director's been hit. I don't know how badly, but we killed one of them."

As if on call, Special Agent Marcus and Mike appeared from behind the equipment.

"We took out one, but Champion took a round in the upper leg," Lance said. "He's going to need some attention in the next few minutes, if he wants to keep it. Let's open this thing up and see what we're dealing with."

The two men opened the doors and were greeted by a small laptop connected to a series of wires that led to several small blocks of white putty. *That's C-4,* Lance thought. The computer and explosives sat on top of a blue drum. Several more blue and yellow drums were scattered in the back of the truck, and a digital red clock counted down: *2:55 . . . 2:54 . . . 2:53 . . .*

Special Agent Marcus let out a small gasp.

Mike reached down and grabbed the radio on his belt, struggling to lift it to his mouth as his strength diminished with the blood loss. Eugene was shouting, but Mike wasn't listening.

"Eugene, I need you to listen to me. There's no time," Mike said, and the frantic voice went silent. *Good man. Knows when to shut up and listen.* "There's a white laundry truck coming your way, and you have to stop it at all costs. Do you understand me? It contains a bomb, and if it gets out, it will kill a whole lot of people. Do whatever you have to do to, but don't let it leave. Kill the driver. Whatever it takes. I'm sending two of my agents to help you, but it's going to be up to you first."

There was a pause. *Please God, let him be brave enough to do this thing.*

"I got it," Eugene said with resignation in his voice. "I'll let you know how it goes."

"You're a good man, Eugene. Once a Marine, always a Marine. Good luck," Mike said, and handed the radio to Lance as he sat down on the floor and studied Matt Stillman's body lying ten feet away facedown on the floor. He'd been shot twice in the back.

"Jesus, Mike, you okay?" Lance asked.

2:33 . . . 2:32 . . .

"There's no time to be thinking about me," Mike said urgently. "Take Chaney and go help Eugene. Marcus can tend to Champion. I'm going to take care of the truck."

"How?" Lance asked, wondering what the hell his boss and long-time friend was thinking.

Special Agent Marcus handed Lance the keys to the Suburban parked out front.

Mike said, "Don't worry about it. It's my problem. Your problem is those two assholes in the truck heading toward Eugene. He needs your help more than I do."

Lance hesitated for a moment, concern apparent on his face, and Mike saw it.

"It's not a request, old friend. Stop wasting time and go help that kid," Mike said.

Lance Foster looked at his boss and friend one last time, nodded, and turned to Special Agent Chaney. "You heard the man. Let's go." As an afterthought, he turned toward Mike and said, "See you when I see you."

"Most definitely, brother," Mike said, uncertain when that would be.

The two HRT members sprinted down the ramp into the afternoon sun.

2:14 . . . 2:13 . . .

"Help me up, Special Agent Marcus," Mike said.

The young agent leaned down and lifted him to his feet, silently struggling with his size.

"Thanks. I know that's not easy. We don't have much time. Help me to the driver's door. We need to move fast," Mike asked.

As she assisted him with the short walk, she said, "Thank you, sir. You saved my life back there. I'd be dead right now if you hadn't seen him. I only turned to look forward for a second."

Almost at the truck's cab, Mike looked down at her. "You're welcome, but I got lucky. You have great instincts, even the way you reacted after I knocked you aside. But sometimes luck is what wins the day. Regardless, I'm glad I turned around. You're a good agent, and we need all of them we can get."

"Thank you, sir," Special Agent Marcus said.

They reached the cab's door, and Mike let out an audible, "Thank God."

"What is it?" Special Agent Marcus asked.

"The keys. I figured they might be here since we interrupted their party and they left so quickly. Like I said—luck."

"What now?"

"Now, Special Agent Marcus, I'm going to ask you to do something you're not going to want to do. But just so we're clear, no matter what you say, I'm going to get my way," Mike said, a genuine smile broadening his paling face.

Special Agent Sheila Marcus suddenly experienced real anguish for the first time that day as she listened to her boss issue his instructions.

CHAPTER 46

Eugene was afraid. Afghanistan had been one thing, but at least there he'd been surrounded by fellow Marines, his comrades and true brothers-in-arms. They were the real reasons he or anyone else who served during wartime stayed in the fight. It might have started out as a war against the Taliban, but by the time Eugene arrived in country, he wasn't sure what the strategic objective was. But no matter how bad things had been—and they'd been pretty bad—he'd always had his fellow Marines at his side.

Those thoughts of his friends, especially the ones who hadn't made it home, finally spurred him into action.

He looked out the rear window of the guardhouse and saw the white truck still several hundred yards away, picking up speed and raising dust as it accelerated toward him. Instinctively, he lowered the barriers on both sides, although he knew it wouldn't do anything to slow the truck down. His only shot was the white Ford F-350 Super Duty pickup assigned to the guardhouse.

He exited the shack and dashed to the truck, catching a glimpse of his target, now less than one hundred and fifty yards away. *This is going to be close. Come on, God, help me now.*

The pickup was parked perpendicularly to the back of the guard-house, facing the incoming lane. His boss had told him that position would make it easier for him to respond to an incident inside the compound. *And this is one big fucking incident.*

Hoping to conceal his movement, he entered the truck through the passenger side. Whoever these guys were, he was counting on the fact that they were in a hurry.

He slid into the driver's seat and secured himself as tightly as possible with the seat belt. What he was planning was going to hurt. *I hope the air bag doesn't break my nose,* he thought absently as he started the ignition, shifted the powerful Ford, applied the brake, and waited.

Seventy-five yards . . . sixty yards . . .

The truck barreled toward him in the outbound lane. He glanced down at the Glock in his right hand, as if its presence could reassure him. He hadn't fired it in weeks, although he cleaned it regularly because of the sand and dust from the desert environment.

Thirty yards . . . twenty-five . . .

He could see two men in the front seat. He experienced a brief flush of fear when he saw that the passenger held some type of submachine gun.

Great, Eugene thought. *Oh well, fuck it. Gotta die sometime. Might as well make it count. Semper fi, motherfuckers.*

Eugene Wabash, Afghanistan veteran, former Marine, college student, and security guard released the brake and slammed the gas pedal all the way to the floor. The pickup truck responded instantly, and the vehicle shot backward, rocketing toward the white laundry truck. He'd timed it perfectly, and the V-8 engine closed the final few feet in seconds.

The bed of the pickup truck slammed into the driver's door with a tremendous *crunch*, and Eugene was flung against the back of the seat, his head crashing into the headrest. He kept the pedal to the floor, and the engine roared, gaining traction as the pickup was pulled backward by the momentum of the laundry truck. The two vehicles merged together for a split second as they crashed through the lowered outbound barrier, locked in battle, driver's sides adjacent to each other yet facing opposite directions. Eugene looked out his window and up into the truck.

An angry-looking man stared at him, shouting words he couldn't hear and didn't care about. Eugene raised the Glock and opened fire. *Go fuck yourself.*

The first bullet tore a hole in the man's left forearm, and Eugene was rewarded with a look of pain and surprise. The second round caught the driver in the shoulder, but it was the third round that ended the one-way conversation. It struck him under the left side of his jaw, and he slumped forward onto the steering wheel.

Just as quickly, the two vehicles separated, and the pickup truck ground to a halt, facing backward in the outbound lane as the white panel truck drove off the pavement and bounced across the rocky terrain before stopping.

Eugene gripped the wheel of the Ford tightly, feeling adrenaline course through him. *Okay. You're alive. You got one of them. Now get the hell out of the car. You're a sitting duck.*

He exited the vehicle and stumbled to a knee to steady himself against the effects of the impact and the blow to the back of his head. He heard the grinding and squeaking of metal and realized what it was a moment too late.

Move! his mind screamed, as he heard the laundry truck's passenger side door open. Eugene scrambled to his feet as the second man appeared at the rear of the truck. He was covered in dark blood that contrasted harshly with the white overalls he wore, but it was the black submachine gun in his hands that captured Eugene's attention.

The man opened fire, and Eugene scrambled around the front of the pickup, scurrying for cover. Bullets punched holes in the skin of the truck, shattered glass, and punctured the tires.

Miraculously unscathed, he hid behind the wheel well and waited for the barrage to end. When it did, Eugene stood up, his Glock searching for a target. The man had ducked behind the truck. *He must be reloading.*

He crouched down and saw the man's legs and figured, *Why not?* Moving to a prone position, he obtained a clear sight picture and opened fire with three methodical shots.

Bam! Bam! Bam!

The first two shots kicked up dirt, but the third struck the man in his left ankle, and he fell to the ground. The submachine gun was still in his hands, and he looked toward Eugene with pure outrage, opening fire from beneath the truck.

Eugene scrambled back behind the wheel well once again and waited for the second fusillade to finish. *Might as well just wait it out until the cavalry arrives. You did what he asked—stopped the truck and killed the driver. Just keep an eye on this fucker and wait, for God's sake.*

The additional bullets that tore into the truck around him reinforced the idea. He prayed that help was close.

CHAPTER 47

Mike Benson didn't have much time left—forty seconds remained on the timer of the enormous truck bomb he was driving.

Initially, he'd thought he'd be okay, but as soon as he'd sent Lance and Special Agent Chaney after the second bomb, he started to experience the first real symptoms of shock—weakness, shallow breathing, and severe chills.

There just wasn't enough time to treat the gunshot wound, which he was fairly certain was fatal. The entire inside of his bulletproof vest was soaked in blood, and his wet shirt stuck to his chest.

He'd made the best decision he could under the circumstances—he'd ordered Special Agent Marcus to tend to Special Agent Champion. He didn't want any casualties other than his own on this operation. Champion was his responsibility, and he felt the weight of that burden on a scale that could only be counterbalanced with his own life.

Just because he was dying, he didn't have to go out with a whimper. He might be removed from the field as was typical of a deputy director of the FBI, but he knew how to fight like the hardest of men. He just concealed it a little more concertedly, only letting the vengeance he felt toward those who would harm the innocent shine through when needed.

And now was one of those times, he thought as he drove the truck down the ramp and sped under the raised door into the midafternoon, high-desert sun. There was only one place that might contain the enormous explosion that was about to consume the facility—the quarry.

He pressed the accelerator to the floor, and his thoughts turned first to Corey, then to his Uncle Jake, and finally to Logan. It was Logan who concerned him most. His friend was fearless, but he struggled with his demons, ghosts from Fallujah and the burning anger that threatened to tear him apart if he allowed it.

He believed there might not be another person on the planet quite like Logan West. He was as loyal and righteous as any man could be in today's world. Mike knew that the anger that Logan harbored wasn't truly anger or mere frustration. It was blinding outrage at the wicked things perpetrated by evil men upon the innocent.

And my death is going to send him on a personal crusade. In spite of himself, Mike smiled. *God help the bastards who'd orchestrated the events of the past few days because Logan's going to find them and make them pay like the Grim Reaper himself.* He just hoped Logan wasn't consumed in the process. He had faith in his friend, though, and that was all he could hope for as he faced his own mortality, barreling purposefully toward his demise.

He focused as the edges of his vision dimmed and the huge vastness of the quarry expanded in his view. He was less than forty yards from the edge of the pit. *Almost time, Mike.*

The truck rumbled forward, devouring the dirt and gravel below it.

Mike cleared his thoughts, not wanting to leave the world with a cluttered mind. He felt the clarity he'd heard survivors of near-death experiences describe, and he watched breathlessly as the edge of the quarry came into view, revealing the vast hole in the earth below that seemed to drop endlessly.

And then it happened—a part of his mind rebelled, refusing to yield to the oncoming inevitability. *It's just like Thelma and Louise. No fucking way I'm doing that.* Life was precious, and if he could buy himself some extra seconds of finite time, he would. In fact, he knew *exactly* what he would do with those seconds.

He grabbed the handle of the door and pushed it open as the speeding bomb closed in on its final destination. *Here goes nothing. Logan would be proud.* With a full heart and clarity of mind, Mike Benson leapt from the cab of the truck and wondered which would kill him first—the gunshot wound or the fall at fifty miles per hour.

CHAPTER 48

Eugene was growing impatient. From his nearly prone vantage point, he couldn't tell if help was on the way. The FBI had told him they'd be here in a minute or two, but not knowing what his enemy was up to on the other side of the truck was maddening. Since the onslaught of bullets had momentarily stopped, he decided to risk it and leaned down further to get a glimpse of the man he'd shot.

He never got the chance because at that moment, the world went from relative quiet—as quiet as the aftermath of a gun and vehicular battle could be—to a roaring soundscape of noise and chaos.

Ba-booooooom!

Eugene jerked upright, his attention fully gripped by the enormous dust cloud rising from the direction of the quarry into the sky in a dark, roiling mass. Small rocks fell onto the road as a hazy darkness swept across the facility, the sun blotted out by the debris cloud. The shockwave reverberated through and across the facility. True terror suddenly gripped him as he thought, *What the hell did these guys put in the trucks?*

A low sound built in intensity as a secondary rumbling shook the earth. *Oh no—an earthquake . . .*

The ground trembled beneath his feet, and he stood up from behind the truck, stepping away in case it suddenly lurched to the side.

His irrational fear gave way to reason when he saw a secondary cloud of dirt burst into the air from the quarry, and the tremors stopped.

It's not an earthquake, you moron. The first explosion triggered a landslide in the pit. Christ . . .

Transfixed by the dust-filled sky, Eugene temporarily forgot he'd just been involved in a shootout, and he failed to notice the wounded man limping and dragging a bloody ankle from around the back of the truck, the black submachine gun raised in one outstretched arm. The man reached the middle of the road, his movement masked by the echoes from the landslide, hatred raging across his face.

Eugene was oblivious to the fact that he had only seconds to live.

Honk-honk-honk-honk!

Eugene looked around as the harsh barks of a car horn broke his trance, and he remembered where he was. Eugene realized his fatal mistake, and he spun around, all thought channeled into one—*where is he?*

The wounded Chinese gunman had him dead to rights. He smiled at Eugene through a mask of pure rage as he pointed his submachine gun toward Eugene.

Way to go, Eugene, he thought. There was nothing left to do but wait for the man to pull the trigger.

Suddenly, a black Suburban shot out from behind the guardhouse. Its speed and momentum drew Eugene's attention to it. He was peripherally aware that the man in white overalls had turned toward it also, identifying the menacing SUV as a more immediate threat.

Eugene cringed reflexively as the man opened fire with the submachine gun. Bullets ricocheted off the glass and tore into the hood, but they didn't slow the vehicle.

Unable to escape thanks to his wounded ankle, the Chinese operative screamed in fury as he fired pointlessly at the SUV.

The scream and gunfire were cut short as the Suburban struck the man at more than sixty miles an hour.

Eugene watched in horror and amazement as the grille of the Suburban shattered the man's pelvis and two legs, driving *through* him rather than over him. His upper torso was smashed against the hood of the car from the violent force of the collision, and a spray of blood washed across the windshield.

The SUV slammed on its brakes as its driver realized the damage was done. The dead man was flung backward into the air just as violently, arms and legs akimbo as he was propelled at least twenty feet. He landed with a sickening crunch in a pile of bones, barely recognizable as the human being he'd been only a second before.

As Eugene stared in stunned silence, the SUV ground to a halt, and the front door opened. Out stepped the large African-American man who'd been in the backseat behind the FBI's deputy director. He looked at the motionless jumbled remains. The passenger door opened, and one of the back-row shooters—Chaney or Champion, Eugene couldn't recall which—emerged, his assault rifle raised and trained on the motionless figure of Eugene's would-be killer.

Satisfied the shooter was no longer a threat, the man with the goatee turned to Eugene and smiled. "You think we forgot about you, Eugene? Not a chance, my friend. Looks like you've been busy. Nice job, son."

Normally quick to respond, Eugene just looked at him in astonishment, searching for the right words of appreciation and gratitude.

"Thanks" was all he managed to say.

"No," the man said, "thank *you*. Believe it or not, Marine, you're a hero."

Eugene nodded in stunned acknowledgment. The battle for Wild Horse Mountain was over.

CHAPTER 49

Special Agent Marcus had initially tried to treat the gunshot wound to Special Agent Champion's upper leg with pressure, hoping the wound might clot on its own until actual medical personnel arrived. After her attempts to stem the flow of blood had failed, she'd secured the operator's black web belt around his upper leg. The bleeding had stopped, and then the world had been torn in half.

The tremendous explosion had shaken the power plant so violently that she'd been sure the tourniquet wasn't necessary—they were both going to die. Pieces of heavy machinery had broken loose from the floor, and one of the immense stacks that soared through the ceiling into the air outside had cracked in a diagonal spiral that ran down to the ground.

But they hadn't been killed, which meant that Deputy Director Benson had succeeded in getting the truck to the quarry, sheltering them from the brunt of the blast.

Once she was sure the building wasn't going to fall down around them, she left Special Agent Champion. He was still conscious and in communication with his boss, who'd informed him that that second truck had been secured.

It's a win-win, she thought as she exited the building, hoping Deputy Director Benson had somehow survived.

The air was still thick with swirling dust, and an acrid smell she didn't recognize filled her nose. She knew the general direction of the quarry and set off into the shifting landscape between the power plant and the giant pit.

The sandy air cleared more and more by the minute as the winds dissipated the heavy cloud of grit, expanding her field of view. After a few more feet, she could see the edge of the pit, as well as the sitting figure of Mike Benson, his back facing her.

Hope accelerated her pulse, and she covered the remaining distance in a sprint, thinking, *He's alive. Thank God, he's alive!*

"Sir, that was an—" was all she uttered as she stopped next to him, realizing her words had fallen on permanently deaf ears. He was gone.

The deputy director of the FBI was in a sitting position, his legs splayed out flat in front of him. His head was bent forward, chin resting on his chest. Sightless brown eyes stared at the chasm of the quarry. A cell phone was gripped in his right hand, which rested on his thigh.

As she studied him, she realized that he must have leapt out of the vehicle, miraculously survived, and amid the chaos of the blast, had the tenacity to make a phone call. Special Agent Marcus choked back a sob.

She looked at the phone and realized the call timer was still ticking upward. *Oh my God. It's still connected.*

She reached down, carefully pried the phone out of his fingers, and looked at the name on the display. She didn't recognize it immediately, but then it came to her, recalling a conversation she'd overheard in Special Agent Hunt's office earlier in the day.

Out of respect for the personal, private nature of his final act, she hit the end button, disconnecting the call. She placed the phone in her pocket, bent over, and closed his eyes. Not knowing what else to do next—the remaining bomb was secure, the bad guys were dead, and Special Agent Champion was stabilized—she sat down next to him and quietly cried for the loss of a man who'd critically impacted her life in a very brief period.

No matter what else transpired, his sacrifice—saving her life and giving his own—would guide her actions for the rest of her days. It would be a tax on her soul that she'd earnestly pay, in both words and deeds.

PART VII

REAP WHAT YOU SOW

CHAPTER 50

US Embassy, Khartoum

"Logan," the voice said urgently. "Logan, wake up."

Logan West, groggy with exhaustion from the day's violent labors, sat up on the leather couch he'd claimed as a bed. The tubular fluorescent lights flickered on, and he squeezed his eyes shut against the onslaught of illumination.

"All right already," he said brusquely. "I'm up. What is it?"

Wendell Sharp stood in the doorway, a peculiar look on his face. *What's wrong with him?* Logan thought.

"There's a call for you in my office. You need to take it," Wendell said, the flat tone of his voice disconcerting.

"What time is it?" Logan asked, instantly knowing better than to ask what was happening. The chief of station wasn't about to tell him. He'd have to take the phone call.

"It's a little after two in the morning," Wendell said.

Whatever it was that required his immediate attention in the middle of the night had to be critical. They'd accomplished their mission, obtained the ONERING, and were just waiting for their flight out of Khartoum. He moved quickly, lacing up his tan tactical Oakley boots and rising from the couch to follow the CIA officer.

They walked down a short hallway that contained several offices, all currently occupied by Logan's sleeping friends. They stepped into Wendell's office, and the man motioned for him to take a seat at his desk, where a black handset sat, ominously waiting for him.

What the hell is going on? Whatever it was, it wasn't good. He had a premonition it was about to be a long night.

"Wendell, can you please wake John?" Logan asked politely. His instincts told him he might need his closest friend and advisor.

Wendell nodded and left the room without uttering a word.

Whatever it is, he already knows.

Logan grabbed the handset carefully, as if by doing so he was about to make some unspeakable horror a reality. He wasn't wrong.

Logan took a deep breath. "Hello?"

"Logan, it's Jake Benson." Mike's uncle and the director of the FBI sounded exhausted, but there was something else in his voice Logan couldn't pin down.

"Sir, what's going on?" Logan asked cautiously. "We heard that the situation was resolved at the MGM, all terrorists dead and hostages secure. As you know, we're on a plane out of here in the morning with the package."

"I know. It's not that," Jake said. "It's about Mike."

The moment the words were spoken aloud, Logan knew. A monstrous steel door slammed down inside his mind—*Mike's dead.*

He closed his eyes as a rushing sensation filled his head, threatening to overwhelm him as he listened to the details. A practical man, Logan didn't try to argue or deny what Jake told him. Death was an occupational hazard, a cliché he simultaneously detested and respected. He'd had more than his fair share of close calls, but somehow he'd always survived. Yet one of his dearest friends—someone he considered family, a fellow warrior fighting a tide of evil threatening the globe, someone who'd risked his life and career to save Sarah, a good man—had died.

The emotional pain was swift, an unexpected visceral punch that threatened to double him over. He struggled to retain control of his emotions. Now wasn't the time to grieve. He breathed deeply and allowed each intake of stale air to calm the intensifying fire burning through him, a raging monster to be unleashed as needed. *Soon, but not yet.*

When Jake said, "Logan, I'm so sorry. I know how close you were," Logan knew the conversation was over.

"Thank you for calling me personally, sir. I appreciate it. I know what Mike meant to you," Logan said. "I'm sorry for your loss."

"Thank you, son," the director of the FBI said. "I'm sorry for *our* loss. He was special, a man of character and conviction. When he was sworn in as deputy director, he took it seriously—deadly seriously. It wasn't just words to him. It was an oath, an oath of honor."

"I know," Logan said. "It's one of the many things I loved about him. It's the same way we felt—the same way all Marines feel—when they first receive that Eagle, Globe, and Anchor, and then finally take the oath. It's a calling, and Mike lived it every day."

"That's good, Logan, because those are the things you're going to need to remember. Dark days are coming," Jake said suddenly, his tone changing, flattening. "We'll talk when you get back. Oh . . . and one more thing."

"What's that, sir?" Logan replied.

"Stop calling me 'sir.' I don't give a damn where we are or who we're in front of. I'm 'Jake' to you, from now until you or I stop drawing breath. You were family to Mike, and now you're family to me."

Logan struggled to respond but emotion seized his voice in its oppressive choke hold. The raw declaration by Mike's uncle had humbled him to the point of nonresponsiveness. *What did I do to deserve this type of loyalty? How could I be so blessed?*

John appeared in the doorway, his appearance a jarring reminder that Logan had to share the news with him next. The weight of that responsibility helped him regain his composure, and he was finally able to respond.

But the fury was back, banging relentlessly at the door, pleading to be let out and unleashed on those who deserved its wrath.

"Thanks. I can't express to you in words how much that means to me," Logan said.

"I know, and don't forget it. I mean every word. Now get some sleep, and like I said, we'll talk when you get back. Safe travels, Logan," Jake said.

"Thanks, Jake. I'll see you soon, but I think there's one more thing we need to do before we head home," Logan said, staring at the floor before lifting his eyes to John.

Jake sensed the implication in Logan's words. "If it has to do with what happened to Mike, then do it. Don't hesitate with these monsters. They set the board for this very lethal game, and it's about time we start playing by the same rules."

"Understood. We'll be careful. See you soon," Logan said, and hung up.

"Logan, what's going on?" John said, obvious concern on his face.

"You're going to want to sit down," Logan said. "It's bad . . . really bad."

Logan told him everything, his voice growing steadier by the moment. He concluded with the battle with the four Chinese operatives at the rare earth elements processing facility.

"More fucking Chinese strikes?" John said, his grief now fully replaced by the same anger that plagued Logan's soul.

"Yup," Logan said, and waited for his friend to ask the question he knew was coming.

"And from the way you ended that conversation, I assume we're not leaving just yet, are we?" John asked.

"As a matter of fact, we're not," Logan said. "But we're going to need a few friends for this one, and we need Amira to talk to Langley ASAP."

"Good. Because I really want to kill the motherfuckers responsible for all of this, and if she can help us identify them, she will," John said, and then added as an afterthought, "She really is the female version of you."

Logan smiled, but it wasn't a smile of warmth. It was a grin that shone through with pure malevolent purpose, green eyes blazing in intensity. It was the face of death itself.

CHAPTER 51

North Side of the Blue Nile, Khartoum

Several recent high-rise construction projects were interspersed among Khartoum's largely poverty-stricken, mostly flat neighborhoods. The buildings had the added benefit of providing security personnel for their residents' protection. The occupants consisted mainly of wealthy foreign nationals in Khartoum on business or local politicians who desired an additional layer of separation from the citizens they halfheartedly served.

Their target was a ten-story building, the middle of three planned luxury towers. The adjacent two were still under construction.

Langley had come through in a big way, providing the location of a cell phone that had been in contact with the one Amira had obtained from the dead operative on the bridge. The activity was significant enough for the CIA analysts to determine with a "high probability" that it had to be either a member of the Chinese clandestine team or someone closely connected to it. Logan disagreed with their "high probability" assessment—his gut told him it had to be the young leader he'd seen in the cemetery.

After their escape from the prison and the raid on Tuti Island, Logan guessed the Chinese bastard had sought refuge at his Sudanese collaborator's residence. The only real question remaining was how high the conspiracy ascended in the Sudanese and Chinese governments.

The analysts at Langley had obtained the list of residents and cross-referenced it with known Sudanese government officials. Once they'd confirmed one name on the list in particular, it'd made perfect sense.

Namir Badawi, the head of the Al Amn al-Dakhili, owned a secure penthouse suite overlooking the Blue Nile and the Republican Palace—which housed his office—beyond. The man's involvement explained the coordination and support the Chinese had received from the government of Sudan, at least in capturing Logan and Cole and using the remote prison to hide them. They needed to discover what exactly the chief of Sudan's internal security knew. Just as important was who was with him in his apartment. In fact, *that* was critical.

But to answer that question, they had to capture Namir Badawi and his guest, a tactical challenge made more difficult by the security of the building. With more time to plan and conduct reconnaissance, they might have found a way to infiltrate the building through the roof, kidnapping him from the suite. But time was not a luxury they had, and since Langley had provided a dossier on Badawi—complete with recent pictures—the plan was simple: they'd take him on the street outside his residence.

Based on the proximity of Badawi's home to his workplace, they'd surmised that he walked to work, had a driver, or took a cab. Driving himself in Khartoum's bedlam of traffic didn't befit a man in his position.

In addition to Logan, John, Amira, and Cole, they'd recruited the assistance of Chief Sorenson and Lieutenant Reed, both of whom had experience in urban environments and could adequately blend in with the local population, thanks to their deep tans and full beards. The fact that the rest of the group hadn't shaved in days made disguising themselves a little easier.

Before leaving the embassy, the men had changed into khakis and long, white button-down shirts. Long, flowing white robes they could easily discard completed the outfits and concealed their weapons. As non-Muslim foreigners, they weren't expected to dress in the conservative, traditional attire of Sudanese men; however, doing so in this case would minimize unwanted attention.

Because of the constant layer of trash on the streets and the abundance of white cars parked around the block in which to blend, setting up surveillance had been easy, especially in the middle of the night. Logan and John had driven a white sedan into the block and found a spot along the road fifty yards up the street on the opposite side of the building. Cole, Chief Sorenson, and Lieutenant Reed occupied a white van on the same side of the street as the apartment complex. Amira had established herself as a homeless woman and created a nest of cardboard and paper at the opening of an alley in between two worn-down buildings directly across from the front entrance to Badawi's building.

The time approached seven o'clock. The first daily call to prayer, the *fajr*, had been a little more than an hour ago, and the sun would soon be rising. As Logan watched the front of the building, his thoughts drifted to Mike and the various operations they'd shared, including the showdown in Iraq two years ago. The memories fueled his desire for justice, although he was also aware that part of his motivation was the predatory bloodlust the loss of his friend had triggered.

"Do you really plan to take them alive?" John asked, his own memories of an insurgent compound in Iraq evoking the question. "You're not exactly keen on taking prisoners."

Logan had considered it, and as much as he needed his thirst for vengeance to be quenched, it was more important that they take Badawi and his friend alive and *then* bleed them—for every ounce of information they had.

"It all depends on how they react. But yes, I do want to capture them. We've got a global conspiracy seemingly led by the Chinese and involving the Russians, North Koreans, and Sudanese, not to mention the four dead assholes in Vegas. We still don't know who *those* fuckers really were. While I don't want to go *X-Files* crazy, this sure feels like some kind of global conspiracy, one targeted directly at our country," Logan said, his voice strengthening with each word. "So as much as I want to wipe these bastards from the face of the earth, I'm going to have to keep my emotions in check." He turned and looked his friend squarely in the eyes and said, "And that goes for you as well."

"Understood, brother," John said. "Only kill 'em if we have no choice. Whether or not they give us one? Well, that waits to be seen."

"The doors are opening," Amira suddenly said quietly across the encrypted channel on their tactical radios. An enemy utilizing SIGINT for force protection purposes might pick up the signal, but they'd never be able to understand what was being said.

Logan and John watched two figures appear under the awning, but at fifty yards, they couldn't be sure they were their targets.

"Can you confirm it's Badawi?" Logan asked.

"Wait one," Amira responded as the two men reached the end of the awning and stepped into the fading illumination of a streetlamp that would soon shut off with the rising sun. "Jackpot. Badawi confirmed. Second male is Chinese, young, short black hair. Looks like the guy we saw on the helo leaving the cemetery."

"Bingo," Logan responded. "Game time. Here we go."

The two men stepped through the black security gate and into pedestrian traffic, which was light at this hour of the morning. People moved back and forth across the sidewalks, oblivious of the cat-and-mouse game unfolding in their midst.

Badawi and his co-conspirator turned right and proceeded up the sidewalk, walking toward Logan and John's position.

"On my mark," Logan said, waiting for the right moment. The timing had to be precise.

A few more seconds . . .

The two men strode casually down the sidewalk, engaged in an animated conversation, their features becoming more defined in the dusky predawn light. Logan had studied the face of Namir Badawi from the photographs Langley had provided, but it was the second man who interested him more.

The short black hair, muscular physique concealed by well-fitting khakis and a white shirt—it seemed like everyone in Sudan wore the same acceptable version of Western clothing—and a youthful face that belied the experience and professional maturity he possessed: it was the man from the cemetery.

Fifteen yards . . .

"Go," was all Logan said, and the two vehicles slowly pulled out of their spaces on the opposite sides of the street.

Had he waited five seconds longer, the operation would have been carried out flawlessly. Unfortunately, luck and circumstance were always the variables that couldn't be accounted for.

Logan and his team never saw the old man until it was too late. On his way to the local mosque in time for the sunrise prayer, he was oblivious of the traffic on the street and stepped out between two parked cars directly in front of the white minivan driven by Lieutenant Reed.

Screeeeeech!

The tires skidded across the asphalt as the man looked up in surprise at the oncoming van. Every member of the team, including Logan, suddenly turned in the direction of the unexpected sound. It was human nature, but it also cost them the element of surprise.

The vehicle stopped less than two feet from the old man, and he continued to stare into the windshield. A moment later, he calmly raised his hand absentmindedly and kept crossing the street, apparently unconcerned that he'd been moments away from a one-way trip to Paradise.

"Oh no," Amira said across the radios, and Logan redirected his gaze at the targets, whose eyes flashed back and forth from the white car moving toward them to the minivan behind them.

Namir Badawi locked eyes with Logan, who was now less than ten yards away, and in that moment that stretched between them, Logan watched recognition transform the intelligence chief's face from a look of casual awareness to urgent action. *We're made,* Logan thought.

"Move now!" Logan screamed as he accelerated the car toward the two men, but it was too late. Namir Badawi spoke hurriedly to his younger companion, and the two men abruptly split apart, sprinting in different directions.

Namir scrambled over the iron gate as his companion dashed across the street in the opposite direction toward the next alley past Amira's position.

"I've got China," Amira said, sprinting down the sidewalk after the target.

"We've got Badawi," Logan said, and slammed the white sedan onto the sidewalk, leaping out of the car and dashing toward the black fence.

"We'll back Amira," Cole said, and the minivan turned across the middle of the street to pursue the Chinese operative.

"Why are we always running after these motherfuckers?" John said as he followed Logan over the fence, memories of the foot chase in Haditha fresh in his mind.

"We're just lucky, I guess," Logan said as he landed on his feet and watched Badawi disappear around the corner of the building. *Where the hell is he going? The Nile is the only thing back there.*

CHAPTER 52

Namir was furious with Gang. The young operative should never have come to his doorstep late last night, especially after the turn of events at the prison. Namir had been trying to keep the lid on that fiasco, ensuring news of the prison escape hadn't leaked to any of the ministers, who might, in turn, inform the president. He'd been able to contain it, but he didn't know for how long.

Several of the guards were dead, and dozens of inmates—mostly rebels from Darfur—had escaped. The irony was that a hostile American force had attacked his sovereign soil, yet Namir was powerless to do anything about it because of the secrecy of the Black Hole and the disastrous ramifications that would come to pass if its existence were publicized.

The assault on Tuti Island had only complicated matters further. Namir was working with the minister of justice to ensure the bodies of the dead Chinese operatives remained unidentified for as long as possible. Locals on the island had been told that Sudanese police had raided a criminal camp and that several of the suspects had been killed. In a city as vast as Khartoum, it wasn't out of the realm of possibility.

Namir had assumed that Gang had alternate plans in place with his own intelligence service. It was well known that the Chinese were expanding intelligence operations across Africa. So he was shocked when Gang arrived at his apartment, seeking temporary refuge. Namir insisted that Gang utilize the Chinese Embassy as his sanctuary instead. It was, after all, how Gang had initially contacted Namir. It was only after he was pressed that Gang had dropped a bombshell on him—although he and his unit were from various organizations inside the Chinese military and intelligence apparatus, the true senior leadership in Beijing hadn't actually sanctioned the operation.

Namir was stunned at the treachery, to the point of outrage, so much so that he'd momentarily considered shooting Gang in his apartment. Gang had expected that reaction, and he'd calmly reminded the director of the Al Amn al-Dakhili that the operation had benefited his country, as he'd promised it would.

Gang had been right, which had infuriated Namir even more. The benefits had definitely outweighed the risks, but the fact that an operative as experienced as he was had been deceived so completely was almost unfathomable.

Namir demanded answers, but Gang had provided none, only revealing the existence of a global organization that had been orchestrating worldwide events for years. It possessed a sweeping global vision that encompassed more than just an oil deal between Sudan and China. Gang emphasized the fact that the organization's interests and those of Namir and his country were intertwined on this part of the continent. Gang assured him that the longer it stayed that way, the more mutually beneficial the relationship would grow.

Realizing it was pointless to press the issue—the young man was more formidable than he'd given him credit for, and he'd given him plenty—he'd dropped it, and both men had turned to a night of restless sleep.

The debate had continued, at least until the white minivan almost struck the old man in the street.

It wasn't the bearded driver and his passenger that gave away the ambush. Westerners with beards were common in Khartoum, trying to blend in as seamlessly as possible, quite often failing. It was the second car in front of them, which *also* had a Western driver and passenger, and the fact that the two were converging directly on them. In his business, seeming coincidences such as these were often fatal, and years of training and professional paranoia had allowed him to identify the ambush.

He'd told Gang to run and reestablish contact later in the day once they were both safe and secure. Namir never doubted they would be. They were both proficient in their field and equally dangerous.

This is why I have a backup plan, he thought as he fled along the side of his building, carefully sidestepping rocks and debris in the dirt. But first he'd have to get to safety, and he needed to outpace his pursuers. He didn't need to look back to know the Americans would follow, and the footsteps behind him confirmed it.

Better run faster, Namir thought, and picked up the pace.

———

Lau Gang sprinted across the street and diagonally moved away from Namir toward an alleyway. A blur of movement from his right caught his attention, and he risked a glance, spotting a homeless woman emerge from another alley and give chase.

It's the same woman from the airfield, his mind registered automatically. It wasn't her appearance that gave her away—she'd expertly changed it—it was the way she moved, the fluidity and grace she employed that made her look like she was gliding as she ran.

Gang had watched the encounter with the mysterious woman outside the airfield from a distance through high-power binoculars. He'd seen how quickly she'd killed Chang, and he'd recognized the rare degree of lethality she possessed. Now, here she was again, this time pursuing him.

He didn't know who she was—he hadn't been provided that information from the American—but he knew she worked for the CIA and was a trained assassin. The American had at least told him that much.

What he didn't know was how the CIA had been able to locate him so quickly, but it didn't matter. They could have been targeting Namir, and he'd just been caught up in the web. Regardless, he needed to find a secure location and escape the country.

The alleyway ended, and he found himself looking across an open area of dirt slated to be the building site of another new apartment complex. More homes and buildings were on the other side, beckoning to him to seek out their refuge. *There's no way I can make it across without getting spotted.*

To his right was another construction site that ran the length of the dirt field. The builders had only reached the initial stages, framing the location with steel girders, several floors, and skeletal walls. At this hour, the construction workers hadn't arrived yet, and the location had a desolate feeling to it. But it wasn't the building's ambience he was seeking. He intended to use it for concealment as he worked his way through to the safety of northern Khartoum beyond.

He dashed down the small street behind the building's skeleton. As he reached the entrance to the construction site, the white minivan appeared forty yards away at the end of the narrow backstreet and slammed to a halt when the driver spotted him.

So much for hiding, Gang thought. Always eager to improvise, he decided on another course of action, one he preferred—stand and fight. The thought of hurting these Americans, especially the woman, sent chills of anticipation and excitement through him. They were no match for him.

Gang suddenly stopped running and faced the minivan. Once he was sure the driver could in fact see him, he did something completely unexpected—he pointed at the minivan, at himself, and then into the building.

The message was clear: *Come and get me.*

The minivan turned up the street, and Lau Gang vanished into the network of concrete and steel.

CHAPTER 53

Crack! Crack! Crack!

Shots ricocheted off the concrete next to Logan's head as he peered around the rear corner of the apartment building. He ducked behind cover and looked at John, who stood next to him along the wall.

"Badawi's twenty yards away on a slope that runs away from the building toward a tree line," Logan said. "I have no idea where this guy's going. Ready?"

"On your count?" John said, his .45-caliber 1911 in his hand, anticipating the next move after years of tactical experience with his friend.

"Uh-huh," Logan said, his Kimber .45 raised and ready for action.

"One . . . two . . . three," Logan said, and wheeled around the corner in a crouch, his pistol up and searching for their enemy.

John stepped out from beside Logan, and large-caliber gunshots echoed across the landscape as he fired the Colt in quick succession.

Logan began to squeeze the trigger in step with John's actions, which were intended as a distraction for Logan to take the real shot, and stopped—Badawi was gone.

"Where'd he go?" John said.

"Let's go find out," Logan said, and sprinted down the pathway toward the trees.

The back of the apartment building contained several concrete patios connected by interlocking stone pathways. In the center of the layout was a large, pristine oval pool, which calmly reflected the morning light.

"There's nowhere for the squirrelly motherfucker to go," John said as they approached a small opening in the trees, weapons up in case Badawi tried to ambush them again.

The sound of a small boat's motor starting solved the mystery.

Logan and John broke into a sprint along the path. They emerged on the bank of the Nile to discover two small piers with an assortment of single-engine motorboats, large wooden canoes, and small sailboats.

Operating a small white boat, Badawi pulled away from the pier, gaining speed. Logan knew there was only one choice.

"You or me?" Logan said calmly.

"I've got it," John said quietly, and Logan stepped aside to provide his friend a clear line of sight.

The Colt tracked the moving boat, and John steadied his aim, sighting on the figure of Badawi at the helm. He relaxed momentarily as he'd done countless times before, exhaling to prevent unnecessary movement. He felt encapsulated by the moment, and he welcomed it, a hunter of men relishing the stillness before he caught his prey. He gently squeezed the trigger, and the cannon in his hand roared with a singular cry across the water.

Boom!

There was a shout of pain, and Namir Badawi suddenly bent over to his right, losing his balance and his grip on the wheel. The boat veered to the left, and the wounded man was thrown into the air. He sailed off the starboard side and landed in the murky waters of the Nile. The boat straightened and kept moving, putting distance between itself and its owner, now struggling to stay afloat in the water.

"My turn," Logan said, and turned to John. "Nice shot, by the way. Here. Hold this." He grinned and handed John his prized Kimber .45 semiautomatic. "I don't want to get it wet."

He ran to the end of the pier and dove into the river, arms outstretched in front of him.

"Show-off," John said as he watched Logan kick and stroke his way across the surface of the Nile.

————

The inside of the construction project was warm, musty, and quiet. The steel girders, floors, and partitions created a partially contained environment. The stench of dust and recently dried concrete hung heavily in the air.

Amira had entered the site as the Chinese operative had ducked into the first floor and disappeared inside the structural maze.

Amira, Cole, and the two SEALs had rallied at the entrance and realized they could cover more ground in teams of two. Engaging in the Hollywood-horror-movie stereotype of running off individually would only get them picked off one by one.

Amira and Cole had found a stairwell and were on the third floor, while the two SEALs remained on the ground floor on the off chance their quarry decided to make a break for it, although his actions outside indicated otherwise. *He wants to confront us. He's either that good, suicidal, or both,* Amira thought. The two stilettos on her belt comforted her, even as she held the black SIG SAUER in front of her and stalked through the building.

She briefly wondered how John was faring with Logan, but then forcibly removed all thoughts of him from her mind, refusing to succumb to any type of distraction. Experience dictated that she be in the moment one hundred percent. Anything less could lead to disaster for her and the team, and *that* was unacceptable.

"This guy's either luring us into a trap, or he's already left the premises," Cole said from her right as he looked through the convergence of metal and wood that seemed to meld into one the longer she stared into it.

"I don't think so. I think he's here, waiting for the right opportunity to strike," Amira responded quietly.

No sooner had she spoken than the sound of a commotion arose from the ground floor, followed by a cry of pain and several clangs as what sounded like pipes fell onto the concrete floor.

"Damnit!" Amira said.

The nearest stairwell was roughly thirty feet in front of them. *Not enough time. They won't last if he's as skilled as I think he is.*

"Take the stairs," Amira said tersely to Cole. "I'm taking a more direct route."

She ran to the edge of the poured concrete floor and looked down—there were no exterior walls erected yet, just the frames and struts necessary to hold the structure together. She glanced back and saw Cole sprinting toward the stairs. *Smart man. Didn't need to be told twice.*

She turned, stepped backward off the edge of the floor and dropped straight down, extending her arms overhead as she did. One benefit of weighing only one hundred and twenty-five pounds—albeit, all taut muscle—was that she was able to execute maneuvers heavier men could only imagine from movies and TV shows. Her relatively light body weight minimized the stress on her joints, and she easily caught the edge of the floor above her head, abruptly stopping her fall. She released her grip and dropped the short distance to the second floor, repeating the same maneuver to reach the ground level as the encounter between the two SEALs and their target was nearing its conclusion.

Less than fifteen feet in front of her in an area full of hardware, tools, and worktables, the young Chinese man she'd briefly spotted at the Khartoum War Memorial Cemetery was engaged in a violent hand-to-hand struggle with the older SEAL, Chief Sorenson. The younger lieutenant was facedown on the concrete, his arms above his head. She wasn't sure if he was dead or unconscious, but considering the two-foot metal pipe the attacker wielded, she hoped it was the latter.

The man swung the pipe in a diagonal slash, and Amira recognized the move for what it was—a feint. Chief Sorenson dodged backward, but the man pressed the attack. He turned to his left, planted his right foot with the heel facing Chief Sorenson, and kicked straight backward with his left leg.

The move was so fast Chief Sorenson never had a chance to deflect it, and the blow caught him squarely in the sternum, driving him backward against a metal bench. His back arched against the table, and as he rebounded forward, the man lashed out with the pipe, swinging in an arc and landing flush on the left side of the SEAL's jaw. Chief Sorenson's body went limp, and he fell to the floor, unconscious.

She knew the SEALs were experts in hand-to-hand combat, but this one was too fast for them. *They never had a chance.*

The man—still unaware of Amira's presence—stepped over Chief Sorenson's body and raised the pipe.

"I wouldn't do that, if I were you," Amira said coldly.

The man's head whipped around, and hard brown eyes burning with fury fixed on her, ignoring the SIG SAUER pointed in his direction.

"You," he said in perfect English. "From the airfield. You killed one of my men. He was an excellent soldier and communications officer."

"Then he should've been faster," Amira said. "You shouldn't have sent him. So his death's really on *you*," Amira replied.

"Who are you?" he said in a low growl. "I know you're CIA, a trained assassin, but that's all."

The question caught Amira off guard more than any blow could have. *There's no way he should have any idea who I am or what I do.*

"We know about you, as well, although we don't have your name," Amira said, and then smiled coyly. "I'll tell you mine if you tell me yours."

"You American women are so arrogant, always overstepping your position, *assuming* you're equal," the man said, and scoffed, lowering the pipe.

"Is that so?" Amira said. "Well. I have an idea, handsome. My name's Amira, and why don't you and I debate the politics of gender discrimination the old-fashioned way—with our fists."

"If you insist," he said as a sinister smile formed on his face. "I am Gang. It will be the last name you hear as you scream for mercy."

"If you say so, Gang," Amira said, and suddenly held the SIG SAUER up toward the ceiling and placed it on a wooden table beside her. "But you're really going to have to work for it."

She withdrew the stilettos from their sheaths and twirled them in front of her, moving closer to Gang.

"They're beautiful," Gang said. "At least now I know what you used at the airfield."

Gang threw the pipe to his side and unsheathed a black fighting knife with a pointed blade and serrated edge.

"Fair is fair," Amira said.

"Enough talk," Gang said, and gripped the knife in his right hand, the blade pointed up.

Amira didn't respond but only moved closer, the left stiletto held in a standard grip, similar to Gang's; however, the right one was held with the blade angled downward. She'd found that mastering this technique—although incredibly difficult at first—afforded her the ability to both puncture and slash.

"Can I please shoot him and call it a day?" a voice said from her left, interrupting the standoff. Cole Matthews had arrived on the ground floor, his M4 trained on Gang's head. "I'll take out his legs. We need him for intelligence."

Gang glared at him, hatred oozing from every pore.

"Absolutely not. No matter what happens. Do you understand me?" Amira said, keeping her eyes on her enemy.

"If you insist," Cole said.

"Good," Amira said, and returned her attention to Gang. "And remember, we don't actually need to get information from this one. We still have Henry."

Gang's eyes changed, widening at the mention of one of his men.

"Yes, Gang. We still have your man. And guess what? He's coming with us," Amira said. "I'm sure by the time we're done with him, we'll know everything about you."

"But this bastard's the ringleader," Cole said. "He's the one we need."

"I agree," Amira said, "but there's no way he's going to come with us of his own free will. Isn't that so?"

The words struck a chord in the young leader, and he responded as only the youthfully arrogant know how—with action.

He sprang at Amira, the blade whistling through the air, as Cole stood by and watched, honoring his promise and thinking, *I swear she's Logan's long-lost sister.*

CHAPTER 54

Logan reached the struggling figure of Namir Badawi as the man wrestled to untangle himself from the traditional robe he wore over his outfit. Splashing as he flailed to stay afloat, he didn't hear Logan paddling toward him until it was too late.

Namir lifted the robe successfully over his head and pushed it aside, setting it adrift. He looked around to determine his proximity to shore and was greeted with a solid punch to the face.

Pain shot through Namir's head, and he felt the bridge of his nose break. *What in Allah's name?* An arm the thickness of a tree branch snaked around his neck, and all thought was interrupted as the oxygen supply to his brain was swiftly cut.

"You've been shot," a voice whispered calmly into his ear. "You're coming with us, Mr. Badawi. If I were you, I wouldn't waste your energy fighting. You're going to need it."

The meaning was clear, but Namir struggled harder, straining to see the face of his attacker. Green eyes flashed by the left side of his face, striking in their clarity and intensity, and a menacing visage briefly appeared in front of him as water splashed over his mouth. *Who is this devil with the eyes of a reptile?*

The arm tightened in response to his silent question, and he felt himself begin to fade inward. Realizing the futility of further resistance, he ceased struggling, and moments later the arm around his neck loosened slightly.

"Smart man," the voice said. "Then again, from Sudan's head of internal security, I'd expect nothing less."

How does this man know who I am? It had to be Gang. Somehow, the Americans tracked him to me.

Namir coughed and struggled to speak, gasping for air as he was dragged slowly backward toward the shore. Whoever the man was, he was a powerful swimmer—the progress was swift and steady.

His initial panic receded, and moments of his life and career flashed through his mind—his subjugation as a child, the odds he'd overcome, the operations he'd planned and executed, the position he now held. Yet here he was, being pulled like a piece of meat through a watery jungle. How had he been reduced to this state of being? Sudan was his homeland, not this arrogant invader's. His confidence quickly resurfaced, even in the face of overwhelming adversity. No matter what, the tide had to be turned, because Namir Badawi would not go quietly. He would not be a puppet on someone else's string.

"Who are you?" Namir spat out, gasping for breath as he completely relaxed his body. He let his arms dangle at his sides, hoping to lull his captor into complacency.

Logan felt Namir's body relax under his grip, but his awareness remained heightened. He operated on a principle of disciplined vigilance at all times. His enemy might have let his guard down, but Logan never would.

"Someone who has a personal interest in the venture you have going with the Chinese," Logan said, the contempt in his voice unrestrained. His legs kicked harder beneath the water, eager to get Badawi to shore.

"You've managed to stir up quite a mess. You've damaged the national security and international standing of my country, and you're somehow involved in multiple attacks on my homeland." Logan's voice changed, his tone menacing and sharp. "I also can't say I enjoyed my brief stay at your prison, but I am glad that I got to *shut that horror show down*. All things considered, I'd personally like to drown you right here. It's what you deserve—swift justice," he finished, squeezing hard one last time for emphasis.

"Then . . . why . . . don't you?" Namir said in between gasped breaths.

"Because you have information we need," Logan said. They were now less than thirty yards from shore, where he saw John waiting expectantly, his arms crossed. "It's really that simple. Your life means nothing to me at this point, but the information—*that* actually is valuable."

Across the city, the harmonious chant of the *adhan*, the preparatory call to the sunrise *salat* and second of the Islamic morning prayers, echoed.

The call to prayer and the dismissal of Namir Badawi's life by his captor triggered his survival instinct, fueled by a religious conviction. *If it's your will I die, Allah, so be it. Then I die with honor.*

Namir felt the grip on his neck suddenly shift, creating a slight gap between his neck and his captor's arm. He quickly reached down to his belt and withdrew a small steel push dagger, closing his fist around the handle so that the blade jutted out between his third and fourth fingers.

Allah is on my side, Namir thought, and wondered how his captor could be so careless.

What he couldn't see was the large dark shape—the source of Logan's distraction—just below the surface, slowly moving toward them with predatory purpose.

———

Gang attacked with a rapid series of slashes and thrusts, his center of gravity lowered in a deep lunge as he shuffled and stepped forward with each strike.

Amira danced away from each move as she parried the knife with alternating stilettos, creating a constant song of *clang-clang-clang* as the metal blades smashed into each other.

Cole watched in rapt fascination as the dueling combatants wielded their weapons with lethal precision. *Jesus. It's like watching an old Jackie Chan movie. If only it weren't so fucking real.*

More than anything, he wanted to put a bullet in Gang's knee, but Amira had ferociously insisted, her intensity and determination forcing him to acquiesce to her demand against his better judgment.

Amira suddenly found herself against a large tool chest on wheels as Gang pressed the attack once again. He feinted quickly toward her face with the blade and attempted the same kick he'd used on Chief Sorenson, but Amira was prepared.

She executed a quarter turn to her left and slashed down with her hand, the blade slicing across and through the khaki material and the calf muscle beneath it.

Gang only grunted in pain, refusing to display any weakness. He planted the wounded leg and lashed out with a spinning back fist, which caught Amira on the right side of the face.

She spun away, positioning the tool chest between them as she shrugged off the effects of his strike. *Don't get caught like that again. He may be wounded, but he's still strong and almost as fast as you are.*

Gang smiled at her maliciously, but she ignored him. She was used to men trying to intimidate her. They had never succeeded before in situations like this one, and she wasn't about to let Gang be the first. She was too well trained, both physically and mentally.

Time to test that wounded leg.

She thrust the stiletto in her left hand toward his face, and Gang moved back instinctively. Instead of following through with another attack, she sprang forward and delivered a blindingly fast low round-house kick that connected squarely with his wounded calf.

"Aghh! Bitch!" Gang spat out as his front leg buckled and he dropped to a knee.

Amira exploited the opening and quickly dashed past and behind him, slicing her left stiletto across his upper arm. She was rewarded with another growl of pain.

She stepped away and moved to the middle of the room, forcing him to turn to face her, a workbench and table now between them.

"Had enough?" Amira asked, a glint in her eyes letting Gang know how much she was enjoying the encounter. "I'm going to throw this offer out one time. Put down the knife, allow us to take you in, and you get to live. Otherwise, you're going to be dead in the next few minutes."

Who the hell is this she-devil? Gang thought incredulously. She'd been lucky with her counterattacks. There was no way this woman would be able to use those tactics again. Her arrogance was infuriating, and it reminded him of a girl he once longed for during his first year of high school.

Yi Sun had shunned his advances, and he'd learned a valuable lesson about women—they all thought that they were better than their male counterparts. Yi Sun had soon started dating a boy—his name escaped Gang's memory at the moment—but what he didn't forget was the two broken arms he'd given the boy, along with a warning to never speak of it to his parents or teachers. The boy had stopped dating Yi Sun, providing Gang with a sense of satisfaction and empowerment that set him on his course into adulthood.

Yet here was another beautiful woman, displaying the same condescension and air of superiority as Yi Sun. He would make the dark-skinned whore pay with her life.

"My father would've known how to handle you. I'm going to gut you, but he's *less merciful* than I am," Gang spat out, but also bracing himself for his next move.

"He sounds like a wonderful man. If I ever see him, I'll send him your regards . . . from beyond the grave," Amira replied coldly.

Gang's eyes darted across the wooden table between them. He

needed something to use to his advantage. If she thought she could use her looks and slithery tongue to lull him into surrendering, he'd teach her a lesson in submission.

He saw what he was looking for, and rather than satisfy her with an answer, he lashed out toward the object he'd spotted.

If Amira was being honest with herself, she was glad Gang had rejected her offer. She'd seen men like this before. There was nothing worthwhile left salvaging in his character. In her experience, men who'd become so cruel at this age had no hope of unraveling the twisted humanity they wore as cloaks of invincibility and used as licenses to wreak havoc on society.

Gang lashed out with his left hand and grabbed the nail gun resting on top of the wooden table. He closed his hand around the grip, but that was as far as it went.

With dazzling speed that Gang's mind barely registered, the stiletto in Amira's right hand skewered his wrist and punctured the wood, pinning him to the table. The blade sliced through tendons and sinew, and his hand reflexively opened as he screamed in pain.

Gang looked at her with a combination of dread, fury, and fear, and Amira realized it was time to end the ordeal.

Refusing to yield to the bitter end, Gang brought his free arm around and tried to slice at her with his knife. The knife attack wasn't even close since the stiletto in his wrist blocked his movement and limited his range of attack. Amira released the stiletto still pinning Gang to the table and spun to her left.

As Amira completed the turn, she found herself exactly where she'd planned—beside Gang. She adjusted the grip on her remaining stiletto, the blade now jutting out and away from her left hand, and executed her own spinning back fist. With her final rotation, she buried the remaining stiletto into the back of his skull with a sickening crunch, violently ending Gang's brief reign of terror in the shadowy world of clandestine operations.

Issuing a brief grunt of satisfaction, Amira withdrew the blade from the back of his head, and Gang smashed face-first into the rough wood. His upper body bounced off the table and hung at an awkward angle, held fast by the first stiletto. She yanked the bloody blade from his wrist, and Gang's corpse crumpled to the floor.

"Jesus," Cole breathed as he looked into the huntress's face. He was in awe at the brutality and skill he'd witnessed.

Amira wiped the blood off the blades and sheathed the stilettos. She reached into Gang's pockets and withdrew a wallet and a cell phone.

"Now let's see if we can wake our friends and get the hell out of here," she said. "Morning prayer's almost over, and the workers will be here shortly."

"What about him?" Cole said.

"Leave him. He's no use to us anymore," Amira said flatly, and bent down to attend to Lieutenant Reed, who, thankfully, groaned. Both SEALs would be hurting once they woke up, likely with at least one broken jaw from the blow she'd seen Gang land on the Navy chief, but at least they would get to go home.

CHAPTER 55

Logan had spotted the crocodile lurking in the water as he'd begun pulling Namir toward the shore. He realized the splashing and blood had attracted the predator.

Even as he'd spoken to Namir, his eyes had never left the large beast that had slowly begun to swim toward them, cutting through the water like a giant serpent. Logan estimated the river monster to be at least fifteen feet long, but he could only see the vague outline of its body. It was the head that had him really concerned. It was almost four feet in length, concealing rows of razor-sharp teeth that could puncture and grab with a viselike grip. There'd be no escaping this animal's grasp.

The crocodile had closed the distance to fifteen feet when sunrise prayer had begun, and Logan had been forced to make a decision—*survive or die.*

For a man of extreme and ruthless practicality, it hadn't been a hard one to make. He wanted to capture and interrogate Namir Badawi, but that wouldn't happen if they were both dead.

Other men would call it murder, but Logan considered it survival. His conscience was the only one that counted, and he knew he'd be able to live with what he was about to do—cut Namir Badawi across the chest and leave him as a morning sacrifice to the reptilian Nile gods.

Logan eased the grip on Namir's neck with his left arm as he reached down to his hip for the Mark II fighting knife in its nylon sheath.

Namir chose that precise moment to act, sealing both their fates. He spun violently in Logan's grasp, and his right arm broke the water's surface, arcing toward Logan's face like an overhand punch. Water cascaded from his arm like a liquid curtain.

The honor graduate of the arduous Marine Corps Combatant Diver Course, Logan had spent countless hours training his Force Recon Marines in underwater hand-to-hand combat techniques. He was at home in the water, an environment he respected and had used to his tactical advantage throughout his career.

Logan took a deep breath as he caught Namir's wrist with both hands. He locked his legs around the struggling man's torso and squeezed as he pulled Namir's wrist *toward* him and down, the momentum driving them both underwater.

Logan snaked his arm over the back of the man's wrist and pushed forcefully with his right hand. He felt rather than heard the crunch as Namir's wrist snapped, and Logan was rewarded with a muffled scream and an expulsion of bubbles. *You brought this on yourself,* Logan thought.

He yanked the push dagger from Namir's now-useless grip and encircled his neck with his left arm, his legs still securing Namir's torso in place.

Aware that he had precious few seconds left before the crocodile reached them, he plunged the dagger into Namir's side. The man's body stiffened as if struck by a bolt of lightning, and Logan kicked down as hard as he could, pushing himself above the Nile's surface and dragging Namir with him.

Logan looked in the direction where the monster had been, and his blood turned to ice. The crocodile was now less than three feet from them, and the sheer horror of its proximity sent a jolt of true fear through him.

The top of its head was still the only part exposed, its reptilian eyes now focused on the two men. But it was the shadow of its immense body below the surface of the water that created a single, solitary thought in Logan's mind—*swim.*

His fear transformed into focus, a physical sensation that fueled him and provided the courage to act in the face of paralyzing terror.

Logan released Namir, turned, and buried his arm into the water in front of him as he began his frenzied stroke, pulling as much water as he could to start his escape.

Namir let out a high-pitched shriek that sent a chill through Logan. *He finally sees it.*

Logan heard a loud splash, followed by a definitive *thwump,* the magnified sound of an oversized briefcase slamming shut.

The scream instantly dimmed, and Logan realized with horror what the predator had done—struck and closed its jaws around Namir's head.

For the love of God, Logan, swim like you've never swum before. You don't want to die like that.

Logan pulled and kicked as hard and fast as any Olympic athlete in the race of his life.

The thrashing continued behind him, but he didn't dare turn around.

The muffled scream was abruptly cut off after several seconds of horrifying, audible terror. *Mercifully,* Logan thought.

"Swim to the dock! *Now!*" Logan heard John shout from nearby.

He didn't look up, and he didn't look back. As he'd done so often in his life, Logan West pressed forward with one objective clearly in mind—reach the pier and safety.

His heart pounded wildly in his chest, but he controlled his breaths and exhaled below the surface of the Nile, inhaling every time his face turned to the side. He sensed the thrashing behind him—now farther away—subside, but he didn't know if that meant the crocodile had turned its carnivorous intentions toward him.

It didn't matter. All that did was the stroke. *Keep pushing. You're almost there.*

John's voice grew louder, and he sensed he was extremely close to the pier. He finally relented and risked a glance up . . .

. . . As two strong arms reached down into the water and grabbed his forearms. Logan grabbed John's in return, and as John pulled, Logan kicked to propel himself upward.

The pier was nearly three feet above the surface, and a moment later, Logan's chest lay on the rough planks, his legs dangling in the water. John reached down behind him and grabbed his pants, pulling Logan's lower half to safety.

Logan rolled over and lay on his back, his chest heaving up and down as he fought to slow his breathing and heart rate. John sat next to him, his hand on Logan's shoulder in reassurance that he was safe from the river monster.

"Where is it?" Logan gasped, and propped himself on his elbows, spotting the location where the crocodile had attacked.

The water was a darker shade of brown and crimson, swirling with the recent commotion. Namir was gone, dragged to the depths of his watery grave, where his body would be consumed piece by piece by the monstrous crocodile.

"After it got him by the head, it thrashed from side to side. I'm pretty sure it broke his neck. It then took him under. I saw it roll a few times, and then it was gone," John said, and looked at Logan.

"He didn't see it until the last second. I spotted it right away. I was going to cut him and use him as bait so I could escape," Logan confessed. "But he made a last-ditch effort to attack with a small push dagger he had on him. So I never got the chance."

John studied Logan for a moment and weighed the moral dilemma his closest friend had faced. "That's the best choice you could've made in that situation. That's what sets you apart pretty much from everyone else—you can make those hard choices."

"I know, but what's scary, even for me, is how fast I made it. There was no hesitation, no consideration for his humanity."

"That quick decision-making is why you survived," John said earnestly. "You made the right call, and you were prepared to do the hard, right thing."

Logan nodded and finally stood, water dripping from his soaked clothing.

"More importantly," John said, a wicked grin breaking across his face, "don't you know you're not supposed to feed the animals?"

Logan couldn't help himself, he laughed, momentarily breaking the fatigue and tension he felt. He shook his head at his friend, grateful for the bond they shared. *I'm humbled to have such companions as these.*

But then he thought of Mike, and his mood sobered.

"Let's find out how our friends are doing and then get the hell out of here," Logan said. "I'm officially ending our Sudanese vacation."

PART VIII

ARES

CHAPTER 56

Arlington National Cemetery, Virginia

In the front of a small, intimate group of friends and family, Logan stood at attention as seven Marines fired three volleys in the traditional twenty-one-gun salute.

Crack!

Crack!

Crack!

Sarah West stood next to her husband, black-gloved hands crossed in front of her. She knew the playing of taps by a live bugler would be next. She'd been to all the funerals for the Recon Marines killed in Fallujah in 2004, and she knew the ceremony by heart, even years later.

John, Amira, and Cole huddled around them in the December air. Even Mike's ex-wife, Corey, and Special Agent Lance Foster were in attendance for the sorrowful occasion. Standing in front of them all was Mike's uncle, FBI Director Jake Benson.

The heartbreaking melody drifted down the hill, shrouding the funeral party with a sense of loss and overwhelming grief. Even the most battle-hardened in the group, including Logan himself, were moved to tears during Butterfield's Lullaby.

When the bugler was finished, two Marines folded the American flag draped over Mike's coffin and presented it to Jake Benson, who reverently accepted it.

A slender man at just under six feet, he cut a distinguished figure with chiseled features, a sloping, hawkish nose, and peppered gray hair. While Mike had had the presence of a linebacker, Jake Benson carried the aura of a statesman. In reality, he and Mike had been cut from the same cloth, but in the same way that Mike had used his physicality, Jake had used his charm and charisma to navigate the treacherous political waters of DC.

Jake stood back and watched through a mask of grief as Mike's ornate casket was lowered into the hallowed ground.

The site was normally reserved for active or retired military members, their spouses and children, elected officials, Supreme Court justices, and a few other select, stringently protected categories, but the secretary of the Army had approved the exception for Mike's burial ground at the urging of the president. A plot had been identified in the southern part of the same section that held President Kennedy. Located just east of the Tomb of the Unknown Soldier, the area had a gorgeous and serene hillside setting befitting the country's national heroes.

The service ended, and the group stood at the coffin, knowing that once they left, the finality would sink in.

Mike's ceremonial interment had been for friends and family only, and they'd all agreed not to say any words over his casket. Anything they said would seem too shallow or artificial for a man such as Mike. The shock of his loss was still too fresh. It'd only been six days since he'd been killed.

The FBI had planned a large memorial for later in the week, and Logan had been told hundreds—if not thousands—would attend. Mike's career had spanned more than two decades, and he'd impacted agents across all organizations in the Bureau, not the least, Special Agent Sheila Marcus, the last person to see him alive. She'd been asked to speak at the service, and Logan had every intention of talking to her after the event. He wanted to know every detail of Mike's last minutes on earth, although he was sure he died the way he had always lived—as a warrior.

As the group walked toward the procession of black stretch limousines, which waited to take them to the Capital Grille—Mike's favorite steakhouse in DC—for a funeral luncheon, Jake appeared at Logan's side and pulled him away from the group.

"Logan, do you have a moment?" Jake asked, his eyes still glistening from the service.

"Of course," Logan answered. "What is it?"

"This is going to sound odd at a time like this, but I need you, John, Cole, and Amira to come with me in my limo," Jake said. "We have to make a stop before lunch."

"Is everything okay?" Logan asked, concern creeping into his voice.

"Yes, but there's something we have to do, and it can't wait," Jake said.

Logan studied the man's face. Whatever it was, it was serious, as well as urgent.

"I'll gather the troops," Logan said.

"Okay. See you at the car." Jake walked away, the flag still held tenderly in his hands.

Logan caught up to his family, who immediately knew from the look on his face that something was amiss.

"What is it, babe?" Sarah asked, gently placing her hand on her husband's arm.

"I'm not sure." Logan smiled at his beautiful, brown-haired wife. "But Jake needs John, Cole, Amira, and me to take a trip with him before we hit the restaurant," Logan said, looking at each person as he said each name. "He didn't say why."

"Sounds like business," John said.

"But what kind of business that it has to be this minute?" Cole asked.

Logan shrugged. "I don't know, but we'll find out soon enough. We'll meet you at the restaurant. I love you," he said, and leaned in and kissed Sarah on the mouth.

"Love you too," Sarah said.

"Come on then, gang. Let's go see what the man wants," Logan said, and the group strode to the waiting limousine.

CHAPTER 57

Fifteen minutes later, Logan, John, and the others found themselves in the Treasury Building's ornately adorned conference room directly across the hall from the Treasury secretary's office.

In addition to the group and Jake Benson, there was only one other occupant—the director of the CIA, Sheldon Tooney. A legendary case officer, he'd earned his stripes during the latter days of the Cold War, serving as the chief of station in Berlin when the wall came tumbling down.

Cole and Amira were momentarily shocked to see the CIA's number one—their ultimate boss—sitting at the table, smiling at them when they walked in.

Known for his interpersonal skills, a trait often lacked by senior officials, he'd stood and greeted them as they entered the room. A man in his early sixties who'd taken care of himself, he moved easily and confidently.

"It's good to see you, Ms. Cerone," Director Tooney said. It wasn't the first time they'd met. He'd shaken the hand of every active LEGION operative. He considered it his personal responsibility to know who his most valuable assets were and to let them know that what they did mattered. "I knew when I sent out the activation message that if anyone had a chance to find that plane, it'd be one of our LEGION." He smiled warmly. "And I was right."

"But sir, how did you know the plane might be coming to Khartoum?" Amira asked. "For a while, I thought LEGION might be compromised and that I'd been sent to fail as part of some sort of diversion."

"Ms. Cerone, have you *ever* failed?" Director Tooney asked, raising his eyebrows.

She didn't respond, accepting the praise with her traditional silence.

"We were lucky. Nothing more," the director continued.

"You're kidding, sir," Cole said incredulously.

"Not at all, Mr. Matthews. You know this business. Sometimes, it's better to be lucky than good. Once we realized the North Korean cargo ship was a wild goose chase, I had our analysts brainstorm where it could go and how it could get there. The 'where' was impossible to know, but they all agreed the safest bet would be via private charter. There was no way they'd go over water after setting up that diversion. So they cross-referenced all private charters and managed to provide a list of potential destinations. Due to the sensitivity of the operation, I decided to activate every LEGION agent near every possible destination. And you just happened to be the one that fate selected," he finished, looking at Amira.

"I'm just a lucky girl, I guess," Amira said.

"You are most definitely *not lucky*. You're one of the most talented agents we have," the director said. "I know it's been a while, and although I know you know it already, I wholeheartedly appreciate everything you've done in your position. You have one of the most difficult and critical jobs, not just in the agency, but in the country, and I can't thank you enough for the way you do it."

He turned to Cole. "The same goes for you, Mr. Matthews. While your position may be a little different, you both possess skills we need, especially now."

"Thank you, sir," Cole said. "Since we just got here, do you have any idea what this is all about?"

Director Tooney smiled, looked at his stainless-steel chronograph watch, and said, "As a matter of fact, I do, and unless my time-telling skills are off in my old age, you'll all find out very soon."

As if on cue, the main doorway to the conference room opened and in walked two Secret Service agents, followed by the last person they'd expected—Preston R. Scott, the president of the United States of America.

———

Preston Scott was an anomaly in the Democratic Party. A former Air Force officer who'd flown A-10 missions during Desert Storm, he understood the necessity of combat and the ultimate sacrifices that war demanded. The descendant of a long line of military leaders and a native of Georgia, it was rumored that one of his relatives had served alongside Robert E. Lee. The legend only added to the popularity he garnered with the country's voters, especially in the South.

A fiscal conservative—or blue dog Democrat—he actually had more in common with the Republican party on defense and economic issues; however, it was the social issues that had held sway over his moral compass, and he'd ultimately entered politics as a Democrat. As much as he respected Republican policies, he believed that their social agenda and the accompanying perception of intolerance it created was an obstacle they needed to overcome. His moderate approach had somehow found the right balance and struck a chord with both parties. It also helped that he was physically fit and extremely good-looking for a man in his early fifties, his thick black hair worn short, clean, and slightly tousled.

He introduced himself and shook each of their hands after he dismissed his two detailed bodyguards with specific instructions—this was a meeting for only those inside the room.

He sat at the head of the table and spoke clearly and directly, with no exaggerated expressions or feigned sentiment.

"Lady and gentlemen, it's been a rough week for this country, but especially for you with the loss of Mike Benson," President Scott began. "Let me start by saying that I didn't know him well at all; however, I know his uncle quite well. As I told Jake and I'm telling each of you now, I'm extremely sorry for your loss. This country lost a hero and a patriot, the FBI lost an excellent leader, and you lost a close friend. And nothing I can say will make up for it."

His sincerity was palpable, and each of them felt a bond grow toward the man they'd just met moments before.

"But that's not why you're all here. First, I chose this location because it's a short walk from my home next door." The east entrance to the White House opened directly opposite the western entrance to the Treasury Department, the convergence of the two buildings already protected by security. "It's easy to cover the distance unnoticed. Additionally, there's no logbook here. I know I don't have to sign anything, but neither do you. There will never be a record that this meeting ever occurred," the president said.

Focusing his attention on Logan, John, Cole, and Amira, the president said, "I've been talking to Jake and Sheldon all week long. They brought me up to speed on what happened to the ONERING, how the Chinese and Sudanese were involved in the hijacking of THOR'S HAMMER, and how it was used to give us a black eye by framing us for an attack on a Chinese oil corporation on Sudanese soil." He paused and placed his hands on the table. "Honestly, it's hard to believe that we could be so careless as to allow something so dangerous to fall into the hands of our enemies, only to have it blatantly used against us. Right now, I've got the State Department in full battle-damage mode, trying to explain to the UN that we weren't responsible. But here's the real bombshell—the Chinese, Sudanese, Russians, and even the North Koreans, if you can believe it, are all denying any role in last week's events. And after what we've learned, it's likely they're all telling the truth. The Russians even acknowledged the existence and identity of the team in Alaska, going so far as to provide us with a file on each man you killed—something the Russian government has *never* done. They insisted they didn't activate their assets, although they acknowledged that the order came from Moscow. They just can't explain how. The same goes for the Chinese."

No one spoke as the president paused. The ramification was clear, but he stated it for the record.

"Whoever and whatever is behind all of this has unparalleled resources and influence. To pull such strings in such high places in *multiple* foreign governments? Well, it's incredibly frightening, to be blunt," he said.

"As for the UN, I could walk in and play a video for the General Assembly showing the Chinese unit launching the attack in Sudan, and they still wouldn't believe it. The organization has become so corrupt, I often wonder why we let its headquarters remain here."

His frank speech had their rapt attention.

I can't imagine what this man must deal with on a daily basis, Logan thought. *It's got to be easier dealing with killers and crocodiles than politicians and world leaders.*

"Here's the crux of the issue, the hard reality we have to face as of this moment: we're at war with a nameless enemy, a secret organization that has the funding and connections to make the types of moves First-World powers make. The first blows have landed—the frame-up for Sudan, the diversionary attack at the MGM Grand set up to look like Islamic terrorists, and the attack on American Elemental."

"Sir, do you have any idea why the attack on American Elemental?" Logan suddenly asked. All the other attacks, as horrible as they were, made sense to him, but the reason for the one at the rare earth elements facility still eluded him.

"Unfortunately, we think we do," Jake said, and added, "which makes it that much harder to swallow." He paused. "Like the attack in Sudan, this was an operation with the reverse motive—an attack on *our* homeland intended to frame the Chinese. We think the fact that knocking out that facility would put the US at the mercy of the Chinese government for rare earth elements was a secondary consideration. The bottom line—someone's trying to pit us against China."

"Jesus," Logan said in a hushed voice. "Two large superpowers duking it out would definitely go a long way in destabilizing not just global security but the global economy as well."

"I know," the president said. His voice hardened, tinged with anger, and they glimpsed the attack pilot he'd once been. "But that's not going to happen, not if we have anything to say about it. As of right now, we start fighting back, and I want each of you to lead the fight for me."

They were stunned. The most powerful man in the free world had just asked for their help. He leaned back and let the weight of the request sink in.

Logan was the first to respond. "What do you need, sir?"

The president smiled, seemingly not surprised it was Logan who had spoken first. "Each of you in this room—and only you, unless you choose to recruit others—will be the most closely guarded secret of my administration, a task force beholden only to me, but with the full resources of the Justice Department, the Intelligence Community, and even the military, if you need it. I'm calling it Ares, after the Greek god of war." His speech pattern changed again, his conviction clear with each syllable. "Because that's *exactly* what we are—*at war*."

The truth of his words sank in around the room. There was no doubt among anyone at the table—the president was all-in.

"Sir, this conspiracy could go back to at least the end of the previous administration and God knows how much further than that," Logan said. "Have you considered that whatever this organization is could have been behind the Cain Frost ordeal?"

"Like you, we think it probably was, which is why we haven't been able to track down the sons of bitches who blew him up in this town. They're ghosts," the president said. "And that has to change. We have to go on the offensive, no matter where, no matter what it takes. We have to draw them out of the shadows. The fate of our democracy, as well as possibly the future of the rest of the world, could hinge on our very actions."

Under any other circumstance, the last statement would have sounded clichéd. Instead, after the events of the previous weeks, it was terrifying.

"So let me be clear. Your president is asking you directly for your help. No one will ever know about this, God willing, and even if they do, I don't care. I want you to do *whatever* you have to do to uncover who's behind all of this. Do not be bound by convention or law or even your own recognition of moral laws. I'm not sure we have that luxury anymore," he said.

"Mr. President, just so I'm clear," John asked bravely, "are you giving us a blank check with all resources at our disposal to hunt down the perpetrators that attacked our country?" *It almost sounds too good to be true,* he thought. *There has to be some kind of catch.*

"That's exactly what I'm doing, Mr. Quick," the president said. "And I'll do you one better. There's a presidential pardon with each of your names on it already signed by me and witnessed by both Jake and Sheldon here. So unless you commit some kind of act of genocide, I've got your back."

Now I understand why people would follow this man anywhere. He has conviction and charisma, an amazing combination if there ever was one, Logan thought. He believed every word the president had just spoken. He'd known men like this before in the military. To say it was rare for a politician was like calling the pope slightly religious.

"So what do you say?" the president asked directly. "Will you help me?"

"Absolutely, sir," Logan said without hesitation. He'd made his decision minutes ago. "It'd be an honor."

The rest of the group followed suit almost as quickly.

"Good, because your work begins tomorrow. Celebrate your friend's life today and begin fresh then. We may see each other from time to time, but due to the sensitivity of this venture, I'll be mostly dealing directly with Jake and Sheldon." The president smiled slightly and added, "Don't be offended if I don't check in every day. I'm a little busy with that whole running-the-country thing."

And a sense of humor to boot? Logan thought. *Will wonders never cease?*

"Unless anyone has any questions, Jake and Sheldon will provide you with everything—and I do mean everything—you need," the president said, and prepared to stand.

"Sir, I do have one question," Logan said, looking around the room. "Something's been bothering me. You've got us, the directors of the FBI and CIA, but for something like this, wouldn't you have your national security advisor on the team?"

A swift sea change washed over the president, and the smile was replaced by a scowl of disgust.

"Mr. West, you are a very smart man, much smarter than my national security advisor," the president said. "Jake can fill you in on the details. Unless there's something else, I need to catch a helo and an airplane for a five-day G8 summit in Greece. I'm going to try and repair some of the damage that's been done to us. It's why we had to do this now."

The entire room stood as the president stepped to the door and reached for the handle. He turned around to face them one last time before grasping the gold knob.

"Thank you, and good luck."

He opened the door and disappeared as dramatically as he'd arrived, an imposing presence whose absence was immediately felt.

For a moment, they looked at one another, and even the two directors felt the heavy burden of the task they'd just accepted. It was a humbling proposition that carried enormous consequences should they fail.

"For the first time in my life, I may be speechless," John said.

"You're talking right now," Amira noted, and smiled at him, pale-blue eyes glittering.

"Yeah, but it doesn't count because I have nothing funny to say," John said.

Logan replayed the president's last comment in his mind, but there was something else he needed to address first.

"What about Henry Cho?" Logan asked both Jake and Sheldon, referring to the young Chinese operative who now rested comfortably in a secured medical facility in Langley. The replantation surgery of his severed finger had occurred near the twenty-four-hour mark, the maximum amount of time allowable before the digit was no longer viable. He'd been lucky, and the doctors gave him an eighty percent chance of recovering most of his original strength and range of motion.

The two directors exchanged a glance, and then Sheldon said, "We haven't decided on what to do with him. His government doesn't know we have him, and based on our interrogation so far, it looks like he really didn't know that there was another organization calling the shots."

"I thought that might be the case," John said. "Can we talk to him?"

"It can be arranged," Sheldon said.

"Good. I think I might have an idea on how to handle him," John replied.

"Does it involve more lost limbs?" Logan asked with a straight face.

"Not this time around," John said. "And it wasn't a whole limb, just a finger, *and* his little one," he added wryly.

"Uh-huh," Logan said, and turned his attention to Jake. "Now that that's settled, what did the president mean by me being smarter than his national security advisor?" Logan asked.

Jake nodded and said, "There's something we need to tell you, and it also happens to be our first order of business."

Thinking the appearance of the president would be the most shocking development of the day was perhaps their biggest mistake.

CHAPTER 58

Jonathan Sommers stepped into the foyer of his renovated three-story brownstone on Dumbarton Street in Georgetown. He was exhausted. The endless hours in the White House—as productive as they were for his cause—were a relentless grind. It was the endgame that made the last four years worth the risk to his life and liberty. A new world order was coming, and he intended to be part of its foundation.

At thirty-eight years of age, he was the youngest of the president's senior advisors or cabinet members, but he held one of the most trustworthy positions in the entire executive branch of government. With boyish charm and a quick wit, he'd insinuated himself into a position of power few could comprehend. The fact that he was working arduously to undermine all of it didn't faze him in the slightest.

A top graduate of the Harvard Kennedy School with a doctoral degree in international relations with a focus on national security, he understood the harsh realities of the new global power structure. Countries could no longer operate in vacuums. The twenty-four-hour news cycle and the advent of social media had shut the door on that archaic way of doing business forever.

His career had been launched into the stratosphere with the rise of the Iraqi insurgency. The White House had recruited him from his prestigious position at one of America's elite think tanks to advise the president on global matters as senior leaders at the Pentagon focused on Iraq. His charge from the last president had been simple—*Don't drop the ball on the rest of the world.* He hadn't, but what the previous president hadn't known was that he'd been juggling many balls since his last semester at Harvard.

On a Tuesday evening at a local pub in Harvard Square as he sat poring over a paper from one of his many talented—although slightly disillusioned—graduate students, he'd been suddenly joined by a mild-mannered man in his midforties. He wore wire glasses and perfectly tailored clothes that blended in with the intellectual elitists at Harvard. He spoke crisp and perfectly enunciated English, but Jonathan had somehow detected that the man was not a native-born American.

Just as Jonathan was known as the American, he referred to the spectacled man as the Recruiter, even to this day.

The man told a tale straight out of a spy movie: he represented an organization whose ultimate goal was the salvation of the planet, not from global warming or theoretical dangers, but from economic and political slavery and its current masters. Jonathan had scoffed at the proposition, nearly laughed, in fact. The man hadn't been offended. Instead, he'd responded by reciting all of Jonathan's personal information, professional accomplishments, and a psychological profile that described and explained his own ambitions more concisely than he could have.

An hour later, when Jonathan had stopped laughing, the reality lay bare before him on the pub table—the possibility of a brave new world. He'd made his decision right there, and he'd had no regrets since, even through the betrayals which he'd coordinated and executed.

Beep-beep-beep.

He closed the front door and entered the code on his alarm panel, the lingering smell of the fire from the night before greeting him warmly.

Home sweet home, for now . . .

He flipped on the lights in the hallway and walked into the kitchen, placing his cell phone on the granite-covered island.

"Welcome home, Mr. Sommers," a voice said from the dark living room beyond the kitchen.

Fear gripped him, and he whirled on his heels to move toward the hallway, where a loaded 9mm Beretta was stored in a console table.

John Quick stepped into the hallway from the front-room library and said, "You looking for this?" He held up the pistol in one black, leather-gloved hand. "Yeah, I don't think so."

Lights turned on in the living room, and Jonathan turned around to see two men he recognized, one standing in each corner. He immediately knew that his life as a double agent was over.

Despite his rapidly racing heartbeat, he tried to regain his composure. He knew the type of men these were. There was no point in begging.

"Mr. Matthews, I'd ask if you'd like a drink, but I don't think you're here on a social call, and I know Mr. West doesn't drink anymore," Jonathan said.

"Put your hands on the counter while I search you." John pushed the national security advisor roughly from behind. "If you make any kind of stupid, dumb-ass move, I'm going to happily kill you. Do you understand, you traitorous sonofabitch?"

The sense of empowerment he'd felt as he'd walked inside was replaced by a desolate feeling of defeat.

"I do," Jonathan said, and spoke no more as his pockets were searched and he was patted down for weapons.

Logan and Cole entered the kitchen, and Logan stood directly in front of him.

Jonathan had read the man's Marine Corps record, as well as the psychological profile the FBI had conducted on him after the events with Cain Frost. As the man studied him, Jonathan felt like he was being scrutinized by some kind of cold-blooded creature. *It's those eyes,* he thought, and felt a chill pass through him.

"You almost got away scot-free," Logan said with steadied nonchalance. "We've known all along—as you well know, since you're it—that there was a traitor in our government, but we couldn't figure out who. Someone tipped Cain off at the Haditha Dam, and only very senior folks back here and us—since we were there—knew about the plan to trap him. I'm betting that guy was you. Am I right?"

Jonathan didn't say a word. He figured silence was his best option.

"Colin Davies gave you up," Logan said.

How? Jonathan thought. *I ensured that his hard drive was destroyed. There was no evidence of our communications.*

"Mr. Davies—even though he believed you—created a file that he kept on a Google cloud server under a false identity. He outlined the three meetings you had, as well as the two cell phone conversations. We've got you dead to rights, asshole."

Jonathan remained silent.

"You know what really pisses me off?" John said quietly. "Until we found that file, we all thought that Colin Davies was a traitor who'd stolen the ONERING to sell to the Russians. But that was your intent, wasn't it?" John's voice was full of cold rage from his position behind Sommers. "That file made it clear you duped him into stealing it, making him believe he was actually helping by testing it before it was ready for prime time. That man died in my arms, looking me in the eyes as he did. I promised him I'd personally find out who did this to him, and guess what, motherfucker? I did. You will pay for what you did to him and countless others."

"But before that, you're going to tell us everything you know about the real organization you've been working for all these years," Logan said, stone-faced. "We know it had to be you that somehow activated the Russian team for the Alaska op."

Jonathan didn't reply.

"I thought so," Logan said. "Don't worry. We'll get it all from you. Trust me. Oh, in case you didn't know it, I'm big into the whole 'Silence is consent' thing. I just want you to be aware now for what's coming later."

True panic smashed into Jonathan's consciousness for the first time. A tight ball in the pit of his stomach threatened to incapacitate him. *What are they going to do to me?*

"So here's how this is going to work. We're taking you out of here to a secure location. No one—and I mean no one—is going to wonder where you are. We've taken care of that," Logan said definitively.

"The president's expecting me for the morning brief in six hours," Jonathan said, a last-ditch attempt at bravery.

John laughed from behind him, and Cole and Logan exchanged amused looks.

"Who do you think sent us, Mr. Sommers?" Logan said.

The finality sank in to every fiber of his being, and Jonathan Sommers hung his head.

"Look at me."

No response.

"I said look at me."

Jonathan lifted his eyes, terrified at what he'd see.

"Good," Logan snarled at him, the blazing contempt and merciless loathing apparent on his face and in his words. "You deserve to feel that way for the rest of your miserable life, as short as that may be."

"Huh?" Jonathan said, barely coherent, the fear finally paralyzing him as he processed Logan's last words. The brilliant academic and traitor had been reduced to unintelligible phrases.

"Do it," Logan said to John.

Jonathan Sommers felt a small pinch in the side of his neck, and his world went black.

Logan looked down at the president's national security advisor.

"Let's get this piece of shit out of here. You two and Amira get him back to the office."

Amira was positioned in an SUV around the corner of the brownstone, waiting for their call. They'd take him out the back of the house into the alleyway, where the SUV would meet them. The camera system that covered the alleyway for the residents had been temporarily disabled.

"I'm going to take a walk around the block to ensure no one saw or heard anything. Once I'm certain we're in the clear, I'll get the other SUV and meet you there." Logan's SUV, a new black Ford Explorer registered to a fake corporation that was untraceable, was parked several blocks away on Wisconsin Avenue.

"It's going to be a long few days," Logan said. "Let's get the show on the road."

John and Cole reached down and grabbed the unconscious man as Logan sent Amira a text. They were on the clock. Their workday had begun.

CHAPTER 59

Logan punched in the alarm code, looked around one last time, and walked out the back door. All three of them had swept the lower level of the brownstone to make sure everything was back to the way they'd found it.

They'd entered the place two hours earlier and searched the entire residence, looking for any evidence of Sommers's treachery. They'd taken his laptop and the contents of a safe he'd had installed in his library. The work had been done by the same security company that had installed his alarm system, which made it that much easier to crack.

A new perk of Ares was that the FBI had ways of requesting information, such as alarm and safe codes, so that the subject never discovered the request. *Terrorism* and *espionage* were still nice buzzwords that went a long way in certain sectors associated with the government.

The door clicked shut. He locked it and walked down the alleyway. Nothing stirred. He faintly heard traffic several blocks away on Wisconsin Avenue, but all was quiet in this suburban oasis in the heart of Georgetown.

He walked for thirty minutes, varying his routes up and down the neighborhood's sidewalks, and stopped to listen for the sound of footsteps just in case someone had followed him.

Confident he was alone, he worked his way up to P Street and cut across the intersection of P and Thirty-First. As he headed toward his SUV, he inserted a pair of earbuds under the black wool hat pulled down to his eyes. He took out his cell phone, found what he was looking for, and hit play.

His ears were assaulted by the loud rushing of wind. He heard two distinct coughs, followed by Mike Benson's voice from beyond the grave.

"Brother, I don't have much time. I know you'll get all the details later. So it doesn't matter how it happened. I'm dying, and I know it."

Logan squeezed his eyes shut. The acceptance in Mike's voice hit him hard each time he listened to his friend's final message. The courage he had to accept his fate in his last moments and the fact that he chose to call him of all people with the little time he had left—it was almost too much for him to bear.

"You and I have known each other for a long time. We're family, and I love you."

Mike had paused briefly, the raw emotion affecting him at the end of his life. Another wave of loss pummeled Logan.

"When you're back—and I know you'll make it back; I think you're impossible to kill—you need to talk to my uncle. He'll tell you everything we know. More importantly, he's going to need you. In fact, this country is going to need you, just like it did two years ago. You and John are the most formidable men I've had the honor of knowing, and you need to find out who's behind all of this because I believe it's only going to get worse. I have faith in you, brother."

Each word slashed another wound deep in Logan's soul. The pure fury he felt that one of his closest friends, his brother, had been taken so soon was unthinkable. He braced himself for the last part of the message.

"Before I leave this mortal coil, Logan, I need you to promise me something when this thing's over—don't lose yourself in the hatred and the violence."

Mike's voice paused, and Logan smiled, not at the words but at the fact that Mike had known him so well and had understood who he was.

"You do what you have to do. God help those who stand in your way. The anger you're feeling, the physical thirst for vengeance you seek, use it. You find this threat to our way of life and eliminate it with extreme prejudice."

There was not one iota of doubt in Logan's being that he'd do exactly that—*eliminate the threat.* That was one promise to Mike he intended to keep at all costs.

"But here's the thing, brother. When it's done, when it's truly done, you need to go back to Sarah and make some kind of life for yourself." Mike laughed oddly. *"Not some normal life. I know that's not possible for you. You weren't meant for that. But some kind of life that you can share with Sarah. You need her, and she loves you. She can help keep the darkness at bay. Don't let the evil and the monsters in this world turn you into something you're not. You're a good man, Logan West. Don't ever forget it,"* Mike said forcefully, and then coughed. *"You owe it to yourself."*

There wasn't much more, and it was as painful this time as it'd been the last twenty.

"I think I'm short on time, brother. I've said what I needed to say. Give my love to John and Sarah. I think I'm going to just sit here awhile. You should see this place. I've got a magnificent view." There was a long pause, and Logan heard Mike take a deep breath. *"I love you, Logan. I'll see you on the other side."*

Logan listened as he heard Mike set the phone down. The rushing wind subsided, followed by a low, rumbling echo. Thirty seconds later, there was the sound of footsteps, and he heard a female voice, but it wasn't discernible with the background noise. He knew the voice had to belong to Special Agent Marcus. She'd found Mike, and he wanted—no, *needed*—to talk to her. And then the call went dead.

He stopped walking for a moment to clear the noise in his head.

He was on Wisconsin Avenue, only a block from his SUV. The lamp-lights flickered, his wet eyes creating a halo effect around each one.

He removed the earbuds, and the normal nighttime sounds of Northwest DC assaulted him. The traffic, pedestrians with their own destinations, the cab drivers mingling on the other side of the street, working the night to earn a living—it was a melting pot of humanity engaged in its normal routines.

Logan smiled, the mundane activities encouraging him and hardening his steel resolve. It was his duty, his *responsibility*, to protect them.

The SUV was parked near a streetlamp that had blown out—with the assistance of a well-aimed rock Logan had thrown the previous day.

What he knew that none of those people did was a simple, fundamental truth—the US was at war. It was a fact, and one that he'd remember every waking moment until it was over. The first blows had landed, and now it was time to respond, swiftly and decisively. A message needed to be sent, one that would be perfectly clear to their enemy.

It's our turn now, Logan thought, and stepped into the shadows.

EPILOGUE

ASSOCIATED PRESS—The White House was stunned at the sudden death of National Security Advisor Jonathan Sommers yesterday. His body was found in the underbrush along the running trail in the Georgetown Waterfront Park. Investigators revealed that Mr. Sommers had been shot twice at close range, and his body had signs of a struggle, indicating he'd fought his attacker or attackers. Mr. Sommers was a prolific runner, and the trail along the Potomac where he was found had reported several attempted muggings in recent weeks.

DC Police Commissioner Albert Paulson said, "At this time, we believe this was a random crime, a robbery that went horribly wrong. We continue to pursue all avenues of investigation, and we are in constant contact with the White House. We are all shocked at this violence, and we will work tirelessly to bring the perpetrator or perpetrators to justice."

———

REUTERS—Citizens in the southern states of Sudan unanimously voted for independence from northern Sudan in the country's first-ever referendum. With 99 percent of the voters in each state voting for independence, it was a landslide victory for a people who have suffered through decades of war and religious and ethnic strife.

Although many struggles remain and fighting along the border with the north is a constant threat, the discovery of the largest oil reserve in the world will help financially. As of this publication, China still retained solitary rights to the oil reserve, but it remains in negotiations with both the north and the south in order to create an environment of peace and prosperity.

ACKNOWLEDGMENTS

Dear Reader,

Oath of Honor was a different kind of runaway train compared to *Overwatch,* which served as an origin story for Logan, John, and Mike (RIP). It's my obligation to be up front with you, since without you, there is no world of Logan West. So here it is—with this novel, my intent was to prep the fictional battlespace for what's to come. And as with all good story arcs, things will get darker before any type of resolution begins to take shape in the murky global conflict occurring both inside and outside the international walls of power. I have a five-book story initially planned, with each book moving the overall story further but also serving as a self-contained novel. I hope you enjoyed this ride, as it is exactly what I intend to deliver each and every time. I owe it to you, and you should demand it of me. Enough said.

Now on to the other important point—thanking all those without whom this novel would not be what it is. First, to Megan Reid, my excellent editor, who has a discerning eye that keeps the story tight and on point, a *huge thank you*. Though we may disagree from time to time, your input and ability to withstand my creative onslaughts are critical to the success of the Logan West thrillers.

Second, to Team West at Emily Bestler Books and Atria, which includes my publicist David Brown; Hillary Tisman, associate marketing director; Emily Bestler; and the rest of the folks behind the scenes, thank you for the countless hours of planning, preparation, and coordination that contribute to the entire effort.

Third, to my agent Will Roberts at The Gernert Company, thank you for letting me vent and serving as a sanity check when I go off the tracks. You manage to bring me back from the edge of my own idiocy.

Finally, to my wife, who has a much harder job than I—raising our children while I play in Logan West's fictitious landscape—thank you for the steadfast support, for putting my eccentricities in check when needed, and for ensuring that the household is fully functional on a daily basis. (The kids thank you, too.) I would not be here without you.

To all, so long for now and until the next time . . .